D0275021

WE'LL SING AT DAWN

Also by Victor Pemberton

Our Family
Our Street
Our Rose
The Silent War
Nellie's War
My Sister Sarah
Goodnight Amy
Leo's Girl
A Perfect Stranger
Flying with the Angels
The Chandler's Daughter

WE'LL SING AT DAWN

Victor Pemberton

headline

First published in 2005
by HEADLINE BOOK PUBLISHING

10 9 8 7 6 5 4 3 2 1

Cataloguing in Publication Data is available from the British Library

ISBN 0 7553 2383 1

Typeset in Bembo by Avon DataSet Ltd,
Bidford-on-Avon, Warwickshire

Printed and bound in Great Britain by
Clays Ltd, St Ives plc

HEADLINE BOOK PUBLISHING
A division of Hodder Headline
338 Euston Road
London NW1 3BH

www.headline.co.uk
www.hodderheadline.com

Dedicated to the memory of all those
who gave their lives in the London Blitz
and in other parts of the British Isles,
on this, the 60th anniversary of the
end of the Second World War

Chapter 1

Oberleutnant Heinz Buchner surveyed the approaching target area from the cockpit of his long-range Messerschmitt Me 109 fighter-bomber. Although London was blacked out, as it was every night, his eyes reflected the glow of endless fires burning down there in the dark, turning the British capital into a raging inferno. With limited fuel in his tanks, Buchner knew that he had only just enough time to drop his two high-explosive 'screamer' bombs on to the target, and head back as fast as he could to his base on the French mainland. It wasn't easy, for the barrage of tracer bullets and ack-ack fire that was streaking up at him from the ground defences below had already shot down far too many of the massive squadron of the *Luftwaffe*'s Dornier bombers, which were overwhelming the night sky like a vast swarm of bats. His target for tonight was the marshalling yards at King's Cross Railway Station, the scene, according to the latest German military intelligence reports, of a great deal of British troop and armament activity.

On the way over above the English Channel, he had carefully studied a scale map of North London; Islington and St Pancras were places he had never heard of, for his only pre-war knowledge of London had been confined to a few days as a tourist visiting the Houses of Parliament, Big Ben, and the Tower of London. Beautiful landmarks, but ones which, in Germany's new world order, would be totally expendable. But first things first. The British had to be taught a lesson; they were far too arrogant, far too stubborn, far too set in their ways. And yet, as he steered his war machine in and out of the clouds, trying to dodge the flak that seemed to be determined to find him, he couldn't help wondering what kind of people they were who were sheltering down there, enduring another night of hell, just waiting for their homes to be destroyed. For one brief moment, he thought of his own wife and family back home in Germany, and how *they* would cope if the enemy were ever to reach the skies above their own tiny village. It was too horrific to contemplate. But when he came out on these dangerous nightly missions, Heinz Buchner, who had so far managed to survive to the age of thirty-six years, thought about his wife and two young children. He thought about them a lot, and wondered if there would ever come a time when he would never see them again.

Outside the cockpit, a vast web of gleaming white searchlights was frenziedly searching the sky for the vast armada of warplanes that carried his fellow pilots and comrades. One by one those menacing but helpless machines were bursting into flames and spiralling down into pieces on the rooftops below. Slowly, breathlessly, Buchner's target for the night came into view. At last he saw what he had come for, and without a second to lose, he jettisoned his two bombs, and sent them whistling down on to the marshalling yards. Then, as fast as it was humanly possible, he steered his aircraft round into a sharp turn, and headed off back through the dark black English clouds towards the coast. There was no time for sentiment, no time to imagine who was caught up in the horror which he himself had just unleashed. He had a family of his own back home waiting for him, desperately hoping they would see him again.

Beth Shanks stared up at the roof of the old factory cellar. The look in her eyes showed real fear. Were those 'screamer' bombs she could hear hurtling down through the night sky – did they have her name on them, and her mum, and the baby, and all her other neighbours who were spending yet another night of misery locked up in the bowels of the earth? As the menacing sound grew shrill and close, she closed her eyes, stiffened, and held her breath. Only after the deafening explosions came did she summon up enough courage to open her eyes and breathe a sigh of relief. Not tonight. Hell had broken loose for some other poor devils, but not for Beth and those sheltering alongside her. Not tonight. But the dust and small flakes of cement that were still floating down on to her upturned face showed what devastation those 'screamers' must have caused not so far away, for the whole shelter had shaken from end to end. But this was nothing new. Listening to all that mayhem outside had become such a nightly ritual for the residents of Hornsey Road that they were beginning to take it all in their stride. After all, this was October 1940, and by now the London Blitz had been in full swing for almost two months, with air raids taking place regularly by night and by day.

The moment the explosions came, the damp, soggy atmosphere of the shelter was pierced by the bawling of Beth's baby brother Simon, whose little legs kicked out so hard against his mum's stomach that the wind was taken out of her. Beth leaned across, lifted him out of his mum's arms, and cradled him in her own. But Simon was having none of it. As far as he was concerned an abandoned piano factory was no place for a four-month-old to spend his nights, and he was determined to let everyone in the shelter know it. 'Simmy, Simmy,' cried Beth, gently rocking the baby in her arms. 'All over now. Time fer beddy-byes.' Only the poor baby's rubber teat shoved into his mouth finally brought the protests to a halt.

'I reckon it's the Cross that's taken *that* lot,' croaked old Jessie Hawks, who lived above the off-licence down the road, but who now was camped down on her usual mattress, covered by two blankets and an eiderdown. 'Those buggers up there've bin after that station ever since the bombs started.'

'It's not the station Jerry's after, Jess,' proffered the Shanks's next-door neighbour, Jack Cutter. 'It's those yards round the back. I 'eard the army's bin usin' those tracks ter move guns and tanks right the way along the coast.'

'Which shows they're expectin' an invasion any minute,' added Bill Winkler, Jack's fellow pensioner mate, whose perpetually glum appearance always irritated his wife Lil, who was at his side knitting what promised to be the longest cardigan in history.

'Stop bein' so gloomy, Mr Winkler,' called Eileen Perkins from the makeshift bed on the cold stone floor that she was sharing with her eight-year-old daughter, Rita. 'We've still got the English Channel between us an' 'Itler. If any of 'em set one foot over 'ere, ol' Winnie'd 'ave their guts fer garters!'

'Oh yes?' retorted Bill, the proverbial pessimist. 'An' wot d'yer fink '*e* could do ter stop 'em? 'Is mum's a Yank, ain't she? The Yanks couldn't care less about the likes of us.'

'That's not quite true,' protested Beth's mother, Connie Shanks, with just a faint trace of an American accent. '*I'm* a Yank, and *I* care a great deal about what everyone here is having to go through in this war.'

'Yeah, well you married one of us,' grumbled Bill, clenching his false teeth on his pipe. 'You're diff'rent.'

'Winston Churchill's mother was American and she married one of you too,' replied Connie, a soft-spoken Texan woman, who although now in her late thirties, looked much younger. 'So I don't see why Mr Churchill should be any different.'

Bill sniffed dismissively, and puffed on his pipe. Fortunately, any further embarrassment was avoided by a frantic barrage of ack-ack fire coming from the streets above, and with the whole cellar shaking from roof to floor, it was some time before anyone had the courage to speak again.

It was two hours or so before the noise outside subsided. Once it was relatively quiet again, Beth handed her young brother back to their mother, and tried to settle down for what was going to be another short night's sleep. Beth hated these nightly visits to the old factory shelter in Upper Hornsey Road. Many a time she had begged her mum to let her stay back home and take her chances. If one of those German bombs had her name on it, there was nothing anyone could do about it. After all, she took a risk every day of her life by travelling up to Finchley on a bus during an air raid; working in a munitions factory was not exactly the safest job to have. But then, in wartime, what job was? She turned over on her mattress, and looked up at her mum, who was stretched out alongside her with baby Simon safely tucked up in her arms. Then she pulled the blanket up to her neck, covering her shoulders. Only her face was showing now, and her modest flock of dark brown hair that, for safety reasons at work, was cut in a short bob style. She hated what old Bill Winkler had said about the

Yanks. Even though she agreed with most people that the Americans should stop sitting on the fence and help the British to fight Hitler, they were good people. Her mum was a good person; she must be because her dad had married her. Yes, Beth hated the war. She hated everything about it, the way it had changed people, the way it had changed their lives, the way it had robbed everyone of the basic necessities of life. Most of all, she hated that cellar. To her, it was more like a tomb, a living hell. Oh, if only she could be out there in the streets with her young brother Phil, who, at the start of the Blitz, had volunteered to become a teenage cyclist messenger in the Auxiliary Fire Service. Phil's job was probably the most dangerous of all, but at least he was doing something constructive, at least he wasn't shut up night after night, like a prisoner in a cold dark cell.

A few hours later, Beth woke up to the distant wail of the All Clear siren. The place now smelt not only of damp but also of urine from the overnight buckets that were placed out of sight in a far corner of the cellar. It was a repellent smell, and Beth couldn't wait to get out of the place. Once she had rolled up the mattress, and stacked it neatly against the wall, she collected her mum's bag and helped her to wrap up the baby against the cold morning air.

When everyone finally emerged from the shelter, it was only just beginning to get light along Hornsey Road. But it was pouring with rain, and the air was polluted with the pungent smell of burning timbers and debris. Beth took a passing look up at the sky and saw thick spirals of smoke rising up from behind the roofs and chimney pots in all directions. The worst area seemed to be a fair distance away, beyond Holloway, towards King's Cross, which seemed to confirm what old Jessie Hawks had suggested down in the shelter during the air raid. Beth felt chilled, pulled up the collar of her coat tightly around her neck, and adjusted the cotton scarf over her head. Her mother followed close behind, still cradling little Simon in her arms, using his thick woollen blanket to protect him from the cold morning air. They had to pick their way carefully, for the pavements were pitted with lumps of jagged metal shrapnel which had rained down during the night from the intensive barrage of anti-aircraft shellfire.

‘I hope Phil got home safe and sound,’ said Connie, as they made their way up Hornsey Road towards their home in Moray Road. ‘I really hate the idea of him being out every night in the middle of all that bombing. He’s too young to be working for the Fire Service.’

‘Don’t you worry about Phil, Mum,’ called Beth, who was walking on ahead struggling with the night’s bedding, a string bag of what had been full of her baby brother’s foodstuff, also their sandwiches, and a vacuum flask of hot cocoa. ‘If I know ’im, when we get ’ome we’ll find ’im sleepin’ it off after ’avin’ a crafty fag.’

‘I hope not,’ replied Connie, her slight Texan drawl contrasting sharply with her daughter’s North London street twang. ‘If his dad knew he was smoking cigarettes, he’d give him a good cuff behind the ear.’

‘Well Dad ain’t ’ere,’ retorted Beth, ‘so there ain’t much ’e can do about it, is there?’

Connie didn’t like the way Beth spoke to her. In fact, she often didn’t like the way her daughter spoke to her at times. Beth was so English, so East End, where she had been born. She was so much more her dad’s girl, who came from the same stock. Beth had nothing in common with her mum, who was from a world that to most people in Islington was as far removed as the moon.

As they turned into Tollington Park, the whole road seemed to be crowded with people rushing all over the place, shouting, waving their hands, pointing this way and that, with an air of utter desperation in the wake of a bomb explosion which had caused immense devastation. At the far end of the road, a tangle of fire hoses were snaked into trailer pumps which were being used by men from the AFS to damp down smouldering debris from a bombed terraced house. It was a scene of utter mayhem, with all the emergency services struggling to free the victims who had clearly been trapped in the rubble there. Beth craned her head to see what was going on, but her mother couldn’t bear to look, and, with little Simon still firmly cradled in her arms, quickly turned the corner into their own road.

The Shanks home was part of a long terrace of red-bricked Edwardian houses, which were set on three floors, and which had clearly once been inhabited by well-to-do middle-class families. However, because of the war, the houses were now in much need of repair and decoration, and matters were made worse by the number of times the windows had been blown in by bomb blast from the surrounding streets. When Beth and her mother arrived home, their hearts sank, because once again the glass had shattered in two of the upstairs bedroom windows, and several roof tiles were lying smashed in pieces on the pavement below. Once inside the house, there was even worse news, for plaster had come down from the ceiling in the front passage, and wherever they moved their feet they walked on broken glass.

'Thank God we weren't here for this,' said Connie with relief, looking around at the mess as Beth opened the front door for her and the baby.

'I'm not so sure,' said Beth, dumping the bedding down on the stair banisters. 'I'd sooner've taken me chances 'ere any day than get stuck down in that 'ole in the ground night after night.'

Connie lowered the sleeping baby into his pram, tucked him up in his blanket, and followed Beth into the kitchen. 'We wouldn't have much chance if we stayed here during an air raid, Beth,' she said. 'There'd be nothing we could do if we had a direct hit.'

Beth shrugged. Only now did she feel the full effect of her night's entombment down in the shelter. She pulled off the scarf over her head, and shook out her hair. She was tired and felt she must look as though she'd been pulled through a hedge backwards. All she wanted now was a cup of tea and a hot bath, but she knew that she only had very little time to do it for she was due to leave for work in less than half-an-hour. First, however, she took a dustpan and brush to clear the fallen plaster and broken glass from the overhead light bulb that was littering the hall. Then whilst her mother fed the baby in the kitchen, she went outside and swept up the broken glass and roof tiles on the pavement. All her neighbours were also out in the street doing the same thing. It wasn't the first time they'd all had to clear up the results of bomb blast since the Blitz started a couple of months before. When she went back in, her mother was once again cradling baby Simon in her arms, gently rocking him to and fro to get him back to sleep again.

Connie waited a moment or so before bringing up the same subject she knew would irritate her daughter. 'You know, Beth,' she said tentatively, 'I think it's now time we got away from all this.'

Beth, halfway up the stairs, stopped with a start and turned. 'What d'yer mean?' she asked.

Connie went to the foot of the stairs and looked up at her. She was still a remarkably beautiful woman, with soft, moonlight features, gentle crystal-blue eyes, and long, strawberry blonde hair which was tied in a bun behind her head. 'It's not safe for us in this house any longer,' she said. 'Why should we put our lives at risk every day and night when we can easily go and stay with your grandma and grandad in Hertfordshire? I wrote and told your dad so.'

Beth's piercing dark brown eyes flashed back a look of total indignation. 'You wrote an' told – Dad?' she asked in disbelief.

'The last letter I had from him,' replied Connie, who knew she had broached a difficult point of disagreement between the two of them, 'he said he was worried about us being in the house all on our own in the middle of air raids.'

'We're not in the 'ouse during air raids!' snapped Beth. 'We're down that ruddy shelter.'

'Only at night, Beth,' insisted Connie. 'The air raids are coming any time of the day and night now. When you go to work, I'm here on my own with the baby.'

'Wot about Phil?' asked Beth, raising her voice. ' 'E only works nights.'

'I hardly ever see him, Beth,' replied Connie in desperation. 'He comes home, sleeps a couple of hours, then goes off the moment he hears the air raid siren. It's not safe here, Beth. Not for me, for you, for Phil, or for the baby. Don't you understand, darling? I'm scared.'

Beth's whole attitude changed. When she looked down and saw the anxiety in her mother's eyes, she knew that there *was* real fear there. 'I'm sorry, Mum,' she said, her voice soft and understanding. 'I didn't mean ter –' She put her arms around her mother, and held her and the baby close. 'I *do* know 'ow you're feelin', 'onest I do. But goin' to Grandma and Grandad's is not goin' to work. Yer know 'ow set they are in their ways. They're just as stubborn as Dad.'

'We'd be safe there, Beth,' said Connie. 'That's all that matters.'

Beth held her at arm's length. 'Yer don't 'ave ter worry, Mum,' she said quietly, smiling sympathetically at her with eyes that were just like her dad's. 'I'll take care of yer. When Dad got called up, I told 'im I'd take care of yer. I told 'im I'd never let anyfin' 'appen ter you or Phil or . . . this one.' She stooped down over the baby in her mother's arms, and kissed him gently on the forehead. 'You're all too precious ter me.'

'You can't protect us from bombs, Beth,' replied Connie. 'Nobody can. Not you – nor your dad. We have to come to a decision soon.'

There was a brief moment of silence between them before Beth spoke again. 'I 'ave ter get ter work,' she said with a faint affectionate smile. 'We'll talk about it when I get 'ome. OK?'

Connie shrugged. She had no alternative. As she watched her daughter hurry on up the stairs, she realised only too well how like her dad she was, the same slight build, the same flashing dark brown eyes, the same rough East End way of talking. And, just like her dad, she had a heart of gold. But it wasn't enough. The family was in danger, real danger, and unless something was done about it soon, it could be too late.

Fortunately, the gas supply to the house had not been disrupted, which meant that the bathroom geyser managed to provide Beth with just enough water to take a quick bath. She was grateful that her father had been such a handyman around the house, for, just before the war started, he himself had converted the small box room on the first floor landing into a bathroom, which was a luxury denied to most of their neighbours. During the few minutes she had available to soak away the grime and dust of the previous night's ordeal down in the cellar shelter, Beth turned over in her mind what her mum had told her about wanting to move out of London to stay with her dad's parents down in Hertfordshire. The whole idea filled her with horror. How could her mother even contemplate such a thing, she asked herself? This was their house, the family's house. How could they just pack up their things and leave it? What about their friends, their neighbours? What about the piano lessons her mum gave to the locals? Was she really willing to give up all that because she was afraid of the air raids? Isn't that just what Hitler wanted? To bomb people out of their homes, to scare the life out of them so that London would become a lost city, and Britain would be wide open for the invasion. The invasion? No. The Germans had managed to walk into Poland and all those other countries in Europe, but they would never have the nerve to set foot on British soil. Oh, if only her dad hadn't been called up; how she missed him, how she *needed* him. She was snapped out of her thoughts with a start. The air raid siren was wailing yet again from the roof of nearby Hornsey Road Police Station.

There was no doubt that it was a nerve-racking experience going to work during an air raid. At the best of times it was quite a journey from the Nags Head in Holloway to East Finchley on the outer fringe of North London, but sitting on the top deck of a Number 609 trolleybus was hazardous in the extreme. To make things worse, Beth always defied reason and sat in the front seat where she could get a grandstand view of any dogfights battling it out in the sky above. She knew it was a reckless and dangerous thing to do, but she had an irresistible urge to know what was going on, and today an awful lot *was* going on. The top deck of the bus was full of the usual smokers, coughing their lungs out, and refusing to let the lady conductor open the windows, which made it difficult for Beth to see the frenzied action that was taking place high above the rooftops. What she did see through the haze of thick, grey cigarette and pipe smoke, however, was an armada of enemy aircraft flitting in and out of the dark grey morning clouds, like a swarm of wasps just waiting to pounce on their helpless victims. As the bus reached the junction of Upper Holloway Road and the main arterial Archway Road, Beth watched people scurrying from all directions down into the safety of the nearby tube station. Oblivious to all this, the bus driver continued on his way, climbing up the steep hill towards the Great North Road, defying the deafening barrage of anti-aircraft fire which, from time to time, caused the bus to vibrate and sway from side to side. When they stopped to let off passengers at the bus stop at the top of the hill, a great cheer went up as one of the intruder aircraft was seen spiralling down in flames through the clouds, to end up in an explosion of thick billowing smoke in the wastes of Highgate Woods on the opposite side of the road.

'Good riddance ter bad rubbish!' yelled one of the female passengers on the lower deck.

'Gord rest 'is soul,' added a more tolerant middle-aged male passenger, sitting quietly in the back seat on the top deck.

The clippie pressed the start bell, and the bus moved on.

Exciting though it was to travel on top of a bus during an air raid, it was at times like this, with hot white shrapnel tinkling down on to the pavements everywhere, that Beth had to admit that her mother had every right to be worried about trying to live any kind of normal life amid such perilous conditions. This reflection took on an even greater significance when, as the trolley bus reached its final destination outside the Gaumont cinema in East Finchley, the blast from an explosion in a street nearby caused the bus to rock to such a degree that for one moment it looked as though it would topple over. When it did recover, however, the conductor immediately called up the stairs, 'All change!'

Beth quickly filed off the bus with the other passengers. Everyone was either shouting angry abuse at Hitler and Goering, or making cheery jokes at the expense of London Transport. The overhead booms of the trolleybus were dangling recklessly after having being de-wired from the overhead electric cables, and within a few moments, other buses came to a stop behind them. Beth's only course now was to get to work as fast as she could without being hit by a lump of steaming white shrapnel, which was by now falling fast and furious from exploding ack-ack fire overhead, and tinkling down on to the pavements everywhere. The noise of aerial dogfights was deafening, broken only by distant explosions from those bombs that the enemy planes had managed to deposit on any target they chose. With several other passengers from the bus queue, Beth took shelter for a moment or so under the main foyer portico of the Gaumont cinema, waiting for a lull in the battle raging in the skies above. When it finally came, she virtually sprinted round the corner to her workplace, which, considering its importance to the war effort, managed to look like nothing more than an old warehouse.

Once inside the ammunitions factory, she knew at once that most of the girls and fellers there were taking cover in the old tunnels beneath the building, for the place was completely deserted, with workbenches idle and littered with spare parts of arms and ammunition. However, she felt heartened the moment she heard a familiar male voice calling to her from the door of the canteen at the other end of the small arms shop.

'Beth! Over here! Quick!'

In a flash, Beth hurried straight into the canteen, and straight into the arms of a burly, muscular young man who immediately smothered her lips with his own. Pinned against the wall and held like that for several moments, Beth had no chance to protest, not that she wanted to, for the young bloke was her 'steady', and had been for the past year or so. 'Thomas!' she gasped, when she finally managed to pull loose. 'Not in 'ere! Charlie 'Atchet'll frow the book at us!'

'Ter hell with Charlie Hatchet!' retorted Thomas Sullivan, with a strong Irish accent, despite the fact he'd only ever visited Ireland once in his entire life. 'Just look at the place. Not a soul around. Who cares *what* we do?'

'*I* care, Thomas!' insisted Beth, easing him gently away. 'In any case, we've got quite enuff problems wiv these bleedin' air raids. If one of those Jerry bombs ends up down our chimney, we'll go up in smoke!'

'So why worry?' asked Thomas, who had the sort of looks which made most girls go limp at the knees, with bright sapphire blue eyes, and flaxen-coloured hair that was far too long for safety in a munitions factory. 'If we've gotta go, let's go havin' a bit er fun, eh?'

'Thomas!' she protested, laughing and pushing hard against his chest as he tried to keep her pinned against the canteen wall.

Fortunately, she was saved in the nick of time by the wail of the All Clear siren, which was followed almost immediately by hordes of girls and fellers streaming up the steps from the tunnels in the backyard outside. Within moments, the whole place was brimming with life and activity.

'Yer won't get away so easily from me the next time, young miss,' called Thomas, as he followed Beth back into the small arms shop. It was a rich remark, coming from someone who, at eighteen, was no more than a month or so older than Beth herself. 'See yers later!' He blew her a very sensual kiss, then, merging into a group of several other male workers, quickly disappeared through another door which led downstairs into the 'Top Secret' mortar workshops.

'It's about time dream boy made an 'onest woman of you, Beff Shanks.' The quip came from Mo Mitchell, a large girl with a doll-like face and puffy cheeks, who was adjusting her workplace hairnet in the changing area. 'Every time I see yer wiv 'im, 'e looks as though 'e's about ter eat yer!'

Beth laughed as she quickly put on her own hairnet. ' 'E can't do that, Mo,' she returned. ' 'E ain't got enuff coupons in 'is ration book!'

Both girls shared the joke, put on their work aprons, and made their way to the small arms bench where they worked together.

'Mind you, I should imagine it's no joke gettin' 'itched to a Paddy these days,' said Mo, who immediately started work on filing down some bullet cases.

'I don't see why,' replied Beth, who at first treated the comment only in passing. But then the penny dropped, and she swung round, giving her workmate a puzzled look. 'Wot d'yer mean?' she asked.

'Well, ever since they let off the bomb up at that 'otel the uvver munff,' Mo continued, 'some er the Paddies ain't got a very good name.'

'*Wot* bomb?' asked Beth tersely. 'Wot yer talkin' about?'

'The IRA,' retorted Mo, who put on a pair of goggles to protect her eyes from the shaved filings she was working on. 'Don't you ever read no newspapers? The Irish Republican Army. They let off a bomb outside Whiteley's store in Bayswater, then anuvver one outside this posh 'otel down Park Lane. Lucky no one got killed.'

Beth wasn't entirely ignorant of the two incidents, remembering that as soon as she had heard the news on the wireless, she had done her best to erase them from her mind.

'Seems a bit nasty ter do fings like that when you're in the middle of a war,' said Mo, rambling on. 'I mean, I know these geezers've got a bee in their bonnet about gettin' 'ome rule or somefin', but there's no need ter take it out on poor innocent people, is there? It's bad enuff 'avin' ter cope wiv bleedin' 'Itler.'

Beth tried not to respond to Mo's comments. She knew how jealous she was that out of all the girls working in the factory, Thomas only had eyes for Beth. But in her mind she knew only too well that there was something in what her workmate had said. In an attempt to terminate the discussion, she went off to collect a new supply of bullet cases. The workshop was brimming with activity, and she had to wind her way in and out of the endless trolleys of machinery that were being unpacked at different workbenches. There was a feeling of urgency in everything the girls were doing, but in their banter with the fellers who were doing the heavy manual work, they treated it all with immense good humour. Beth had never got over the fact that since the start of the war, most of the male workers were either middle-aged or elderly. As each day passed, the absence of young men who had been called up was becoming more and more noticeable. Until this moment, however, it hadn't really crossed Beth's mind to ask Thomas why *he* hadn't been called up with all the others.

'I 'ear they gave the Cross a bit of a bangin' last night,' called Charlie Hatchet, foreman of the smalls arms workshop, referring to the bombs dropped on the King's Cross marshalling yards during the night. 'Looks like there's quite a lot er dead.'

Beth shuddered at the thought. When she heard those explosions with her mum and the baby down in the shelter, she tried hard not to think about all the poor innocent people who had lost their lives. 'Terrible, Mr Hatchet,' was all she could say.

'Yer know, Beff,' said Hatchet, who was actually quite a mild-mannered and kindly person, quite unlike the picture Thomas always painted of him, 'you should watch yer step coming up 'ere in the middle of an air raid. Fings're 'ottin' up in this blitz. Jerry knows exactly wot 'e wants ter get rid of, and this factory's one of 'em.'

Hatchet's remark caused Beth to take a quick look around the workshop. There were girls crammed into every foot of the place, into every corner, every crick and cranny. It was true. If the Germans ever managed to pinpoint the place, they could cause such devastation, and a huge loss of life. She looked at one of the wall posters which showed a police constable in uniform and tin helmet, with fingers to lips and the legend in thick black letters: CARELESS TALK COSTS

LIVES. 'I thought we was s'pposed ter be top secret,' she said to Hatchet. 'Jerry could never find a place like this.' Then she turned her statement into a guarded question. 'Could 'e?' she asked.

Hatchet shrugged. 'London's full er spies, Beff,' he replied.

'Spies?'

'This is war,' continued Hatchet. Then he looked around the human mass of activity. 'It ain't a very nice fing ter fink about, but anyone er them people out there could be a traitor, workin fer Jerry – fer one reason or anuvver.'

Beth was taken aback. She slowly cast her eyes around the vast number of people working all around her, many of them her friends, friends she had made from the first moment she started working in the factory soon after the start of the war. Traitors? These people weren't traitors; they could never be. Like her, they loved their country. No. They were just hard-working girls and fellers who all shared the same common purpose: to help the boys at the front and in the air to win the war.

'Anyway,' continued Hatchet, before walking off to inspect a fresh truck of machinery that had just arrived outside, 'mustn't put the fear of God inter yer, Beff. All I'm sayin' is, just take care of yerself. But if yer 'ear somefin' goin' on that don't sound right, just pop a word in my ear.' With those last ominous words of advice, he hurried off.

Beth watched him go. For a moment, she just stood where she was, thinking carefully about what Hatchet had just said. It would be wrong to say that she was concerned, but she certainly didn't take his words lightly. Fortunately, the tannoy speakers all around the walls of the workshop suddenly burst into life, allowing *Music While You Work* on the wireless to break the gloom of the morning after the night before. But for Beth, after all Mo had been saying to her, the first song seemed to take on an added significance. It was 'When Irish Eyes Are Smiling'.

Chapter 2

Connie Shanks liked teaching young Freddie Cooper. He was certainly the most attentive of all her pupils who took piano lessons from her once a week, and, even though he was barely ten years old, he had consistently shown a great aptitude for classical piano music. Not that Connie had many pupils at all these days, for quite a lot of children in the neighbourhood had been evacuated, and ever since her husband Ted had been called up for active duty in the army at the start of the war, it had been difficult making ends meet. Connie's one disappointment, however, was her own daughter Beth, who had never shown any real interest in learning how to play the piano in the same formal way Connie herself had been taught as a child by her own mother back in her native Texas, opting instead to play by ear all the popular tunes of the day. But then Beth's brother, Phil, was no different; he couldn't care less about either Chopin or Bing Crosby, preferring his old bicycle to musical instruments. All Connie could hope for now was that young baby Simon might at least inherit some of her love for what she considered was 'real' music. Nonetheless, disappointed though she was by her family's lack of enthusiasm for anything cultural, she loved them all dearly. After all, the day she married Ted Shanks a little over twenty years before, she knew that he was an East End boy through and through, and she took him for better or for worse because she loved him, not because of who he was or where he came from, but because he was a warm and generous-hearted man.

Connie stood behind young Freddie in the ground-floor front parlour of the Shanks family house in Moray Road, and watched him with a glow of quiet satisfaction. His small hands seemed to glide along the piano keyboard quite effortlessly, whilst his slender little fingers produced the most lovely, almost perfect sounds of a Brahms lullaby. For those few moments, Connie was in her seventh heaven; listening to anyone playing anything vaguely classical on her beloved upright piano was one thing, but when it was being played by a child she herself had taught, it seemed as close to sheer joy as she had ever dared hope.

'Mum says I'm to ask you to teach me how to play "Onward Christian Soldiers".'

Connie looked down at the boy with a start. ' "Onward Christian Soldiers"?' she asked, taken aback. 'But – that's a hymn,' she said.

'I know,' replied Freddie, with a shrug. 'We sing it in church on Sunday mornings. Mum says I ought to be able to play it for the family when they come over to tea.'

Connie's mind was reeling, because she knew the boy's mother was forcing him to learn how to play the hymn. However, Connie thought it wasn't her place to ask any more questions, especially about a family that were such regular churchgoers. 'Move over, Freddie,' she said, sitting beside him.

For the next few minutes, Freddie listened enraptured as his piano teacher sat alongside him playing through the music of the hymn, at the same time singing the words. Teaching the boy to play something by ear was not something she approved of, but as she had no music sheets for any hymns, she had no alternative but to do what she could.

Whilst this was going on, Beth quietly peered into the room. She knew better than to make her presence known, for her mother hated to be interrupted during one of her piano lessons. After a quick glance at young Simon in his pram on the other side of the room, she quietly closed the door again, and went off to the kitchen. Starving hungry after a rough day at the munitions factory, she looked around for any scrap of food she could find. But there was very little on offer, for it was becoming harder and harder to make the measly food ration last out a whole week. However, there was hope, as always, with the good old dried egg powder, and, despite the fact that it was no alternative to the real thing, Beth opened the tin she found in the kitchen pantry, and took it and a small mixing bowl over to the pine table. Once she'd mixed two tablespoons of the dried egg with four tablespoons of water, she then prepared the ingredients for her somewhat sparse omelette. As the weekly ration of approximately two ounces of cooking fat didn't go too far, she used the barest minimum she dared in the frying pan on the oven range hob. After rummaging around in the pantry, she found the remains of some potatoes and sprouts left over from the previous night's supper, so she warmed up some of them in the pan with a little seasoning before pouring in the dried egg mixture. A few minutes later she sat down at the table and ate her omelette, or what was an excuse for one, but when she tasted it, she began to think that she would have been far better off to stay hungry.

'You should have waited for me, Beth,' said her mother, at the kitchen door with little Simon in her arms. 'I was just coming to get supper ready.'

'I'm sorry, Mum,' said Beth, her mouth full. 'I was so hungry. And in any case, you were busy with Freddie. It sounded like I was just coming into church!'

'What d'you mean?' asked Connie, carefully lowering Simon into his kitchen cot.

' "Onward Christian Soldiers"?'

'Freddie's mother wants him to learn how to play it – for the family.'

'Wow!' exclaimed Beth. 'There's dedication for yer.'

Connie came across, and sat at the table with her. 'The Cooper family *are* dedicated, darling. They believe in their religion. I don't blame them for that. With the way we're all living now, it's good to have *something* to believe in.'

'I've got plenty er fings *I* believe in,' said Beth, finishing the last of her dried egg omelette.

Connie raised her eyebrow. 'Oh?' she asked, surprised.

'Not in the way you fink,' replied Beth. 'Not religion an' all that. I mean, the war. I believe it's somefing we've got ter get on wiv. The sooner we face up to it, the sooner it'll be over.'

'You really think this war will be over soon?'

Beth put down her knife and fork. 'Well, let's face it,' she replied, running her fingers through her short, bobbed hair, 'it can't go on fer ever, can it?'

Connie wasn't so sure. She sat back in her chair, and pondered all the questions that had been plaguing her since the bombing started. 'It's going to get much worse before it gets better, Beth,' she said. 'We have to be prepared.'

Beth looked up at her. 'Yer mean – run away?' she asked, with an irritable sigh. 'Run away and bury ourselves in the country with Gran and Grandad?'

'Protecting ourselves is not about running away, Beth,' returned Connie, leaning forward in her chair. 'It's about survival. We owe it to your dad to stay alive – you, me, Phil and Simon.'

Beth got up from her chair, went to the sink and washed her hands. She knew what her mum was saying was right, but she just couldn't accept that they'd be any more better off in the country, living with two elderly people with whom she had absolutely nothing in common.

Connie got up from her chair at the table, collected a hand towel from a hook by the sink, and gave it to Beth. 'You mustn't be angry with me, darling,' she said softly and caringly. 'I know you don't want to leave your home any more than I do. But we can't go on spending night after night in the air raid shelter.'

'I've told you, Mum,' replied Beth, subconsciously irritated by her mother's half-Texas half-North London drawl, 'I'd much rarvver take me chance any time in the 'ouse. That air raid shelter down in the cellar's a real death-trap. If a bomb fell on the place, we wouldn't stand a chance.'

'If a bomb fell on this house,' replied Connie despairingly, 'we'd have even less chance of protecting ourselves. I've asked the Town Hall over and over again to let us have an Anderson shelter for the back garden, but all they keep telling me is that they've used up every one of their allowance, and they have absolutely no idea if and when they'll be able to get one for us.'

'That's becos we never applied fer one when they came round ter check,' added Beth reprimandingly.

Connie was stung, and turned away from the sink.

'It's all right, Mum,' said Beth sympathetically, putting her arm around her waist. 'You're not ter blame. No one's ter blame. When the war started, 'ow was we ter know we was goin' ter be bombed out of our minds night an' day.'

'That's the trouble, Beth,' replied Connie. 'We *should* have known. Everyone else in the road knew. It's my fault. When you come from a country that doesn't know what it's like to have bombs exploding on its own soil, you can't imagine that such a thing could possibly happen anywhere else in the world.'

'Hey, Mum! Can I 'ave some bread an' drippin'?'

The teenage boy who had just burst into the room was Beth's young brother, Phil. His Auxiliary Fire Service uniform was filthy dirty from what seemed like endless duty out on the roads during the air raid carrying messages by bicycle all over the borough of Islington. Phil was already taller and lankier than his sister, but for a sixteen-year-old, he looked much younger.

'Phil!' gasped Connie, hurrying to the pantry. 'Just look at the state of you. As soon as you've eaten, get yourself upstairs into the tub.'

Phil followed his mum anxiously to the kitchen table as she brought across a bowl of beef dripping and a half-loaf of bread. 'Not much use gettin' washed up in two inches of lukewarm water,' he said, feverishly cutting himself a thick slice of bread. 'In any case, Jerry's on 'is way over. I'm on standby. I've got ter get back ter the station.'

Connie grabbed the boy's cap, pulled it from his head, and threw it down on to the chair. 'Tub first!' she demanded.

'Wot d'yer mean Jerry's on 'is way over?' asked Beth, also cutting herself a slice of bread. 'I didn't 'ear no air raid siren.'

'No, but yer will!' insisted Phil, digging down to the bottom of the bowl of dripping to get a spoonful of the tasty beef jelly. 'They was sayin' up the station this one's goin' ter be a real big'un. Over a 'undred planes, they reckon.'

Beth resisted the urge to exchange a glance with her mum.

'Oh God,' said Connie, immediately bustling around to collect their belongings for what looked like a long night ahead. 'Beth, can you make up the cocoa flasks? I'll go and get Simon's clean diapers.'

'Oh Mum!' protested Beth as her mum rushed to the door. ' 'Ow long 'ave yer been in England now, an' yer still can't speak the King's English. They're nappies – not wot you call 'em!'

'Or whatever!' Connie called back, quickly hurrying out of the room.

Beth sighed, and joined her brother at the table spreading beef dripping on to their slices of bread. 'Is it true?' she asked. 'Is there really another raid on the way?'

Phil, mouth full of bread and dripping, nodded emphatically. 'Everyone's on full alert,' he said darkly.

'Bloody sods!' exclaimed Beth, also munching as she talked. 'They won't be satisfied 'til they've burned down the 'ole er London.'

'They won't do that!' insisted Phil, full of bravado. 'Not while *I'm* around!'

Beth took this in for a split second until she suddenly realised how daft her young brother was. Smiling broadly and protectively at him, she couldn't help noticing the likeness between him and their mum; the same blue eyes and flaxen-blonde hair, the same winning smile, but large ears and a boxer's square chin that were just like his dad. Beth was very fond of Phil. They had been mates ever since they were small kids. If one of them ever got in a scrap, the other would always come to his or her rescue. 'I wish I was out there wiv yer,' said Beth. 'Much better than being cooped up in that ruddy shelter all night.'

'I wouldn't be so sure if I was you,' replied Phil, stuffing the last bit of bread and dripping into his mouth. 'After wot I saw last night, you're much better off where yer are.'

Beth watched him with some apprehension. 'Wot yer talkin' about?'

Phil wiped his mouth with the back of his hand. 'They got the T.A. barracks up the Archway last night. Nine blokes killed, plus two gels in the canteen. Five 'undred-pound high explosive bomb. They didn't stand a chance.'

'Blimey!' gasped Beth. 'But – 'ow did Jerry find it? I fawt that barracks was s'pposed ter be top secret.'

'It was,' replied Phil, getting up from the table, and going to the sink to rinse his hands. ' 'Til someone split on 'em.'

Beth's face stiffened with shock. 'Split on 'em?' she asked uncomprehendingly.

'Jerry's got plants all over, ain't 'e?' he called, over his shoulder. 'The boys up the station said there are spies all over London. They're watchin' everyfin' they can set their eyes on.'

'Spies?' It took Beth a moment to take this in. 'Here – in 'Olloway?'

' 'Olloway, Islin'ton, King's Cross – anywhere. There's a war on, Beff. Jerry aims ter win it in any way 'e can. 'E can get anyone 'e likes who's got a grudge against us. Bleedin' traitors all over the place. If I got *my* 'ands on 'em, I'd string 'em all up from Tower Bridge.'

After the conversation she'd had with Mo at the munitions factory that morning, Beth suddenly felt quite numb. The stories that were going around about traitors who were spying on military installations around London were gaining momentum. It was a horrible feeling; to think that someone you might actually know, have known all your life, was willing to pass on information, no matter how minute, to an enemy whose only aim was to destroy all the good things that Britain had ever stood for. 'Do they 'ave any idea who told them about the barracks?' she asked tentatively.

Phil shrugged. 'Could've bin anyone. There are still a few wops an' huns around the place who 'aven't bin locked up in the nick. Who knows – it might even be a Paddy. I mean let's face it, one or two er them don't like us much, do they?'

Beth hardly had a moment to react, when the air raid siren wailed out from the roof of nearby Hornsey Road police station.

'What'd I tell yer!' spluttered Phil, rushing to the door. ' 'Ere we go again!' In a flash he was gone, back to another hectic, perilous night of messenger duties.

Connie passed him briefly in the passage outside, then hurried in to join Beth, who was just lifting baby Simon out of his cot. 'I knew this was coming!' she gasped, bustling around quickly to collect all the things they would need for yet another night in the air raid shelter.

'Don't panic, Mum!' urged Beth, wrapping her baby brother up in his blanket, and tucking him up neatly into his pram. Simon was not amused that his beauty sleep had been disturbed, and he immediately let out a yell of disapproval. 'We've got plenty of time before they get overhead.'

'I don't care!' insisted Connie. 'I don't want to be out on the street once those ack-ack guns start up! Hurry, Beth! Hurry!'

Beth crammed the baby's pram with as many things as possible that they would need for the long night ahead. For her, it was a deeply gloomy thought. Yet another air raid, yet another night of sheer agony down in the bowels of the earth.

Thomas Sullivan had only just managed to get home with the fish and chips before the sky exploded with the sound of anti-aircraft shellfire. Although he and his father Joe lived in a fairly vulnerable residential area close to King's Cross Station, neither of them ever used the Anderson air raid shelter in the backyard that had been provided by the Borough Council at the start of the war. The ground-floor flat they lived in was serviceable rather than comfortable, but at least there was the advantage that the tenants who used to occupy the top two floors upstairs had evacuated to the country, leaving the house virtually empty for Thomas and his father. Like most people they hardly ever used the front room, and usually ate in the back parlour close to the scullery, which was handy for Joe Sullivan, for whenever he had the time, he was actually quite a good cook. This was a skill he had been forced to develop over the years after his wife left him and returned to their former home in Ireland for what she had called 'a bit of peace and sanity away from anger and politics'. What she had been referring to was what she had seen as her husband's obsession with 'the troubles' of Northern Ireland, an issue which had dominated their family life since Thomas was a small boy. Thomas himself, however, had always distanced himself from his father's somewhat extreme views on politics. Despite the Blitz, despite the hardships of rationing and trying to dodge the Nazi bombs, he loved living in England, loved the people he worked with, no matter who they were or where they came from.

'I must say, there's nuttin' I like better than eatin' cold fried fish fer supper,' grumbled Joe, with an Irish accent that was, unlike his son's, as thick as the day he first arrived in England more than twenty-five years before. He quickly shovelled cod and chips into his mouth as though he hadn't eaten for a week, and paused only briefly to remove a lock of his rapidly greying hair which had fallen across one eye. 'These people have got a nerve chargin' money fer this muck!'

Thomas, eating opposite him at the table, gave his father no more than a cursory glance. 'It was no one's fault but my own,' he replied. 'All hell broke loose just as I was leavin' the chip shop. There was so much shrapnel comin' down I had ter take cover fer a few minutes down the gents' lav.'

Joe threw a concerned look at his son, put down his knife and fork, and wiped his lips and full white moustache with the back of his hand. Despite his complaints, he had left nothing on his plate. 'It's all right, son,' he said, with a fond smile. 'I'm not blamin' you. You do yer best.' He sat back in his chair briefly and waited for Thomas to finish eating. 'What about a smoke?' he asked.

'Sure,' replied Thomas, getting up from the table, crumpling up the newspapers he had brought the fish home in, and going out into the scullery to wash his face and hands at the old stone sink. By the time he came back, his father had lit two Players cigarettes for them from a packet he kept on the mantelpiece over the small fireplace. Thomas took one of them, and settled down to smoke it in an easy chair just in front of the old brown varnished dresser.

With a fag dangling from his lips, Joe stood in front of the fire warming his hands. His collarless striped shirt looked in need of a wash, and although he was wearing braces, his trousers were also held up by a thick belt. 'I had a letter from yer mother terday,' he said, quite suddenly. 'She wants ter know when you an' me're comin' home.'

Thomas looked up with a start. 'Why would she ask a thing like that?' he asked. '*This* is our home.'

'Not to her it isn't,' replied Joe. He returned to the table, opened a quart bottle of brown ale, and poured two pint glasses. As he did so, the sound of ack-ack gunfire shook the place from ground to ceiling. Ignoring the intrusion, he took one of the glasses to Thomas, and kept one for himself. 'What she really wants to know is when am I going to let her have her freedom.'

'You mean – divorce?' asked Thomas, taking the glass of brown ale.

'*She* means divorce,' replied Joe, 'but not me. There are a lot of things wrong with me, but one thing I'll always remain is a good Catholic. As far as I'm concerned, when I married your mother it was for life.'

Thomas took a gulp from his glass, whilst at the same time sneaking a look at his father. Joe Sullivan was a rough diamond, with his shirt sleeves rolled up just high enough to reveal his fading tattoos, which showed a map of Ireland with no national boundaries, and a striking sketch of the Madonna. But Thomas knew that he had been a good father, and in many ways blamed his mother just as much for being so intransigent during her married life, for just walking out on him without any care for the son she was leaving behind. 'So what are you going to do?' he asked.

'Do?' asked Joe. 'I'm going to write back and tell her that one of these days we *will* go back home to Ireland, but it won't be to her. She made up her mind what she wanted to do, and she'll have to live with it. But I'll never give her what she wants, not as long as there's breath in my body.' He took a vast gulp of his brown ale, almost emptying the glass. 'No. We'll go home, son – one of these days. But not until the war's over.'

'Not me, Dada,' said Thomas, leaning forward in his chair. 'I'll never go back to Ireland – not to live. *This* is my home. *This* is where I'll marry and settle down.'

Joe's face stiffened. 'Marry?' he asked. 'Are you tellin' me yer've got someone *particular* in mind?'

'As a matter of fact, yes, I have,' replied Thomas. 'Mind you, I haven't asked her yet, but I intend to.'

'You're talkin' about – an English girl?'

'Yes,' replied Thomas, with a shrug.

Joe put down his empty glass, and got up from the table. 'Are you sure you know what yer're doin', son?' he asked grimly.

Thomas looked at him with some puzzlement. 'I've never been so sure of anything in my whole life,' he replied. 'In fact, I was thinkin' I'd like to bring her over to tea one day. I'd love her to meet you, Dada.'

'What's wrong with a girl from the old country?' asked Joe, cutting straight across him. 'There must be plenty of them in the dance halls around King's Cross.'

Thomas was taken aback by his father's narrow reaction. 'I suppose there are,' he replied. 'But I don't see what difference it makes. As a matter of fact there are some great Irish girls around, but it just so happens that I've fallen for someone else.'

Joe paused awkwardly before saying, 'I've got to get back to the hospital. I'm on duty at eight o'clock.'

As his father reached the parlour door, Thomas called to him. 'Will it be all right then, Dada?'

Joe turned at the door. 'Will what be all right?'

'Can I bring Beth over to meet you?' he asked, rising from his chair. 'Maybe a cup of tea on Sunday afternoon?'

'I'm sorry, son,' replied Joe ungraciously. 'I may be workin' on the wards on Sunday. Some other time, maybe.'

Thomas watched him go without further comment. Although he had always known that his father had a fixation on anything or anyone from 'the old country', he found it hard to understand why he remained so stubbornly narrow-minded when it came to mixing with people from the country he had chosen to live in for so many years. Once again, the whole place rocked with the sound of ack-ack fire bursting directly overhead. But Thomas didn't even notice it. His mind was far too preoccupied with thoughts about the darker side of his father's nature.

At the start of the war, Abe and Bernie Lieberman vowed never to spend the night in an air raid shelter. Abe, the older of the two brothers by three years, suffered from asthma, and the thought of spending even a few hours down in the dusty, damp cellar of an old piano factory was enough to bring on one of his attacks. But the relentless, practically non-stop Blitz was turning into a nightmare, and if it was a choice between dying of asthma or one of the *Luftwaffe*'s bombs, both brothers, who were themselves German Jewish refugees from the Nazi 'putsch' in 1923, knew what choice they would prefer. That's why they had finally turned up in the shelter beneath the old piano factory, joining all the regulars who had long since claimed their own special places in which to kip down for the night. Fortunately, Abe and Bernie were well-known to the residents of Hornsey Road, for they ran a small tailor's shop near the old Star Cinema further up the road, but despite the fact that they never stopped arguing with each other, their good Jewish humour endeared them to everyone.

However, the main talking point in the cellar tonight was not the Lieberman brothers, or indeed the fierce noisy air raid that was going on in the streets above. It was the dark, varnished upright piano that had suddenly been waiting for them when they filed down into the shelter earlier that evening.

'I can't believe it,' said Eileen Perkins, who positively purred with approval. 'Fancy old Stocker actually givin' us one of 'is pianos. I never knew 'e 'ad such a big 'eart.'

'Ol' Stocker ain't got no big 'eart, Mrs P,' sniffed Bill Winkler, who, to the irritation of everyone, was smoking them all out with the stale tobacco in his pipe. 'Yer can bet yer life there's a reason fer 'is madness. 'E din't own a string er factories like this fer nuffin'.'

'Too true!' agreed Jessie Hawks, settled down in her usual pitch at the foot of the stone entrance steps, her hairnet holding in her tight white curls. 'I bet 'e's makin' a fortune outer this war. I 'ear 'e's bin flogging pianos and Gord knows wot ter the NAAFI. Don't miss a trick, that one.'

'Oh, I think that's a bit unfair,' said the more conciliatory Jack Cutter, whose dog-end was in danger of dropping on to the closed lid of the piano keyboard. 'I'm sure Mr Stocker just wanted to bring a little bit of joy to us down 'ere in the shelter.'

'Wanted to dump it off, more like!' grumbled Bill.

Jack gently raised the piano lid. Surprisingly, the 'old girl' looked in good condition, for the notes on the keyboard were not too faded. Jack looked closer, and read out loud the maker's trademark inscription which was set out in gold lettering: '*G.E. Little, Chapel Street, Islington.* It's got a good pedigree, this one.'

'What is it – a dog?' asked Abe Lieberman wryly, his elderly midriff bulging over the edge of the deckchair he was trying to sleep in.

'Don't be such a chump, Abe!' scolded his young brother, Bernie, squatting uncomfortably on another deckchair next to him. 'It's not a dog. It can't bark!'

As Bernie spoke, Jack poked one of the notes with his finger. The sound it produced was pure, and echoed throughout the curved walls and ceiling of the long, narrow cellar.

Everyone turned to look at the 'old girl'.

'Oooh Jack,' squealed Eileen. 'That's beautiful!' Her daughter Rita, who was fast asleep in her arms, tossed and turned irritably.

'It sounds as if it's in good condition all right,' said Jack, striking another note. Then he turned to Connie Shanks, who was watching from her pitch nearby, whilst Beth rocked baby Simon to sleep in her arms. 'Wod'yer fink, Mrs S?'

Connie eased herself up from her mattress on the floor against the wall, and went across to take a closer look at the piano. She slowly slid the tips of her fingers all over the 'old girl', almost caressing it as though it were a thing of great beauty. 'She's seen better days, that's for sure,' she proclaimed, endearingly.

'She's not the only one!' mumbled Bernie, with a sly look at his brother.

Abe grunted back at him contemptuously.

Standing in front of the 'old girl', Connie ran her fingers along the keyboard. The sound it produced caused everyone to look on with awed fascination. She tried a few scales; the result was not tinny as she had expected, for the strings seemed to be perfectly tuned. 'Hmm,' she said half to herself, 'not bad, not bad at all.'

'Go on, Con,' called Eileen, urging Connie on enthusiastically. 'Give us a tune. It'll cheer us all up.'

'I don't think so,' said Connie, turning away from the piano. 'I don't want to keep the children awake.'

'Don't be silly!' insisted Eileen. 'We can join in. A good old sing-song'll 'elp us all ter get some kip.'

Connie smiled back. 'I'm sorry, Eileen,' she replied sweetly. 'I don't really play sing-songs.'

' 'Course yer do!' added Jessie Hawks. 'Yer're a piano teacher, ain't yer? Wot about a bit er Vera Lynn?'

There was a chorus of agreement from Eileen, Jack, and even Bill and his missus, Lil. But there was a sudden dead silence, as a bomb came screaming down nearby, shaking the cellar to its foundations. Everyone automatically covered their head with their hands as dust fluttered down from the ceiling, but as soon as the noise outside had subsided, Jessie called: 'Come on, Jack! Get the lady somefin' ter sit on!'

Jack immediately brought over his own collapsible wooden chair, and placed it in front of the piano. Connie tried to decline, and looked across at Beth for support. But all Beth could do was to shrug, and do her best to get young Simon to sleep again. Connie sighed. 'Well, I'll do my best,' she said. She sat down on the chair Jack was holding out for her, then, only too aware that all eyes were turned towards her, she placed her fingers delicately on the keyboard.

Amidst a background of distant ack-ack gunfire, explosions, and the roar of aircraft overhead, Connie's talented fingers persuaded 'the old girl' to produce a sound that was gentle, soothing and romantic. The trills were precise, the tones and semi-tones were effortless, and the piano strings accepted Connie's challenge with pride and gratitude. For several minutes, the arched ceilings and dank atmosphere was echoing to a classical piano composition that brought nothing but awe and admiration from the small group of astonished faces that were sheltering from the harsh world above. But there was nothing to sing to, no musical words to raise their spirits, nothing to urge them to get up on their feet and dance through the night. This was music, real music, the music of the concert hall, a world that most of those listening in the cellar had never experienced.

'Chopin,' whispered Abe, turning quietly to his brother as Connie played on.

'Brahms,' countered Bernie, with the utmost confidence.

'Rubbish!' insisted Abe, furious to be contradicted. 'You don't have to be an expert to know it's Chopin!'

'Brahms!'

'Chopin!'

Beth looked on, from time to time anxiously watching everyone's reaction. She was proud of her mum, there was no doubt about that.

The way Connie's fingers glided effortlessly back and forth along the keyboard was an absolute joy; if only circumstances had been different, Beth was convinced her mum could have been a famous concert pianist. But the cellar shelter was no concert hall, and she was not sure that the type of music she was playing was quite what her neighbours had in mind to distract them from the horrors of what was going on in the skies above.

Beth's uncertainty was more or less confirmed when Connie finished the short piece she was playing. After a noticeable silence, there was a slight ripple of applause, led by Abe and Bernie, who were joined eventually by the others.

'Bravo!' called Abe. 'I've never heard Chopin played so beautifully!'

'Actually,' replied Connie, getting up from the chair at the piano, 'it was by Schumann, Robert Schumann. It was one of his preludes.'

Bernie swung a smug glance at his brother. Abe sniffed and turned the other way.

'You got a way wiv those ol' ivories all right, Mrs S,' said Jack Cutter. 'I reckon you could give ol' Charlie Kunz a run fer 'is money!'

'Charlie Kunz?' added Jessie Hawks, tucking herself up in her blanket. ' 'E ain't a patch on Rawicz and Laundaur!'

'It was lovely, Mrs S,' said Eileen appreciatively, as Connie stepped carefully over her and Rita to get back to Beth and their own pitch. 'You made that ol' Joanna sound like a dream.'

'Actually,' said Connie, settling down alongside Beth, and taking the baby from her, 'Beth plays the piano far better than me.'

Beth swung her a look of total astonishment.

Connie smiled at her. 'She has a real ear for music.'

Beth's eyes were transfixed on her mother. She was stunned.

'Why don't you play something for them, darling?' asked Connie.

Before Beth had a chance to answer, everyone started to settle down in their makeshift beds, indicating that they had had enough culture for one evening.

'That'll be somefin' ter look forward to termorrer evenin',' said Jack Cutter tactfully, before snuggling down in his own blanket.

Nearby, Bill Winkler turned off the solitary electric light, and, but for the flickering of a small night-light candle, the place was plunged into darkness.

In the streets above, a strange silence seemed to have descended, and the only sounds that prevailed now were from the distant rumble of anti-aircraft gunfire.

'What d'yer do that for?' whispered Beth to her mum in the dark. 'You're the one who plays the pianer, not me.'

'I wouldn't be too sure about that if I was you, darling,' Connie whispered back. 'I wouldn't be too sure.' She tucked little Simon down under the blanket between her and Beth, and settled down for what she hoped would be a relatively undisturbed night.

In the sky above the South London suburbs, Heinz Buchner headed his beloved fighter-bomber out towards the French coast. Compared to most nights, it had been an uneventful mission, with no real target other than to cause havoc and fear amongst the civilian population who were curled up in their tiny rabbit-hole air raid shelters down below. But it wouldn't always be like that. There would soon be another target, more pressure, more danger. There was always tomorrow, and the day after, and the day after that . . .

Chapter 3

'The thing about a green cabbage,' said Uncle Horace as he dug up the biggest one he could find in his tiny back garden, 'is that you should always steam it. Your Auntie Maudie used to say that if you boil a cabbage, you lose all the natural flavour.'

Beth loved her Uncle Horace. Of course he wasn't her real uncle, but that's what both she and her brother Phil had called him ever since they were kids, and even though he was really old enough to be their grandad, that's the way they had always thought of him. Horace Ruggles and his missus Maudie had been friends of the Shanks family for donkey's years, right back to the time when Horace was serving as a soldier during the First World War and had shared a fag in the frontline trenches with Beth's paternal grandad, Percy Shanks. Although Horace had lived in London for the best part of his life, he had been born in Essex, where he had spent his early years, and where people speak with a lovely twang in their voice that seems to be a cross between rural life and nearby East and North London.

'There you are, my girl,' said Horace, proudly holding up the cherished cabbage, hands black with thick well-manured soil. 'You give this to your mum, and see what she says about *that*!'

'Oh she'll love it, Unc,' said Beth, with a broad smile. 'She always says your veg taste better than anyfin' yer can buy in the shops.'

Uncle Horace beamed, and wiped his hands on his old work dungarees. 'Only trouble though these days,' he continued, 'is this ruddy stuff.' He stooped down again and picked up a piece of jagged shrapnel that was lodged in the middle of one of his well-formed pumpkins, a remnant from the barrage of ack-ack gunfire during the previous night's air raid. 'Every mornin' I come out here an' find I've lost somefin' or uvver. Causes havoc with me Brussels, I can tell yer.' He threw the piece of shrapnel to one side, and with muddy shoes, picked his way carefully off the cabbage patch on to the narrow flagstone path. 'Let's go in and get some newspaper ter wrap this up.'

Beth followed him into the scullery through the back garden door. She had always loved going to visit Uncle Horace each Sunday morning at his small terraced house in Tottenham, not out of duty, but because she thought the world of him, especially as he was the one person in the world she knew she could always confide in.

A widower for nearly ten years, Horace had long since retired from his job as a fitter with the Gas, Light and Coke Company to take up his passion for growing vegetables in both his own garden and also the small allotment he rented from the local Borough Council, a hobby he worked on with so much love and care even though he had never actually won any local gardening competitions. 'So what's the trouble today?' he asked, whilst searching for an old newspaper in a cardboard box under the sink.

'Trouble, Unc?' asked Beth.

He looked up briefly with a grin. 'You're not goin' ter tell me yer've come to see yer ol' Uncle without havin' something on yer mind?' He spread the newspaper on the scullery table, and started wrapping the cabbage up in it. 'What's yer mum done this time?'

'She's impossible!' replied Beth, sitting at the table. 'D'yer know wot she wants ter do now? She wants us all ter pack up an' go an live wiv Gran an' Grandad.'

'Oh yes?' replied Uncle Horace, without so much as a raised eyebrow.

For some reason, Beth was surprised by his reaction. 'Well – don't yer fink that's a terrible idea?'

Uncle Horace took off his flat cap and put it down on the table. He had a thick flock of pure white hair. 'I'd say it depends,' he said.

'Depends? On wot?'

'Well let's face it,' said Uncle Horace, his face weather-beaten from years of working out in his back garden vegetable patch, 'you can understand why yer mum wants ter get out of London. With yer dad away, it ain't exactly the safest place ter bring up a family.'

'But *you're* not gettin' out, Unc,' Beth reminded him. '*You're* not worried about the bombs.'

'Ah, but *I'm* an ol' man, Beff,' replied Uncle Horace, as he finished wrapping up the cabbage. 'I've *had* the best years of *my* life. And in any case, I've got me Morrison shelter in the front room. If the whole house fell in on me, I wouldn't get a scratch.'

Beth wasn't too sure about that. To her, indoor air raid shelters were an absolute death-trap. 'The point is,' she said, 'I don't *want* ter leave London. And neivver does Phil. This is our 'ome, this is where we belong. An' in any case, the last people I'd want ter stay wiv is Gran an' Grandad.'

'That's a bit unfair, Beff,' said Uncle Horace. 'Yer gran and grandad are good people. They were absolutely wonderful to yer mum when she first came over ter England. Yer mum's a very cultured woman, Beff. She gave up a good life over in America ter marry yer dad.'

'Yes, I know all that, Unc,' said Beth. 'But let's face it, she din't 'ave to, did she? I mean, she could've stayed in America and carried on wiv 'er piano playin', instead er troopin' all the way over 'ere er live below 'er station.'

This time Uncle Horace did raise his eyebrows. 'Yer know, Beff,' he said, 'when you're in love with someone, I mean *really* in love, nothin' else matters. Believe me, I *do* know. But I'm tellin' yer, yer mum's a good woman. She loves yer dad, and she loves her family. If anythin' happened to any of yer, it'd break her heart.'

A few minutes later, they went into the front parlour where Uncle Horace poured them both a glass of his home-made rhubarb wine, which he kept in the sideboard close to the old upright piano on which his late wife Maudie occasionally tinkled a popular tune of the day. On the other side of the room, Uncle Horace's bed was made up inside the cumbersome steel Morrison shelter which took up much of the space beneath the bow window, and, proudly displayed on the wall in one of the two recesses on each side of the tiled fireplace, was a framed sepia photograph of Horace and Maudie outside the church on their wedding day.

'Yer know, yer musnt' blame yer mum fer not wantin' any harm ter come to you and Phil and young Simon,' said Uncle Horace, settling down in his favourite easy-chair. 'She's got somethin' on her mind that's scarin' the daylights out of her.'

Beth, sitting on the piano stool, looked up at him with a puzzled start. 'Wot d'yer mean?' she asked.

Uncle Horace sat back in his chair and sipped his rhubarb wine. 'Did you know yer mum was psychic?' he asked.

Beth looked even more baffled. 'She's wot?'

'Psychic,' said Uncle Horace. 'She reckons she can see things that can happen in the future. She told me that ever since the war started, she's been havin' nightmares that come true.'

'You're – jokin'?' said Beth dismissively.

'Not accordin' to yer mum,' he insisted. 'Apparently, some of the things she's seen *did* come true. She saw this cat run over in a nightmare. A couple of days later she saw it happen for real – in Seven Sisters Road.'

'I don't believe all that stuff,' said Beth, sipping her rhubarb wine. 'Most of it's just coincidence.'

'Maybe so,' replied Uncle Horace. 'But somethin's on her mind, that's fer sure. She won't tell me what it is, but it's somethin' ter do with the family, somethin' that's givin' 'er sleepless nights.'

In her mind Beth dismissed what her uncle had just told her as a lot of old boloney.

At the piano a short while later, Beth played Uncle Horace's favourite song, a wistful, romantic lullaby called ' 'Til We Meet Again'. It was a tune she always had to play for him when she visited him on Sunday mornings, partly because it was always a popular favourite at family sing-songs, but also because he and Maudie used to sing it when they sat alone together at the piano. On this occasion, however, Beth didn't join in singing the words with her uncle. It was that cat she was thinking about, the cat that had been run over in her mum's nightmare.

Sunday was turning out to be a day of rare peace and quiet for the people of London. It was the first time for ages that the air raid siren hadn't wailed out across the rooftops, giving everyone the chance to visit friends and relatives, go to church, or simply take a relaxed stroll along pavements strewn with the fallen leaves of autumn. In Finsbury Park, autumn was also much in evidence. Now that it was almost November, there were very few leaves left on the trees, the last stubborn rose blooms were wilting beneath an early previous night's frost, and a watery sun was hiding behind a maddening layer of haze.

Beth always cherished the rare moments she could spend alone with Thomas, for their independent patterns of shift work at the munitions factory made it difficult for them to get together on a regular basis. There was no doubt that she loved him, and in her heart of hearts hoped that he loved her too. However, even though they had been a couple now for over a year, there was still a lot she didn't know about him, and as they strolled together hand in hand through the park, watching hardy groups of volunteers working on what had once been the most beautiful formal gardens, now converted into vegetable plots, she made up her mind that this was the right time to ask Thomas one or two questions. 'Yer know,' she said quite out of the blue, 'yer've never told me wot it's like in Ireland, I mean where you was born an' all that.'

Thomas turned a grin at her. 'That's because I haven't the faintest idea *what* it's like in Ireland,' he replied. ' 'Cos I wasn't born there.'

Beth brought them to a halt. 'Yer wasn't?'

'Not at all,' said Thomas. 'I was born in Edmonton, before we moved across ter King's Cross. I only ever went to Ireland once in me whole life. That was when I was seven, when Dada had to go across to County Donegal ter see me mam after she'd walked out on us. I don't remember much, just that it seemed ter rain an awful lot – just the same as here.'

'But most of yer mates I've met are Irish,' said Beth inquisitively.

'So what's so wrong about that?' asked Thomas, somewhat surprised. 'Most of the fellers where I live happen ter be from Ireland. We're always swappin' jokes from the old country.'

'The *old* country,' said Beth. Her eyes flicked down to his lips, which were full and sensuous. 'That's a funny name ter call a place where yer weren't even born.'

'It don't mean nuttin' really, Beth,' he replied, in the soft Irish brogue that Beth loved so much. 'Just a term of affection, that's all. I s'ppose I love the place really.'

'Then why don't you live there?' asked Beth.

'Well fer a start,' he replied with a twinkle in his eye, 'I'd never've met you, would I?' He leaned forward, rubbed his lips gently against hers, then kissed her.

Despite the fact that two disapproving middle-aged ladies glared at them as they passed by, Beth did not object, and gave in to him willingly. 'Wot about your dad?' she asked, as they moved off.

'What about him?'

'Yer never talk about 'im much,' said Beth. 'D'yer get on wiv 'im?'

She felt him stiffen slightly, his eyes fixed firmly ahead along the path. 'What makes yer ask that?'

'Well – I remember yer once sayin' 'ow strict 'e could be.'

Thomas shrugged. 'Aren't all fathers like that?'

'Mine isn't,' insisted Beth. 'Never 'as bin. I fink the world of 'im.'

He swung a look at her. 'I love my dada too,' he said quite forcefully. 'I know he's got some funny ways, but that's because he gets so worked up about what goes on in the North.'

'The North?' asked Beth, puzzled.

'Northern Ireland,' replied Thomas. 'He gets a bit hot-headed about it all, hates the fact that Ireland isn't just one country, like over here. But it don't mean much. When it comes to the push, he's just a big ol' softie at heart.'

'And where does he work?'

It took Thomas a moment or so to answer because he was suddenly aware that Beth seemed to be taking more than just a passing interest in his dad. For some reason it unnerved him, mainly because of the problems he had had in the past with his dad being arrested some years before at a political rally which called for the British to get out of Northern Ireland. 'He's a ward porter at the Royal Northern Hospital. Any more questions?'

Again Beth brought them to a halt. She was taken aback by his touchiness. 'Thomas!' she exclaimed. 'Yer don't 'ave ter tell me anyfin' if yer don't want. It's just that – well, we've bin walkin' out now fer quite a time an' – an' I just thought I'd like ter get ter know yer better.'

Thomas unwound and relaxed. He suddenly felt guilty for being so defensive. 'I'm sorry, Beth,' he said sheepishly. 'I don't know why I always get so touchy about Dada. It's just that, well – he's not the easiest person ter get on with. I try ter keep him away from my friends.'

'Does that include me?' asked Beth.

Thomas tried to smile at her, but it was a weak smile. Fortunately, he was distracted by something in the sky above. 'Hey!' he cried. 'Will yer look at that!'

As Beth turned to look up, they could just see a huge silver shape rising up from the ground behind the trees on the other side of the road, its umbilical cord taut and unyielding. It was a barrage balloon, one of the many aerial defences designed to stop enemy aircraft flying low over the capital's rooftops.

'Come on, Beth!' cried Thomas excitedly. He grabbed her hand, and virtually yanked her at speed across the road, where, on a great stretch of grassland on the Seven Sisters Road side of the park, the Royal Air Force were raising the first of three cumbersome balloons that looked like a bloated airship with ears. Attached by heavy cable to its mobile truck below, it rose slowly, majestically into the sky bobbing up and down in a gentle breeze.

'Bleedin' 'ell, Thomas!' protested Beth out of breath, as they reached the boundary fence of the special RAF unit, which displayed a large Ministry of Defence warning notice showing: ENTRY FORBIDDEN. AUTHORISED PERSONNEL ONLY.

'Wot d'yer want ter see these fings for?'

'But they're beautiful, Beth!' gasped Thomas, eyes bulging with awe and fascination as he watched the cables unravel, and all three balloons rising up from their trucks one after the other. 'Yer see 'em bobbing up and down in the sky over yer head all the time, but yer never stop ter think where they come from, and how they do all this.'

Beth craned her neck up to look at the three bulging shapes climbing higher and higher into the hazy sky. She really couldn't understand why Thomas was so fascinated by them.

'I mean,' continued Thomas, his arm grabbing her round the waist, eyes eagerly following the balloons' steady ascent, 'just look at 'em. They're a real work of art – beautiful, just beautiful!'

Now Beth was convinced he was bonkers.

'But just imagine what Jerry would do,' said Thomas, who seemed to be miles away, 'if he could land a coupla bombs in the middle of all this.'

Startled, Beth swung a look at him. 'Wot d'yer mean?' she asked.

Thomas turned to look at her. He had a strange, distant look in his eyes. 'I mean, let's face it,' he said, 'if Jerry could find a way to knock out a place like this, all these huts and trucks and things, their planes would have a much better chance of getting through the flack. And yer know wot that would mean for London town, don't yer? It wouldn't stand a chance!'

Beth was suddenly numbed by what he was suggesting. As their eyes turned to look up at the balloons which were gradually reaching their final position in the slowly fading light of day, she began to understand what he was trying to say. This site *was* a sitting target, a *prime* target for enemy planes – *if* they knew enough about it. It was a chilling thought, and it disturbed her that Thomas had taken such an interest in it.

Connie Shanks looked up at the sky through her front bedroom window and watched the three barrage balloons rising up slowly from Finsbury Park in the distance, beyond the grey sloping rooftops of Moray, Fonthill and Stroud Green Roads. They were a comforting sight, for although they seemed bizarre, bobbing up and down against a deepening red sunset, she knew that they at least offered some defence against the *Luftwaffe*'s nightly aerial onslaught. She peered over her shoulder briefly to see baby Simon gurgling happily in his cot at the side of her bed. It brought an affectionate smile to her face, for she was grateful that she had been blessed with a child who had accepted the rigours of war as though there had never been any other way of life. Then her eyes moved to the old double brass bedstead, where she and her husband Ted had spent so many wonderful nights together, where all three of their children had been planned and conceived, and where they had so often solved the problems of the world before going to sleep. These days, with both Beth and Phil out at work all day, Connie spent far too many days on her own, with only the baby to keep her company. In many ways she felt it was a dreary existence for someone who had been brought up in the splendours of a well-to-do family back in Houston, Texas, whom she had not set eyes on since she left America to marry Ted nearly twenty years before. She had often wondered how different her life would have been if it hadn't been for her falling so helplessly in love with such a rough and ready young East End boy whilst she was studying for a music degree in London. Spending so much time alone was so depressing; it forced her to sit for hours just dwelling on the past, present and future, especially the future, which, during such hazardous times, seemed bleak and uncertain.

A short while later, Connie went downstairs to start preparing for another night in the piano factory air raid shelter, although no siren had yet sounded. Ever since the Blitz first started it had become something of a ritual amongst many of the population in London to seek the regular safety of the public shelter each night, regardless of whether or not an air raid was in progress. Although some people welcomed the chance to get together with their neighbours, Connie hated it, not only because of the claustrophobic atmosphere of the deep cellar shelter itself, but because it seemed such a totally unnatural existence. However, the one person who despised using the shelter more than anyone else was Beth, who resented being dragged off night after night to sleep on a mattress on a cold stone floor amongst a whole lot of other people. And if Beth's constant resentment wasn't enough, the news Phil brought home with him from the fire station was, for Connie, yet another cause for concern.

'They want to transfer you?' she asked, ashen-faced, as she watched Phil at the kitchen table, tucking in to a fried kipper she had managed to get him for tea. 'What exactly does that mean?'

Trying to shrug off her concerns, Phil continued to pick at the kipper bones. But he was careful not to catch her look. 'It just means they want me ter be based at anuvver station, that's all.'

Connie sat opposite him at the table. '*Which* other station?'

'Up the City,' replied Phil hesitantly. 'Moorgate.'

'Moorgate!' Connie's eyes widened with horror. 'That's one of the most dangerous areas to be in the whole of London. There's been a hell of a lot of damage up there.'

'Not really,' said Phil, quite matter of fact. 'Moorgate's no diff'rent ter Islin'ton. It's busy durin' the Blitz wherever yer go. Anyway, they're short of one messenger up there.'

'Why?'

Connie's direct question took Phil off-guard. 'Wot d'yer mean?' he asked, flicking a quick glance up at her.

'I'm asking *why* they're short of one messenger boy?' she demanded.

Phil only had a split second to give a convincing reply. 'I dunno,' he said with a shrug. 'We're all volunteers. We don't 'ave ter do the job if we don't want.'

'Precisely!' insisted Connie, glaring at him. 'So why does it have to be you?'

This time he looked at her directly. ' 'Cos, I want to, Mum,' he said. ' 'Cos I volunteered ter do somefin' ter 'elp out. There are plenty of uvver blokes like me.'

'You're not a bloke, Phil,' she said pleadingly. 'You're only sixteen years old, and you're my son. Each night you go out through that door, I'm worried sick about you. Can't you understand, Phil? I love you.' She stretched out and covered his hand with her own.

Again Phil shrugged, and returned to his kipper. 'I love you too, Mum,' he replied. 'But if they need someone urgent up at anuvver station, I can 'ardly say no, can I?'

'Maybe not,' replied Connie, withdrawing her hand. 'But *I* can.'

Phil looked up at her with a start.

'You're under-age, Phil,' said Connie. 'I'm still your mother. I still have some say in what you may or may not do.'

'That's not wot Dad'd say!' snapped Phil defiantly. ' 'E's doin' 'is bit fer 'is country, an' so am I. In the last war blokes er my age joined up and went off ter fight in France.'

'The last war was a long time ago, Phil!' insisted Connie, getting up angrily from the table. 'One can only hope this country has learned something since then about using children to go to war.'

This last remark of his mum's cut Phil deeply. As far as he was concerned, to be called a child was just about the most stupid thing anyone could ever say to him. He didn't *feel* like a child night after night, whilst he was racing his messenger's bicycle through streets of falling masonry, risking his life to save other people's. His mum didn't understand. How could she? Despite all her years in England, she was still a Yank. *They* weren't fighting a war. *They* didn't know what it was like to have their homes blown to pieces. He slowly eased himself up from the table. 'I'm going to get changed,' he said, turning to the door.

'Phil!'

He stopped briefly, and turned.

'Please try to understand how I feel, son,' she pleaded, her face wrought with anguish. 'What sort of a mother would I be if I didn't worry about you?'

Phil nodded with a weak smile, and left the room. As he closed the door, he paused in the passage outside and took a deep breath, relieved that the scene with his mum which he had been dreading all day was over. But he still wasn't sure if he had got away with it. He still wasn't sure what she would do if she really was determined to stop him doing what he knew he had to do. But then, how could he have told her the real reason he was being transferred to one of the most dangerous areas in the Fire Service, that the messenger boy he was being asked to replace had been killed during a heavy bombing raid there just a few nights before.

Chapter 4

When Beth arrived at the munitions factory for her morning shift, she found the place buzzing with excitement. In an effort to help raise the morale of war workers, the BBC had decided to try out a series of thirty-minute variety programmes, which would eventually be broadcast from factory canteens in the lunch-hour throughout the country. The programmes, which as yet did not have a title, would consist of two or three variety acts, including comedians and singers, who would be accompanied by a single pianist. Beth and her mates were thrilled to discover that their factory was one of the first to be used as a try-out for the programme, and even more thrilled when the show was performed in their own canteen whilst they ate their midday meal. During the show, Beth sat with Thomas and her mates, and they all roared with laughter as the much-loved comedian Jack Warner told stories about 'My Little Gel', which was his well-known catch-phrase on the music halls.

When it was all over the producer asked if anyone would like to sing or play a musical instrument, and to her horror, Beth's mates immediately pushed her up to the piano on the platform. After her initial reluctance, and aware that the eyes of all the workers in the canteen were watching her, Beth launched in to a medley of favourite tunes of the day, including. 'Let the Rest of the World Go By', 'Shine On, Harvest Moon' and 'Run, Rabbit, Run'. Unfortunately, her rousing performance was cut short when the air raid siren wailed from the factory roof, but just as everyone was making a dash to the shelter, she was thrilled to be thanked by Jack Warner, who then asked her if she had always played by ear. 'Oh no, sir,' replied Beth, quick as a flash. 'I always use me fingers!'

*

Down in the factory shelter, and against the background of overhead ack-ack gunfire, Beth was again the life and soul of the party, cracking jokes about Hitler and Mussolini, and, much to Thomas's disapproval, making up silly stories about her experiences with previous boyfriends, which confirmed her reputation as the 'firecracker'. However, the situation became more serious when one of the factory's air raid wardens called down into the shelter that two barrage balloons had just been shot down and were now bursting into flames in the distance, somewhere in the direction of Finsbury Park. Although this provoked no reaction from Thomas, it immediately dampened Beth's high spirits. Fortunately, the air raid lasted little more than forty-five minutes, after which the workers streamed back up to their respective factory benches.

It was not until later in the afternoon that Beth first heard the rumours that had been sweeping though the factory all morning. She was working alongside her mates, Mo Mitchell and Elsie Tuckwell, at the time, and when another of her mates, 'Midge' Morton, came over to break the news, it was not at all welcome.

'Movin' out er London?' exclaimed Beth, completely shocked, whilst trying to take it all in against a background of *Music While You Work* on the tannoy system. 'I don't believe it!'

'Neivver did I,' replied Midge, who was given her name by the other girls because she stood no more than four feet six in height. ' 'Til I 'eard 'Atchett talkin' about it wiv the General Manager. Apparently it ain't confirmed yet, but it looks as though it's goin' ter 'appen.'

'They can't do that!' insisted Mo haughtily. 'We all live in London. They can't just force us to go an' work wherever they want.'

'I wouldn't be so sure of that,' added Elsie, whose flaming red curls were just visible beneath her white work turban. 'There's a war on. If there's a chance of a place like this bein' in any kind of danger, they'd 'ave the powers ter do wot they want.'

'Danger?' asked Beth sceptically.

'Just think wot this place is for, Beff,' replied Elsie. 'We ain't exactly makin' kids' toys, are we? If Jerry dumped a bomb down our 'ooter, there wouldn't be much left of *us*.'

'But we're s'pposed ter be top secret,' said Midge. 'Jerry wouldn't know where ter find us.'

Mo laughed. 'You've got an 'ope, Midge Morton!' she cried. 'London's full er spies and traitors.'

Elsie agreed. 'I 'eard they knocked out a factory like this down in Streatham the uvver week. Loads killed, gels workin' on plane parts or somefin'. Needless ter say, it was all 'ushed up.'

Beth was getting more depressed by the minute. 'Where do they want to move us to?' she asked, dreading the answer.

'Somewhere up Norf,' replied Midge. 'Gord knows where.'

'But there must be plenty er gels up there who could take over this work?' asked Beth.

Midge shrugged. She hadn't a clue.

'It's time that's the problem, I'd say,' said Mo. 'They'd need time ter train up new people. Keepin' us on they could make sure there'd be no hold up in supplies.'

Whilst the others carried on talking, Beth looked around the factory at the hive of industry, a sea of white-coated girls slaving away at their respective workbenches. She was utterly dismayed by the suggestion that the place could be a target for enemy aircraft, even though it was perfectly obvious that it would be. She was also unnerved by the thought that if the workers' safety was to be protected, then the only way was to move them all to the depths of the country. But as far as Beth was concerned, such a move would be out of the question. How, she asked herself, would she be able to look after her mother and young baby brother if she was transferred to some distant rural area? It was bad enough that her mum wanted the family to go and stay with Beth's grandparents, but now this! No. She would never agree to abandon her home, not for the Government nor her mum. There was too much talk, too much panic. The Germans would never bomb this factory because they would never know how to find it.

'An' did yer 'ear we're all goin' ter be questioned?'

Beth was snapped out of her thoughts by Midge's latest bit of gossip. 'Questioned?' she asked irritably.

'After wot 'appened down at Streatham the uvver week,' continued Midge, revelling in the attention she was getting, 'the management 'ave asked the police in to question everyone ter see if they 'ave any suspicions about anyone.'

'Suspicions?' asked Mo sceptically.

'Careless talk cost lives,' said Midge grandly, reminding them of the posters all around the factory walls. 'Yer never can tell. One of us might be a saboteur or somefin'.'

Both Mo and Elsie raised their eyes in bored disbelief at Midge's stupidity. 'Use yer common sense,' snapped Elsie. 'We'd 'ardly be likely ter pass on secrets ter Jerry when we 'ave ter work in the place ourselves – now would we?'

Midge shrugged snootily. 'I'm only sayin' wot I've 'eard,' she replied, before going back to her bench.

The other girls watched her go, and shook their heads. 'Questioned by the police!' said Elsie dismissively. 'Who does she fink we are – Lord 'Aw-'Aw?!'

Both girls roared with laughter and returned to their work. But Beth didn't feel very amused. She had too much on her mind.

Connie Shanks wanted to get to the Lieberman brothers before they closed up shop for the night. Although it was only a short walk along Hornsey Road, it was almost blackout time, and pushing Simon's pram uphill was always quite a struggle. In the far distance, Hornsey Rise and Muswell Hill were already blanketed in the dark of early evening, and in the sky above, army searchlights were criss-crossing the sky, practising for what seemed sure to be another all-night air raid. With this in mind, Connie quickened her pace; getting caught out in the street during ack-ack gunfire was something she always dreaded, especially with so few places to shelter from falling shrapnel on the way. She resisted the urge to join the long queue outside a greengrocer's shop, where excited shoppers were hoping to buy an allowance of two oranges per person, which, since the start of the war, had become a real luxury. But the wet fish shop had a large notice in its unlit window, which showed quite clearly: NO FISH UNTIL FRIDAY. Every time she went shopping these days, Connie found it a deeply frustrating and depressing experience. Even the most ordinary necessities of life, such as eggs and meat, were in short supply, and when they did suddenly become 'available', there was such a mad scramble to get them, a queue could take anything up to an hour to clear, and Connie often left the shop empty-handed. But today, Connie's main preoccupation was to collect Ted's grey flannel trousers, which she had taken in to Abe and Bernie's tailor shop the week before to have a patch put on a small hole in the seat. She didn't know why she had waited so long to have them repaired, for they had been hanging in the bedroom wardrobe ever since Ted had been called up. But Connie had woken up one morning with a firm desire to get the job done. She had no idea why, only the feeling that it would somehow make her feel close to Ted again.

'Frankly,' said Abe Lieberman, handing over Ted's trousers to Connie at the counter, 'I've never understood why people are always having their clothes repaired and altered. Better just to buy something new. Saves so much time and trouble.'

Connie thought that a fairly extraordinary remark considering the first thing one saw upon entering the tiny tailor's shop was a huge notice which proudly proclaimed: REPAIRS AND ALTERATIONS. AT YOUR SERVICE. 'The way things are going, Mr Lieberman,' said Connie, 'buying new clothes will soon be a thing of the past. There's a rumour going around that the Government are going to introduce clothes rationing.'

'Clothes rationing!' scoffed Abe dismissively, whilst wiping a dew-drop from his nose with a handkerchief, which he always kept tucked into the top pocket of his jacket. 'I blame it all on Chamberlain.'

'Chamberlain?' called his brother Bernie, metal-rimmed spectacles on the end of his nose as he sat at his sewing machine. 'What's clothes rationing got to do with Neville Chamberlain? He's not Prime Minister. He resigned months ago.'

'I don't care,' insisted Abe, neatly folding up Ted Shanks's trousers. 'If Chamberlain hadn't done a deal with that house painter in Munich, there wouldn't be any need for any kind of rationing.'

'You're crazy!' retorted his brother, with a dismissive wave of the hand. 'Chamberlain tried his best. As a matter of fact, I think he must have had some Jewish blood in his veins.'

Abe was so outraged at such a suggestion, he chose merely to sniff indignantly and ignore it.

Connie, sorting through her purse for the payment, thought that both brothers were quite incongruous in their grey tin helmets, which they always insisted on wearing whilst they worked, whether there was an air raid in progress or not, and which displayed their names scrawled in white paint. Connie handed over the one shilling and sixpence in coins. 'I hope you don't mind rather a lot of pennies and ha'pennies?' she asked. 'Unless you can change a ten-shilling note?'

'Pennies, ha'pennies,' replied Abe, taking the coins. 'What does it matter? It's all money.' Even so, he counted out every coin, raising his spectacles to inspect each one individually.

'By the way, Mrs Shanks,' said Bernie, calling across to her. 'If I may say so, I think you played the piano beautifully in the shelter the other night.'

Connie looked up with a start, and smiled gratefully at him. 'Thank you very much, Mr Lieberman,' she replied. 'That's most kind of you.'

'*I* was going to say exactly the same thing,' added Abe, with a sidelong glare at his brother. 'I haven't heard music played like that since Bernie and I were kids in Leipzig.'

'Oh really?' asked Connie appreciatively.

'Mama used to take us to this place called the Café Rosa,' continued Abe, in his thick German Hebrew accent. 'There was this man there called Domino.'

'That was his nickname, you fool!' growled Bernie, without looking up from his sewing.

'His name was Domino,' insisted Abe, ignoring his brother's intervention. 'He used to play Mozart . . .'

'Beethoven!'

Abe talked straight through his brother's interruption. 'He used to play Mozart as though the sound was coming from heaven itself. I remember watching his fingers on the keyboard. They moved like magic. Mama loved it! She drank black coffee with small sweet biscuits, and listened in a state of total enchantment. There's something about a piano. It has a way of talking to you, of sending you off into a different world.'

Connie smiled sweetly at him. She was very impressed by his observation.

'*You* can do that too, Mrs Shanks,' continued Abe, once he had come down to earth again. 'When I heard you play the other evening, I thought of Domino. He was a Jew. I often wonder what the Nazis did to him.'

Connie's smile faded. She could feel Abe's pain. 'Thank you very much, Mr Lieberman,' she said, picking up Ted's trousers and putting them into Simon's pram.

'But I still don't know what a nice lady like you is doing in a place like this.'

Bernie's odd remark caused Connie to look round with a start at him. 'What did you say, Mr Lieberman?' she asked, with some curiosity.

Bernie removed his foot from the pedal of the sewing machine, took off his spectacles, and looked across at her. 'Where did you learn to play the piano, Mrs Shanks?'

'My mother taught me,' replied Connie. 'Back home in the States. Then I came over here to train at a music college in St John's Wood.'

'But why here?' asked Bernie, to his brother's intense discomfort. 'How come you end up here – in Islington, of all places? Why not Kensington, or Knightsbridge, or Mayfair? If I may say so, Moray Road is hardly the kind of area for a lady of – *your* talent.'

Connie was quite taken aback by Bernie's strange attitude. 'The reason I came to England, Mr Lieberman,' she said gently, 'the reason I came to Islington, was because I fell in love, I fell in love with someone who was unlike anyone else I had ever met in my entire life, someone who cared for me, treated me as though I was someone who meant something to him. When he brought me to live in Moray Road, I was proud, am *still* proud. And d'you know why? Because it gave me the chance to meet people like you and your brother, to know our neighbours in Moray Road, and the people who work in the shops, who know how to serve, how to smile, how to make you feel welcome. Believe me, if it wasn't for this wretched war, it would never be a hardship for me to live in Moray Road – or anywhere else.'

Once she had left the shop, Abe Lieberman turned to his brother and asked: 'Why do you always have to open your big mouth?'

Beth had a lot to think about. Despite her personal triumph playing for Jack Warner and the BBC people back at the factory canteen during the lunch hour, she was full of concerns not only about rumours that the factory might move up north, but also about the prospect of being interviewed by the police about anyone she might know who had been asking questions about security matters that might be seen as being just a little *too* inquisitive.

Thinking about all this whilst she waited for Thomas to travel back home with her to Holloway from the Tally Ho bus stop, she had no idea why her mind kept focusing on that walk through Finsbury Park with Thomas, and how he had been so fascinated with the RAF unit that was operating the barrage balloons. But then her other self told her that she was being obsessed by something that was just too stupid for words. What if Thomas *had* taken an interest in the barrage balloon site. After all, wasn't Finsbury Park a public place? It wasn't exactly hidden behind bushes, or kept out of view. There must be similar sites like that all over London, probably all over the country; it would hardly be difficult for Jerry to pinpoint them from either the sky or the ground. Thomas was no spy. He was just like any other young bloke who liked watching trains from railway platforms or men using pneumatic drills at road works. In other words, it was ridiculous to even think that there was anything odd or suspicious about Thomas, even if he did have an Irish mum and dad, and was unlikely to be called up in England. And in any case, if the factory had had any real worries about using someone like Thomas, they would hardly have allowed him to work in such a highly sensitive job.

The bus queue was down to just two or three people when Thomas finally turned up. Beth couldn't actually see him coming towards her in the pitch dark, but she knew it was him because he always flicked his torch on and off as soon as he turned the corner at the Gaumont cinema.

'Sorry ter keep yer waitin',' said Thomas, directing his torch beam on to Beth's face, and immediately giving her a quick peck on the cheek. 'I've had quite an interesting half-hour.'

'Wot d'yer mean?' asked Beth.

At that moment, a 609 trolleybus drew to a halt at the stop. It was hard to see it in the pitch dark, for, during the blackout, its headlights were dimmed and half-masked. Thomas put his arm around Beth's waist, and before answering her question, gently eased her on to the bus platform. As usual, they climbed the stairs to the upper deck, where they were relieved to see that the back seat was free.

'So wot's 'appened?' asked Beth, the moment they had settled down.

Thomas slipped his arm around Beth's shoulders, and leaned her into him as much as he could. The interior light was so dim, they could hardly see each other. 'I've been questioned by the law,' he replied, voice low.

Beth panicked. 'Wot?' she gasped.

'Nothin' ter worry about,' he assured her. 'I just got called into the security office to answer a few questions, that's all. Purely routine.'

'Routine?' asked Beth sceptically. Again she had to wait for an answer, for the clippie came up the stairs with her torch to collect their fares. Once she'd moved on, Beth continued to press Thomas. 'Wot d' yer mean *routine*?' she asked.

'They're checkin' on everyone, Beth,' he replied. ' 'Specially people like me. Not a hundred per cent British, if yer get my meanin'!' He shone his torch briefly on her face, and could see her anxious look. 'It's nothin' ter get worked up about, Beth,' he insisted. 'I'm not the only one. They've bin goin' in an' out of that office all day. They'll probably get round ter you sooner or later.'

'Wot *exactly* did they ask yer, Thomas?'

Thomas found Beth's inquisitiveness unsettling. He pulled his arm away from her shoulders, and took out a fag from his duffle-coat pocket. 'They just wanted to know a bit about my background, where

I was born, my family, where I live, that sort of thing.' He put the fag in his lips, but didn't light it. 'As far as I could tell, they were just checking up on who I know, my mates, the people I mix with. They even asked about you.'

Beth stared hard at him in the dim light. 'Me?'

He gently turned her face towards him, and took the unlit fag from his lips. 'You *are* my girl – aren't yer?' he asked.

Beth didn't reply. Of course she was his girl, but all the rumours and questions about careless talk had unnerved her. She sat back in her seat again, and listened to the quiet electric whir of the trolleybus engine. In the dim interior light, she could see by the red glow of fags, that there were only a handful of passengers on the top deck, which was always the smoker's safe haven, and as the bus made its way downhill towards Archway Junction, through the window she could just make out shadowy elongated figures stretching out along the pavements, their flickering torch bulbs lighting the way as they scurried home. There was a sudden flash of light reflected in the window at her side, followed by a pungent waft of smoke, which meant that Thomas had lit his fag. Gradually, his arm slid over her shoulders again, and once he had exhaled, his lips searched for hers, and he kissed her.

'Did they ask yer why you ain't bin called up?' Almost the very moment she had asked the question, Beth regretted it. But to her surprise, Thomas didn't pull away.

'Now why would they do a thing like that?' he asked quietly, without any sign of irritation.

'Well –' said Beth, fumbling for words, 'there ain't many boys your age workin' in the factory, are there? I just fawt—'

'I've told yer before, Beth,' explained Thomas calmly, 'I'm Irish as well as English – if yer get my meanin''. They can't call up someone from a foreign country. But if it wasn't fer me dad, I'd go termorrow.'

This took Beth by surprise. 'Yer would?'

'Of course I would!' said Thomas firmly. 'I feel just as much British as I do Irish.'

Suddenly, Beth felt a wave of affection for him, and she leaned her head on his shoulder. With that one brief assurance from Thomas, all her doubts had been brushed aside. He was no traitor, he was no spy. She felt ashamed of herself for being so muddled in her thinking. She blamed it all on going to too many pictures. 'Wot about yer dad?' she asked. 'Wot would '*e* say if yer went into the army?' This time, she did feel him stiffen. She felt herself tense and shrivel up inside. There I go again! she said to herself.

'I don't think Dada would take very kindly to me goin' off ter the war,' he said tactfully. 'But then I guess, it'd be the same with any father or mother – wouldn't it?'

Beth tried to hide her embarrassment by snuggling up closer to him. She was relieved when he responded by kissing her again.

Within the next few minutes, the bus reached Archway Junction, where two passengers from the upper deck got up, and with torches already turned on, went downstairs. Once the clippie had pushed the start button, the bus moved off again, winding down across the Junction into Upper Holloway Road.

As she leaned into him, Beth loved the warmth of Thomas's body; it made her feel as though they were one person. It made her think back to the time when she had given herself to him, that oh so wonderful warm summer afternoon some months before, when Beth's mother had taken the baby down to see Gran and Grandad Shanks down in Hertfordshire, and Beth had brought Thomas home. She remembered how strange but excited she felt as she took Thomas up to her bedroom. She felt so guilty, so ashamed, but so thoroughly happy. It was the first time she had seen the naked flesh of a man, the first time she had given herself to a man, and although in many ways it was a traumatic experience, Thomas had treated her with so much care and understanding, she felt as though he was making love to her for herself, and not just for the moment. It was also a moment she would cherish for the rest of her life.

'I've got an idea.'

The sound of Thomas's voice took her by surprise. She looked up at him.

'I think it's about time you met my dada,' he said.

Beth sat up with a start. 'Wot?' she replied, taken aback.

'Well why not?' he continued. 'You took me home to meet your mum and brother, so why shouldn't I return the compliment? As I don't intend to ever let you go, you'll both have to meet one of these days, so I don't see why it shouldn't be now.'

Beth was too stunned to reply.

'Well yer do *want* ter meet him – don't you?'

Beth slowly sat up. ' 'Course I do!' she returned. 'If you fink 'e'd like ter meet *me*?'

'Good!' he exclaimed, after a quick draw on his fag. 'Then that's settled.'

'But 'ow?'

'Well it's no use comin' back home,' said Thomas. 'It's a bit of a man's patch, and neither Dad nor I are much of a cook.'

'So where?'

'The pub.'

'Pub?'

'Our local,' said Thomas, with a grin. 'It's second home ter Dada. He's always in a good mood there.'

'Yer mean, yer fink 'e might not be in a good mood after 'e's met *me*?'

Thomas was stung. That's not what he thought at all. As far as he was concerned, his dada would, like himself, fall in love with Beth the moment he laid eyes on her. In any case, he couldn't care less *what* his dada felt about her; Beth was *his* girl, and that's all there was to it. And yet, there *was* a nagging doubt in his mind. Joe Sullivan was not an easy man to deal with at the best of times, especially where the English were concerned. The thing he feared most was that if his dada took against Beth once he'd seen her, he would show it, and be as intractable as the Rock of Gibraltar. Nonetheless, this was something that had to be done, and until it was done, Thomas knew that his relationship with Beth would always be under strain.

'No one could be in a bad mood after meetin' you,' Thomas said, pulling her close to him.

Beth leaned her head on his shoulder. She was in her seventh heaven.

The trolleybus purred its way down Holloway Road, passing the Royal Northern Hospital on the way.

At the emergency ward in the hospital, Thomas's father, Joe Sullivan, returned from taking his final patient to the X-ray department before knocking off for his evening meal break. With no air raid during the previous twenty-four hours, it had been a quieter day than of late, which gave Joe and his fellow hospital porters a chance of a little more relaxation. The meal break for Joe, however, did not mean sitting down to an actual meal, but time for a pint or two in the local pub just down the road near the Nag's Head. But before that, he had one task ahead of him, an important task that could not be left unattended, especially as the man he had arranged to meet had come all the way from Streatham in South London.

After exchanging a few casual words with one or two of the nursing staff and some of the patients, Joe left the hospital by the Manor Gardens entrance, and made his way across the road to the old Holloway Empire cinema, which had closed and been boarded up just two years before. There was quite a chill in the air, not a time for someone to be out in shirtsleeves. But Joe Sullivan was a hardy man, who was more concerned about the man he was meeting than the sharp early evening frost.

'You're late,' said a tall shadowy figure waiting for him on the stone steps of the old cinema. The husky, deep-throated voice was more Northern Ireland than Islington.

'Sullivans are always late,' replied Joe, who, like the man he was meeting with, had refrained from using a torch. 'It's our code of practice.'

The man lit a cigarette, but it was done so quickly that Joe only caught a brief glimpse of his face, which was lined, and older than his voice suggested. 'D'yer have anythin' for me?' the man asked.

'Not yet,' replied Joe, carefully checking all around to make sure they were not being watched. 'It's much too early.'

'Too early for what?' came the retort.

'These things have to be done when the time is right,' replied Joe. 'I don't intend to take any chances.'

After a slight pause, which seemed to Joe to be interminable, the man replied: 'We can't wait for ever, Sullivan. This thing is urgent. There are people waiting on it.' He paused again to let the sound of a tram rattle past them along the Holloway Road. His cigarette glowed as he inhaled a lungful of smoke. 'So what seems to be the problem?'

'The war,' Joe returned, without a second's thought. 'In case you hadn't realised, it's not easy moving around in the Blitz, with shrapnel fallin' down from the sky every few minutes.'

Another long, ominous pause. 'So when *can* we expect some sort of result?'

'When I'm good and ready,' replied Joe fearlessly. 'Tell yer people.'

'As you wish, Sullivan,' replied the man. 'As you wish.'

Without another word, Joe turned, and started to walk off.

'Oh by the way,' called the man. 'How's your boy? How's your Thomas?'

Joe came to a brief halt. Although it was pitch dark, his face was as hard as steel. He wanted to reply. He wanted to go back. He wanted to go back and choke the hell out of that faceless weed. But he resisted the temptation. He knew what the suggestion was, he knew he was being deliberately provoked. But he decided against reacting. He decided that the best way to treat filth was to ignore it. And so, resisting the temptation to look back over his shoulder to try to catch a last glimpse of the shadowy figure, he walked off, and made for the pub for what was still left of his evening meal break.

Chapter 5

The freezing fogs of November were proving to be almost as much of a problem as the air raids, which were now coming on a fairly regular basis every evening. Hit and run daylight raids were also on the increase, and aerial dogfights between the superior power of the German *Luftwaffe* and a handful of plucky RAF Spitfire and Hurricane pilots were becoming a feature of everyday life in the skies above London. However, despite the drudgery of having to spend each night in the cellars of the old piano factory, the residents who sheltered there were astonished to find that the local authorities had agreed to equip the place with a dozen bunk beds, which meant that, once they had been delivered and installed, the groans and grumbles became less and less frequent. Even more of a godsend was the portable lavatory that had also been provided, which was placed behind a hanging blanket, replacing the enamel buckets that were none too conducive to getting a good night's sleep. However, during the second week of November, there was an unexpected lull in the air raids, caused, according to the Civil Defence teams, by the massive aerial assault on the provincial city of Coventry, which had sustained the most devastating loss of life and property. During this time, the people of Islington were able to go about their daily lives, with most people, including Connie, Beth and little Simon, temporarily forsaking the damp atmosphere of the shelter in favour of some peaceful nights in their own beds. In other words, life was gradually beginning to return to normal. Even Arthur the postman was back to delivering the post on time.

'You're in luck terday, Mrs Shanks,' called old Arthur, who had come out of retirement to resume his job with the Post Office after all the younger men had been called up at the start of the war. 'Got a speshull for yer!'

Connie, peering out from the front door, practically ran to the garden gate to meet him. 'What is it?' she asked excitedly.

'Don't ask me, ducks,' replied the old codger, who was weighed down with the sack of post he was carrying. 'But it's got OHMS all over it, so I reckon it's somefin' important.'

As Connie reached the gate, her heart sank. An official letter. Oh God, was it bad news, she asked herself? Has something happened to Ted? But the moment she took the letter from Arthur, her eyes lit up. The writing on the envelope was Ted's handwriting; she'd know it anywhere, the same neat hand he'd always used ever since the time when he wrote his first letter to her soon after they met. 'Oh thank you, Arthur!' she gasped, with a mixture of joy and relief. 'Thank you so much!'

Old Arthur's eyes lit up as he watched Connie rush back into the house clutching her precious morning delivery. Another satisfied customer.

'Beth! Beth, come down here! It's from your dad! There's a letter from Dad!'

Hearing the front door downstairs slam, and her mum calling up to her, brought Beth hurrying out of her bedroom and down the stairs. 'Wos wrong?' she asked, doing up the buttons on her dress as she came into the kitchen. ' 'As anyfin' 'appened to 'im?'

Connie was shaking her head ecstatically. She had already ripped open the envelope and was reading the contents of the letter with unbounded joy. 'No! There's nothing wrong!' she spluttered. 'He's well! He's really well! Oh my God! He may be coming home!'

'Wot!' Beth couldn't believe what she was hearing.

'Here!' said Connie, holding out the letter for her. 'Read it!'

Phil came into the room, in pyjamas, scratching his head, still half asleep. 'Wos all the noise?' he groaned.

Beth started to read out loud from the letter her mum had just given her:

Dear Gang (Con, Beth, Phil *and* the newest member!),

Well, here I am. Can't tell you where I am, but I'm thinking of you *all* the time. Got your last letter, Con, and I can't tell you how it cheered me up. It's funny, but though I'm miles away from home, I can still see you all – you, Beth, with your cheeky grin, you, Phil, grumbling and groaning about not getting enough grub, and my dear Con, sitting at your old piano, your hair tied behind your head, making sweet music that I hear every night when I turn in. And young Simon. It's hard to think that he don't even know me. But I know him. Oh yes, I know him, all right, even though I've only ever seen him in that snapshot you sent me. What's he doing now, I wonder? I wonder who he looks like? Hope he looks like you, Con.

'He don't look like either of you,' mumbled Phil, half asleep and with his face resting on his arms on the kitchen table. ' 'E looks just like a baby ter me!'

Beth ignored him and carried on reading her dad's letter:

Anyway, not much to report from this end, and even if there was, I'm not allowed to tell you. All I can say is that my mates with me here are the salt of the earth. They come from all parts of dear old Blighty and we all look after each other like we was one big family. I tell you one thing though: it's . . . cold here! Enough to freeze the knackers off a brass monkey.

Got to go now. It's first bugle and we've got things to do. Oh and by the way don't be surprised if you see me suddenly walk through that front door one of these days. Don't bank on it, but from what I heard, it could just happen. Take care of yourselves – *all* of you, and if the raids are getting any worse remember what I said about going down to Gran and Grandad's. I worry like hell about you.

Cheers for now.

Your loving husband and dad,

Ted xxxx (one for each of you!)

As soon as Beth had finished reading, Connie, whose eyes had welled up with tears, practically snatched the letter back from her. 'I wish 'e'd tell us where 'e is,' said Beth. ' 'E hasn't even put the date.'

' 'Course 'e aint, yer mut!' mumbled Phil, sitting up, eyes dazed. 'Din't 'ear wot 'e said? 'E can't tell us where 'e is 'cos it ain't allowed.'

'We must get the place cleaned up!' announced Connie, clutching Ted's letter ecstatically to her chest. 'When your dad gets home, I want this place spick and span!' She immediately started to bustle around tidying up plates and saucepans.

'Come off it, Mum!' said Beth. 'It ain't certain Dad's comin' 'ome. 'E only said it *could* 'appen.'

Connie came to an abrupt halt at Simon's pram. 'And did you also hear what he said about going to your gran and grandad's?' she replied sharply.

Beth came back at her immediately. 'That's only if the raids are gettin' worse. An' they ain't. We 'aven't 'ad one fer nearly two weeks. For all we know, Jerry may've given up.'

'If you think that,' replied Connie, lifting Simon out of his pram, 'then you're greatly mistaken. As soon as they've finished with Coventry, mark my words – they'll be back.'

'I still don't think we need ter go runnin' off ter the country.'

'Well *I* do!' insisted Connie, gently stroking Simon's back. 'As a matter of fact I've already mentioned it to your gran, and we're all going down there on Sunday.'

Both Beth and Phil threw a horrified look at each other.

'I can't!' protested Beth. 'I'm seein' Thomas on Sunday. The only chance I 'ave ter see 'im is when 'e's on night shift.'

'I can't help that,' insisted Connie, displaying a rare note of firmness. 'I've already made arrangements with your grandmother. We're going to catch the early morning bus to Hatfield, and I want no arguments!'

'But wot about Thomas?' asked Beth gloomily. 'Wot am I goin' ter tell 'im?'

'Frankly, I don't care *what* you tell him, Beth,' called Connie, as she moved with Simon to the door. 'If you want to, you can bring him with you.'

Beth exchanged another astonished look with Phil. 'Bring Thomas to Gran and Grandad's?' she asked.

'Why not?' Connie called back over her shoulder. 'At least he'll know where to find you after we've moved there.'

Beth watched in astonishment as her mum left the room. Then she turned to Phil, who seemed just as nonplussed.

'Well, don't blame me,' said Phil with a shrug. 'Looks like we've got a fight on our 'ands!'

Anderson's fish and chip shop in Hornsey Road was having a busy Friday evening. Despite the first real fog of the season, which was bringing traffic to a crawl, a long queue had formed inside, and in front of the shop on the pavement outside. Half way along the queue was Jessie Hawks, clutching her torch, free for once from her nightly vigil down the air raid shelter in the old piano factory. Just behind her, standing in the light of Jessie's flickering torch bulb, was Abe Lieberman, so wrapped up in an overcoat that was too big for him, a flat-cap and scarf, that he looked as though he was about to journey across the North Pole.

'Din't know Jewish folk ate fish 'n' chips,' croaked Jessie, edging closer to the shop door. 'I fawt yer only ate them raw 'errings.'

'Raw herrings!' retorted Abe indignantly. 'What d'you think we are – cannibals?'

Jessie felt a bit put out. She'd known a lot of Jewish people in her time, and always got on well with them. In fact her employer at the tin factory where she used to work was Jewish, and Jessie always said that a nicer woman never walked the face of the earth.

'Anyway,' said Abe, 'what does it matter? These days we have to eat whatever we can get our hands on. I just wish I was someone like that Mrs Shanks. She knows how to feed a family on practically nothing.'

'Why d'yer say that?' asked Jessie with curiosity.

'She told me so,' replied Abe. 'She said that the way her boy eats, the family's food ration disappears by the beginning of the week. After that she has to make do with left-overs, any old scraps of meat done up with vegetables. She's got guts, that woman. You'd never think she was a Yank.'

'As a matter of fact,' returned Jessie, 'Yanks've got a lotta guts. My 'usband fought alongside them in the last war. 'E said they never gave up 'til the job was done.'

Abe grunted. In front of them, a quick shaft of light escaped from the front door as one of the customers left clutching his fish and chips. When the door closed, the road outside was again plunged into the dark of the blackout.

'I still say Mrs Shanks is something special,' continued Abe, dabbing a dewdrop from his frozen nose with his handkerchief. 'It can't have been easy having a baby with her husband away on call-up. If anything happened to him . . .' he shook his head, 'I can't imagine how terrible it would be, not ever being able to see the child.'

'Well from wot *I've* 'eard,' said Jessie, who now only had one person in the queue in front of her outside the shop, ' 'e'll soon 'ave a chance ter do just that.'

'What?' spluttered Abe, in the dark. 'What's that you say?'

'I said,' continued Jessie, 'Ted Shanks'll soon 'ave a chance ter see his boy. Sounds like 'e's comin' 'ome.'

Standing just behind them was the silhouette of a woman in her thirties, whose features were completely masked in the pitch dark. The mention of Ted's name had clearly attracted her attention.

'Are you sure about this, Mrs Hawks?' asked Abe. 'Who told you Mrs Shanks's husband is coming home?'

'Never you mind,' replied Jessie, who felt very superior to know something that Abe didn't. 'I know a lot of folk around 'Ornsey Road. There ain't much goes on wivout my 'earin' about it.'

Abe had no doubt about that. Even up his end of the track, old Jessie was known as the 'fountain of knowledge', someone who never let a good bit of gossip pass her by without making something of it. 'So – what a wonderful thing!' he said. 'To see your baby months after it's been born!'

'My ol' man', said Jessie, 'said 'e wished 'e'd never seen *me* after *I'd* been born!'

Abe believed her.

The front door of the shop opened again, and this time there was room enough inside for both Jessie and Abe. But once Jessie had ordered her sixpenny piece of cod and pennyworth of chips, she received a scolding from Mr Anderson behind the counter. 'Where's yer newspaper, Jess?' he said. 'Don't tell me yer've forgotten it again?'

Jessie looked guilty. 'I'm sorry, Bert,' she said. 'I must be gettin' old. I put it out on my dresser ter bring, an' fergot all about it.'

'You know the rules, Jess,' replied Mr Anderson. 'No fish unless yer bring yer own newspaper ter wrap it up in. Old papers are too 'ard ter get.'

'I'm sorry, Bert,' said Jessie. 'I promise I won't ferget next time. As I said, I must be gettin' old an' senile.'

Mr Anderson shook his head, and quickly wrapped up Jessie's fish and chips in some of his last remaining old newspaper.

'Don't you worry, Mrs Hawks,' added Abe. 'Even *I* forget things all the time.'

' 'Ow old are *you*, then?' asked Jessie, quick as a flash.

'As a matter of fact, I'm seventy years of age,' replied Abe, proudly.

'Well *I'm* eighty-four,' boasted Jessie. 'Nearly old enuff ter be yer bleedin' muvver. So *I've* got an excuse!'

A short while later, Abe walked with Jessie as far as the turn-off at Andover Road. Once he'd continued on up the hill, Jessie made her way home slowly in the dark, with only her flickering torch bulb to guide the way. It was a perilous journey on foot, even at the best of times, but tonight was even worse, for the fog was beginning to freeze, making the pavements treacherous to walk on. It was easy to see that the fog itself was very low-lying, for just above it all there was a clear, crisp sky, with occasional glimpses of the moon. But Jessie wasn't interested in looking up at the moon; she was far more concerned in getting her fish and chips warmed up in her oven back home, for the smell of them was driving her mad. Her taste buds were already anticipating what the cod would taste like, and she sucked her old false teeth in the hope that she would not be disappointed. A bit of salt, some vinegar, a slice of bread and marge – there was nothing finer in the whole wide world! But as she started to cross the road, she had the uncomfortable feeling that there was someone behind her. If it hadn't been for the fog she wouldn't have worried, but for some reason or another her mind went back to Jack the Ripper, and how he had crept up on unsuspecting women and slit them up. It was clear that Jessie had a vivid imagination, for even in her wildest dreams, she would never have been considered a woman of 'ill-repute'. Nonetheless, she stopped at the kerb's edge, and started to cross the road.

'Excuse me.'

Jessie froze. She hardly dared to turn and see who was standing behind her.

'I'm sorry ter trouble yer,' said a soft-spoken woman's voice. 'I wonder if I could 'ave a word with yer?'

Jessie slowly turned, and shone her torch up into the woman's face. What she saw in the dim light was a face that, although pale and pallid, was utterly beautiful, with deep-set dark eyes, a clear unblemished complexion, a slight but perfectly shaped nose, and the suggestion of jet black hair beneath her headscarf.

'Wot d'yer want?' Jessie asked nervously.

'I hope yer won't mind my askin',' replied the woman, whose voice was straight out of East London, 'but I was in the queue at the fish shop, at Andersons. I over'eard yer talkin'.'

Without being aware of what she was doing, Jessie stepped back a pace. She didn't like this. She didn't like it at all.

'I know this must sound strange,' continued the woman, 'but – well, I got the feelin' you an' the gentleman were talkin' about someone – I might know.'

'Who?' snapped Jessie.

'Ted Shanks,' replied the woman. 'I used ter know someone by that name – oh, it was some time ago now, but I just wondered if it was the same person?'

'I 'ave no idea,' replied Jessie, turning and starting to move off.

'He married someone called Connie, I think it was,' said the woman, hurrying to catch her up. 'She was an American.'

Jessie came to a halt. 'Who are you?'

The woman hesitated. 'Oh – no one in particular,' she replied. 'But I would just like ter know that Ted's safe. If 'e is comin' 'ome, it'll be such a relief.'

'Fer who?' asked Jessie shrewdly.

'Fer everyone,' replied the woman. 'I 'ope I get the chance ter see 'im. Just fer a minute. Just fer ol' times' sake.'

Jessie was deeply sceptical of the woman, of her reasons for wanting to know so much about Ted Shanks, a man she hadn't seen for such a long time. 'Me fish is gettin' cold,' she grumbled. 'I'll bid yer goodnight.'

'Goodnight, Mrs Hawks,' returned the woman. 'An' thank you.'

Taken aback that the woman knew her name, Jessie came to an abrupt halt again. But when she turned to look, all she could see was the shadowy figure of a woman disappearing into the dark fog of a cold November evening.

Lossheim was barely a village. Set in agricultural countryside just ten miles from the north German port of Lubeck, the entire area consisted of no more than three or four turn-of-the-century red-bricked houses, with grey-slated roofs, and long, tall chimney stacks. Although the houses were set far apart, the residents of each of them could get an occasional glimpse of each other, especially during the winter months when the trees and hedges were stripped of their leaves and foliage. During the summer, the surrounding fields were bristling with wheat crops, which rustled and swayed in a gentle breeze, and struggled against any unexpected inclement weather.

The house Heinz Buchner and his family lived in had once had a thatched roof, but when Buchner bought the place five years before, like the other residents, he did away with the straw cover in favour of a slated roof. The house itself, with four bedrooms, a spacious sitting/dining room, a country kitchen, two bathrooms, and a conservatory, which looked out over a large well-stocked garden, showed every sign of opulence, for Buchner had come from a wealthy background, his father being the owner of a small arms factory in the Ruhr. On the other hand, his wife Helga had been born of modest Bavarian stock, her father being an accountant's clerk in the local Town Hall, but after she had met Heinz at an airman's dance in Munich, she travelled to Lubeck, where she married and settled down. They had two children, both boys, Richard, who was born in 1933, and Dieter, who arrived in the middle of a thunderstorm in 1935. Over the years the two boys had become very proud of their father, who was, to them, a symbol of the new, modern Germany; a fighter pilot with the *Luftwaffe*, someone to look up to, someone they could boast about at school, even though it was only a small village school. Helga was also proud of her husband, but she had always secretly harboured certain reservations about the dangerous work he was doing, especially now that Germany was at war, which meant that she and their children had to spend many nights without him, not knowing whether he would ever return home to them. But, for the first time since the *Luftwaffe* onslaught on London had begun back in August, Helga was at least relieved to have Heinz back home with them for seven days' leave – one whole, glorious week!

On Sunday morning Heinz drove his family to church in the ancient nearby town of Lubeck. As it was now the middle of November, the roads were covered with fallen leaves, and the heavy rains of the past two weeks were now replaced with frost, which had settled on the barren, flat landscape turning it into a dazzling white wonderland. On the way, Heinz led his family in their usual sing-song, a raucous medley of current popular songs which were being pumped out of all the favourite German radio programmes day and night. They were a happy, complete family, who, for just a short space in time, were far removed from the rigours and trauma of war.

In the Lutheran church, the pastor's address talked of triumph over adversity, of love and support for those nearest and dearest, and of compassion for one's foes. But this last appeal did not go down too well with the men in military uniform amongst the congregation, such as Heinz Buchner, who had all lost comrades in battle during the previous few months. But it was a beautiful service, one that Helga in particular always enjoyed, for it reminded her of Sunday morning visits to church with her parents when she was a little girl, and the feeling that someone 'up there' was looking after her.

When the service was over, the family strolled along the river bank and watched the tug boats chugging by, some of them making their way to the sea port on the Baltic sea, destined for any number of different wartime duties. Before the war, the river had been a riot of colour, pleasure boats in abundance, with the sound of concertinas and xylophones and happy day-trippers singing their heads off, drinking beer, and eating their wurst and sauerkraut picnics. As they strolled, the two children chased one another up and down each flight of stone steps that they came to, never tiring, always remembering not to make too much of a nuisance of themselves lest they incur the wrath of their father, who had a temper to match any man. For Helga, however, it was sheer bliss to have Heinz home with her, to have him holding her hand, and pointing out the beautiful landmarks on each bank of the river; the ancient spires of the cathedral, the old town with its museum and concert hall, and the dozens of tiny cafés that seemed to be everywhere, but whose owners were finding it difficult to survive on the meagre rations of the Fatherland at war.

Helga loved being with Heinz; this was the Heinz she identified with most of all, relaxed, carefree, no sign of the tearaway young air force officer he used to be. Now he was mature, sensible, and practical about the world as it existed today. Nonetheless, she did have certain anxieties about the philosophies he had adopted, the same philosophies that had been adopted by so many of his contemporaries. Germany was a country that had changed so much since the end of the First World War, and it concerned her that so many men, including Heinz, had embraced that change with so much enthusiasm. However, it was the look in his eyes that occasionally told a different story, a look of uncertainty, a look of foreboding.

'You know something,' said Helga, trim and pretty in the navy-blue overcoat with the fox fur that Heinz had bought her for one of her birthdays, 'you've never told me what it's like up there?'

Heinz turned only a brief, casual glance at her. 'What do you mean?' he asked in his clipped north German voice as opposed to Helga's rural Bavarian drawl. 'Up where?'

'Over England,' replied Helga, almost nervous to ask the question.

Heinz brought them to a gradual halt, and whilst the children continued to play tag up and down the steps leading to the river, he looked out at the ice-cold waters below, and took off his uniform cap, which revealed a flock of military-cut blond hair. 'I don't think of it as any particular place,' he replied, his eyes flicking from one part of the river to the next. 'It's the enemy. That's all that matters in war.'

Helga thought about this. 'Who *are* the enemy, I wonder?' she asked, more to herself than to Heinz. 'I mean, they're people, aren't they? The same as you and me and the kids.'

'They're the enemy, Helga,' said Heinz firmly, turning to her without actually raising his voice. 'That's the only thing we are told to think of, the only thing I ever think of when I fly over them.'

'I know, darling,' said Helga. 'I *do* know what you're saying. But I just think it must be an awful feeling when you drop bombs on people, knowing that they're just ordinary people – like you and me?'

'I don't bomb *ordinary* people, Helga,' Heinz assured her unconvincingly. 'Our targets are always military.'

'But in air raids, isn't it nearly always civilians who get the worst of it?'

Although Helga's question irritated him, he knew it had to be answered. 'Not necessarily,' he replied blandly. 'But in modern warfare, it's inevitable that *some* civilians are going to get hurt.'

Helga hesitated before saying anything. Now both of them were looking out at the river, where a gunboat carrying the iron cross insignia on its flag was racing at speed in and out of the slower tug boats. When she spoke again, she seemed to address her words to the waters below. 'They say people take cover in shelters that are no better than rabbit holes,' she said. 'It seems awful. I've never liked the English, but they must be so scared.'

'And what about *our* people?' countered Heinz. 'We have air raids too. You only have to walk through the town to see the damage. Thank God we live in the country. At least you don't have to worry about going down into a shelter.'

'No,' replied Helga. 'But if we did, I would hate the person who was trying to kill me and our kids.'

Heinz swung her a sharp, indignant and surprised look.

Helga turned to face him. Hers was drawn and anxious. 'I hate it, Heinz,' she said. 'I hate it when I say goodbye to you, and never know whether I'm going to see you again. I hate it when I know you're going off to kill innocent people.'

'When are you going to realise that the enemy are *not* innocent people, Helga?' protested Heinz.

'They're people, Heinz,' insisted Helga. 'People like you and me, and our kids, and all our family and friends. If men have to fight wars, it shouldn't be against us. Just think of what it must be like down there when you drop bombs on them. The look of fear on their faces, the hopelessness, the frustration, the dread that they might not last another night.'

Heinz knew that whatever he said would make absolutely no difference to his wife. It worried him. It worried him very much. If such talk got around, questions might be asked about the Buchners' allegiance to the party, to the country. But in all the years he had known his wife, he knew that her only concern was for him and their kids. There was nothing subversive about Helga. She was as patriotic as any other fair-minded German. But she was naive. This war was against a tyrant, an enemy who crushed the German nation in one war, and was now trying to do so all over again. War is war, he told himself, and if the rules had to be changed to meet circumstances, then so be it. 'It's getting cold,' was all he would say. 'I think it's time we went home.'

Helga grabbed his arm, and held on to it. 'Don't be angry with me, my darling,' she said, her eyes forlorn and pleading. 'You've no idea how much these past two days have meant to me and the kids. Having you home again is the most wonderful treat we could possibly have. I pray to God you never have to go back to those dark, foreign skies again. I pray to God this week goes on for ever and ever.'

As they stood there, Helga was not to know that the moment they got back home, the telephone would be ringing, with orders from his own *Luftwaffe* squadron that the rest of his leave was cancelled, and that he was to return to his unit as soon as possible.

Chapter 6

The bus took for ever. At least that's what it felt like to Beth as she joined her mum, Phil, baby brother Simon and Thomas Sullivan on the long journey down to Hatfield in Hertfordshire. They had all set out from home at eight o'clock on Sunday morning, taken the 609 trolleybus to Barnet, and then waited an hour for a petrol bus that would take them all the way to Gran and Grandad's. Fortunately, the front seats were free on the upper deck, so they all managed to sit together, with Beth snuggled up to Thomas, and Connie nursing baby Simon in her arms, with Phil at her side.

The journey was pleasant enough, for, despite the cold, the countryside on the way looked absolutely ravishing in all its autumn colours, with dead chestnut, oak and elm leaves strewn across every road and lane, an endless carpet of faded brown and purple, which seemed to come to life as they fluttered into the air in the cold morning breeze. It was also a joy for once to have a sky that could actually be seen, unblemished by the cumbersome silver barrage balloons that constantly bobbed up and down over the rooftops of London. And what a sky it was! So blue, such a deep azure blue, as though it had been specially painted for a Hollywood Technicolor musical film, and the fields were newly ploughed and sewn, waiting for the first crop of wheat or corn to appear during the eagerly awaited spring of next year.

If it wasn't for the despair she felt about their final destination, this would have been a day of sheer bliss for Beth. Having Thomas by her side for one whole day was more than she had ever dared hoped for during those long periods they had to spend apart because of the Blitz. Nonetheless, she still wondered why Thomas had not yet taken her to meet his 'Dada', and the longer that meeting was delayed, the more uneasy she became.

Percy Shanks and his wife Edie moved to Hatfield in Hertfordshire during the height of the great depression in 1931. It hadn't been an easy decision to abandon their small terraced house in Bow, East London, where they had lived since they got married nearly forty years before. But during those chaotic years, London had become a place of deep industrial and social unrest, and when Percy retired from his job at the sheet metal factory in Leytonstone, it came as no real hardship to seek the peace and quiet of a rural setting that was only a short train journey back to London on the LNER.

Their 'dream home' turned out to be a bungalow at the far end of Green Lanes, which they had rented for seven and sixpence a week, gradually rising to the current princely sum of ten bob. For them it was an ideal place to live in, a 'real Dook an' Duchess' said Percy, the moment he walked through the front door. But their two modest bedrooms and sizeable box room, dining/sitting room, kitchen, and, for the first time in their lives, bathroom, were not the only reason for the move, for the rich, bracing country air had done Edie a world of good in her constant struggle against bronchitis. Beth, however, couldn't bear the place, partly because it always seemed just *too* neat and tidy, and partly because her grandad was a dedicated do-it-yourself fanatic, who never finished any job he had started. Beth also never really got on with her grandad because he was so set in his ways, always insisting that his opinion was the only one that should be considered. However, although Beth did get on with her gran, it always irritated her that she was so passive, and never stood up to her husband. Therefore, the prospect of coming to live with her grandparents filled her with horror and apprehension, which made this Sunday visit something she had dreaded ever since her mum had first mentioned it.

'Oh it's really lovely here, Con,' said Edie, who was at least three inches shorter than her husband, and who had a sweet little face with wrinkles that actually suited her. 'It's always so quiet. Yer wouldn't even know there's a war on.'

'Quiet?' spluttered her husband Percy, who was busy dunking his biscuit in a cup of tea.'Wiv planes takin' off an' landin' at that bleedin' airfield night and day?'

Both Edie and Connie glared at him. Even though it was true what Percy had said about warplanes always taking off and landing from the airfield of the nearby De Havilland aircraft factory, he was not helping their efforts to show what a perfect haven the bungalow would be for the family to escape to during the Blitz.

'Oh it's not *that* bad, dear,' said Edie, who was twitchily peeling Brussels sprouts into a saucepan at the polished dining table. 'We don't *really* notice 'em, an' in any case, it's all in a good cause. They say there's a lot er 'ush 'ush work goin' on over there.'

'Hush, hush?' asked Thomas, who was sipping his cup of tea with Beth at the other end of the table. 'What does that mean, Mrs Shanks?'

Edie lowered her voice as though someone outside might hear her. 'It's all experimental work over there,' she said.'We've 'eard some very strange sounds comin' from that factory.'

'Is that a fact?' asked Thomas, quite casually.'What kind of sounds?'

'It's 'ard ter say, really,' replied Edie.'Sort of 'igh pitched. It's all top secret of course.'

Beth quickly changed the subject.'So 'ow far d'yer 'ave ter go to the shops?' she asked.

'Oh, we've got a greengrocer's at the bottom of the road,' replied Edie enthusiastically.'An' there's a lovely shop where Grandad gets 'is fags *an'* 'is newspapers.'

Connie was carefully watching Beth's reaction.'You've also got a good butcher nearby, haven't you, Mum?' Connie said.

'Oh yes,' returned Edie, dropping a Brussels sprout into the saucepan of water.' 'E's a luvely man. 'E gets us anyfin' we want – beef, pork, chicken. We don't 'ave ter worry about coupons out 'ere. In the country we can get just *anyfin'*.'

Beth wasn't impressed. In fact, she had heard all this before. In fact, she had heard the same old thing every time she had visited her grandparents. But as she looked around the space that was half dining and half sitting room, she became more and more depressed. Maybe it was the unfinished tiling around the fireplace, which her grandad had started working on more than two years before but still hadn't completed, or perhaps it was Edie's endless collection of china cats, which were crowded on to every available space, from the dark varnished sideboard, to the mantelpiece above the fireplace, and even on top of the wireless set in the corner. Could she live in such a place, Beth asked herself? Could she really give up all her mates back at the munitions factory for a life in which she woke up to the sound of birds singing in the dawn every morning? The answer was, and always had been, 'not on your Nellie!' Beth was no country girl; she was pure East End, North London, whatever folk liked to call her, but despite the fact that her grandparents were harmless enough, no one, not even her own mum, was going to lock her away in a bungalow a million miles away from her true home patch. Her brother Phil felt much the same way. He had already decided that if his mum tried to drag him away from his job with the Fire Service, he would run away, lie about his age, and join up. For the time being though, he was aimlessly passing his time by teasing Oscar, his grandparents' elderly tabby cat, who took refuge under the sideboard and hissed at Phil every time he came near.

'So, still no word from Ted, then?' asked Percy, who was scooping out the remains of his dunked biscuit from the bottom of the cup. 'I fawt 'e was s'pposed ter be comin' 'ome on leave?'

Beth swung a look at her mum, who was sitting alongside Edie at the table, gently rocking little Simon in the cot that Edie and Percy provided for him whenever he was brought on a visit to them. 'So did I,' replied Connie with a sigh. 'But I guess the army have other ideas.'

'The army!' snorted Percy dismissively. 'Don't talk ter me about the army. All wind and no sail.'

'I don't fink that's a nice fing ter say, Perce,' said Edie, scolding him. 'I tip my 'at ter those boys after wot they 'ad ter go fru at Dunkirk.'

Connie felt herself tense. Although the evacuation of the British Expeditionary Force from Dunkirk in Northern France had been a momentous achievement, it had resulted in an enormous loss of life, and the fact that she had not heard from Ted for nearly two months after the event had given her plenty of sleepless nights. 'He's beginning to grizzle,' she said, lifting Simon out of his cot. 'Might as well give him his feed now.'

'I'll come wiv yer,' said Beth quickly, looking for a perfect excuse to get out of the room.

'No, darling,' said Connie, who had always felt that the feeding of her baby was a private matter. 'I can manage perfectly well, thank you.' She wrapped Simon's blanket around him, and went off into one of the bedrooms.

Left alone with her grandparents, Beth feared the worst.

'So 'ow d'yer feel about comin' ter live out in the country?' Edie asked her granddaughter. 'Bet yer'll be glad ter get away from that 'orrible air raid shelter?'

'The air raid shelter doesn't really worry me, Gran,' replied Beth. 'We've got nice neighbours we meet every night. We all get on.'

'But it's not the same, is it, dear?' said Edie. 'I mean, it must be terrible bein' shut up in a dark cellar like that every night. I know 'ow yer poor mum feels. Especially 'avin' those dreams – or wotever they are.'

Beth swung her a startled look. 'Dreams?' she asked sharply. 'Wot d'yer mean, Gran?'

'Oh, she's always 'avin 'em,' replied Edie. 'She says 'er mum back in Texas used ter be the same. Apparently, she could often tell wot was goin' ter 'appen in the future. She's got somefin' on 'er mind, all right. I dunno wot, but I reckon that's why she wants ter get yer all ter move out 'ere. Er course, your grandad an' me'd love it. We've got plenty of space.' She turned to Phil who was sorting through his grandparents' collection of gramophone records. 'You wouldn't mind sharin' the room wiv yer sister, would yer, Phil? We can get the two of yer in quite easy. Just 'til the Blitz is over?'

'Wot makes you fink the Blitz is *ever* goin' ter be over?' he mumbled, without bothering to look up at her.

Edie exchanged a crafty look with her husband. 'Well, the war won't go on for ever, dear,' she replied. 'Churchill says that one of these days our boys are goin' ter get back to France, an' when they do, it won't be long before it's all over.'

Phil looked up at her with a look of disdain. 'Bleedin' lot er cods!'

he snapped. 'We're not winnin' this war, Gran. If you was to come out wiv me on my rounds each night, you'd see wot this war's all about. Fings are goin' ter get much worse before they get better. Everyone up my station says so.'

'Even more reason why yer should all come an' live out 'ere,' replied Edie, who looked rather hurt that she should have been spoken to in such a way by her young grandson. 'You'd be as safe as 'ouses out 'ere.'

Realising that his wife was beginning to irritate both Phil and Beth, Percy got up from the table. 'I reckon the best way we can ferget this war is fer us blokes ter go an' down a good pint up The Fiddle. Wot d'yer fink, Tom?'

Thomas was baffled, and turned to Beth for some kind of explanation. '*The Fiddle?*' he asked.

'It's Grandad's local pub,' said Beth, with a sigh. 'It's a kind of ritual on Sundays – blokes to the pub, leave the women to get on with the cookin' an' 'ave a good gab.'

'Now don't be like that, Beff,' said Percy. 'Women prefer their own company, an' so do us blokes. Wot say you, Tom?'

Thomas shrugged. He hadn't a clue what was going on. 'Sure,' he said. 'Why not?'

'Come on, Phil,' said Percy, collecting his jacket from the door. 'You might as well come along too. You look older than yer age. It's time yer got the taste of a pint er bitter.'

Thoroughly fed up, Beth watched Thomas and Phil reluctantly leave the bungalow with her grandfather. Ever since she was a child she had always hated this splitting up of the sexes at Sunday lunchtimes. It seemed so unnatural to her. After they had gone, she helped her gran peel the potatoes for the roast pork meal. Despite her grand-parents' kind intentions, it was clearly going to be yet another grim afternoon.

It was quite a long walk to The Fiddle. Despite his seventy-six years, Percy Shanks set the pace, leaving both Thomas and Phil way behind, panting for breath. But it was a crisp, cold afternoon, and although the hedgerows on the way were stripped of their foliage, the autumn sun was quite dazzling, helping the occasional scattering of autumn crocuses to open up their hearts after a cruel, frosty night.

As it was Sunday midday, the saloon bar of The Fiddle pub was full of the usual crowd, most of whom were middle-aged or elderly men who came there not just for the booze, but for the company of their fellow regulars. The absence of young men who had been called up was noticeable, although there were one or two of them amongst the customers, either farm labourers or skilled workers from De Havilland's aircraft factory on the Great North Road who had most likely been exempt from national service by the very nature of the war-work they were doing.

Once Percy had introduced Phil and Thomas to his drinking partner mates, all three watched the rowdy darts match that was in progress on the far side of the bar. Despite Percy's determination to introduce his grandson to the pleasures of a pint of bitter, Phil stubbornly kept to his favourite drink – a glass of Tizer. But Thomas always enjoyed a pint, and he soon found himself the centre of favourable attention from Percy's mates, who all enjoyed ribbing him as 'a good Paddy!' However, Thomas and Phil were soon to know the real reason why Percy had left the women back home.

'Yer mum needs help,' he said, addressing his remark straight to Phil. 'Gran and I fink she's flipped.'

'Wot yer talkin' about?' asked Phil, staring at his grandad as though he was potty.

Percy took a long gulp from his pint of bitter, and lowered his voice. 'She told yer gran she's bin 'avin' nightmares. She says she knows somefin' terrible's goin' ter 'appen.'

Phil swung a look of alarm at Thomas.

'I don't follow you, Mr Shanks,' said Thomas. 'Somethin' terrible? What does she mean?'

'She means that she's 'avin' the same nightmare every night,' continued Percy. 'She can see every detail as clear as daylight. The trouble is, she's so convinced that wot she sees is goin' ter really 'appen that she's bin ter see a doctor about it.'

'Yer mean, she's got somefin' wrong wiv 'er?' asked a thoroughly startled Phil.

'P'raps, p'raps not,' replied Percy gloomily, again addressing his remark to Phil. 'But wotever it is, she's takin' it seriously. She wants us *all* ter take it seriously. That's why she wants you and Beff ter get out er London as soon as possible.'

Thomas was a bit wary of the old man's intentions. Beth had often talked to him about her grandad. She told him that on one occasion her dad had alluded to the fact that Percy had always been a bit of a mischief-maker, which was apparently the reason why, when he was a young man, his first marriage had failed after only a year. It was also one of the reasons why Beth was so reluctant to go and stay with her grandparents. 'Are you sayin',' he asked, 'that Beth and Phil are part of these nightmares?'

'From what Edie says,' replied the old man, 'it's worse than that. Much worse.'

Despite the chill in the air, Beth strolled around her grandparents' back garden looking at what was left of the late, soggy plants. It always amazed her how retired people spent so much time in their gardens, as though their lives depended on it, but then she was grateful that her grandad, just like Uncle Horace, had at least something to occupy his mind.

Knowing that her mum and her grandmother were watching her through the dining-room window, she tried to show some interest in what she was aimlessly looking at. But she had other things on her mind, mainly the thought of how she would keep her sanity if she and Phil were forced to leave London to move in with their grandparents. She kept thinking of the boredom of watching her grandma cleaning and dusting and bustling around the bungalow each day, how being house-proud seemed to be at the centre of the old lady's life. Was it just a generation gap, Beth kept asking herself, or was her grandma really such a completely boring person?

She looked over her shoulder towards the bungalow, where Edie was waving to her. Beth waved back, and immediately felt a sense of guilt. Her grandma wasn't such a bad person, she tried to tell herself. After all, the old lady had never asked much from life, and despite her devotion to her husband, by all accounts it had not been plain sailing for her during almost forty years of marriage. Beth didn't need anyone to tell her that her grandad had always had a wandering eye for the girls; it was obvious by the excited way in which he looked at the pin-ups in the newspapers. Oh yes, he had been a bit of a lad in his time, all right. But Edie – poor Edie. What *did* go on in that humdrum mind of hers? Why did she *always* have to accept life without any questions? She flicked another look over her shoulder to the bungalow window. Now her mum, nursing little Simon in her arms, had joined Edie. Beth's heart sank. Seeing the two of them together made her wonder what they had been talking about, as if she didn't know! How *could* they expect her to give up her own active life in London just because of a few bombs? Worst of all, how could they expect her to leave Thomas behind? Thomas meant the world to her. If she lost him now, if she had to leave him behind, her world would come to an end. But then, she thought about her mum. Life wasn't easy for her now that Beth's dad had been called up. It was hard enough for *any* woman to have to endure such a hardship, but for someone who, in Beth's mind, was still a stranger in a foreign country, it must be absolute hell to cope with, especially with a four-month-old baby to look after. Was that why her mum was such a nervous kind of woman, she asked herself? In many ways Connie was such a beautiful woman, so cultured, and so loving, but she was surely out of her depth in a situation like this. War was an endless crisis, and living through the Blitz was not an easy thing to do. But Beth kept telling herself that, even though she loved her mum very much, she herself was of much stronger stock. She wasn't frightened of Hitler's bombs. In her heart of hearts she was East End through and through, and wasn't going to be hounded out of her own patch. But how, how was she going to combat these combined efforts of both her mum and her grandparents to banish the family into a place that meant absolutely nothing to either her or her brother Phil?

A few minutes later, Beth was back in the bungalow, helping her grandmother to lay the table. The only redeeming feature of all this was the scrumptious smell of pork roasting in the oven in the tiny adjoining kitchen. She looked up at the clock on the mantelpiece. Thomas and Phil had been gone for over an hour. Was her grandad trying to work on them in the same way that Edie had been trying to work on her?

'Yer mum's absolutely right,' said Edie, setting the table in her own meticulous way. 'Wot's the point in lockin' yerself up every night in a dark cellar, when yer can breave our luvely fresh air out 'ere?' For a brief moment, she stopped what she was doing and looked up at Beth. 'We'd take care of yer, yer know,' she said reassuringly. 'I said to yer grandad, we're all family. It's wot yer dad wants. 'E's said so to yer mum loads er times, 'asn't 'e, Con?'

Connie, rocking Simon gently to and fro in her arms, smiled back weakly at her.

'An' yer don't 'ave ter worry about puttin' us out,' continued Edie relentlessly, unwilling to let Beth get a word in. 'It's at times like this that we all 'ave ter pull tergevver.' Again she looked up briefly at Beth. 'In any case, it's the least we can do fer yer mum – especially in 'er condition.'

Beth swung a look at her mum, expecting some kind of explanation from her.

'Anyway, we're not goin' ter force yer,' continued Edie. 'Gord forbid we'd ever do anyfin' like that. But yer *are* our kiff an' kin. If we can't 'elp out in times like this, we ain't worf very much – are we?'

Before Beth had a chance to answer, Edie had gone off to collect a clean pinny from her bedroom.

Connie waited a moment before speaking. 'Granma means well,' she eventually said, the remains of her Texan drawl somehow more pronounced. 'Looking after us would give her a new meaning in life.'

'Wot does she mean by "especially in your condition"?' asked Beth, ignoring what her mum had just said. 'Wot condition is that, Mum? Are yer ill or somefin'?'

'No!' said Connie, coming back at her immediately. 'Of course I'm not ill – well, not exactly that.' She looked up at Beth, to find her staring at her. 'I just fear for what might happen to us, that's all.'

'Wot makes yer fink somefin' *is* goin' ter 'appen to us?' asked Beth cuttingly.

Connie looked agitated, and removed a strand of hair that had fallen across her left eye.

'Is it 'cos of yer nightmares?'

Connie swung a startled look at her. 'Who told you that?' she asked.

'It don't matter who told me, Mum,' replied Beth. 'Is it true?'

Connie moved away, and stared out through the window into the back garden. 'I'm scared, Beth,' she replied, still gently rocking Simon to and fro in her arms, using him as an excuse to give as vague a reply as she possibly could. 'I owe it to your dad not to let anything happen to us. I'll do anything to help us survive this war.'

'Mum,' said Beth firmly, 'millions er people're goin' ter survive this war. We just 'ave ter keep our 'eads down, that's all.'

'Keep our heads down?' retorted Connie. 'And how d'you think we're going to do that, Beth – when we're all blown to pieces . . .'

'We're not goin' ter be blown ter pieces, Mum!' sighed Beth, in despair. 'Why d'yer fink we go down that bleedin' shelter night after night? You're always sayin' no 'arm can come to us down there.'

Connie's face stiffened. 'I know,' she replied, distantly. 'Now, I'm not so sure.'

Beth stared in disbelief at her. 'Mum!' she demanded. 'Wot's this all about? Wot're yer seein' in these nightmares?'

'That's *my* problem, Beth!' snapped Connie. 'Could you please stop asking me so many questions!'

Beth was getting angry. 'If it's somefin' concernin' *us*,' she insisted, 'then we 'ave a right ter know!'

'Beth!' retorted Connie. 'I did not say that my nightmares had anything to do with the way that I feel. I just have genuine fears about what could happen to us if we continue to stay on in London. Fears that Dad may one day come home and find that he no longer has a family. I'm a mother, Beth. I love you and Phil and Simon. I have a mother's feelings. I have every right to be afraid of what's going on in this war. Why can't you understand that, Beth – why?'

'I *do* understand, Mum!' replied Beth forcefully. 'But you mustn't get yourself so worked up just because of a silly nightmare!'

'Don't talk to me like that!' snapped Connie, face crumpling up, close to tears. 'Don't ever talk to me like . . .' With Simon still in her arms, she started to sob.

Beth was horrified, and rushed across to her. 'Oh Mum!' she said guiltily, throwing her arms around both Connie and Simon, and hugging them tight. 'I don't wanna 'urt yer. I would never wanna 'urt yer. I love you too. We're worried about yer, that's all. Me an' Phil are really worried about yer.'

Connie looked up. Her face was streaked with tears.

'Please, Mum,' Beth implored. 'Wot is it? Wot is it that's *really* scarin' yer so much?'

But Connie wouldn't say.

The sun was already dipping down into the barren fields at the end of Green Lanes, flooding the Hertfordshire countryside with a deep golden glow, which would soon embrace a twilight the colour of blood.

'Red sky at night, shepherd's delight. Red sky in the morning, shepherd's warning,' Beth quoted.

'And where d'yer get *that* old boloney from?' asked Thomas, as he and Beth gazed up at a vast, cloudless sky that seemed to stretch to eternity.

'It's wot my auntie Maudie used ter say when me an' Phil were kids,' replied Beth, whose face was reflected in the gradually fading light. 'She said it was an old farmer's warning.'

'And you believed her?'

Beth, snuggled up to Thomas as they strolled, looked up at him with a surprised expression. 'Why shouldn't I?' she asked. 'As a matter of fact, I believed practically anyfin' my Auntie Maudie used ter say. I loved 'er. She was speshul – just like Uncle 'Orace. They was boaf the salt er the earth.'

'I thought you said your uncle Horace was still alive?' said Thomas, who was relishing his first chance of the day to be alone with Beth.

' 'E is, fank Gord,' replied Beth. 'Dunno wot I'd do wivout 'im. 'E's the only one I know who knows how I feel about fings, who actually listens ter me when I 'ave a problem. 'Onest ter God, I don't know wot I'd do wivout 'im.'

'As a matter of fact, I don't know what I'd do without *you*,' countered Thomas, as they strolled on.

Beth brought them to a halt, and turned to look at him again. He had that look in his eyes that told her how much he loved her, how much he wanted to hold her in his arms in just the same way that he had done on that wonderful summer afternoon when she had given herself to him for the first time. And she wanted him too. She wanted him for the rest of her life, to make her feel like a whole person, someone who would one day help her to bring up a family of their own. For the next moment or so they just stood there on the muddy path, which cut right across the middle of the barren cornfields, staring into each other's eyes, just the two of them, two isolated figures, isolated from the rest of humanity, inhabiting a world that was all their own. It was so peaceful, so perfect. He slipped his arms around her waist and gently pulled her close. She could feel the warmth and power of his body, the soaring heat beneath his duffle-coat. He put one hand behind her head, slowly eased it forward, and kissed her long and hard. His lips felt good, and she groaned with silent ecstasy. 'Oh Thomas,' she sighed, 'yer've bin so wonderful the way yer've helped me fru today. I'm sorry I've got such a mixed-up family. I don't know wot's the matter wiv Mum. She got so upset when I asked her about 'er nightmares. She just won't tell me wot they're all about.'

Thomas didn't have the heart to tell her that he knew, that her grandad had told him what it was that Connie was 'seeing' during her sleepless nights. 'You don't have to apologise to me about *anything*, Beth,' he said, holding her close, and whispering into her ear. 'Even *my* ol' man isn't exactly the easiest person in the world ter deal with.'

She hugged him, and pushed her face into his shoulder. A gentle breeze whistled across the fields, and made straight for the thin row of terraced houses all the way along Green Lanes in the distance.

'Actually, *I* feel quite sorry for her,' said Thomas.

'Who?' asked Beth.

'Your mum. Did you know she's been seeing a doctor?'

Beth sprang a startled look up at him. 'Mum?'

Thomas nodded.

'Wot about?' she asked, completely taken aback.

Thomas shrugged. 'Headaches, one thing and another.'

'Yer don't just go ter see a doctor 'cos yer've got a bleedin' 'eadache,' replied Beth. 'Is it 'cos she's goin' ter 'ave a nervous breakdown?'

'What makes yer say that?'

'I don't know,' said Beth. 'It's the way she looks sometimes, always on edge, always gettin' worked up. It's the war. It's this bleedin' war. It's gettin' 'er down. Who told yer about it? Was it Grandad?'

Thomas nodded.

'So that's why 'e dragged yer off ter the pub.' Beth was suddenly quite irritated by what her grandad had done. 'Wot about Phil?' she asked. 'Did 'e tell 'im too.?'

'In a manner of speakin', replied Thomas.

'Oh Thomas,' pleaded Beth. 'Don't play games with me. Is Mum ill? Is she in trouble?'

'No, Beth,' replied Thomas reassuringly. 'Your mum's not ill, not in the usual sense of the word. But she does need advice. That's why she's been seein' a doctor.'

'D'yer mean *our* doctor?' Beth came back at him immediately. 'Ol' Roberts down 'Ornsey Road?'

'I don't know, Beth,' said Thomas. 'I really don't know. All yer grandad would tell me is that these nightmares are beginning ter get her down.' As he watched her anxious expression, he suddenly felt very sorry for her. 'Hey,' he said, gently raising her chin so that he could look into her eyes directly, 'it's nothin' ter worry about – believe me. It's just a passing phase. As soon as this war's over, as soon as yer dad gets home, she'll be as right as rain again.'

'Yes, Thomas,' she replied. '*When* the war's over.'

He kissed her tenderly. 'Yer know somethin'?' he whispered. 'Yer've never told me how you got yer name, "Beth"?'

Beth tried to smile, but it wasn't easy. 'Dad said it was Mum's idea,' she said. 'It came from this book *Little Women* she read when she was young back 'ome in America. There's this gel named Beff. In the story, she gets ill and later she dies.'

'Charming!' retorted Thomas. 'And your mum called you after a kid who died young?'

'The gel in the book,' continued Beth, 'was Mum's favourite character. She said everyone loved 'er – all over the world.'

'Ah! *That* I can believe,' replied Thomas.

This at last brought the smile back to Beth's face. She hugged him, and as they stood there without saying another word, the peace of a gradually approaching twilight seemed to engulf them.

Thomas finally spoke again. 'Don't worry, Beth,' he said softly. '*I'll* take care of you. You're my girl, and I'm your feller. I won't ever let anythin' happen to you. Believe me, the war won't go on for ever . . .'

As he spoke, his words were totally drowned by the most deafening sound they had ever heard, so much so that they both automatically threw themselves down on to the muddy earth. As the sound of a plane's engine roared at speed from behind and then above them, they just managed to catch a glimpse of the strange shape as it skimmed the tops of the trees and hedgerows, to disappear into a hasty landing on the runway of the nearby De Havilland's airfield.

'B'Jesus!' gasped Thomas. 'What the hell was *that*?'

'I dunno!' spluttered Beth, shaking from head to foot. 'But fank Gord it's one of ours!'

As they lay there, huddled against each other in the mud, they began to hear the distant rumble of anti-aircraft gunfire. It was the first sign that the peace of an idyllic few moments was about to be shattered yet again by the renewed sound of war.

Chapter 7

The rumble of ack-ack gunfire was now a cacophony of explosions, engulfing the night sky over Islington with the terrifying drone of enemy aircraft, which seemed to be releasing their deadly cargo of bombs on to any unspecified targets. It was a night of chaos and fear, ending the short interlude of tranquillity with a ferocity that shook every building to its foundations. Fire engines, with bells clanging, raced to every 'incident' with frenzied determination, followed by ambulances and rescue teams, struggling to keep fires and damage under control. But, despite the grim determination of the civilian population to keep their nerve, they were only too aware that they were under intense aerial bombardment, and that there was always the horrifying possibility that they would never see the start of another day.

The Shanks family's journey back from Hatfield soon after dark became a frightening ordeal the moment their bus approached Barnet High Road from the autumn woods of Cockfosters. Ahead of them was the glow of fires in the distance over what must have been the City of London and the East India Docks, and as they were drawn closer and closer into the deafening barrage of overhead gunfire, the bus rocked from side to side in the vibration, and by the time they were heading down Upper Holloway Road, the familiar sight and sound of hot white shrapnel tinkling down on to the pavement alongside automatically prompted Connie to smother little Simon to her chest as close as she possibly could. With the constant bright flashes that frequently streaked across the sky, Beth snuggled up to Thomas, leaving Phil sitting alongside his mum, casually finishing off a piece of the bread pudding that his grandmother had made for them all before they left. However, ignoring his mum's frantic pleas, as soon as the family got off the trolleybus at the Nag's Head, Phil continued on the bus on his way to report for emergency fire service duty at Moorgate, whilst Thomas reluctantly left at the same time to make his way back home to King's Cross.

Back once again with the regulars in the makeshift air raid shelter in the bowels of the old piano factory after almost a week's respite, Beth and her family did their best to keep up their spirits. But it wasn't easy. Perched on the edge of their bunks by the light of only a couple of paraffin lamps, the strain and fear was there in their eyes, as they frequently looked up at the curved brick ceiling, where tiny fragments of cement filling were becoming dislodged during the endless shaking of the entire building above them.

For almost an hour nobody spoke a word. It was as though they were all holding their breath, praying that the noise above would soon subside, giving them at last a chance to get some sleep. Eventually, the intense aerial barrage came to an end, leaving only the sounds of the emergency services racing up and down outside along Hornsey Road. Beth gave her mum a breather by nursing Simon in her arms, leaving Connie time to make up the damp bed-clothes on their bunks. Jessie Hawks, hair in curlers, sat completely immobile on the edge of her own bunk, eyes closed, hardly daring to move, even resisting the urge to pour herself her usual cup of hot cocoa from a flask. Bill Winkler, grim-faced as ever, puffed aimlessly on his unlit pipe, whilst his wife Lil clutched on her lap the never-ending cardigan she was still knitting after God knows how many months. The smell of whisky came from Jack Cutter whose small metal flask was kept tucked away in his jacket pocket for what he always insisted were 'emergencies'. Eileen Perkins, hair in a net, and wearing a shabby old woollen dressing-gown given to her by her husband Ernie before he had been called up, hugged her daughter Rita tightly, a way of trying to reassure the child that everything was going to be all right. Even the old Lieberman brothers were sombre, sitting side by side wearing their tin helmets on Abe's lower bunk, with blankets around their shoulders. They all looked a sorry bunch, and the one person who noticed it more than anyone was Beth. 'Come on all of yer!' she called, breaking the woeful silence. 'Fer Gord's sake, cheer up!'

All eyes turned towards her.

'Well, it's true, ain't it?' she insisted. 'It's all over.'

'Oh yes?' asked Bill Winkler, gloomily. 'An' fer 'ow long, may I ask?'

'Blimey, Mr Winkler,' retorted Beth. 'It's bein' so cheerful as keeps you goin'!'

Bill grunted haughtily and turned away, unimpressed with Beth's attempt to be jovial by echoing Mrs Mopp's catch-phrase from the BBC's much-loved *ITMA* show.

'Come on now, everyone!' pleaded Beth. 'This ain't a wake, yer know. If Jerry could see us down 'ere now, just imagine 'ow good 'e'd feel.'

'If Jerry was down 'ere now,' suggested Jack Cutter, perched on the edge of his upper bunk with a roller fag dangling from his lip, 'I'd separate 'im from 'is bleedin breff!'

'That's wot I like ter 'ear, Mr Cutter!' replied Beth rousingly, at the same time getting up from her own bunk to place her baby brother into his carrycot alongside their mum. 'That's wot we need down 'ere – a bit er life! I mean it's no use lyin' down an' carryin' on as though we're all 'eadin' fer the knacker's yard, now is it?'

'So wot d'yer suggest we do?' groaned Bill Winkler, irritated by Beth's boisterous attempts to raise everyone's spirits. 'Do a soft shoe shuffle or somefink?'

'Hey!' returned Beth, quick as a flash. 'That's not a bad idea, Mr Winkler. You, me an' Mr Cutter could do a real Wilson, Kepple an' Betty – me in a yashmak an' you two wearin' a fez!'

Bill glared angrily at Jessie Hawks when she let out a loud guffaw.

But the gloomy atmosphere returned immediately when a sudden burst of anti-aircraft gunfire rumbled above, causing everyone to hold on for grim death to the posts of their bunk beds.

'No, but seriously,' continued Beth, shouting above the din, 'why don't we 'ave a sing-song or somefin'? A bit of a knees-up?'

The two old Jewish brothers exchanged a bewildered look, convinced that Connie Shanks's girl had gone off her head.

'A knees-up?' spluttered Abe. 'With *my* rheumatism?'

'Do it the world er good, Mr Abe!' Beth assured him. 'Get the ol' circulation goin'!'

'It's already come *and* gone!' added his brother Bernie acidly.

If looks could kill, Bernie's glare was enough to do just that.

'All *I* want,' said Eileen Perkins with a loud yawn, 'is a good night's kip!'

The others agreed, and once the noise up top had subsided again, all of them settled back in their bunks.

Beth looked at them all in despair. It was obvious that they were determined to make the worst of an already depressing night. How could they possibly turn in when it wasn't yet even nine o'clock! Even her mum was combing her hair ready for bed. But when the ack-ack barrage started up again, everyone sat up with a start and stared up at the ceiling with a sense of deep foreboding. Soon, the shelter was being rocked by the distant blast of high-explosive bombs. Rita Perkins, Eileen's girl, screamed, and Connie had to comfort baby Simon, who was starting to bawl. Beth could see that the situation was getting desperate. If these air raids were going to go on, she asked herself, how would these people ever be able to cope with them? Sooner or later their nerves would break, and that's exactly what Hitler and his gang wanted. In a moment of impulse, Beth swung round and went straight to the old upright piano. Plonking herself down on the wooden box that served as a piano stool, she opened the lid, put her fingers on the keyboard, and launched straight into a rousing version of 'My Old Man Said Follow the Van', singing out the words as loud as she could above the sound of all hell breaking loose in the streets above them. Completely startled, the tension and fear of everyone in the cellar turned to astonishment, as they all turned to watch and listen to Beth's performance.

'Come on, all of yer!' she yelled, as she played on vigorously, loudly singing out the words.

For the first few moments, everyone greeted Beth's impromptu performance with silence. But then old Jessie Hawks was first to respond, and with the words of the popular song gradually forming on her lips, she let rip, as though competing with every ack-ack shell that was exploding in the sky above. In fact it was the women and girls who got the whole thing going, with Lil Winkler belting out the song as loud as she could, much to her husband Bill's glare of disapproval. Then Eileen Perkins joined in, with her young daughter Rita swaying to and fro on her lap, clapping her hands excitedly in time to the music. After that, of course, it didn't take long for the men to join in, and, despite the fact that he had a terrible tuneless voice, Jack Cutter's baritone could be heard above everyone else, which, for one moment at least, helped him to forget the large goitre on one side of his forehead, which always made him feel so unnecessarily self-conscious.

The Lieberman brothers, both wrapped up in their striped winceyette pyjamas and heavy woollen dressing-gowns, and clutching their hot-water bottles to their stomachs, were at first a little reluctant to take part in the raucous goings-on, but the happy, defiant and unexpected sing-song soon became too infectious for them to ignore, and they too systematically joined in, waving their hands and hot-water bottles in the air in song and in unison.

Last to be convinced, however, was Bill Winkler, who did his best to show that he didn't go along with all the fake hilarity, but when the sound of a high explosive bomb once again rocked the cellar, he quickly slipped a protective arm around Lil's waist, and sang out loud with her.

When the song finally came to an end, everyone yelled out, 'Good ol' Beff!' and 'Well done, gel!' They clapped and cheered, but most of all, for just a few moments, they were able to forget about all the horror that was going on in the streets above them – thanks to the girl who didn't seem to play a bit like her mum.

Beth woke up at about three o'clock. As usual, the cellar shelter was filled with the unmistakable sounds of sleep, snores light, snores deep, groans, even Bernie Lieberman humming what could have been some Viennese waltz from his childhood. But at least all seemed to be quiet up above, no barrage of ack-ack gunfire, no droning of enemy raiders on yet another hit-and-run mission, only the very distant sounds of the emergency services tackling yet another 'incident', but

God only knew where. There was so much on Beth's mind that she knew that once awake, she would never get to sleep again, so she quietly put on the thick woollen jersey her mum had bought for her before the war, eased herself down from her top bunk, put on her shoes, and collected her torch. She couldn't wait to get out of the place for a few minutes, for the air in the shelter was as thick as ever with fag and pipe smoke, and the portable lavatory behind the curtain was emitting its usual pungent smell of urine. She carefully tiptoed her way to the foot of the steps at the far end of the shelter, and took one last look over her shoulder. Exhausted by their burst of musical energy earlier in the evening, the 'rabbits' were now safely tucked away into their deep hutch, hopefully oblivious for once to the worries of a dangerous world.

Once she had climbed the flight of steps and pulled back a thick blackout curtain, Beth passed through a door that took her to the next level up in the building, which was a large area that had for years been used as a storage space for new and second-hand pianos waiting for sale or repair. These days it housed nothing more than an old electrical generator, a few broken office tables and chairs, and quite a lot of broken wooden floorboards. It was much the same when she reached the ground floor level of the building, where the only difference was that it was completely bare, with all the windows boarded up on the outside to prevent the risk of injury from flying glass during an air raid.

By the light of her torch, she found her way to the main double front doors, which, for the benefit of the people sheltering below, were kept unlocked. However, if she had hoped for some pure fresh air in the street outside, that illusion was soon shattered, for the moment she pulled back the blackout curtain, she was practically overcome by the choking smell of burning timbers which was drifting over the rooftops from fires that were blazing all over the borough.

For a moment or so she stood at the door, staring out at the red glow lining the horizon for miles beyond the junction of Hornsey and Seven Sisters Roads, where it was clear the attack of the night had clearly been directed once again at the London Docks and the City of London. She shuddered at the thought of what had been going on, the poor people who would be emerging from the public air raid shelters only to find that they had no home left to return to. She rubbed her eyes wearily with both hands, crossed her arms, and leaned against the brick wall alongside the front door, which was still pitted with machine gun bullets from a rogue enemy fighter plane a few weeks earlier. And then she thought about her mum and baby Simon, and all her neighbours whom she had brought together in such a rowdy sing-song just a few hours before. Why did she do it, she asked herself? Why did she have to keep putting on this show of courage, when in fact she was far more scared of the bombs than the whole lot of them. It was bad enough to be called a 'firecracker' at the munitions factory, but now to be known as the 'life and soul of the party' was more than she could possibly cope with. Oh, if people only knew the truth about her, she told herself, knew that everything she did was only an act, a cover-up to disguise her own anxieties.

As she stood there, an ambulance with bells clanging wildly, approached at speed down the hill from Hornsey, and quickly disappeared to the right along Tollington Way in what would seem to be a race against time to reach the Royal Northern Hospital in Holloway Road. She felt so alone, so cut off from reality. The whole day had been a terrible ordeal for her, having to deal with her gran and grandad's pulverising but well-meaning attempts to persuade her and Phil to go and live with them, and her mum's constant anxieties about the nightmares she was having each night. If it hadn't been for Thomas, Beth couldn't imagine how she could have ever coped with such a day. Oh Thomas, she sighed. How she wished he was there with her now, holding her in his arms, and telling her that everything was going to be all right. But was it, she asked herself? Despite the politicians' assurances that things would soon get better, she found it hard to believe. The Blitz was getting more intense every day and night. More and more people were going to die, and no one, not even Winston Churchill, could do anything about it.

'Wish I 'ad a fag or somefin'.'

Beth turned with a start, and by the light of her torch picked out old Jessie Hawks, who had followed her up from the shelter below and was now standing in the open doorway behind her.

'They say it 'elps yer to cope,' continued the old girl. 'Not that I go along wiv smokin'. Never took to it meself. Not like my Albert. 'E always 'ad a fag on, said it calmed 'is nerves, though it didn't do 'im much good. That's wot took 'im off in the end. They say 'is lungs was full er black. Still, 'e 'ad a good life. I always fink of 'im when someone else's got a fag on.'

For a few moments, the two women stood there in silence, arms crossed, staring up at the dark night sky, with the early November moon drifting in and out of small puffs of clouds that looked like cotton wool, but tinted red from the flickering glow of fires amidst the eerie columns of thick black smoke that spiralled up from every part of the city.

'That was a good fing yer did down there,' said Jessie. 'Livened up the place.'

'Fanks, Mrs 'Awks,' Beth replied, with a comforted smile.

'No, I mean it,' said Jessie. 'It's no use feelin' sorry fer yerself, carryin' on as though we're rats caught in a trap. If we let ourselves go under, there's nuffin' left, is there?'

Beth shrugged.

'It's funny about a sing-song, in't it?' continued the old lady. ' 'Speshully fer ordinary folk like us. I mean, it don't matter 'ow lousy yer voice is, it makes yer feel good, makes yer feel as though yer ain't got a trouble in the world.' For one brief moment, she hummed the first line of 'My Old Man Said Follow the Van'.

'My trouble,' she said when she'd stopped, 'is I can never seem ter remember the words. Even though me an' Albert used ter sing 'em a 'undred times, I always get lost in the middle.' She chuckled to herself. 'But it's lovely when folk get tergevver an' sing their 'eads off. A good ol' sing-song makes life worf livin', don't it?'

Beth smiled. She had always had a lot of time for the old lady. Jessie was no fool. Like so many other widows who had to live on their own, each day was a struggle to survive. But no one ever heard Jessie complain about what she never had. After her much-loved hubby Albert died after nearly fifty years of marriage, she refused to spend the rest of her days grieving; she just got on with her life, and made do with what she *did* have. With her grey curls that were once bright red, Jessie was a pillar of defiance. She was a true fighter. Her indomitable spirit would allow nothing and no one to get her down.

'Funny about your mum though, ain't it?'

Beth turned to look at her. 'Wot d'yer mean?' she asked curiously.

'Well – the way you're so diff'rent to 'er. I mean, just look at the way she plays the pianer. Oh it's luvely stuff all right, but – well – yer can't sing along wiv it, can yer?'

'Mum plays the piano the way it *should* be played, Mrs 'Awks,' replied Beth. 'All *I* do is put me fingers on the keyboard an' 'ope fer the best.'

Jessie chuckled. 'Oh, I ain't knockin' yer mum,' she replied assuredly. 'No – not at all. Your mum's one of the best. In fact I love ter watch her. When I see 'er walk down the street sometimes, she seems ter – float on air, so light, so graceful. She's got a lot er class, Beff, there's no two ways about *that*. I mean, it's always amazed me 'ow she's fitted in.'

'I don't foller yer?' said Beth.

'Well,' continued Jessie, 'she ain't ruff and ready like most of us lot, is she? I mean, I know she's a Yank, but your mum's a *real* lady. You can always tell, by the way she talks, the way she eats. I've watched her down this shelter a coupla times I can tell yer – the way she peels an apple with a knife, all in one piece. It's beautiful – a real work of art.' She sighed. 'If all Yanks are like 'er, then I tip me 'at to 'em.' She paused just long enough to look at Beth, whose face reflected a bright white glow from the moon every time a cloud raced by. 'Not like yer dad, though,' she continued, her voice carrying real warmth in the dark night air. 'One er the boys, your dad, one er the best. My Albert always said Ted Shanks was a real rough diamond, do anyfin' fer anyone, never crossed anyone, 'onest as the day is long.' She paused a moment. 'By the way,' she said, quite out of the blue. 'Who's that woman who's bin askin' after 'im?'

Again Beth turned with a start. 'Woman?' she asked. 'Wot woman?'

'Followed me 'ome from the fish 'n' chip shop the uvver night,' replied Jessie. 'Said she knew yer dad years ago. Wanted ter get in touch wiv 'im. She give me quite a turn, I can tell yer. It ain't no joke 'avin' someone come up be'ind yer in the blackout.'

Beth was curious. 'Wot did she want ter talk ter Dad about?' she asked.

' 'Aven't the foggiest, dear,' replied Jessie. 'All she said was years ago she knew someone by yer dad's name, an' just wondered whevver he was safe an' well. But she knew 'e was married to yer mum – or so she said.'

'Wot did she look like?' asked Beth.

' 'Ard ter tell in the dark. An' the battery in me torch was nearly run out. But she was a good looker all right, a bit pasty, wiv dark eyes. Mind you, she looked 'armless enuff, but these days, yer never know, do yer?'

By the time Beth had emerged from the air raid shelter with her mum and baby brother, a freezing November drizzle was fluttering down relentlessly from a dark grey sky, and to make matters worse, water was cascading down the gutter from a fractured water main in Upper Hornsey Road. Wrapped up warm against what was clearly promising to be a very cold day, the rest of the neighbours still squinted in the morning light after having to spend so long in the dark cellars below.

Everyone dispersed, and quickly scuttled off to the comfort of their own homes, including the Shanks family, who were accompanied on the way to Moray Road by their next door neighbour, Jack Cutter. Despite the ferocity of the previous night's bombing, it was clear that the local kids had been up bright and early, for they had already been around with their buckets to collect all the fallen shrapnel that had been scattered menacingly along every pavement and street in the neighbourhood. Hornsey Road was as busy as any other normal weekday morning, with the number 14 petrol bus conveying commuters back and forth to their jobs in Holloway, King's Cross and the West End. Further down the road, the usual queue of people was forming outside the Public Baths, waiting to get in to pay twopence for their weekly early morning ration of six inches of lukewarm water.

It had been yet another long and wearisome night for Beth, and she was only grateful that she was on split turn at the munitions factory that week, which meant that, providing there wasn't another daytime air raid, she could at least grab a few hours genuine sleep. Her mum looked all in too, as the two of them struggled along clutching one handle each of the baby's carrycot.

They stopped only briefly to wait for Jack to buy a newspaper at the shop on the corner of Tollington Way, where Peg, the middle-aged owner, was sweeping up the remains of her broken shop window. 'I'm sick er this!' she growled, her dyed blonde curls quivering with rage. 'This is the third bleedin' time I've lost my window this munff. I know wot I'd like ter do ter bleedin' 'Itler if I see 'im – *if* 'e's still got any left!'

For the last few remaining minutes before they reached home, Jack continued his usual irritating habit of reading out loud bits and pieces from his beloved *Daily Mirror*, which consisted mainly of disapproving grunts and groans and outraged murmurs of 'Typical!' Today there were the gradually developing rumours of an imminent Nazi invasion of Britain, and the measures the Government were putting in place to help the civilian population defend itself. However, the one news item that did make Beth take notice was the report of possible IRA activity in London that could point to collusion with German intelligence.

'That's the trouble with the Paddies,' said Jack, as they turned into Moray Road. 'They can't make up their bleedin' mind who's side they're on!'

Beth tried to dismiss the report from her own mind. Nevertheless, it still left her with uneasy feelings which just wouldn't go away.

Once they had finally got home, Beth and Connie bid farewell to Jack who quickly disappeared into his own house next door. For some unknown reason, seeing him go always made Beth feel guilty, because Jack, a lifelong bachelor, never seemed to have a life outside the four walls of his house. Even when she and Phil were kids together, Beth remembered how, during the summer months, they often watched him sitting in a deck chair in his neat and tidy backyard, reading his *Daily Mirror* over and over again, never going out except for an occasional trip round the corner for a pint at the pub in Andover Street. It was such a solitary life, and Jack must have been quite a good looker when he was young, thought Beth, so it seemed strange that no girl had ever snapped him up.

Inside the house, the place was freezing cold, so the first thing Beth did was to go straight into the kitchen to light the paraffin stove. It was a frustrating job, for, owing to the damp, the matches solidly refused to ignite. Her next priority was to make a cup of tea, but when she went to the sink to fill the kettle she was puzzled to find a dirty cup with tea dregs there. But as she quickly came to the conclusion that her brother Phil had probably got home from his night duty, she carried on filling the kettle, before taking it across to the cooker to light the gas ring. Then she went into the front parlour, where Connie was changing baby Simon's nappy. Surprisingly, the room was slightly warmer than the rest of the house, and she soon discovered why when she went to light the fire.

'Mum?' she asked. 'Did you lay this fire last night?'

Connie looked up only briefly from what she was doing. 'Of course I did,' she replied. 'You know I always do. I did it before we left to go to Gran and Grandad's yesterday morning.'

Beth looked at the fireplace. There was no fresh newspaper or wood or coke, only ashes that were still smouldering. She slowly turned to look across at her mother. 'Are you sure?' she asked sceptically.

Connie looked round, and met her gaze. As she did so, they heard a door opening on the first floor upstairs.

Beth immediately rushed out into the hall. Her frozen body was suddenly consumed with searing warmth, for standing on the first-floor landing looking down at her was her father. 'Dad!' she yelled out loud.

The moment he saw his daughter, Ted Shanks, a towering six-footer, unshaved, and wearing only his khaki army trousers, braces and vest, spread out his arms, and with a wide welcoming grin called out, 'Beff!'

Beth leapt up the stairs two at a time, and threw herself straight into his arms. 'Oh Christ, Dad!' she gasped, half laughing, half crying. 'Bleedin' 'ell!'

Ted grabbed hold of her, lifted her into the air, and hugged her so tight that she could hardly breathe. 'Beff!' he said, over and over again, eyes tightly closed in deep affection. 'Beff, Beff, oh Beff . . .!' But when his eyes opened again, over her shoulders he suddenly caught sight, at the foot of the stairs, of that other special person he had also been yearning to see. It was Connie, baby Simon clutched in her arms, tears streaming down her cheeks.

Gently leaving Beth behind, his face crumpled with emotion, Ted Shanks slowly walked down the stairs to greet his wife, together with the baby son he was seeing for the very first time . . .

Chapter 8

Uncle Horace couldn't believe his luck. On Tuesday morning he received confirmation that the huge pumpkin he had grown with such love and care over the previous months had qualified for entry in the Walthamstow Town Hall's winter 'DIG FOR BRITAIN' vegetable competition, which was due to take place, air raids permitting, on the following Saturday afternoon. And if that wasn't enough, Beth's breathless unexpected midweek visit brought him even more joyous news. 'Yer dad's 'ome?' he gasped in disbelief, eyes nearly popping out of his head. 'Yer mean, yer've seen 'im? Yer've actually *seen* 'im?'

'Of course I've seen 'im!' Beth was so excited she could hardly breathe. ' 'E got 'ome', she babbled, 'while me an' Mum an' Simon was down the shelter last night. We nearly died when we got 'ome an' saw 'im at the top of the stairs! Oh, isn't it wonderful, Uncle 'Orace!'

'Wunnerful?' he returned in the rural Essex twang that he would never lose. 'It's bloomin' marvellous! I can 'ardly believe it. I didn't fink any of the boys would get 'ome 'til the war's over.' As absent-minded as ever, he was hobbling around his back parlour wearing one carpet slipper and one muddy shoe. But then a worried thought suddenly occurred to him. 'There's nuffin' wrong wiv 'im, is there?' he asked anxiously. 'I mean, 'e ain't bin injured or nuffin', as 'e?'

Beth's initial exuberance became slightly subdued. 'No,' she replied. 'Not exactly. But somefin' must've 'appened, becos they've given 'im seven days compassionate leave.'

'Compassionate leave?'

Beth warmed her hands in front of the old oven range, where a pair of kippers were on the stove smelling the place out. 'Don't ferget, we ain't seen 'im since Dunkirk. In fact we don't even know fer sure if 'e was there, but – well, the way 'e looks . . .' She slowly shook her head.

'Wot d'yer mean, Beff?' asked Horace.

Beth shrugged. 'Oh, I don't know,' she replied with a sigh. ' 'E looks so much older. 'Is eyes look sort er – far away.'

Horace knew exactly what she was saying. The evacuation of the British forces from Dunkirk had been a traumatic period not only for the men themselves, but also for the entire nation. The images of what those men went through, the desperate attempt to stay alive as the great armada of little boats struggled to get them back across the English Channel, would be something that would remain in their memories for the rest of their lives. And Horace knew what Beth had never been told, that her dad had indeed been one of the lucky few who had made it back home, but no one would ever know at what price. 'Don't you worry,' said Horace reassuringly. 'Once 'e's been wiv yer mum an' the family for a day or two, 'e'll soon be back to 'is old self.'

'I hope you're right, Unc,' said Beth. 'I hope you're right. Still,' she continued brightly, 'wait 'til I tell Mum an' Dad about your pumpkin. They'll be over the moon!'

' 'Ang on, gel,' returned Horace. 'I ain't won that prize yet.'

'But yer will!' insisted Beth emphatically. 'Yours is the best. There won't be anyone in that competition to touch yer.'

'Don't you believe it,' replied Horace, who finally sat down and exchanged his muddy shoe for a carpet slipper. 'Some of those veg are top class – 'speshully the Brussels sprouts. Take Stan Pakeman, fer a start. 'E wins practically every year. It'd be real fluke if I pipped '*im* ter the post.'

'Well, you're goin' to!' insisted Beth. 'An' wot's more, we'll all come over on Saturday an' see yer take the prize!'

Horace roared with laughter. But inside he longed for such a dream to come true. He had never won a prize before, *any* kind of prize, and if he did, he would feel that he had made his dear late wife Maudie so proud of him. 'Tell yer wot,' he said with restrained exuberance. 'If I win that prize, we'll 'ave such a booze up, my neighbours'll go on talkin' about it fer years!'

They both roared with laughter, realising only just in time that the kippers Uncle Horace was cooking for his midday meal were about to become charred remains.

Ted Shanks looked at his baby son and couldn't believe his good luck. When his wife Connie had first written to him about the day young Simon arrived, he was convinced that he would never set eyes on him. As one of the last thousand or so British troops who had been trapped on the beach at Dunkirk, the journey back on a small civilian motor launch had been hazardous and death defying, and by the time he had reached the quayside at Dover, he was in such a collapsed condition that he never remembered a thing about the previous few days until he woke up and found himself in a military hospital somewhere in the South of England. By then he had no energy, no reason to go on living, not after all he had seen, not after the friends he had lost in the bloody fields of France. But when that letter from Connie arrived, it was as though someone had given him an injection that had brought him back to life again; he could feel the warmth of home and family seeping through his veins, so much so that he began to cry. This was something that he had not done in his entire life. Ted Shanks was no cry baby, he was a man, a man of the East End, where there was no time to cry, where working to make ends meet was what life was all about. Crying was for the weak, not for someone who had always been strong physically *and* mentally. And yet, and yet there he was, crying like a baby, a tough six-footer who only a few years before had played centre-half with his mates in the regular Sunday morning football matches up on Hackney Marshes. There was no doubt that, until he had received that letter about the baby from Connie, he had almost given up the will to live, because he hadn't wanted any of his family to see what had happened to him. But that letter had changed everything. It was as though he had been given a new lease of life, a family to go home to, *his* family, who would see him through the worst of everything.

'Most people think he looks like Phil,' said Connie proudly, as she watched Ted cradling the baby in his arms at the kitchen table.

Phil scowled at the thought. Although he was over the moon to see his dad again, he'd only just got home from a gruelling night's AFS messenger work during the air raid up in the City of London, and he didn't take kindly to being compared to a baby – *any* baby.

'Don't listen to yer ma, Phil,' said Ted, looking up from cooing helplessly to his baby son. 'You don't look like no one *I* know. An' that's just fine wiv me. Be yer own fing, mate, and yer won't go wrong.'

Phil liked that. His dad always had a way with words, always had a way of makin' him feel good. 'I wish yer could stay 'ome, Dad,' he said. 'Seven days ain't very long. Yer've done your bit. Somebody else should take a turn.'

Ted looked serious for a moment. 'We've *all* got to do our bit, son,' he said to Phil. 'Once the invasion comes, every one of us is goin' ter 'ave ter defend ourselves.'

Connie, horrified, looked across the table at him. 'The invasion?' she asked anxiously. 'You really think they'll come?'

Ted shrugged, got up from the table, and lowered the baby carefully into his pram. 'Ever since we got out of Dunkirk,' he said, 'Jerry's massed all 'is troops along the French coast. It's only a matter of time.' He came back to her. 'We've got to be prepared, Con. They'll carry on bombing the daylights out of us until they're ready to move in.'

'But what can *we* do to stop them?' asked Connie. 'We're not soldiers. We don't know how to fight.'

'*I* do!' insisted Phil emphatically, thumping his fist on the table. 'If I see a Jerry coming down in our back garden, I'll annihilate 'im!'

Ted smiled at the boy. 'I don't fink that's goin' ter be likely, son,' he said. ' 'Cos I want you an' Beff ter do wot yer muvver says. Go down an' stay wiv yer gran an' grandad.'

Phil let out a loud groan.

'Now listen ter me, Phil!' said Ted sharply. 'When Jerry comes, *this* is where 'e'll be makin' for. London's wot 'e wants. This is where the big fight's goin' ter take place.'

'But we 'ave ter stand up to 'em, Dad!' insisted Phil defiantly. 'Nobody's goin' to get *me* ter just run away.'

'Yer'll do as you're told, Phil,' said Ted quietly, but firmly. 'You're still our son, an' when yer mum an' I fink somefin's right for yer, then you do wot we say. Right?'

For a brief moment, Ted stared at the boy, waiting for his response. But Phil remained sullen and silent. He flicked a quick glance at his mum, then back at his dad again. In those few short seconds his whole world seemed to fall apart. He had waited for this moment for so long, waited for the time when he could sit and talk with his dad again, not as a kid, but as his equal. In Phil's eyes, his dad was a hero; he had always worshipped the ground he walked on. But his dad was no different to his mum. They were just two of a kind. All they wanted to do was to treat him as though he had no mind of his own, no right to an opinion. There and then he decided that if they tried to get him to go and live with his gran and grandad, then he would be forced to do something drastic.

'Did you hear what I said, son?' said Ted reasonably.

Phil shrugged, calmly got up from the table, and left the room.

'You see what I mean, don't you? He's out of control. Both he *and* Beth are out of control.'

Ted looked at his wife and saw the look of fear and vulnerability in her eyes. He smiled affectionately at her, because he loved those eyes; he'd loved them from the very first moment he had first seen them. 'They're growin' up, Con,' he said, sitting opposite her at the kitchen table. 'They've got a right to start thinking for themselves.'

Connie watched him light up a fag. In fact she had watched his every movement since she had first set eyes on him that morning. Just seeing him sitting there made her forget about all her worries and anxieties. Her face was a picture of warm, loving smiles, and smiling was something she hadn't done since the day he was called up. 'Oh Ted,' she sighed, stretching out to hold his hand on the table, 'you've no idea what it means to us all to have you back. We've missed you so much.'

Ted looked across at her, straight into those crystal-blue eyes. He took the fag out from his lips and placed it in the small glass ashtray Connie had bought him for one of his birthdays. Then he took hold of her other hand; her hands were warm, and throbbing with life. 'Yer know somefin'?' he said, not taking his eyes off her. 'You look more pretty than I've ever seen yer. A bit tired, a bit under the wevver, but just as I always remember yer, just as I remember yer night after night wherever I am.'

'Seven days is no time at all, Ted,' replied Connie, as Ted's fingers gently stroked hers. 'I can't bear the thought of you going back into any more danger.'

Ted shook his head. 'After that din I 'eard round 'ere last night,' he replied, 'I reckon *I'm* the one that should be worried. I was up in the bedroom when this bomb come down – Gord knows where. So d'yer know wot I did?'

Connie shook her head.

'I 'id under the bleedin' bed.'

Connie laughed. Ted had always been one to make her laugh when things were in fact quite serious.

'Bleedin' 'ell, Con!' he retorted, half laughing himself. 'Scared the daylights out er me!'

Connie grabbed his hands, gently rubbed them against her cheeks, and then kissed them. She looked up at him. 'I've been having such nightmares, Ted,' she said, the smile now dissolved into strain, her Texan drawl only just noticeable. 'Night after night I dream of exactly the same thing.' She paused a moment. 'I dream that Beth, Phil, Simon and I are down in the shelter.' Her words were slow and faltering. 'I dream that . . . that a bomb comes down – and kills all of us.'

'Bleedin' 'ell, Con!' gasped Ted, turning his face away in horror.

'That's not all, Ted,' continued Connie, holding on to his hands. 'I dream that you come looking for us. But we're not there.'

Ted slowly turned back to her. 'Yer know wot they say, Con,' he replied reassuringly. 'They say that when yer dream somefin', it's nearly always the opposite of wot *really* 'appens.'

As they looked at each other, Connie's smile gradually returned, and for one brief moment, she looked absolutely radiant.

This was one morning that Beth wished that she didn't have to come to work. Seeing her dad for the first time in months had made her long to stay at home and be with him, to hear all that had happened to him since Dunkirk. But after sending a telegram to her gran and grandad, and then making a quick bus trip up to Tottenham to tell Uncle Horace, it seemed as though she had already missed several hours of being in her dad's company. However, once she had arrived for her morning shift at the munitions factory, she soon found that quite a lot was going on there too.

The first thing that happened was that her mate, Mo Mitchell, was secretly selling illegal half-pound bars of Cadbury's milk chocolate on the black market. 'You're a bleedin' dope, Mo,' said Beth, trying to ignore the selection of goodies that Mo was offering her beneath their workbench. 'Yer know wot they'll do if they catch yer. Six munffs in the jug.'

'Git off!' replied Mo dismissively. 'Fer sellin' a few bars er chocolate?'

'It's against the law, yer silly cow!' retorted Beth. 'Don't yer fink they don't know where the stuff's come from?'

'It's fallen off the back of a lorry,' insisted Mo. 'There's nuffin' wrong wiv that.'

'Who're *you* kiddin'!' snapped Beth, looking over her shoulders from side to side to make sure no one was watching them. 'They've got ways of checkin'. I'm warnin' yer, if you get shopped, yer've 'ad it!'

Mo shrugged. 'Please yerself,' replied Mo haughtily, placing the bar of chocolate back into her carrier bag of goodies. 'If *you* don't want it, I've got plenty of uvver customers.'

'It's not that I don't want it,' explained Beth. 'My mum loves chocolate, so do me an' Phil, but I just don't want ter end up in the clink, that's all.'

'That's your trouble, Beff Shanks,' replied Mo, carrying on with her bullet case filing. 'You're scared er yer own skin. Just look round the place. D'you fink anyone cares a monkey's about buyin' a bar er chocolate on the black market?'

No sooner had she spoken than Charlie Hatchet the foreman called from just behind. 'Beff, you're wanted.'

Both girls froze, but when Beth turned round to look, she found Hatchet hurrying towards her. 'Wot d'yer mean?' asked Beth, conscious that Mo was quickly hiding her bag of goodies beneath the workbench. '*Who* wants me?'

'Security office,' replied Hatchet. 'You're next.'

'Next?' asked Beth warily, reluctantly getting up from her stool. 'Fer wot?'

'Fer questionin',' returned Hatchet. 'Get a move on, gel! They ain't got all day.'

Beth's expression was like stone as she started to move off.

'Stop lookin' so worried!' called Hatchet as she went. 'It's only routine.'

This was the moment Beth had been dreading. Although most of her workmates in the factory had already been questioned by the security police, she had somehow dismissed the idea that she would also be called. As she wound her way through the small arms workshops, with music blaring out from the tannoys, some of the girls stopped briefly to give her the thumbs-up sign. She smiled back weakly at them, and hurried on her way. In the reception area outside, various staff were gathered around waiting to have interviews with the personnel office and medical unit, and the tense atmosphere unnerved her.

'In here please, Shanks!' called a middle-aged man from personnel who was waiting for her at the open door of the security office. She glared at him as she went in, deeply resenting the way he always referred to the employees by their surnames.

'Please sit down, Beth,' said a uniformed, middle-aged woman sitting at a trestle-table bench, flanked on either side by a male police officer and a younger woman in civilian clothes. 'It *is* Beth, isn't it?' she asked, with a warm informal smile that was in contrast to the bigoted reception Beth had received outside.

'Yes, it is,' replied Beth, taking the seat which was being indicated to her by the male officer.

'I remember there was a lovely girl with the same name in *Little Women*,' said the smiling policewoman. 'Have you read that book?'

Beth shook her head. 'Afraid not, miss,' she replied formally. 'But my mum 'as.'

'Ah!' replied the woman, immediately connecting the two. 'We shan't keep you a moment, my dear.'

The woman began a whispered consultation with her colleagues, who were all referring to a file on their desk. Beth was convinced this was some kind of tactic to unnerve her, so she looked away, looked at anything that didn't really register around her. Like every other room in the building, it was all pretty bleak, with distempered green walls that hadn't been painted for years, and were covered mainly with wartime propaganda posters, mostly about careless talk costing lives, but also about other bizarre issues such as 'MAKE DO AND MEND' and 'DIG ON FOR VICTORY'.

'You're probably aware by now', said the smiling woman, peering at Beth over the top of her metal-rimmed spectacles, 'that we're having a little chat with all the employees of this factory. Nothing to worry about. Just routine.'

Now Beth was really worried.

'The fact is,' continued the woman, whose speaking voice to Beth sounded like cut glass, 'with the war at such a crucial stage, a munitions factory is naturally a prime target for the enemy. Therefore, I'm sure you'll appreciate how imperative it is that we keep security on maximum alert.'

Beth didn't really know to answer, and so she merely shrugged.

'Which means that we have to know thoroughly who our employees are,' continued the woman, 'and what backgrounds they come from.' She referred to the file on her desk. 'I see you're a London girl. Your father was born in the East End – Bow.' She looked up briefly with a smile. 'A cockney – born and bred.'

'I put that all down on the paper,' replied Beth irritated, 'when I first come 'ere.'

'And your mother's an American?' continued the woman, again referring back to Beth's file. 'She teaches the piano. How interesting.'

'What can you tell us about Thomas Sullivan?'

The sudden, rather impatient question from the male police officer, took Beth completely by surprise. 'Thomas?' she asked.

'You've been close companions for nearly a year,' continued the man, much to the obvious disapproval of the smiling woman, who was glaring at him sideways.

So that was it. Beth now knew why she was there. At last they were getting to the point. It wasn't her they were interested in, it was

Thomas, Thomas who had to be checked up on because he was Irish. 'Thomas ain't my *companion*,' Beth replied tersely. ' 'E's me boyfriend.'

'So what can you tell us about him?' pursued the male police officer.

'Wot d'yer wanna know?' asked Beth, crossing her arms and sitting slackly back in her chair.

'Does he ever talk about the war?' asked the young female, who was wearing a two-piece checked suit with a woollen scarf around her shoulders.

' 'Course 'e talks about the war,' replied Beth. 'Who don't?'

'What kind of things do you discuss with him?' pressed the male officer.

Beth sighed, and took a brief moment to answer. She flicked a quick glance up at them and thought what a ripe old bunch they were. Except for the smiling woman, who clearly stood head and shoulders above the other two. 'We talk about all sort er fings,' she replied finally. 'About where we can get fings that yer can't buy in the shops any more, about comin' ter work an' the risk of getting coshed by a bit er shrapnel. We talk about the planes that Jerry sends over every night, the way they just seem ter bomb anyfin' they like.'

'And what does Thomas Sullivan think about that?' asked the male officer.

'Wot d'yer fink 'e finks!' snapped Beth. ' 'E 's just the same as anyone else. 'E 'ates the war!'

'And what do you know about his friends?' asked the male officer.

Beth swung a puzzled look at him.

'He must have a lot of friends?' continued the officer, with a shrug. 'You must have met some of them?'

'As a matter of fact,' replied Beth casually, 'I 'aven't.'

The three members of the team remained silent.

'Isn't that a little strange?' asked the younger woman.

'Why?' asked Beth resentfully.

'You've known this man a year,' said the male officer. 'I find it hard to believe that he hasn't introduced you to any of his friends.'

'Thomas lives up King's Cross way,' said Beth. 'I don't get up there very often, 'cos when Thomas an' I leave work, we usually meet up later down the Nag's Head.' She was now intensely aware that they were staring at her. Even the smiling woman was beginning to get on her nerves, because the smile was becoming just a little too shallow and repetitive. 'Look,' she continued, 'the only mates of 'is I '*ave* met 'ave bin really nice.'

'In what way?' asked the male officer.

Beth shrugged. 'Just – nice,' she repeated. 'They din't ignore me like some of the blokes I know. They're just ordinary Irish fellers, who like a pint er beer an' a good laugh. Is there anyfin' wrong wiv that?'

'Well,' continued the male officer, as though he hadn't been listening to a word Beth had said, 'let me put it another way. Does Thomas ever talk to you – or his friends – about politics?'

'Not ter *my* knowledge,' replied Beth. 'Unless you're referring to who's playin' fer the Arsenal or the Spurs.'

'No, I'm not referring to that, Miss Shanks,' returned the male officer, who clearly did not appreciate her humour. 'What I'd like to know – what we'd all like to know – is whether you've ever heard Thomas talking with his friends about his place of work – this factory?'

Beth froze. After a moment of shock she replied adamantly, 'No. I've never once 'eard Thomas talk about this factory, *or* what 'e does 'ere.'

'And what about his father?'

Again Beth was taken aback by the male officer's question. 'Wot about 'im?' she asked.

'Does Thomas ever talk to his father about the kind of work he does at this factory?'

Beth was now getting irritated by the man's relentless interest in Thomas. ' 'Ow would *I* know?' she snapped. 'I've never even met the man.'

Beth could feel the wariness of the three people facing her across the desk.

'You've never met Thomas's father?' asked the younger woman, who was from the personnel unit, and was now leaning forward in her chair. 'You've never met Joe Sullivan?'

Beth shrugged. 'Never,' she replied quite openly. 'Why should I?'

'You've been walking out with Thomas for nearly a year, and you've never met his father?' asked the woman. 'Don't you find that a little – well, shall we say – out of the ordinary?'

Beth was utterly bewildered by the question. ' 'Course I don't,' she replied. 'Thomas says 'e wants ter take me 'ome ter meet 'im some time, but so far –'

'So far?'

Beth now hated this man who was interrogating her as though she was some kind of criminal. The more he looked at her, the more she thought what an intensely ugly and unpleasant man he was, with his wisp of grey hair, staring dark eyes, and a nose that seemed to jut out into a point. What *was* he getting at, she asked herself? What were all three of them trying to get at? But in her heart of hearts she knew exactly what they were trying to suggest: that Thomas was Irish, and therefore because the IRA had been mixed up with Jerry, then *he* must be some kind of collaborator too, someone who was prepared to give information to the enemy. The very idea made her angry, because being Irish didn't mean that you were a traitor. It didn't mean that good honest Irish people like Thomas wanted to see Hitler's troops marching down Whitehall and taking over the country. What kind of prejudice was this? she asked herself. Why don't these three stupid mugs just come right out and tell her straight what they're trying to get at? 'I'll meet Thomas's dad one of these days,' she replied. '*When* Thomas is good an' ready.'

A short while later, Beth left the security office. What had been promised as nothing more than a 'routine' interview, had turned out to be an interrogation. She hated the three people who had sat in judgement on both her and Thomas. She hated the smug way that they just sat there and presumed that she was trying to conceal something from them. Most of all she hated what they were trying to suggest, that if she was patriotic, if she loved her country, then she should keep an eye on the boy she was walking out with, and report anything unusual about the way he talked or conducted his life. But she decided there and then that she would do nothing of the sort. She loved Thomas, and she trusted him. Nothing and no one in the whole wide world was going to get her to become an informer, a spy. She was angry, really white-hot angry, and as she stormed out of the office, regardless of the consequences, she found herself slamming the door behind her. She should have gone straight back to her workbench in the small arms workshop, but for the moment, she was just too angry to see or talk to anyone. She felt tainted, as though she herself was now some kind of a suspect – and all because she was in love with an Irish boy. She found herself at an exit door, and marched out into the backyard of the factory, which was totally deserted but for a couple of vans and trucks. Despite the freezing cold, she felt so hot she wanted to rip off her protective hairnet and white work-coat. She made her way across to the back entrance to the yard, which was heavily protected by sandbags, barbed wire, and two armed security guards, but before she could do anything rash, she heard someone calling to her.

'Beth!'

She came to a halt, and swung round to find Thomas hurrying across to her.

'Beth!' said Thomas, coming to a breathless halt. 'What the hell's goin' on? What are yer doin' out here?'

Beth stared at him, and for one brief moment didn't know what she was going to say. 'Nuffin's goin' on,' she replied brusquely. 'Nuffin' at all.'

Without another word, and with Thomas watching her in absolute bewilderment, she turned and hurried back into the factory.

Chapter 9

Heinz Buchner was grateful he was back on night raids. The last time he had flown on a mission over London during daylight hours, he had been engaged in fierce aerial combat with an RAF Spitfire, an irksome British fighter plane that was proving far too troublesome for what had until now been the superior power of the German *Luftwaffe*. He hated cat and mouse chases, he hated to be challenged. In a few moments he would again be dropping his bombs on the railway marshalling yards at King's Cross before making a hazardous escape back to his air control centre in northern France. He was anxious to get it over and done with.

Despite what his wife Helga had said about dropping bombs on innocent people, in a war everything and everybody was a target, including civilians. Part of his training had been to erase from his mind the people down below. Innocent or not, they were the enemy, and until the enemy had been eradicated, there could be no successful outcome to the war. Nonetheless, he *did* have misgivings, especially about tonight. As he approached the target area, he had a nagging feeling in his stomach. It was partly because of the November moon, which was full, with its white luminous glow turning the dark night clouds into terrifying ethereal figures that seemed to reach out at him as he tore through them at speed.

Once he had jettisoned his deadly cargo of weapons, he turned his aircraft into a swift curve, and raced off back towards the coast as fast as his engines would carry him. He left behind a series of blood-red explosions and a spiral of thick black smoke that curled up relentlessly towards the moon. He breathed a sigh of relief only when he approached the Essex coast for the last dash across the English Channel to safety. But his misgivings about the night's mission were to be realised when a sudden burst of anti-aircraft fire from the ground below suddenly clipped the tail of his plane, and sent it into a dive, heading directly towards the ice-cold waters below.

Ted Shanks was beginning to think he had been safer wading in the sea under enemy fire at Dunkirk than making a wild dash with his wife and family along Hornsey Road in the middle of an air raid. Dodging in and out of falling shrapnel was no laughing matter wherever it came from, but somehow it seemed much more terrifying as it tinkled down on to the pavements of a London street than it ever did in the cold and muddy fields of France. He also didn't feel much better, cooped up down the old factory shelter in Hornsey Road, where the entire foundations shook every time a bomb fell in the distance, or a barrage of ack-ack gunfire split the heavens apart high above them.

'Those sods are determined ter get poor ol' King's Cross,' growled Jessie Hawks, as she perched on the edge of her bunk, rolling up one of her curlers which had come loose under her hairnet. 'Gord knows wot we'll do if they knock out that station.'

'I'd like ter bet it's not the station Jerry's after, Mrs 'Awks,' said Ted. 'It's the marshallin' yards. That's where all the loadin' up goes on.'

'Loadin'?' asked Jessie.

'Armaments, weapons,' replied Ted. 'They're always movin' stuff up an' down the country.'

Jessie didn't ask anything more. Like the others, she knew that you just didn't ask a soldier those sorts of questions during wartime. But that didn't dampen the huge welcome everyone had given Ted the moment he stepped down into the shelter, so much so that bottles of brown ale and stout appeared out of nowhere, mainly from Jack Cutter, Bill Winkler and old Jessie, turning the place into a veritable underground pub.

To the gang sheltering there, and to the immense pride of both Connie and Beth, Ted was a hero, not just because he was a survivor of the great Dunkirk evacuation, but because he was one of them, fighting for his own people. But Ted was proud of them too, proud especially of his girl Beth, for there she was, keeping up their spirits by belting out song after song on the old Joanna, getting them all to sing their hearts out, defying everything Jerry could throw at them up above. He was proud also of his boy, Phil, who was out there in the streets night after night, putting his young life at constant risk.

As he sat perched on the edge of the bunk, watching in awe and admiration as Beth's fingers flitted energetically back and forth along the keyboard, and with baby Simon snuggled up comfortably in Connie's arms at his side, Ted felt that he was the luckiest man alive to have such a family. Beth was a beautiful girl, with a personality that could compare with any of the Hollywood glamour-pusses. She had a way with people, a way of cheering them up, of making them feel that life was worth living. However, his one regret was that Beth sometimes treated her mum as though she was a foreigner. It wasn't that she didn't love Connie, but that she considered herself to be different to her, to be part of the East End of London without any recognition that she had her mum's American blood running through her veins too. Ted knew only too well how sad his wife had always felt that Beth had turned her back on the formal way her mother wanted to teach her how to play the piano, and how she had insisted on going her own way. Beth was stubborn all right, which was a pity, because she had so many other good qualities.

To a hail of cheers and applause, Beth finished playing her final song. Exhausted, she made her way back to her mum and dad, and perched on the edge of the bunk alongside them.

Bernie Lieberman shook his fist triumphantly up at the ceiling. 'Well I hope you heard *that* – you schmuck!'

Abe Lieberman was absolutely horrified to hear his young brother use such language in front of the ladies. 'Bernie!' he scolded, quickly grabbing hold of his brother's fist and pulling it down. 'Are you a crazy man or something?'

'Wot's wrong with you?' growled Bernie indignantly, pulling his arm away. '*I'm* not the crazy man. It's that schmuck who dropped the last bomb on those yards!'

Amused by the brothers' customary banter, Beth called across to them. 'What does "*schmuck*" mean, Mr Bernie?' she asked.

Abe Lieberman froze with horror to hear Beth repeat the word. 'Don't mention it!' he replied nervously. 'It's a Yiddish word, not a *nice* Yiddish word. Don't listen to my brother.' He turned and gave Bernie a penetrating glare. 'He doesn't know any better!'

Bernie shrugged and sniffed dismissively.

'Well, whoever 'e is,' called Eileen Perkins, who was combing out her young daughter Rita's long straight hair, 'anyone who can drop bombs on innocent people oughta be 'ung, drawn an' bleedin' quartered!'

'You're right Eileen, dear,' said Bill Winkler's wife, Lil, amidst murmurs of agreement from the others. ' 'E ain't 'uman!'

'We don't know that,' returned Connie Shanks, who had finally managed to get Simon back to sleep in her arms. 'For all we know, he's probably just a family man like anyone else.'

Everyone swung an astonished look at her.

'Family man?' gasped an outraged Bill Winkler, who practically bit through the stem of his pipe.

'Come off it, Mrs S!' retorted Eileen. 'D'you 'onestly fink a man like that 'as any conscience at all before 'e drops that bomb?'

'I don't know, Eileen,' replied Connie in her soft Texan drawl. 'I honestly don't know. But I imagine they have to do as they're told – much as our own boys have to do when they're on missions over Germany.'

'*Our* boys would never knowingly kill innocent civilians,' replied Eileen indignantly.

'I know that, Eileen,' said Connie, who was beginning to feel a little uncomfortable. 'All I'm saying is that not every German is without a conscience.'

At the end bunk, Abe Lieberman muttered something which was practically inaudible.

'Do wot, Abe?' asked Jack Cutter, who was already tucking himself up in his own bunk for the night. 'Wot was that yer said?'

Abe lay down on his lower bunk, eyes staring up aimlessly to his brother above him. 'I said, once a German always a German.' Although unemotional, his quiet voice was tinged with cynicism.

For obvious reasons, nobody wanted the older of the two Jewish brothers to elaborate on what he had just said. Abe and Bernie had both been born in Germany, and they knew only too well how much the brothers had suffered at the hands of the Nazis when they fled from their repression back in the 1920s.

'So wot der *you* fink, Ted?' asked Bill Winkler who was perched on the edge of his bunk smoking a fag close by. 'Bet *you* din't fink Jerry 'ad much of an 'eart when 'e was poundin' away at you an' yer mates down those beaches?'

Ted took a moment before he answered. 'Nah,' he replied without expression. 'Din't see many 'earts around over there, mate. Din't see many faces eivver. It's all a bit of a blur ter me – couldn't tell who was who. I reckon a Jerry face don't look much diff'rent to anyone else.'

As he spoke, a distant barrage of gunfire broke what until then had been a few moments of silence. Beth's eyes slowly looked up towards the ceiling, hoping that whoever dropped that last bomb would eventually get what he deserved.

Heinz Buchner's luck was certainly with him that night. As his aircraft plunged out of control towards the cold waters of the English Channel, he said a final prayer to God, pleading with him to take care of Helga and the kids, hoping that they would remember him not only as a proud member of the *Luftwaffe* who had served his country well, but also as a husband and father who had loved his family to the end. However, with his mind on the verge of blackout, an inner voice told him that it wasn't time to go just yet, and so, as if galvanised into consciousness by an electric charge, he suddenly sat up, shook his head, grabbed hold of the stricken aircraft's steering stick, and with a firm grip struggled to pull the machine out of its relentless dive.

Despite the bitterly cold air outside, his entire body was engulfed in sweat. Heart thumping harder and harder and harder, and with one last desperate yell of triumph, '*Ja . . . !*', he gradually succeeded in pulling the machine out of its dive, levelling it out to no more than fifty feet or so above the dark, murky surface of the water. But the danger was still far from over, for the aircraft was shuddering too much to climb again, which meant that he had to head towards the nearest flat stretch of land on the French coastline where there were no cliffs or high ground. With six or seven miles to go, and the smell of fuel leaking from a ruptured oil tank, the dim header lights from his fuselage gradually picked out the approaching shoreline. As he skimmed the long stretch of white sandy beach, the fields and solitary farmhouses seemed to be rushing straight at him, but beyond was his salvation – a vast muddy agricultural field which seemed to extend for miles. Slowly, precariously, he brought the aircraft down. This was going to be a forced landing and he knew it, but the impact of virtually sliding along a sea of November mud was more than he expected, and when the aircraft finally came to a halt, it spun round and round like a spinning top.

When it was all over, the silence that followed seemed almost ethereal, until gradually, he heard voices, and out of the dark he saw a confetti of lights hurrying towards him. In a few moments he was engulfed by a crowd of country peasants, each one of them directing the beams from their torches into his face. But the language they used was not one he had ever embraced.

This was not England. This was France, occupied France, now under the complete control of the Third Reich. He had come home! He was alive! He was safe – at least until the next mission over enemy territory.

At about eleven o'clock that night, Ted Shanks realised he had run out of fags. It wasn't that he was a chain smoker, but after all that he had gone through up front in France, smoking was the only thing that calmed his nerves. The only light left on in the old factory dug-out was a solitary paraffin lamp which stank the place out and cast sinister shadows on the crumbling plaster and brick walls and curved ceiling, and as he sat up on his mattress on the stone floor, looked around and listened to the snores echoing around the place, it was easy to assume that everyone in the place was fast asleep. He hadn't slept a wink himself, for the moment he finally managed to close his eyes the All Clear siren sounded, and there had been an unholy silence ever since. He quietly sat up and pulled off the blanket covering him. He got up, found his khaki army tunic and uniform cap, and put them on. After one last look at Connie, who was snuggled up on the lower bunk with baby Simon tucked under her arms, and then Beth, who, even in the half-light and with her eyes closed looked radiant, he picked up his boots, and carefully tiptoed his way up the stone steps.

In the street outside it was immediately obvious why there was no enemy activity in the skies above, for a heavy autumnal fog was so thick it was barely possible to see the opposite side of the road. For one moment, Ted wished he'd brought his heavy army greatcoat with him, for although his uniform was reasonably warm, the ice cold fog quickly settled on the fabric and made him feel damp and chilled. He pulled up the tunic collar, put his hands in his trouser pockets, and hurried off as fast as his legs would carry him.

There was an eerie silence along Hornsey Road and the streets behind and beyond, for the earlier air raid had long since passed, giving the hardy workers of the emergency services a rare chance to see a night through without incident. On his way, he got to thinking about young Phil, and the terrifying dangers his son faced each night. It made him resolve to get the boy out of the job as soon as he possibly could; in Ted's eyes it was wrong for a boy of sixteen to have to face up to such an ordeal night after night. He wasn't a man, he wasn't a soldier. Only soldiers fought wars. And yet he was proud of the boy, proud that he had a son who wanted to do his bit to help people survive.

'Dad.'

At the corner of Tollington Road, Ted came to an abrupt halt, and turned to find Beth hurrying after him out of the fog. 'Beff!' he called. 'Wot yer doin'?'

'Wot're *you* doin'?' returned Beth. 'I 'eard yer get up.'

'I've only come back to get a packet er fags, replied Ted. 'Yer shouldn't've come out in this wevver, gel. You'll catch yer deff er cold.' He immediately drew her to him, and tucked her under his tunic.

Although she couldn't see him too well in the fog and dark, Beth looked up at him with total devotion. As they moved on round into Tollington Road, she snuggled up to him, her arm tucked around his waist. She was in her seventh heaven to have him home again. 'Oh

Dad,' she sighed. 'I don't want yer ter ever go away again. Yer've no idea 'ow I miss yer, 'ow we *all* miss yer.'

Ted held on to her, and smiled down warmly at her. 'I miss you too, gel,' he replied. 'The 'ole bloomin' lot er yer.' He sighed deeply. 'But I worry about yer. Yer've no idea 'ow much I worry about yer. Every time I listen ter the news or look at the newspapers, I know wot 'ell you an' yer mum've bin goin' fru. An' Phil too. It shouldn't be like this, Beff. It just shouldn't be like it.'

She looked up at him. 'Wot d'yer mean?' she asked, puzzled.

'All this,' replied Ted. 'Livin' in fear of yer lives each day, each night. Never knowin' from one day to anuvver wevver you'll be alive the next mornin'. When I got called up, I never fawt fer one minute that me own family was goin' ter be in more danger than meself.'

' 'Ow can yer say that, Dad,' replied Beth, dismissing what he had said. 'After all *you've* bin fru?'

'It's not the same, Beff,' Ted replied. 'A soldier's taught 'ow ter stand up fer 'imself. 'E knows wot 'e's up against. 'E can fight back.'

'So can we, Dad,' insisted Beth, her face only just visible beneath his tunic. 'We've got ack-ack guns, barrage balloons, an' the RAF are amazin' the way they keep Jerry on the run.'

'It's not the same, Beff,' said Ted. 'When a bomb comes tearin' down outer the sky at yer, yer never know whose name it's got on it. I can't take a chance like that. Not with *my* family. Yer mum's right. We've got ter get you out of all this.'

Her dad's words sent a cold chill right through Beth, and by the time they got home, she feared that she would have to have it out with him. Whilst her dad collected his packet of fags from the bedroom upstairs, she waited in the kitchen, turned off the light, and drew back the blackout curtains. 'Yer can't be serious, Dad,' she said, the moment he came into the room. 'Yer don't really expect us ter give up everythin' in London – just becos er Mum?'

Ted's fag glowed in the dark as he stopped dead, taken aback by what she had said. 'It's not just becos er yer mum, Beff!' he snapped. 'It's becos er me!'

'It's not true, Dad,' she countered. 'Yer know very well it's Mum's idea for us all ter go and live with Gran and Grandad. She's so scared all the time. That's why she makes us troop down that shelter night after night.'

Ted strode across the room and in the dim light from the fog outside stood right in front of her. 'Don't *ever* let me 'ear yer talk about yer mum like that, Beff!' he said angrily. 'Yor mum's a good, plucky woman. She only ever does wot's right for 'er kids.'

'But Phil and I *ain't* kids any more, Dad,' she returned. 'That's the trouble. Mum keeps treatin' us as though we're the same as the kids where *she* comes from.'

This infuriated Ted. 'Watch wot yer sayin', Beff!' he growled. 'Just remember you're 'alf Yank wevver yer like it or not!'

Her dad's outburst completely shocked Beth. It was the first time he had ever talked to her like that before, and she didn't know what to say to him. Totally flummoxed she turned round to the sink, and stared out through the window into the back garden.

Ted waited, then went to join her. Realising that he had hurt her, he gently slid his arm around her waist, and stood in silence, trying to peer through the dark grey fog that had completely engulfed the small back garden outside. For a moment or so, there was complete silence between them. 'I wanna tell yer somefin', Beff,' he said softly. He pulled on his fag, and exhaled away from her. 'When I first met your mum, I was workin' on a buildin' job up in St John's Wood. It was this big red-bricked 'ouse which'd bin a music college fer – oh I don't know 'ow long – donkey's years. Anyway, I was up on the scaffold on me own doin' a bit er trowellin', when suddenly I 'ear this pianer comin' from down inside somewhere. It was a funny ol' sound, not my kind er music, all posh an' serious, an' yet – an' yet it was kind er, oh I dunno, kind er – beautiful.' He chuckled to himself. 'Up 'til then I'd never really fawt of music as "beautiful". Ter me, music was fer 'avin' a good ol' sing-song, a good ol' knees-up, not somefin' that yer actually stopped an' listened to.

'Anyway, me curiosity got the better er me, so I put down me trowel, wiped me 'ands down me trousers, and climbed up on the windersill just above where I was workin'. Inside was this big 'all, wiv a stage, and loads er seats – there weren't many people there, just five or six sittin' in seats about 'alfway back. But on stage was this gel, playin' this great big pianer. I managed ter get the winder open wivout anyone noticin'. The sound comin' from down there was – well, I can't really describe it. It was as though I'd died an' gone up fru the pearly gates! But that gel – d'yer know wot she looked like, Beff? She looked just like you, just like yer are now. I can still see 'er. She 'ad long 'air that was done up be'ind er 'ead, an' it was tied up wiv a pinky coloured ribbon. But it was 'er 'ands . . . yer couldn't take yer eyes off 'er 'ands. 'Er fingers went up an' down that keyboard like there was no termorrer, an' the sound they got out er those ol' pianer strings – well, I tell yer, it was like somefin' I'd never known before. And when those few people down in the 'all clapped, I clapped too.' He paused, and took another pull from his fag. 'Anyway,' he continued, 'at the end of the day, I saw 'er when she come out, carryin' these music sheets under 'er arm. So I did somefin' I fawt I'd never 'ave the guts ter do – I went up to 'er and said: " 'Scuse me, miss. I 'ope yer won't mind my sayin', but I 'eard yer playin' the ol' Joanna in there terday, an' I fawt it was – well, it was just – amazin'!" An' yer know wot? She smiled. She smiled just the way I've seen you smile lots er times, all wide an' bright, like she was really chuffed. An' yer know wot she said? She said, "That's the nicest thing anyone has ever said to me." Of course, you know the rest,' he continued, ' 'ow we got chattin', 'ow we started walkin' out tergevver. She was so diff'rent to me. I was so diff'rent to '*er*. Ter me, Yankeeland was somefin' I knew nuffin' about. But it din't make no difference. It din't matter ter me the way she talked, an' it din't matter ter 'er the way *I* talked. We just – felt somefin' fer each uvver. We *still* feel somefin' fer each uvver. That's the way it is, that's the way it'll always be. An' yer know why, Beff? Becos we respect each uvver. Becos we always try ter listen an' understand each uvver's point er view.'

He stubbed his fag out in the sink, took hold of Beth and gently turned her towards him. He could only see her dim outline in the blackout, and so his fingers softly traced the outline of her face. When he reached her eyes, he realised that tears were rolling down her cheeks, and so, with his fingers, he dabbed them away. 'All I'm askin', Beff,' he said quietly, 'is that yer give yer mum a chance. Take my word fer it – she's worf it.'

She slid her arms around his waist and leaned her head against his shoulder. Just as she did so, however, the air raid siren echoed in the street outside.

As Beth and her dad left the house, a barrage of anti-aircraft gunfire could already be heard approaching from the suburbs east of London, with shells bursting intermittently against the dark night sky above the grey November fog. The distant drone of enemy aircraft brought an incessant rumble of ack-ack fire, shattering what had been just a few moments ago an interlude of peace and calm. Once he had closed the front yard gate, Ted wrapped his arms around Beth, and hurried them off back towards the safety of the shelter in Hornsey Road. By the time they got there, all hell had broken loose in the skies above them, as though a violent thunderstorm would soon tear the place apart. But just as they were about to disappear through the front door of the old warehouse factory, a woman's voice suddenly called to them from behind.

'Ted!'

Both Beth and Ted turned with a start to find a woman calling to him as she stepped out from the shadows of a shop doorway on the opposite side of the road.

'Ted!' the woman called again, trying to be heard above the crescendo of ack-ack fire. Even as she approached, her features could hardly be seen, for her head was swathed in a thick black woollen headscarf, and the high collar of her heavy winter coat was buttoned up to her chin. 'Oh Ted!' she cried, her voice shivering with emotion. 'It really *is* you, ain't it?' She immediately turned to Beth. 'An' I bet I know who *you* are. You're Beff, ain't yer?'

Ted was completely shocked to see the woman. 'Vera!' he replied. 'Wot *you* doin' 'ere?'

Realising that her dad clearly recognised the woman, Beth swung a startled look up at him.

'I 'eard you was comin' 'ome,' said the woman, in between the blast of ack-ack gunfire. 'I met one of yer neighbours. She said yer was comin' 'ome.'

Ted was so taken aback to see the woman, all he could do was to splutter. 'Nice ter see yer,' he said. 'Better get in out of all this.' He put his arm around Beth, and tried to lead her through the front door of the factory.

'A coupla minutes, Ted,' called the woman. 'Just a coupla minutes. I've *got* ter talk to yer.'

Both Ted and Beth froze. 'You go on down,' he said to her. 'I'll join you as soon as I can.'

Beth's pained expression showed that she was not only shocked, but feared the worst.

'It's all right, gel,' he said. 'Nuffin' ter worry about.' He kissed her gently on the forehead, and opened the factory door for her.

Reluctantly, Beth went inside.

'Yer shouldn't've come,' said Ted to the woman, once Beth had left. 'I told yer before, there's no need fer this. I've got a wife, a family. They wouldn't understand.'

'A coupla minutes, Ted,' replied the woman, slipping her arm through his. 'That's all I ask.' With that, she led him off to the safety of the shop doorway where she had been waiting for him.

Inside the abandoned top-floor area of the old warehouse, Beth leaned her back against the door. She felt her body consumed by an ice-cold chill. Who *was* that woman, she asked herself? What was she doing waiting in the dark up there, in the middle of the night, waiting for her dad? What did it all mean? Once she had composed herself, she started to make her way down the stone stairs to the cellar shelter below. The whole building shook as a bomb exploded somewhere in the distance. She didn't know where, and didn't really care. All she knew was that the way things looked, the way she felt, nothing was ever going to be quite the same again between her and her dad.

Chapter 10

Beth felt as though she had a hangover. As she hardly ever drank more than a half-pint of shandy, it was a somewhat bizarre notion, but after one hell of a night tossing and turning in her upper bunk down in the old factory air raid shelter, her head was bursting with anxiety. The thought of her dad's meeting with that woman out in the street in the middle of the night had knocked her for six. Vera? Vera *who*? Who *was* she, Beth asked herself over and over again, what was it all about, and why had the woman been hanging around in the fog waiting to talk with her dad? Her mind was throbbing with so many possible explanations, but no matter how hard she tried to dismiss what she really thought, the only conclusion she kept returning to was that her dad must have at some time had a relationship with the woman.

On the top deck of the bus the next morning, it was all she could think about, not the air raid the night before, not about the happy look on everyone's faces in the shelter as she thumped out their favourite tunes on the piano. No, It was that face, the face of a woman in the dark, in the fog, a desperate woman with a haunted look, who had at last found who she was looking for. Beth stared out at the pavements below, but didn't really take in any of the commuters who were waiting wearily in bus queues. All she could think about was her dad, how he had deceived her, how he had deceived his wife and the rest of his family, even though just a short while before he had talked with so much love and affection for the woman he had first seen playing a piano on the stage of the old music college in St John's Wood. What would happen when she saw her dad again that evening? How would he explain that meeting in the street outside the factory warehouse? It was an encounter she was dreading.

★

It was not until she had reached Tally Ho Corner that she first became aware of the commotion in the streets. There were people hurrying about all over the place, shouting and waving to each other, cars, buses, and emergency vehicles piled up in a long queue along the main road for as far as the eye could see, and the distant sound of voices booming out frenzied warnings through loud-hailers.

Beth's first thought was to get to work as fast as she could, but even though she managed to ease herself through the crowds surrounding the Gaumont cinema, the moment she turned the corner and was within sight of the munitions factory, she was shocked to find her way barred by a major security barrier which was strictly guarded by Special Constables, a unit of the local Home Guard, and several air raid wardens. Stuck in the middle of the crowd, she just couldn't see what was going on, for everyone in front of her seemed to be a giant. Finally, however, she managed to squeeze through to the roped barrier, where she was horrified to see the first sign of bomb damage along the small back road outside the perimeter of the factory. The road was littered with debris and broken glass from windows that had been blown out of their frames, and a burnt-out black taxicab was lying on its side on the pavement. The factory! They've hit the factory! Beth's alarm was immediate, and the first thing she wanted to do was to get under that barrier and find out if any of her workmates had been injured. But just as she was about to do so, she heard her mate Mo calling to her from the barrier nearby.

'Over 'ere, Beff!'

Beth pushed her way through the crowd, and by the time she reached Mo, she realised that Mo was just part of a large group of factory workers who had gathered along the barrier. 'Mo!' she cried, as soon as she reached her. 'Wot's 'appened?'

'We're bleedin' lucky sods!' growled Mo, the large frame of her body heaving with indignation. '*That's* wot's 'appened!'

' 'Ave we bin 'it, then?' Beth asked urgently. 'Is the workshop—?'

'No, it's not us,' returned Mo, who was wrapped up in a heavy coat and headscarf, with a face blood-red from the cold. 'The factory ain't bin touched.'

'So far!' called a voice behind Beth, who turned out to be Midge Morton, who was so small she could hardly be seen amongst the others. 'If that bomb goes off, there won't be much left of poor ol' Tally 'O!'

'Oh shut up, Midge!' barked Elsie Tuckwell, whose red hair-curls were tumbling out from beneath her knitted hat. 'It's bein' so cheerful that keeps you goin'!'

'Wot d'yer mean "*if that bomb goes off*"?' asked Beth anxiously. '*Wot* bomb?'

'There's a big unexploded bomb stuck in the ground in the backyard,' said Mo, 'just be'ind the canteen.'

A cold chill ran down Beth's spine. 'Oh Christ!' she gasped.

'It'll be all right,' insisted one of the other girls amongst the group. 'They've got the army in there. *They* won't let us all blow ter kingdom come.'

'Not if *I* go in an' give 'em a 'and or two!' called one of the other girls, to gales of laughter.

'I'll give 'em more than a 'and!' came another bawdy call from one of the girls in the crowd.

Beth was the only one who was not amused by the roar of jeers and laughter. This was far too serious a situation to joke about. This was emphasised even more when a series of frantic shouts from the men on guard at the barrier brought the laughter to an abrupt halt.

'Move back, please!'

'Right the way back, please, everyone! Fast as yer can!'

The girls from the factory groaned and tried to protest, but the guards were having none of it.

'Come on now!' yelled a particularly irritated Special Constable. 'Unless yer want ter get yer 'eads blown off!'

'Right back now!' yelled a Home Guard corporal. 'Right back past the pitture 'ouse! Back ter the main road!'

Foolishly unaware that their presence was putting themselves and everyone else in great danger, and reluctant to miss out on any of the high drama that was unfolding inside the munitions factory, with loud groans the girls turned and made their way laboriously back towards the cinema and the main road beyond.

'Well I fer one ain't 'angin' round in the bleedin' cold!' insisted a very disgruntled Mo. 'I'm going down the caff ter get a cuppa. Wot say you, Beff?'

'No, I'll 'ang around a bit if yer don't mind, Mo,' replied Beth. 'I just want ter check if Thomas was on duty last night. 'E's probably in the crowd somewhere.'

'See yer later, then!' called Mo, as she and the other girls headed off en masse to the worker's café on the main road.

For the next few moments Beth searched the crowd, hoping to catch a glimpse of Thomas. But it proved to be a useless exercise, for the tide of human flesh seemed to be pushing and shoving against her. However, once the crowd thinned out and she had managed to cross the road behind the cinema, she suddenly felt someone take hold of her arm.

'Hallo, Beth.'

Beth turned with a start and came to a sharp halt. She immediately recognised the middle-aged woman clutching her arm, who was one of the three security officers who had interrogated her about Thomas.

'It's a nasty business, isn't it?' continued the woman in her cut-glass voice, and withdrawing her hand from Beth's arm. 'This is such a terrible war. We never know what's going to happen from one day to another.'

Beth was absolutely startled to find the woman talking to her. Although the woman seemed to have a perpetual warm, sweet smile on her face, as she had done during the interview back at the security office, Beth had been around long enough to know exactly how much a sweet smile could conceal.

'D'you mind if I walk with you?' asked the woman. 'Just as far as the main road. I have a car waiting for me.'

Beth shrugged and walked on. The woman went with her.

'Oh by the way,' said the woman. 'My name is Jane. Jane Grigsby. It's awful not knowing what the future holds, isn't it?'

Beth came to another abrupt halt. 'What's this all about, Miss Grigsby?' she asked irritably. 'Am I bein' followed or somefin'?'

The woman looked surprised, or at least pretended to. 'My dear child,' she said, taken aback. 'Why on earth should you think that?'

'I'm not a child, Miss Grigsby,' retorted Beth. 'I've bin around longer than yer fink.'

The woman realised that it was no use trying to play games with the girl. 'As I said,' she replied, moving them on again, 'it's a nasty business, isn't it – I mean, what's happened to the factory. It looks as though you and your friends will have a bit of a holiday until the place is made safe again. Mind you, it's quite a mystery how it all happened.'

They turned the corner by the cinema, where the crowd of factory workers and onlookers were streaming out on to the main road.

'A mystery?' asked Beth, as they waited to cross the road. 'Wot d'yer mean – a mystery?'

The woman turned to look at her. 'The munitions factory you work in, Beth,' she replied, 'is like all the others throughout the country: top security. Once the enemy have knowledge of its precise location, well – I don't think I have to tell you what the consequences would be. The problem is, our friends in the *Luftwaffe* now seem to know rather more about the factory than we'd like them to know.'

'If you're tryin' ter suggest that it's got anyfin' ter do wiv Thomas,' Beth said immediately, 'then you're wrong. Thomas was on night shift last night, so 'e'd 'ardly give information away if Jerry was goin' ter drop a bomb an' blow up the 'ole bleedin' place – now would 'e?'

The woman turned to Beth and gave her another of those sweet, excruciating smiles. 'As a matter of fact, Beth,' she insisted, 'Thomas *wasn't* on duty last night. It appears he missed the night shift. But don't worry; I'm sure he had a perfectly logical reason for doing so.'

Ted Shanks didn't feel good about what had happened the previous night. His unexpected meeting with Vera Jeggs had thrown him into total confusion, and the fact that it had taken place in front of Beth had only made matters worse. But even though Vera was a good woman, how was he going to explain who she was, not only to Beth, but also to Connie? Nonetheless, for the last few remaining days of his one week's compassionate leave, he was determined to get his family out of London and into the comparative safety of his mum and dad's place out in Hertfordshire. But from what Connie had already told him, it wasn't going to be easy.

Moorgate Fire Station looked as though it had been under heavy bombardment all night, for the forecourt was covered with debris from a bomb explosion in the street nearby. By the time Ted got there, half the neighbourhood seemed to have turned out to help clear the way for returning fire engines, which was becoming so characteristic of ordinary folk who were determined to give the emergency services as much help and support as they could. As Ted hadn't seen young Phil since he left the house the previous afternoon, he was immediately concerned for the boy's safety, so he clambered over the rubble and found his way in to the station to see if Phil was there.

'A *kid*? Don't call your boy a kid, mate. *All* our boys are ruddy heroes. The way they get on their bikes and ride 'round fru streets bein' blown up all over the place – I tell yer, them boys've got more guts than the rest of us put tergevver!' Suddenly realising Ted was in army uniform, the exhausted fire crewman patted him admiringly on the shoulder. 'No offence meant, of course, mate!'

The answer Ted got from his enquiry may not have been what he expected, but it did make him feel immensely proud of his own boy. 'Is he around, mate?' he asked the crewman. 'Is 'e still on duty?'

'On duty?' replied the crewman, taking off his helmet and wiping his face which was blackened from a night of fighting thick black smoke from fires all over the City of London. 'Young Phil ain't been *off* duty since 'e came on at five last night. But 'e is now. We practically 'ad ter drag 'im upstairs for a kip. 'E took about fourteen messages durin' the night. 'E was just about ready ter drop, poor little bugger.'

Even before he had reached the top of the stairs, Ted could hear the snores of the night crew coming from the station's dormitories, and once he had got there he could see why. Several exhausted crewmen were flopped on their beds, faces swollen and smeared with smoke from tackling endless fires all around the City during the night, some of them too tired to take off their uniforms, which had been covered in wood ash and smelt foul. They were all in, out for the count, as though they would never have the strength to wake up again, which, of course, they had proved time and time again to be most unlikely.

He looked around for Phil, but for the time being couldn't find him anywhere. But just as he was about to leave the dormitory, he suddenly caught sight of a crumpled figure tucked up tightly under a blanket in a crew bed at the far end of the room. When he got there, he found the boy sound asleep, his head hardly visible beneath the sheet and blanket.

Ted quietly perched on the edge of the bed, and leaned down close to the boy. 'Phil,' he whispered into the boy's ear. 'Wake up, son.'

Phil didn't stir; he was in a deep sleep, with just the suggestion of a teenage snore.

Ted tried again, and very softly smoothed his hand over the boy's forehead. 'Come on, son,' he whispered again. 'Time ter go 'ome.'

Phil stirred, his eyes gradually opened. For a brief moment, he couldn't quite focus, but when he looked up and saw his dad looking down at him, he sat up with a start. 'Dad!' he gasped. 'Wot *you* doin' 'ere?'

Ted was shocked to see the boy's face streaked with thick black wood ash, his eyes protruding from their sockets like a frightened animal. 'Mum's waitin' fer yer, mate,' he replied. 'Get yerself up. We're goin' 'ome.'

Phil panicked. ' 'Ome!' he pleaded. 'I can't go 'ome! Not yet! I've got ter cover fer Johnny Rickman. 'E's the uvver messenger. 'E got blown off 'is bike last night. Don't yer understand, Dad? I've got ter cover fer 'im. They ain't got no one else!'

Anxious that Phil's voice might wake up the crewmen, Ted put the tips of his fingers over the boy's mouth. 'It's all right, son,' he said. 'I'll speak to yer boss. 'E'll find somebody.'

Phil, really upset, shook his head and leapt out of bed. He was still fully clothed but for his tunic which was lying on the floor alongside. 'You don't know wot you're sayin', Dad!' he spluttered. 'You just don't understand!'

Nearby, one of the sleeping fire crew groaned and turned over. Ted quickly put his arm around the boy and led him out through the door at the end of the dormitory.

'Now listen ter me, Phil,' he said, the moment they were on the landing outside. 'This is no place fer a boy your age. Not that I'm not proud of yer, 'cos I bloody am, but it's too dangerous for yer, son. Yer mum's scared out of 'er life every time yer leave the 'ouse. Phil, yer only sixteen fer Chrissake!'

'Sixteen now,' retorted Phil. 'But in less than a coupla years I'll be eighteen, I'll be called-up!'

Ted took hold of both the boy's arms. 'Now listen to me, Phil,' he said firmly. 'Yer mum loves yer. *I* love yer. Yer sister loves yer. We all want the 'ole family out of London . . .'

'I don't want ter stay wiv Gran and Grandad,' returned Phil, who was now really agitated. 'An' neivver does Beff. Yer *know* she doesn't! Our place is 'ere in London, wiv our mates, an' all the people we know.'

'To 'ell wiv yer mates, Phil!' snapped Ted, whose head was suddenly bursting with tension. 'What about yer own mum an' dad? Don't yer care 'ow *we* feel?'

Phil avoided his dad's eyes. He looked chastened. 'There's a war on, Dad,' he said wearily. 'Everyone 'as ter do their bit.' He looked up at Ted. 'You're doin' *your* bit, so why shouldn't I?'

Ted was stung by Phil's remark. As he looked at the boy – *his* son, standing there in his vest and uniform trousers that were really too big for him, large staring eyes that made him look so vulnerable, and face smeared with the smoke of yet another night of interminable death and destruction, he found it hard to dispute the fact that what the boy had said was true. Despite his youthful looks, Phil was no longer a boy, he was a man. War, and the terrifying onslaught on London had done that to so many youngsters of his generation; they were being forced to grow up before their time.

Phil smudged the smoke grime on his face with the back of his hand. 'Yer know, Dad,' he said. 'It's no use lookin' back. When I was a small kid, I didn't know nuffin' about people dyin' – except that ol' bloke on the uvver side of our road, the one who 'ad a 'eart attack or somefin' an' snuffed it – remember?'

Ted shrugged.

'But since I've bin doin' this job,' continued Phil, 'I know all about death, 'cos I see it every day, an' every night.' He smiled wistfully to himself. 'D'you know the first dead fing I saw?' he asked. 'It was this cat – a big fat tabby fing. I watched some ARP bloke pullin' 'im out of the rubble from these 'ouses up Whitechapel. I looked at 'is collar. 'Is name was Charlie Chaplin. Stupid name ter call a cat! But I reckoned Charlie must 'ave meant somefin' ter somebody, an' they'd be very upset ter lose 'im. The only fing is, when they dug 'round the debris, they found quite a lot of uvver bodies; not cats, but people. So – chances were Charlie wouldn't be missed by anyone. Since then I've seen a lot er dead people bein' pulled out of bombed-out buildings, but some'ow I always remember Charlie. I s'ppose it's becos, until then, I'd never seen anyfin' *really* dead before. But it don't matter now. I've kind of – accepted it.' He looked at Ted with an assuring smile. 'You see, Dad,' he pleaded. 'I really ain't a kid any more.'

As he spoke, the air raid siren wailed out from the roof of the nearby police station. Simultaneously, a fire officer called out from the door of the watchroom below. 'Messenger!'

Phil immediately yelled back down the stairs. 'Comin', sir!'

'Phil!'

Ted tried to grab the boy's arm, but before he had the chance, Phil had rushed back off into the dormitory, where the other crewmen were already leaping out of their beds.

'Gotta go, Dad!' the boy yelled as he collected his uniform and cap from the floor, and rushed off along the dormitory. He stopped only briefly to call back, 'Tell Mum I'll try an' get back fer tea. See yer later, Dad!'

Knowing only too well that there was now nothing he could do to stop the boy, Ted hurried to the window, and watched the officer down below passing him a message, which Phil grabbed, and put in his leather shoulder pouch.

A moment later, to the accompaniment of an approaching barrage of ack-ack gunfire, and the drone of enemy aircraft overhead, Ted watched his son get on to his bike, and peddle furiously down the main road. It was a sight that, for as long as he lived, he would never forget.

★

Beth had only ever been to King's Cross once in her life, and that was just before the war, when she went with her mum and dad to the railway station to meet one of her mum's cousins from America, who had been to visit some old friends in Scotland. Beth thought King's Cross a funny old place; some of the buildings were really quite elegant, especially the posh red-bricked St Pancras Hotel, and even the grand Victorian station itself, with its giant arch-shaped façade, massive concourse and high, glass-covered platforms. But beyond the hustle and bustle of train stations and official buildings, there were the contrasting terraces of Victorian and Georgian houses, some for the rich, some for the poor, some beautifully maintained, and others in a state of crumbling disrepair. Even under normal circumstances, Beth would have found the house where Thomas lived difficult to find, but in the middle of an air raid it was an unnerving experience. Even as she left the bus stop, with the air fractured by the sound of ack-ack fire, and skies droning with aerial dogfights, Beth had had to rush into the doorway of a Chinese café as someone yelled, '*Take cover!*' – and only just in time, as the pavements were riddled with machine-gun bullets from a marauding enemy fighter plane which was skimming the great Euston Road thoroughfare with guns blazing. She found herself cooped up there longer than she imagined, listening to the incessant excited chatter of Chinese voices coming from inside the café, but at least it gave her time to turn over in her mind how to get to the back street where Thomas lived.

A few minutes later, it was safe enough to be on the move again. Clutching the piece of paper with Thomas's address, which she had got some time ago with the help of her friend Linda, who worked in the personnel department at the factory, she scurried as fast as she could away from the main road, turned the corner by the Gaumont picture house, and found her way to what at first sight looked like a fairly seedy looking area behind the Pentonville Road.

The street she was searching for proved to be fairly elusive, but, despite the mayhem still going on in the sky above, she eventually found it, tucked away behind a small pub which had windows that had been shattered by a bomb blast, and was boarded up with the words BUSINESS AS USUAL scrawled in white chalk in large letters all over it. Beth quickly found Number 21, the house she was looking for, halfway down the street, and, to her surprise, the place looked much better kept than she had imagined. Set on three floors, there was no front garden, and the street door was at the top of three small stone steps. She slammed down the heavy iron door-knocker as hard as she could. Several moments passed, but there was no reply. A bomb suddenly whistled down on to a street in the distance, which made her fall to her knees and shield herself against the door. Struggling against a cacophony of fire engine, ambulance and police car bells, she slowly recovered herself, and got up. Once again she knocked hard on the door but, as she did so, a salvo of anti-aircraft fire coming from what sounded like a 'Chicago piano', the local name given to a multi-barrelled naval weapon, launched an endless deafening trail of shells into the sky from just a few streets away. Falling to her knees again, and pressing as hard as she could against the bottom of the door, Beth shook with fear from head to toe, and wondered what madness had brought her to such a place at such a time. However, just when she was on the point of getting up and running off, the door opened slowly, only slightly, just enough to reveal to Beth a man's feet standing on the doormat inside. But she only summoned the courage to look up after the explosion of anti-aircraft fire had finally subsided.

'Who the hell're *you*?'

Beth looked up. She was looking into the hardened face of a middle-aged man, with short, white, cropped hair, a surly expression, bull-neck, and who was wearing braces over his shirt and trousers.

'Wot the hell're you doin' there?' repeated the man in a broad Irish accent.

For a moment, Beth was embarrassed and at a loss for words. 'I – I'm sorry. I – I'm looking for Thomas. Thomas Sullivan.'

Joe Sullivan's face softened just enough to open the door. 'Who wants him?'

'My name's Beth,' she replied, still shaking, and finding it difficult to get to her feet. 'Beth Shanks. Thomas and I work at the—'

'I know who yer are,' interrupted Joe, offering Beth his hand. 'I'm Tom's dad.'

'Pleased ter meet yer, Mr Sullivan,' said Beth, taking his hand, and letting him help her up to her feet. Another burst of ack-ack fire caused them both to look up with a start to the sky.

'Yer'd better come in,' said Joe dourly.

'Fanks,' said Beth, as he held the door back for her to enter.

'This way,' said Joe, going off to the kitchen at the rear of the passage.

Beth followed him. Although it was daylight outside, the place was remarkably dark and uninviting, and there was an unmistakable smell of beer as she reached the kitchen.

'Yer can sit down,' said Joe, casually, returning to his half-finished fag which was smouldering in a tin-top ashtray. 'If yer want a cup of tea, I'll put the kettle on.'

'Fanks all the same, Mr Sullivan,' replied Beth. 'I've got ter get back. I 'ave ter go down the shelter wiv my mum.'

'There's an Anderson in the backyard,' replied Joe dismissively. 'Never use the ting meself. But my neighbours the Finnegans from the top floor are down there. You can join them if yer want.'

Beth shook her head, and smiled back gratefully. 'No – really. Better get back. I just came ter see Thomas. Is he around anywhere?'

'If he is,' replied Joe, '*I* haven't seen him.'

Beth felt herself tense. 'He didn't turn up for his night shift,' she said, waiting carefully for Joe's reaction.

Joe shrugged. 'Is that a fact?' He collected his fag from the ashtray, and picked up a half-finished glass tankard of beer.

'You don't know where he was?'

'I'm his dad, young lady, not his keeper.'

For one brief moment, Beth looked at the man and tried to determine whether there was any physical resemblance between him and his son. Apart from his chin, which was really quite bony, there wasn't, so she presumed Thomas took more after his mum. But she did find Joe Sullivan an unresponsive man, hiding himself behind a totally unyielding personality. She felt awkward in his company. 'There was quite a bit er damage round the factory last night,' she said. 'When I left, they were still trying to deal wiv an unexploded bomb. Looks like we'll all be off work fer the rest er the week.'

For one brief moment, Joe went quite still. But he quickly took a pull on his fag, exhaled it, and gulped down some beer. 'Nobody killed, I hope?'

'Not so far,' replied Beth. 'As luck 'as it.'

Joe swung a look at her. 'Quite,' he replied awkwardly.

Suddenly, the whole house shook when a bomb whistled down to a massive explosion in the far distance. Beth clutched the table and held on, but Joe tried to reassure her by putting his arm around her shoulder. 'Sure you don't want to go down the Anderson?'

Beth shook her head. 'Better be goin',' she replied. 'Could yer tell Thomas I called?'

'I'll do that,' replied Joe. As Beth made a move to leave, he put his hand on her arm. 'I'm not as bad as I seem, young lady,' he said. 'My trouble is I just don't have any manners. Don't ask me why. I s'ppose I've never worked at it like you English.'

Beth took note of this last remark. 'English people ain't much diff'rent from anyone else,' she replied. 'We're all the same, really. Ter *my* way of finkin' we should all stop gettin' at each uvver fer no reason at all.'

'Oh there are a lot of reasons why people get at each other, young lady,' replied Joe, to a background crescendo of ack-ack fire. 'The way *I* see it, it's all about trust. I mean, if you can't trust a person, then what's the use? That's why you English have this war.'

Beth came straight back at him. 'This ain't just a war against England, Mr Sullivan,' she said. 'It's a war against *everyone* – wherever they come from.' She smiled politely. 'I'll be off, then.' She turned and went out into the passage.

'Don't you tink you should wait a bit?' asked Joe, calling after her. 'Just 'til it calms down?'

'Don't worry,' called Beth from the front door. 'I can take care of myself.' She opened the door, went out and looked up at the sky, which was suddenly silent, but for the distant droning sound of enemy aircraft making a quick getaway. 'Looks like it's all over,' she said, turning from the front doorstep. ' 'Til the next time, anyway. Fanks a lot, Mr Sullivan.'

'D'you have any message you want me to pass on to Thomas?' he called, as she went.

'Just tell 'im I've got a few important fings I want ter talk over wiv 'im,' she called back over her shoulder. 'Anyway, 'e knows where I live.'

'OK, then!' called Joe. 'Thanks for calling – Beth.' He watched her go, hurrying down towards the end of the road. As she went, in the distance she seemed to him to look petite and quite insignificant. But the more he thought about her, the more it struck him that the little girl his son was so hooked on was someone who was just as solid as a rock. He went inside and closed the front door. For a moment he just stood there, thinking about that munitions factory, and about what might have happened if things had gone a different way.

Chapter 11

Connie Shanks looked at herself in the mirror and, for the first time since Ted had gone away, liked what she saw. In fact she had such a good, unblemished face, that she needed little, if any make-up, and her eyes were so crystal-blue it was as though they were reflecting a full horizon out at sea. But the light touch of lipstick she was applying made her feel good, made her feel that she was a real woman again, and in any case, she now had her man back home, and that was a good enough reason to *want* to look good. For just a few moments in time at least, she was forgetting about those nightmares, forgetting about the horrors she could see, and which had haunted her for so long. After checking her face and tying and pinning her strawberry blonde hair back into its bun behind her head, she left the bathroom on the first-floor landing and went back into her bedroom next door. Baby Simon was lying on his back in his cot, kicking his legs furiously, and making frustrated gurgling sounds which were just a hint that it wouldn't be long before he expected Mama to give him a decent feed. 'Come on then, Simmie, Mama's little baba,' Connie said affectionately in her own soft Texan drawl, as she lifted him out of his cot and held him up to look at. 'Now that your dad's back, you and I have got to start changing our ways. For a start, we're not going to keep being afraid of the air raids, are we? We're going to take it all in our stride, so that when we all move out to stay with your grandma and grandad we'll be good and strong, and enjoy that good country air. What d'you say to that, honey bun? Deal?'

Simon gurgled and kicked his legs. But by the scowl on his face, there was no hint of agreement to such a deal there!

'OK, OK,' said Connie, holding him back in her arms again. 'Anything you say, boss.' She took him to her bed, perched on the edge there, unbuttoned the top of her dress, slipped it down to her waist, unclipped her bra with one hand behind, then positioned the baby for his favourite treat. 'Hey!' she barked with a jump, as his gums took too firm a grab. 'Take it easy, young man! You'd better not do that when you've got teeth!' Despite the somewhat rough start to Simon's feed, his mum was in her seventh heaven. It wasn't that anything had changed all that much, but the very fact that Ted was around had somehow given her a new-found confidence to face up to all the horrors around them. In other words, she didn't feel so alone any more; she wasn't going to sit around and mope. At least, not for a few more days. After that – well, as Scarlett O'Hara said in that *Gone With the Wind* movie she and Ted saw the night before he went away, 'I can't think about that today, I'll think about it tomorrow.'

A short while later, Simon had finished his one o'clock feed, and was tucked up again in his cot beside the bed. It wasn't long before his eyes started to flicker, and once Connie was satisfied that he was asleep, she quietly made her way out of the room, leaving the door open. But as she came down the stairs, she was surprised to see Beth just coming through the front street door. 'Beth?' she called. 'Darling? What are you doing home so early?'

Beth shook her head, took off her headscarf.

'Is anything wrong?' asked Connie.

'There's an unexploded bomb in the backyard er the factory,' replied Beth, taking off her topcoat and hanging both that and her scarf on a clothes hook in the passage.

Connie clasped her hand to her mouth in horror.

'They bombed all the roads round the Tally 'O last night,' continued Beth. 'It's a miracle the place wasn't blown ter smithereens. For all I know, that's wot's 'appened if they ain't bin able ter diffuse that bomb.'

'Thank God you weren't on night duty,' gasped Connie, as she went across to her. 'I don't even want to think about what might have happened if . . .'

'I'm not the only one who works in the factory, Mum,' replied

Beth tactlessly. 'There's 'undreds of gels an' fellers up there. We was just lucky, that's all.'

'What about Thomas?' asked Connie. 'Was *he* on night duty?'

Beth didn't answer. She turned and went off into the front room. 'Is there any paraffin in the stove?' she asked as she went.

'Just a little,' replied Connie, following her. 'I'm afraid we've used up the last of the coke. Your dad's gone up to see Phil's fire station manager. As soon as he gets back he's going to pop round to see Jim Thorley in the coal yard to see if he can let us have a bag of coke.'

Beth went straight to the fireplace where there were still the faint remains of some coke glowing in the grate. She quickly retrieved a box of matches from the mantelpiece, knelt down beside the small paraffin stove, which was placed on a sheet of plywood nearby, and carefully raised the outer covering. After struggling for several moments with the rusty mantle, she finally managed to raise the wick and light it. Although the sour smell of paraffin immediately filled the room, the stove provided the first real warmth Beth had felt since she left home that morning. She stood up, and held her hands over the rising heat.

'So,' said Connie. '*Was* Thomas on duty last night?'

Beth paused before answering. 'No,' she replied without turning to look back. ' 'E wasn't.'

'Oh, what a relief!' sighed Connie.

Beth swung round to her. 'Mum,' she said tensely. 'I've just been up to Thomas's place ter try an' see 'im. 'E wasn't at home. I saw 'is dad. 'E's an 'orrible man. It's the first time I've met 'im. 'E said Thomas ain't bin 'ome all night.'

Connie looked puzzled.

'Mum,' said Beth, going to her, 'don't you understand? Our factory was bombed last night, and Thomas wasn't on duty even though 'e was s'pposed ter be.'

Connie was now bewildered. 'I'm not sure what you're trying to tell me, Beth?' she replied.

Her hands now warm again, Beth went to sit at the polished parlour table nearby. 'Our factory,' she began, '*all* munitions factories right round the country – they're s'pposed ter be top secret. Nobody's s'pposed ter know where they are.'

'I appreciate that,' said Connie, joining her at the table.

'Not even the locals,' continued Beth. 'They're s'pposed ter fink the place is a paint factory or somefin'. That's why yer never find any notices or sign boards or anyfin'.' She paused just long enough to look directly up at her mum. 'An' yet – an' yet, Jerry found *our* place last night. Why?'

Connie thought about it, and drew an obvious conclusion. 'You think they were – tipped off?' she asked anxiously. 'Someone working for the enemy, inside the factory? A secret agent or—' Aware of the way Beth had brought up the subject, she stopped dead, and again clasped her hand to her mouth. 'Thomas?' she gasped. 'You can't possibly think that –'

Beth sat forward in her chair, and stared hard at her mum across the table. 'Mum,' she said, lowering her voice. 'Last week, I was called inter the office an' questioned by three different security people. Practically every question they asked – was about eivver Thomas or 'is dad.'

Connie was astonished. 'But why?'

'It's obvious, in't it? Becos they come from Ireland.'

'What!'

'I know. I felt just the same way as you,' said Beth. 'Even so, that's wot 'appened. Thomas is definitely under suspicion. The trouble is, I don't know if they're right or not. I don't know whevver they're pickin' on Thomas and 'is dad just 'cos they're Irish.'

Connie stared at the girl in disbelief. 'Beth!' she gasped. 'That's an outrageous thing to say! Do you really think that boy could be involved with passing information to the Germans? The same boy that you've waxed lyrical about ever since you met?'

'I'm not sayin' *anyfin'*, Mum,' insisted Beth. 'All I know is, this 'ole fing 'as bin keepin' me awake at night ever since those people talked about it. An' let's face it, there's no smoke wivout fire. Look at the IRA plantin' those bombs in that hotel up the West End. There's some real nutcases amongst 'em.'

'If you say things like that, Beth,' said Connie intensely, 'then you're no better than these people yourself! You're not like that. You're not one of them. How can you possibly think that all Irish people who live in London are spies?'

'I'm *not* sayin' that, Mum!' insisted Beth. 'I'm sayin' that *some* of 'em are capable of bein' troublemakers. Look at old Lord 'Aw-'Aw. The girls up the factory were sayin' the uvver day that *'e's* 'alf Irish.'

'As a matter of fact,' said Connie, correcting her, 'Lord Haw-Haw's father was Irish, but his mother was English.'

'It makes no diff'rence,' snapped Beth, getting up from the table. 'The fact is, there's a war on, Mum. An' it don't matter where people come from, they could be spies or – or anyfin'!'

Connie got up from the table and went to her. 'And you think Thomas – *your* Thomas – could be capable of giving away information, knowing that *you* could have been working in that factory last night?'

Beth was exasperated. 'That's not the point, Mum,' she replied. ' 'E *knew* that I wasn't on night duty last night. But even more important was that *'e* was s'pposed ter be there, but fer some reason or uvver – wotever reason – 'e didn't turn up.'

'What is it they call you at the factory, Beth? *Firecracker*. I'd say that means you give your mates quite a few laughs. You make a lot of people happy down the shelter each night, too. When I listen to you playing that piano, and watch the way our neighbours respond to you, and the enormous pleasure you give them, I often wonder why I always tried to bully you into learning music the way *I* was taught. Your way is so natural, so – from the heart.' She put her hand up to Beth's cheeks and stroked them gently with the back of her knuckles. 'You have such a heart of gold, Beth,' she said. 'Don't ever let people try to change that. Don't ever let them poison your mind into making snap judgements. Before you do that, make quite sure of what you're doing. There's always a logical reason for *everything* in this world, Beth. Whatever you do, don't ever forget that.'

In the piano warehouse shelter that evening, Beth played so many 'old favourites' for the neighbours on the old Joanna, that she was beginning to feel she was neglecting some of the popular hit tunes of the day. So with her mum and dad watching, she launched into a medley that included 'The White Cliffs of Dover', 'Somewhere Over the Rainbow', and 'I'll Be Seeing You'. But her mind was still churning over her meeting with Thomas's father, and the remote way he had greeted her. She was also deeply concerned at how the security people at the factory seemed to be keeping such a close watch on her, as though she herself had something to do with the factory being singled out as a target. Was it really possible, she asked herself, that Thomas had been passing information to the Germans? It was a thought that had come to haunt her. Fortunately, the siren, known as 'Moaning Minnie', hadn't yet wailed out, but it would be a miracle if it didn't do so at any minute, and in any case it was becoming a good idea to keep everyone's spirits up before, as well as during an air raid, especially as the morning's newspapers were full of Churchill's warnings that an invasion by the enemy was not only 'inevitable' but 'imminent'. The thought of German jackbooted troops marching through the streets of London horrified everybody, and she prayed that if it ever happened, they would be resisted by every man, woman and child.

Once Beth had finished her stint at the piano, everyone started to get ready for another long night. The place already stank to high heaven of Jessie Hawks's medicated '*Zube*' sweets, which she sucked all night long as a substitute for her beloved boiled sweets, which were no longer available, and this evening, Eileen Perkins's daughter Rita ponged with the smell of cheap carbolic soap, after a late-afternoon visit to the public baths down Hornsey Road. The Lieberman brothers had at last discarded their tin helmets, and were now taking turns changing into pyjamas and heavy woollen dressing-gowns behind a makeshift changing area, which had been set up discreetly behind a tatty old curtain provided by Lil Winkler, and strung up by Jack Cutter. At the moment, Jack was the only member of the nightly residents gang who had not yet turned up, but no one was unduly surprised by that, for just lately he had taken to popping in to the Eaglet pub at the corner of Seven Sisters Road for a couple of 'quickies' before turning in for the night.

Ever since Ted Shanks had got home from seeing young Phil up at the Moorgate Fire Station, Beth had avoided having any real contact with him. She knew that sooner or later he would have to do some explaining to her about his meeting with the mysterious 'Vera' the night before, but how and when he did it was clearly going to have to be *his* responsibility and not hers. However, the manner in which the subject was eventually brought up, took both her, and her mum and dad by surprise.

'By the way, Ted,' called Jessie, who was filling her hot-water bottle from a kettle she'd just boiled up on top of the paraffin stove. 'Did that gel ever get in touch wiv yer?'

Beth and her mum looked round with a start, but Ted, flat on his back on a mattress on the floor straining to read *The Daily Mirror*, tried not to react. 'Wot gel's that, Jess?' he called back, without turning round to look at her.

'That one that come up ter me a while back,' replied Jessie, careful not to spill any of the boiling water on to her fingers. 'Before yer come 'ome. It was on my fish 'n' chips night down at Anderson's. Scared the daylights outer me in the fog. I fawt she was the Ripper or somefin'. Funny sort er geezer.'

Beth carefully watched her father's reaction.

'Dunno who you're talkin' about, gel,' replied Ted, concentrating hard on his newspaper.

'Well, she knew you, all right,' persisted Jessie, twisting on the stopper of her hot-water bottle. 'Said she knew yer a long time ago or somefin', that she'd 'ope yer was safe and well, an' that if she got the chance, she'd like ter talk wiv yer. Just fer ol' times' sake, I s'ppose.'

Ted shook his head, and continued to read. ' 'Aven't the faintest, gel,' he replied. 'Probably someone I used ter work wiv up the depot or somefin'.'

Jessie shrugged, and tucked her hot-water bottle under the top sheet and blanket on her bunk. 'Well, don't say I din't pass on the message,' she sniffed.

Connie grinned down at Ted. 'Looks like you've got a fan, darling,' she said.

Ted smiled up at her briefly. 'Reckon I've got all the fans *I* want,' he replied.

Beth watched this exchange with scepticism. What would her dad say now when she approached him about the woman who came up to him in the dark the previous night?

Everyone suddenly turned with a start as they heard a commotion coming from the warehouse above. The door at the top of the stone steps was flung open, and Jack Cutter appeared. More than a little tipsy and very unsteady on his feet, he took off his trilby, and waved it triumphantly in the air. 'Ah! So *this* is where yer've all bin 'idin'!' he called, slurring his words wildly as he addressed the astonished residents below. 'Me dear friends an' neighbours! Come on! Let's 'ave a knees-up!' He started to bellow out, 'Knees Up, Muvver Brown', but as he did so, he missed his footing, and but for the hasty intervention of Bill Winkler who rushed to catch him, he would have tumbled down the stairs from top to bottom. Ted Shanks went to Bill's aid, and together they led Jack off to his bunk. On the way, he caught a glimpse of Jessie in her curlers. 'Hedy Lamarr,' he called, 'I love yer!'

'Drunken sot!' growled Jessie, as Ted and Bill plonked Jack on to his bunk. 'If you break wind down 'ere again ternight, Jack Cutter, yer'll 'ave my bleedin' brolly over yer 'ead!'

Beth stifled a laugh, but was not expecting what Jack called to her. 'There she is!' he spluttered boisterously. 'Our very own Paderewski of 'Ornsey Road!'

'Get ter sleep, Jack!' growled Eileen Perkins, reprimanding him from the far end of the shelter.

'Not much chance of that!' groaned Abe Lieberman.

'Not much chance of that!' bemoaned his brother Bernie, in agreement, sitting on the edge of his bed and cleaning his reading spectacles with the tail of his pyjama jacket.

'Come on now, gel!' wailed the almost incomprehensible Jack, as Bill tried to pin him down on to his bunk. 'Don't keep Paddy waitin' for yer!'

Beth swung with a start. 'Wot's that, Mr Cutter?' She leapt up from the edge of her bunk, and rushed across to him. 'Wot did you say?'

Even as she got to him, he was flat on his back, eyes closed, but with a huge tipsy smile on his face. 'Show Me the Way Ter Go 'Ome,' he started to sing, prompting groans from everyone.

'Wot was that you said?' repeated Beth, calling to him over Bill's shoulder. 'Wot did you say about Paddy?'

Jack grinned back without opening his eyes. 'Don't keep 'im waitin' in the cold, gel!' he burbled. ' 'E'll catch 'is deff!'

'If you don't shut up,' barked Jessie from her bunk, ' *'e's* not the only one who's goin' ter catch 'is deff!'

By the time Jack had started singing again, Beth had already grabbed her scarf and topcoat, and was halfway up the stone steps.

In the street outside, there was no sign of Thomas. But as she frantically looked around and called his name, she suddenly caught sight of him just along the road, hands deep in his duffle-coat pockets, moving from one foot to another to keep warm.

'Beth!' he called, the moment he saw her. They rushed to each other, and he hugged and kissed her. 'Oh Beth,' he said, kissing her repeatedly. 'Thank God I've got a chance ter speak to yer. The moment Dad told me you'd been ter the house, I came rushing up here as fast as I could.'

'Where *was* yer last night?' Beth asked immediately, before allowing him to say another word. 'You was s'pposed ter be on night duty.'

Thomas was ready for the question. 'I'll tell you,' he said, sliding his arm around her waist. 'Let's walk.'

Although bitterly cold, in contrast to some of the previous night's weather, it was a crisp, clear evening, so much so that the half-moon was casting a white glow all along Hornsey Road. As they strolled up the hill in the direction of Hornsey Rise, it seemed an unreal sight, with the entire road deserted for as far as the eye could see, a dazzling picture of white, undisturbed for once by the ravages of war that continued to plague the streets of London ever since the Blitz had begun. Thomas delayed answering Beth's question until they had reached the junction of Tollington Way, and were just passing the Lieberman brothers' tailoring repairs shop close to the Star cinema. 'There was no way I could have gone in to work last night,' he said.

'Although I can assure you, Beth, I'd sooner have been there than where I actually had to go.'

'Certain people fink it was too much of a coincidence, Thomas,' replied Beth awkwardly. 'The fact that yer just 'appened to be away on the night the factory nearly got blown ter smithereens.'

Thomas brought them to an abrupt halt. 'Certain people?' he asked, resenting the implication. '*What* people?'

'From security,' she replied. 'One of 'em follered me ter the bus stop an' asked me all sorts er questions about you.'

'Jesus Christ!' snapped Thomas. 'Who the hell do they think they are? They think I'm a criminal or somethin'?'

'You know the rules, Thomas,' Beth reminded him. 'If yer don't report in fer duty, yer s'pposed ter phone in an' let 'em know why. It's the war, Thomas. They 'ave a right ter know wot's goin' on.'

'They don't 'ave a bloody right ter know about my private life!' growled Thomas, striding off ahead of her.

'*I'm* s'pposed ter be yer private life, Thomas!' she called. 'Ain't *I* got some kind er right ter know too?'

Thomas came to a dead halt. He slowly turned and looked at her. She had remained in exactly the same spot where he had just left her, a diminutive figure bathed in the frosty moonlight of an ice-cold November evening. And as she stood there, it came back to him, that night no more than a year before – the night that he had first seen her, looking much the same as she did now, standing at a bus stop at the Tally Ho just before blackout, waiting to go home. He remembered the first thing he had said to her as he went to join her: 'Hope you don't mind company?' He remembered her chirpy reply too as though it was only yesterday: 'Don't mind at all, mate, as long as yer pay yer own fare!' He had loved her from that moment onwards. She had turned out to be not just the 'firecracker', the name that all her mates called her, the life and soul of the party, the one who always had an answer for anything and anybody, but more than that, much, much more. She was a girl with a heart, a girl who knew how to love with more than just her body, but also her mind.

As he looked at her now, he remembered that meeting only too well, and the reason why he wanted to be with her for the rest of his life. He walked slowly back towards her and came to a halt. He paused, and looked straight at the face drowned in a white glow and the sharp, deep shadow of his own body. 'Beth,' he said softly. 'The day before yesterday, one of my best mates was killed by a bomb that came down on a block of flats where he was working. His name was Johnny, Johnny O'Halloran. His family came from the next village where my dad was born back in the old country. He was the same age as me – and a plumber's mate. We've known each other since we were kids. We went to the same school, played football together, and once a week we always sneaked in together through the back door of the Angel cinema up at Islington. Most people thought we were so close, we were brothers. But we weren't. We just – liked each other a lot.' He stopped, and paused with difficulty before continuing. 'I got the news when Dad was at work, and I was having a nap at home yesterday afternoon. Johnny's young brother Sean came round to tell me; his eyes were blood-red from cryin'. He's twelve years old.' Quite spontaneously, he took hold of Beth's arm and walked her slowly on.

'Anyways, bein' Irish, the O'Hallorans had Johnny brought back home, and they held a wake. That's a kind of watchin' over a dead person before the funeral. They put his coffin in the front parlour. All the family were there – his mam and dad, aunties, uncles, cousins, all the relations – and a lot of friends too, some of who had known Johnny ever since he'd been born. Dada never came. He's always said that the only wake he ever wanted to go to was his own! Mind you, there was one hell of an air raid goin' on outside; the place was shakin' to high heaven, but nobody took the blindest bit of notice. Of course, there were too many of us to sit in the room at the same time, but we took turns – just starin' at Johnny in his open coffin as though he was just fast asleep. It was peculiar, really. There wasn't a mark on him – as far as I could see, and at any moment I expected him to sit up and scare the livin' daylights outer me. Johnny was like that – a real joker if there ever was one.' He paused again. 'So yer see, even an Irish boy can get bombed – just like anyone else.'

Beth, upset, and holding firmly on to his arm, brought them to a halt. 'You don't have ter go on, Thomas,' she said. 'Now I understand.'

'Do yer?' he asked. 'Do yer really, Beth? D'you feel any diff'rent to the way you were when you told me about those security people asking you questions about me?'

Beth was suddenly feeling awkward and uneasy. ' 'Ow was I to know, Thomas?' she pleaded. ' 'Ow was I to know? We've bin tergevver fer a year now, an' yet I don't really know nuffin' about yer. I mean, look at the number of times yer've promised ter take me ter meet yer dad, but yer never 'ave. Yer've never even given me yer address. All yer've ever told me is that yer live up King's Cross somewhere; I practically 'ad ter bribe one er the gels in personnel ter dig it out for me. An' as fer yer dad – well, I 'ave ter say *'e* wasn't exactly 'elpful. Probably 'ated me on sight.'

'That's not what he told *me*,' added Thomas. 'He told me you're a fine girl, and that he'd like to meet you again for longer next time.'

This really took Beth aback. 'Well,' she said half jokingly, 'he could've fooled *me*!'

Thomas looked away. He didn't really like that remark. 'I'm sorry you feel that way, Beth,' he said.

Aware of her tactlessness, Beth put her arms around his waist and looked straight into his eyes. 'I din't mean nuffin', Thomas,' she pleaded, ' 'onest I din't. 'It's just that – well, your dad wasn't exactly warm wiv me, an' the way 'e talks, 'e don't sound as though 'e likes the English very much eivver.'

'Excuse me.'

Both of them turned with a start to find an elderly ARP warden calling from the other side of the road.

'Don't want ter break up the party,' said the man, 'but we've just bin told that Jerry's on the way over again. If I was you, I wouldn't 'ang around too much. Sounds like it could be quite a hot night again.'

Both Beth and Thomas called back their thanks, turned around, and quickly made their way back towards the piano warehouse shelter. Before they had even got there, the deafening sound of the air raid siren wailed out from the top of Hornsey Road police station. 'Why don't yer come and spend the night down wiv us?' asked Beth. 'There's plenty er room. We've got some extra blankets; you could kip on the floor.'

'No I won't, thanks all the same,' replied Thomas, pulling her to him, and sliding his arms around her waist. 'I promised I'd pop round to see Johnny's family. It's just something I want to do.'

Beth nodded that she understood.

He hugged her, and she tucked her head against his chest. 'Beth,' he asked, in a whisper. 'Do you trust me?'

Beth hardly let him finish the question before answering. 'Thomas!' she protested. ' 'Ow can yer ask such a fing?'

'No – I mean it,' he insisted. 'You see, if there's no trust between two people, then what else is there? I love you for who you are, and I've always hoped that you'd feel the same way about me.'

'But I do, Thomas!' insisted Beth, hugging him tightly. 'I do!'

'Then just remember,' he continued softly, 'that when people start tryin' ter put crazy ideas into yer mind, just stop and ask yourself if what they say is – anything like the person you know – I mean *really* know. You see, Beth, I trust *you*, but if I thought at any time that you didn't trust *me*, I'd feel really miserable. Can you understand that?'

Beth looked up at him. 'I trust yer, Thomas,' she replied. 'I can't say more than that.' She leaned forward and kissed him warmly and passionately.

In the distance came the first rumbling sound of ack-ack gunfire. For a moment or so, they ignored it, and stood there in the full glare of moonlight holding on to each other.

'You'd better go,' said Thomas, gently pulling away. 'Depending on the way things are, I'll try and come down to see you again tomorrow evening. OK?'

Beth smiled and nodded. 'Okey doke,' she replied chirpily, giving him one final kiss.

'Catch yer later, then,' he replied, as he hurried off down the hill towards Seven Sisters Road.

Beth pulled her coat collar around her neck, and watched him go. She felt a surge of warmth inside her as she strained to see his tall, wiry figure shimmering in the crescent-shaped moonlight. But as she did so, a dark approaching night cloud suddenly blotted out her view, and by the time the moon had emerged again, the tall figure had disappeared. With the barrage of gunfire closing in, she stood there at the warehouse entrance just long enough to take in all Thomas had said to her, and for one brief moment, she thought of her mum's words earlier that afternoon: '*There's always a logical reason for everything in this world, Beth. Whatever you do, don't ever forget that.*' But then, she thought about the forced smile on the face of that security woman, and as she turned to go back down into the warehouse shelter, all the nagging doubts she had felt about Thomas just wouldn't go away.

Chapter 12

The moment the All Clear sounded, Uncle Horace emerged from his Morrison shelter in the front room. Although it was only just after six in the morning, it was still dark outside, and so cold that he had to wrap his spare blanket around his shoulders when he went into the scullery to put the kettle on.

Horace hated the long, dark winter mornings, which seemed to go on for ever. Of course, it was different when his late wife Maudie was alive, because they would snuggle up together in their old double bed upstairs, and only get up when the first chink of light sneaked through the curtains. However, whether Maudie had been alive or not, Horace would still not have slept a wink that night, knowing what lay ahead of him today. As the blackout was still on, and would not be lifted until nearly eight o'clock, he had to use his torch to make his tea in the scullery, where the blackout curtain had been found to be a bit threadbare in places.

His feet were freezing on the cold lino, mainly because he had not put his socks on when he got out of his Morrison shelter bed, having thrown away the old worn-out carpet slippers Maudie had bought him before she had passed away more than ten years before.

Once he'd made his first cup of tea of the day, he carried it back to the front room, but paused just long enough to shine the beam of his torch on to a small paper ticket which was propped up on the mantelpiece. The printing on it showed that day's date, and the words: GRAND WINTER VEGETABLE COMPETITION. TOWN HALL, WALTHAMSTOW. ENTRANCE FEE 6d. Horace picked up the ticket and looked at it for the umpteenth time since he had bought it two weeks before. His hand was shaking with excitement. 'Oh Maudie,' he said softly to himself. 'Be with me terday, my sweet girl.' He gently kissed the ticket, and replaced it on the mantelpiece. Then he put the cup of tea on the floor alongside the bed, turned off the torch, discarded the spare blanket around his shoulders, and got back in. His feet suddenly touched the hot-water bottle under the sheet, but it was cold, so he quickly kicked it out.

Snuggling down again, he pulled the sheet and blanket up to his chin, rested his head on the pillow, and closed his eyes. Soon, there was a big smile on his face. He could see that pumpkin – *his* pumpkin – the one he had grown with such love, care and attention. Was it going to win the big prize in that competition, he asked himself? Even though it would be the first time ever for him, could he really take that prize from Stan Pakeman, who had won it for the last four years in a row? He sighed, sighed with deep pleasure and elation at the thought of seeing himself up on that platform, shaking the judge's hand, being congratulated for a job well done, and holding that gold cup, even if it was only made of brass plate. And he could hear the audience applauding, cheering – applauding and cheering for *him*, applauding and cheering for him *and* Maudie. A few minutes later, he fell into a deep sleep, leaving his cup of tea to get cold, and missing the first sparrow song of the day from the drooping bare branch of the tree in the street outside.

Saturday was quite an important day also for the Shanks family, for not only were they all going along to Uncle Horace's vegetable competition, but it was the one and only Saturday that Ted Shanks would be spending at home before he returned to duty on the following Tuesday. Fortunately, Ted had managed to talk Phil's station manager into letting the boy have a few days off, for it was quite obvious that he was suffering from exhaustion and was in desperate need of a break. This meant that for the first time since Ted had gone away, the whole family would be together and be able to do some of the things they always used to do before he was called up. However, the day had started on a grim note when the BBC morning news reported that the city of Coventry was under a massive aerial onslaught from the *Luftwaffe*, and that casualties were expected to be high. As soon as she heard the news, Connie had a terrible feeling of foreboding, until Ted assured her that, despite Beth and Phil's objections, he was determined to make arrangements for the family to get out of London as soon as possible. For the time being, however, he was content to enjoy the day just being with them, and trying to forget that when he rejoined his unit in a few days' time, he was going to be posted to a distant part of the world where he might not get the chance to see any of them for a considerable amount of time. His other concern was Beth. He knew only too well that she was waiting for some kind of explanation about Vera, the woman he had met with in the street outside the warehouse just a couple of nights before, and he knew only too well that, for the time being at least, Vera was someone he just didn't want to talk about. Therefore, it wasn't going to be easy, for Beth was clearly avoiding him, something she had never done in her entire life; she was putting two and two together, and thinking the worst. How then, Ted wondered, was he going to resolve such a delicate situation without telling her the truth? And what would happen if she passed on her fears about the woman to her mum?

After breakfast, Ted found a suitable moment to talk to all the family, addressing his remarks mainly to Beth and Phil. 'Now listen, you two,' he said, half jokingly. 'Yer mum and I are goin' off ter see Gran an' Grandad termorrer. I'm goin' ter tell 'em that you're all goin' ter move in wiv 'em from next weekend onwards.'

Phil, still in his pyjamas, nearly exploded. 'Dad!'

Ted held up his hand to prevent any protests. 'It's no good, son,' he said. 'I've made up me mind. The way fings're goin' wiv these air raids, I'm not 'avin your lives put in danger any longer. You all 'eard that racket goin' on last night. God only knows who copped it, but it sounded like I was back at the front again. It's not goin' ter stop all this, not 'til we've sorted out Jerry one way or anuvver. I won't get a minute's sleep 'til I know you're all out of it.' He took a quick glance at Beth, who refused to look up at him. 'It's the right decision, Beff,' he said weakly. 'I promise yer.'

Connie, gently rocking baby Simon back and forth in her arms at the kitchen table, came to his support. 'Your dad's right,' she said to both Beth and Phil. 'When he leaves us on Tuesday, he'll have quite enough to contend with without worrying about us all the time.' She gave Ted an encouraging smile.

'What I want yer ter do in the next coupla days is ter get some of yer fings ready,' said Ted. 'Just take wot yer need fer the time bein'. When fings calm down a bit, yer can always come back an' pick up wot more yer need. I'm goin' ter get Dave Gilbert ter come over an' collect yer all in 'is van next Saturday. 'E says 'e can get enuff petrol on the black market ter get yer all down ter Gran an' Grandad's.'

'I don't want ter go, Dad,' protested Phil. 'Yer know I can't go. They need me up at the station.'

'Phil,' replied Ted firmly. 'Yer might as well know that I've 'ad a word wiv yer superintendent, an' we boaf agree that you're whacked out, and badly need a break. An' yer 'ave no need ter worry, 'cos 'e's gettin' a replacement for yer next week.'

'Wot!' Phil was close to tears. 'But they don't 'ave anyone ter cover fer me now. I can't go. They won't let me go!'

'You're a volunteer, son,' Ted reminded him. 'You're not in the army. Anyway, it's final. I'm makin' all the plans.'

Phil, utterly defeated, flopped back in his chair at the table.

Ted slowly turned to look at Beth, who remained sullen and silent. 'OK, Beff?' he asked tentatively.

Beth, also at the table, slowly looked up at him. 'Is wot OK, Dad?' she asked sourly.

'You're not at the factory any more,' he said. 'So can yer manage ter get ready by next Saturday?'

'If that's wot yer want, Dad,' she replied coldly.

Ted exchanged an anxious look with Connie. 'That's settled then,' he said, getting up from the table.

'Can I ask just one question though?' Beth asked.

' 'Course,' replied Ted.

'They've removed that unexploded bomb from the factory,' said Beth. 'Wot 'appens when they open up the place again? Do I take it that yer want me ter quit?'

'Yes, Beff,' said Ted. 'I do.'

'Even though I'm over eighteen, and I'm expected ter do some kind of war work?'

'You're under twenty-one, Beff, an' yer mum and I still 'ave the right ter say wot yer can an' can't do.'

'You'll 'ave ter tell that ter security,' replied Beth tersely.

'Do wot?' asked Ted.

'The security people at the factory are keepin' an eye on me,' said Beth.

'They seem ter fink I'm walkin' out wiv someone who's bin passin' information ter Jerry.'

Ted turned and stared at her in disbelief.

'So if yer take me away from the factory, Dad,' continued Beth, 'don't be surprised if they carry on watchin' me. It seems like me an' Thomas are quite a security risk.'

Ted exchanged a startled look with Connie.

Still clutching baby Simon in her arms, Connie got up from the table. 'I think it's time we were going,' she said. 'If we're going over to give Uncle Horace some support at the competition, we don't want to be late.' She turned and left the room.

Phil got up from the table and followed her out.

Once they were alone, Ted went to the table and sat there opposite Beth. 'Wot's this all about, Beff?' he asked.

'I wish I knew, Dad,' she replied, with a touch of irony. 'In fact there're a lot er fings I'd like ter know.' Beth stared at him, hoping that she had at last given him the opportunity to say something about the woman he had met. She felt utterly crushed inside – this was her own dad, the man she had been longing to see ever since he had been called up, the man she had idolised ever since she was a kid, who used to take her piggy-back practically everywhere they went. But because of that one fleeting moment outside the warehouse, she felt she didn't know him any more. Ever since that night, she had been tormented by the thought that he was not, after all, the father she had always thought he was. What had happened to him, she asked herself? Was the reason he had been sent home on sick leave because the trauma of Dunkirk had left him in some way mentally unstable? And if this was so, would it account for his change in personality since the last time he was home? For in *her* eyes, he definitely *had* changed, changed in the way he looked, gaunt and restless, unable to maintain eye contact for more than a split second, changed in the way that he had become scruffy and didn't seem to care whether he shaved or combed his hair. The fact was, she just didn't seem to know him any more, and she couldn't really understand why. Who *was* this woman he had never spoken of before? Why had she come out of the shadows so suddenly, so mysteriously? She longed to know, longed to have him tell her face to face right now. But, for a moment or so, there was silence between them, and when her dad took the dog-end from behind his ear and lit it, she was convinced that he was going to avoid the subject she had tried so desperately to bring up.

'There're fings better left alone,' Ted said, after taking a deep puff of his dog-end. 'Fer the time bein', anyway.'

Connie's voice interrupted them from the passage outside. 'Come on, you two! Time to go!'

Ted hesitated, then got up and slowly left the room.

Beth waited a moment, then followed him.

It took the family the best part of an hour to get to Walthamstow. Most of the time was spent waiting for a trolleybus at the stop outside the North London Drapery Stores in Seven Sisters Road, but when it finally came, Moaning Minnie suddenly wailed out from the roof of Hornsey Road Police Station, which meant that most people either made a rush for the nearest public air raid shelter in the basement of the store itself, or took cover in what they hoped would be safe shop doorways. As it so happened, it was only a few minutes later that Moaning Minnie wailed out again signalling the All Clear, so there was an immediate scramble by all the travellers to resume their place in the bus queue.

The Town Hall at Walthamstow was a fairly modern, white-stone building, which, since the start of the Blitz, had not entirely escaped its share of bomb blast, and was only waiting for building work to finish on the brand new Civic Centre next door, which had been started before the war, and would, despite the current ban on new building work, be completed in time for its opening in 1941. Nonetheless, the old building had hosted many prestigious events in its time, including the Winter Vegetable Competition, a regular firm favourite with the locals. Today's Saturday afternoon competition was especially important because Uncle Horace's beloved giant pumpkin had been accepted by the competition committee as a likely contender for a prize. Needless to say, by the time the Shanks family had arrived, he was a bundle of nerves. 'Didn't sleep a wink last night,' he said breathlessly, whilst Connie greeted him with a hug and a kiss. 'Couldn't get Stan Pakeman's face out of me mind.' He shook his head despondently. 'An' I was right,' he said. 'I've just bin to have a look at the pumpkin he's entered. It's the same size as my one, but streaks better.'

'Don't believe yer, Uncle 'Orace,' said Beth supportively. 'I saw it when it was out in your back garden. 'I'm tellin' yer, yer've got nuffin' ter worry about.'

'Well, let's face it,' said Ted, 'it's only a competition, ain't it. All yer'll get is a bit er brass plate or somefin''.'

'Oh Ted!' said Connie, uneasy that he had been so tactless.

But Beth threw her dad a look which confirmed what she had been thinking about him before they left home that morning. However, Uncle Horace took it all in his stride; he was far too overjoyed to see Ted home again to take offence.

Whilst they waited for the start of the competition, Horace took the family for a cup of tea at the indoor refreshments stall. It was certainly very welcome, for the place was freezing cold, so much so that every time anyone spoke their breath came out as condensation from their mouths. All around them stood competitors and their friends, local borough council officials, a St John's ambulance brigade nurse, and several special constables and air raid wardens, all wearing tin helmets. And to make the atmosphere less formal, in the background the tannoy system was belting out gramophone records of Vera Lynn, Anne Shelton and Donald Peers. Horace pointed out his main rival, Stan Pakeman, who was mingling with as many of the competition judges and officials as he could manage. He looked a pompous little man, wearing his Home Guard uniform and metal-rimmed spectacles, and when he suddenly caught a glimpse of Horace chatting with people at the tea stall, he made sure he gave him a look of total confidence. As the clock ticked away, Uncle Horace became more and more nervous, which seemed to loosen him up, allowing him to tell his dear friends the Shanks family something he had never mentioned before. 'I'm goin' inter business,' he revealed quite suddenly.

All the family looked at him aghast.

'Business?' asked Ted incredulously. 'Wot kinda business?'

'Ter me,' replied Horace proudly, 'there's only *one* business I know – vegetables.'

'Vegetables?' asked Connie, rocking little Simon back and forth gently in her arms.

'I don't know if any of yer remember my mate Terry Barlow?' asked Horace. 'We play darts tergevver on Tuesday nights up the Horse and Whistle. We're in the same team. Anyway, Terry's got a fruit and veg stall up Chapel Market, and he wants me to go into partnership with him.'

Beth was thrilled. 'Oh Uncle Horace!' she exclaimed. 'That's wonderful! Yer mean, you're goin' ter grow the veg, an' 'e's goin' ter sell 'em?'

'Right first time!' replied Horace.

'Yer don't mean yer can grow enough veg in yer own back garden ter keep a stall goin' all through the year, do yer?' asked a sceptical Phil.

'Not only from 'is own back garden, stupid!' said Beth. 'Uncle 'Orace 'as got 'is own allotment up near where 'e lives at Tottenham. Yer rent it from the Town 'All or somefin', don't yer, Uncle?'

'Almost a year,' replied Horace. 'Up 'til now I've bin givin' most of the stuff away, but Terry says I ought ter start makin' a bit er cash fer meself. Not that I need it at my time er life, but at least it'll keep me out er mischief.'

'I think it's a wonderful idea, Horace,' said Connie enthusiastically.

'So do I!' declared Beth. 'An' if yer want 'elp some time, yer can count on me. If our factory moves outer London, I'll be out of a job.'

'Done!' said Horace. But when he looked at Connie and Ted, he remembered that they had other ideas for the family. 'Anyway, I just wanted yer ter know what I'm up to. Of course, if by any chance I *should* win that prize for me pumpkin, ol' Terry'll be able ter charge a bit more for his veg!'

'Double!' proclaimed Beth, without any hesitation.

'Ladies and gentlemen!'

The male voice booming out from the tannoy silenced the lot of them.

'The judges are now inspecting the entries for large winter pumpkins.'

'That's it!' gasped Horace, nearly choking on a mouthful of tea. 'This way – quick!'

In the main hall, with its walls plastered with DIG FOR VICTORY posters, and watched by both standing and seated competitors, the judges had already started their inspection of all the numbered pumpkins lined up on long wooden benches. Not surprisingly, there had been dozens of entries, for the London boroughs were now brimming with small allotments and back-street vegetable gardens, all of them now helping to fill the gap left by so many wartime shortages. The three judges themselves, one woman and two men, all carrying clipboards, were fairly elderly, and as they slowly walked around the benches, they were clearly being very careful about showing any preference for any particular entry. Just occasionally, however, they would lightly prod the hard orange skin of one of the pumpkins, score the entry on the clipboard, then make a hurried whispered comment to each other before moving on. At one point, however, the veil on the ancient hat of the elderly female judge suddenly flopped forward over her face, causing titters from amongst some of the younger spectators.

Uncle Horace and the Shanks family gathered as close as they could to the benches, watching every movement, every gesticulation from the judges. 'That's Alderman Woolley,' whispered Horace. 'He's never given me a good point. Most people know he's got his own favourites.'

Hearing this, Beth spent the next few minutes glaring at the unsuspecting Alderman.

'Who's the old bag?' asked Phil, who was shifting from foot to foot with boredom.

'Ssh!' hissed Uncle Horace, who nearly had a fit. 'That's Mrs Fitzherbert. Her husband sponsors this competition every year.'

The judging continued slowly and methodically, and only came to a brief halt when baby Simon, who was being nursed in his dad's arms, suddenly let out a loud yell, announcing that he had done something in his nappy, and wanted a quick change. Watched by some very disapproving people around them, Connie quickly grabbed the baby from Ted's arms, and rushed out to the ladies' toilets to do the necessary. By the time she got back the judging was over, and Alderman Woolley was just stepping up to the microphone in front of the stage platform to announce a decision.

'Ladies and gentlemen!' He called so loudly that the microphone whistled and boomed. 'I am pleased to announce the judges' decision on the preliminary eliminating final for this afternoon's pumpkin competition. He fumbled in his hand for the piece of paper that contained the necessary information. 'Place Number Three goes to Mrs Dotty Wilkinson . . .'

A great cheer, coupled with jeers and boos from the spectators.

Alderman Woolley was not amused by the interruption. 'As I was saying,' he repeated, 'Place Number Three goes to Mrs Dotty Wilkinson from Hamilton Road, Higham Hill . . .'

A ripple of polite applause.

'Place Number Two', continued the Alderman, taking rather longer than necessary to refer to the next name on the list, 'goes to . . . Mr Horace Ruggles of Beardsley Street, Tottenham . . .'

A groan of disappointment from the Shanks family, mixed with jeers and disappointed groans from the other competitors.

'Don't worry, mate,' said Ted, putting a comforting arm around Horace's shoulder. 'You're still the best in my book!'

'It's not over yet, Uncle,' insisted Beth. 'Don't yer see, you're down ter the last three. You'll win in the final.'

Horace shook his head. As far as he was concerned, it was all over for another year, and it came as no surprise when the Alderman announced the winner of the preliminaries.

'And first place', continued the Alderman, 'goes to Mr Stan Pakeman of Ulverston Road, Walthamstow.'

A roar of cheers from the winner's family and friends, was accompanied by a round of courteous applause from everyone else in the hall.

It was half an hour or so before the final of the pumpkin competition took place. Whilst they waited, Connie and the baby, Ted and Phil went for a quick look around the other vegetable entries, leaving Beth alone with Uncle Horace. Beth was the only one in the family who really knew how he felt. She knew it wasn't easy to be rejected, especially when you've pinned your hopes on something. She remembered only too well when, soon after leaving school, she herself had been rejected for a job as a clerk in the office of a local builder's merchant. How she had wanted that job! Not that it was wonderful pay, but it would have given her the chance to prove to everyone that she did have a brain in her head, especially to her headmistress, who, in her final school report, had dismissed Beth as someone who hadn't known how to concentrate on school studies, and was therefore destined to roll on through life doing menial work. The only thing was, Uncle Horace wasn't just leaving school. Although winning a prize in a vegetable competition wasn't exactly everyone's ambition, to him it was something he had wanted badly for so much of his lifetime. 'Don't you worry, Uncle,' she said, as they strolled around the site of the new Civic Centre next door. 'It's not over yet. I bet when yer go back inside that 'all, it'll all be diff'rent. Now they're down ter three places, you're in wiv a chance – you mark my words.'

Horace smiled gratefully at her, and put his arm around her shoulders. It was at times like this that he knew why he had always had such affection for Beth. She had such genuine care for him, and made him laugh whenever he was feeling low. He also remembered what his dear Maudie had once said about her: '*I've got a lot er time fer that girl. She's got so much love in 'er.*' They came to a halt, and spent a moment or so watching a huge crane lifting some gleaming white stone blocks into place on top of the new Civic Centre next door. 'I'm not going back inter that 'all, Beth,' he said. 'There's no point. It's a foregone conclusion who's going to win that prize. Stan Pakeman's goin' ter walk away wiv it.'

Beth was horrified. 'Uncle!' she gasped. ' 'Ow can yer say such a fing! Yer know wot they say: "Fer gordsake don't close the door 'til the fat lady's sung 'er song!" '

Horace had to laugh. Trust Beth. She was the only one who could cheer people up when things were looking bad.

'It's true,' insisted Beth. 'If yer want somefin' bad enuff, yer'll get it.' Although she didn't actually believe a word of her own home-spun philosophy, she knew it was right to say it.

'It's not that I want that prize 'cos I want ter show off,' said Horace in his slow Essex drawl. 'I want it fer yer Auntie Maudie, 'cos she was like you – she always gave me such encouragement.' He turned and looked at her. 'But I s'ppose I also want it 'cos it'd give me such a lift up, a real new start in life. Just imagine the look on Terry Barlow's face when I turn up at 'is stall carryin' that prize cup. I can 'ear 'im shoutin' out: "*Come on now, ladies and gents! Get all yer prize-winnin' veg terday! Only the best quality!*" '

Beth lowered her eyes. She couldn't bear the look of hope and disappointment in Uncle Horace's eyes.

'It'd be such a start for me, Beth,' continued Horace. 'Instead of diggin' away in that clay up at the allotment, knowin' that it was nuffin' more than a 'obby, I'd be doin' it for a reason.'

'Yer will anyway, Uncle,' said Beth, slipping her arm around his waist. 'Whevver yer win that prize or not.'

A short while later, the Shanks family joined all the other contestants in the hall for the final of the pumpkin competition. The judging seemed to take for ever, with the Alderman and his colleagues going from one to the other of the three pumpkins, sniffing them, measuring them, tapping them with their pencils, then rubbing their chins in deep thought. Ted, Phil and even Connie, were now glaring at them, convinced that Uncle Horace was right and that the judges would inevitably find in favour of Stan Pakeman's giant, healthy-looking pumpkin. Beth, however, was more interested in the turmoil and despondency Uncle Horace was going through, whilst he waited in the entrance lobby outside. After spending just five minutes inspecting the three pumpkin entries, Alderman Woolley stepped up to the microphone. 'Ladies and gentlemen!' he announced. 'We are pleased to announce the result of this year's competition for the best-grown pumpkin in Walthamstow and surrounding boroughs, and I am pleased to announce that the winners are as follows: In third place, Mrs Dotty Wilkinson from . . .'

The rest of his announcement was immediately drowned out by cheers, jeers and boos from the spectators.

'In second place,' continued the Alderman, rather tersely, 'is . . . Mr Horace Ruggles from . . .'

Amidst more cheers, jeers and applause, Phil Shanks groaned out loud, and Ted and Connie shook their heads despondently. Beth didn't wait for the inevitable result. She turned and hurried straight out to see Uncle Horace.

Uncle Horace himself was seated on a bench just outside the front entrance of the building. His face was blood-red from the ice-cold breeze. When Beth reached him, he looked up at her and smiled. 'Don't worry,' he said. 'Yer don't 'ave ter tell me.'

Beth sat down beside him. As she did so, a deafening roar went up from the spectators inside the hall, clearly indicating who had won first prize. 'Yer know wot I fink yer should do now?' she said, slipping her arm around his waist. 'I fink yer should start plannin' fer next year. There are uvver fings besides pumpkins yer can put in the competition. I'ad a shufty at the Brussels sprouts. They're not a patch on the ones you showed me in your back garden.'

'No, Beth,' he replied. 'I don't think so. I reckon I've 'ad enuff er competitions. I mean, when yer think about it, they're a bit of a waste er time, ain't they?' They both stared out aimlessly at the traffic hurrying along Forest Road in front of the Town Hall, and just over the rooftops, two barrage balloons could be seen rising up into the light grey cloud that had persisted all morning. 'As a matter of fact,' continued Horace, 'I've bin giving it quite a bit of thought since I got up this morning, and I think what I'll do is ter give up me allotment. At my age it's becomin' much too back-achin'.'

'Uncle 'Orace!' protested Beth. 'I never 'eard anyfin' so daft in all me life! You're an Essex man, remember, an' don't you forget it! You an' Auntie Maudie loved workin' out in that garden er yours, an' it's bin the same ever since yer came ter live in Tottenham. Yer've got soil in your veins, Uncle, not blood!'

The moment she had finished speaking, there was a huge roar from the crowd inside the hall, followed by what sounded like a great deal of barracking and cat-calling. Neither Beth nor Uncle Horace reacted. As far as they were concerned, the competition was over, and that was that.

'Come on!' said Beth quite suddenly. 'We ain't goin' ter take this lyin' down. Let's 'ave a sing-song, and ferget all about bleedin' pumpkins.' With that, she launched straight into the words of Uncle Horace's favourite song, ' 'Til We Meet Again'.

Horace turned and looked at her, his face immediately lit up, and he joined in the song in perfect harmony with her. They were only a few lines into the song, however, when Phil came rushing out of the hall, breathless, and bursting with excitement. 'Uncle Horace – come quick!' he roared, suddenly grabbing hold of Horace's arm and tugging him up to his feet.

Horace was absolutely flustered. 'Wot's goin' on?' he asked.

' 'Urry up! 'Urry up!' insisted Phil, dragging his uncle off. 'They wanna see yer!'

Beth looked on in amazement, and followed them both back into the hall.

In the hall itself, there was general mayhem. People were waving their fists in the air, and others were cheering and applauding, including Connie and Ted. And the moment everyone saw Horace being dragged in by young Phil, the place erupted into roars of delight, wild cheers, wolf-whistles and applause, mingled with some boos and shouts of 'Fix!' Despite the fact that she had the baby in her arms, Connie, tears in her eyes, was first to hug Horace, followed by Ted who put his arm around Horace's shoulders, saying: 'Well done, mate!'

Horace, absolutely astonished at the proceedings, hadn't the faintest idea what was going on, but as he looked across to the other side of the hall, he could just catch a glimpse of Stan Pakeman glaring angrily at him. Meanwhile, Phil continued to push Horace up towards the stage, where the three judges were waiting for him.

Beth was just as dumbfounded as Uncle Horace. 'Wot is it?' she asked her mum and dad. 'Wot's 'appened?'

'They found a big split or somefin' underneaf Stan Pakeman's pumpkin,' said Ted, who had his hands over his head applauding Horace as he climbed the few steps on to the stage. 'They said 'e deliberately tried ter 'ide it, so 'e's bin disqualified.'

'Uncle came in second,' proclaimed Connie deliriously. 'So he's now the winner!'

Beth swung a look of total disbelief and elation at Horace, as he approached the judges.

'Ladies and gentlemen!' proclaimed Alderman Woolley, whose chain of office was twisted out of shape in a very undignified way around his neck and chest. 'Owing to the disqualification of this award to the winner in this category previously announced, it is the unanimous decision of myself and my two colleagues that the award should now go to the runner-up . . .'

Another roar of approval from the crowd.

'I therefore ask Mrs Fitzherbert', contined the Alderman, 'to make the presentation of first prize to Mr Horace Ruggles . . .'

As Horace stepped forward to receive the small brass-plate cup, the hall once again erupted into wild applause. Mrs Fitzherbert stood back to let him say something into the microphone, but he was too overcome with emotion to say anything more than, 'Thank you – everyone.' When he got off the stage, people everywhere were patting him on the back and congratulating him for at last winning the prize he had been denied for so long. When he reached the family, all of them hugged him. But his special hug was reserved for Beth, whose eyes were streaked with tears. 'Looks as though the future's rosy after all,' he said croakily.

As he spoke, 'Moaning Minnie' wailed out from the roof of the nearby Walthamstow Police Station. Within minutes, everyone had evacuated the hall to take cover in the Town Hall shelters below.

Chapter 13

It took Helga Buchner quite some time to find the hospital for *Luftwaffe* officers, which turned out to be in a secluded rural area just outside Hamburg, and as she had never learned to drive she had to take a bus to Lubeck, a train to Hamburg, and then another bus to the village of Marstein. It was Sunday morning, and as she had managed to leave her two young sons with their grandparents for the day, on the journey she was able to reflect on all that had happened within the past forty-eight hours, starting with that terrifying message from Heinz's field headquarters that he had been 'slightly' injured on active duty, and was being confined in an air force hospital for a few days. How 'slightly injured', and what kind of 'active duty' had he been on had dominated her thoughts from the moment she left home. Each day the newspapers and radio were reporting heavy raids on London and the British mainland, but she knew only too well that the German propaganda machine had been careful not to mention that the 'specific targets' of the air raids had been on the civilian population. It also omitted the fact that casualties amongst the *Luftwaffe* air crews were growing day by day, night by night, and if it hadn't been for the rumours flying around, the German public were clearly not going to be told. When she finally got to the hospital, she found the place was some kind of a castle set in a rolling valley that had been requisitioned by the authorities, and was now heavily camouflaged and fortified. This proved, if any proof were needed, that air raids by the British on German targets were now a fact of life; only the week before, the RAF had bombed a military training depot not more than twenty kilometres from the Buchner home in Lossheim.

'Stop looking so worried, woman!' was the first thing Heinz said to his wife the moment she entered the ward where he was recovering. 'The only wound I have is a strained back, and that's almost back to normal. In any case, I'll be out of here tomorrow, so you'll have to put up with me for a couple of days.'

'A couple of days!' protested Helga. 'Is that all the time they can give you when you've nearly got yourself killed?'

Embarrassed, Heinz looked around the small ward to see if anyone was paying any attention to them. 'Sit down, Helga,' he said affectionately, but firmly.

Helga did what she was told, and sat in a chair at the side of the bed.

Heinz motioned for her to draw close. She did so. 'Helga,' he said calmly, 'you have to remember Germany is at war. Everyone has to play their part. There's very little time for any of us to feel sorry for ourselves.'

Helga was astonished by his attitude. For all she knew he could have been killed out there on 'active duty', and all she would be expected to do was not to feel sorry for herself. 'How did you come to get this injury, Heinz?' she asked blankly. 'What happened?'

'Darling,' he said, propping himself up in the bed. 'You know as well as I do, I can't pass on information like that.'

'Can't pass on information?' Helga protested. 'For God's sake, I'm your wife, Heinz. I have a right to know.'

Heinz was aware that one of his fellow officer patients had turned to see why voices were raised. 'How are the boys?' he asked, blocking any more of her questions. 'Has Richard finished that model of the Dornier bomber I bought him?'

'Yes, he has,' replied Helga, with little enthusiasm. 'It's hanging over his bed. Every night before he goes to sleep, he salutes it, and says, "*Heil, Führer!*"

Heinz roared with laughter.

'I don't think it's funny, Heinz,' said Helga. 'If you must know, I'm worried about the boys. There are times when I feel I've lost them.'

Heinz, serious again, watched her carefully. 'What does that mean?'

Helga drew closer. 'Oh darling,' she pleaded, 'you *know* what I mean.' She looked around the ward, then lowered her voice. 'There are things going on in that school that their teachers never tell us about. I heard from Frau Lechter that people from outside come to talk to them.'

'Oh really?' said Heinz casually. 'What do they talk about?'

Helga leaned in closer. 'You *know* what they talk about, Heinz. Don't you see? They're far too young to be involved in the youth movement, too young to be involved in politics.'

'Don't be foolish, my dear,' returned Heinz, showing some irritation. 'The youth movement has nothing to do with politics. It's just a way for young people to show how much they love their country.'

'That's not true,' insisted Helga, whose voice was now down to a whisper. 'I've heard them in the village square at Lossheim. They talk about winning the war against bolsheviks and Jews. They talk about bombing the British until every man, woman and child is annihilated. If that isn't politics, I don't know what is.'

Heinz took her hand and caressed it gently with his fingers. 'My darling,' he said. 'You worry too much. Richard and Dieter are still our boys. There's nothing wrong with being patriotic, no matter *what* age they are.'

'It's wrong to want to kill people, Heinz,' said Helga, careful to keep her voice as low as she could. 'Especially innocent people.' She took his hand and kissed it. 'I love you, Heinz,' she said. 'If anything were to happen to you, I don't know what I'd do.'

Heinz paused a moment. His expression hardened. 'Go home, Helga,' he said coldly.

She looked up at him with a start.

'We'll talk later.' She was about to protest, but he stopped her. 'Go home, Helga.'

Beth spent Sunday morning sorting out the few things she would need once the family had moved out to her gran and grandad's place in Hertfordsire the following weekend. Knowing that leaving London was going to change her life, perhaps for ever, she did the chores with the utmost resentment, blaming her mum for putting the idea into her dad's mind in the first place. Her brother Phil, however, was not so obedient. As soon as his parents left the house to go to Hertfordshire in the morning, he went off to see his station superintendent at Moorgate. Before he went, he even told Beth that he was so upset at being forced to give up his job as a fire brigade cycle messenger that he was thinking about running away. Beth warned him not to do anything so stupid, saying that no matter how much they both hated doing what their parents were making them do, they had a duty to obey, and in any case it was for their own good.

A short while later, Beth left the house herself. After yet another night in the warehouse shelter, she craved some fresh air and the chance to get out into the streets on her own. As she strolled down Seven Sisters Road, the fire brigade from Mayton Street Fire Station were hosing down a fire that had been smouldering all through the night, the result of an oil bomb which had ripped down through the roof of a shoe shop, causing immense damage. For some unknown reason, she found herself wandering towards the bus stop outside the Marlborough cinema where she had always caught her morning bus to the Tally Ho, and without thinking, when a 609 trolleybus came along, she rushed after it, and got on.

The journey up to Finchley was fairly dull, mainly because it was difficult to see out through the bus windows which were all blacked out and, being a Sunday, there were very few passengers on either deck. When the middle-aged bus clippie came up to collect her fare on the top deck, the woman looked and sounded the picture of misery, for she had a terrible cold, and her nose was so red Beth reckoned it could be used as a traffic light. 'I won't charge yer all the way, dear,' said the poor woman, blowing her nose for the umpteenth time. 'We're 'avin ter turn round one stop before the Tally 'O 'cos somefin's goin' on up there somewhere. I just 'ope I get some 'elp ter transfer me poles fer the return journey, 'cos if I don't, the bleedin' fing can just stay in the middle er the road!' She took Beth's fare, and clipped a ticket for her. 'This bleedin' war!' she sniffed. 'Remember when it all started? Remember what all the smart arses said about it all bein' over in a coupla weeks?' She grunted, and made herself sneeze again. 'Some 'opes!' she spluttered. 'Just look at wot they're doin' ter poor ol' Coventry. The way fings're goin' up there, there won't be nuffin' left.'

As she heard the clippie thumping off down the stairs, Beth found herself agreeing with everything the woman had said. Despite the Government's attempts to keep the catastrophic news to a minimum, the word going around was that the city of Coventy had been practically demolished. But as the bus finally came to a halt at the stop before Tally Ho Corner, her thoughts quickly turned to what was going on around there. When she got off and walked up towards the Gaumont cinema, she was surprised to see the security barriers in place, and when she attempted to get closer to the munitions factory, once again she found herself stopped by a Special Constable. 'Sorry, miss,' he said. 'Yer've got ter keep back.'

'But I work in the factory over there,' Beth tried to explain. 'I want ter collect some of me fings.'

'No way yer can do that, I'm afraid,' insisted the constable. 'Not without special permission.'

'Permission from who?' asked Beth irritably.

'Security office.'

'Well 'ow can I get permission if I'm not allowed in ter see them?'

The constable thought about this for just a brief moment. 'Got an identity card, young lady, I presume?' he asked.

'I've got one,' replied Beth, 'but not on me.'

The constable shrugged. 'Then I can't 'elp,' he replied. 'Sorry, miss.' With that, he turned away, leaving Beth fuming behind the security cordon. But she refused to move, and did everything she could to see what was going on around the factory in the distance. As far as she could make out, a busy group of soldiers were loading a series of large wooden containers on to a cluster of military vehicles that were entering and leaving the backyard.

'Looks like we're on the move.'

Beth looked up with a start to see who had joined her. 'Thomas!' she spluttered. 'Wot're *you* doin' up 'ere?'

'Same as you, I reckon,' he replied, slipping his arm around her waist. 'I came up ter see what's goin' on.' His attention was transfixed on all the comings and goings outside the factory. 'Looks like we're being kicked out or somethin'.'

'Yeah,' growled a voice just coming up behind them. 'No fanks ter the likes er *some* people!'

Both of them swung round with a start. It was Beth's mate from the factory, Mo Mitchell. 'Mo?' said Beth, taken aback. 'Wot's goin' on?'

'They're closin' the place down, that's wot!' she barked. 'It's apparently too dangerous for any of us ter work in there any more.'

'But I fawt they diffused that UXB,' replied Beth. 'Surely the place is safe now?'

'It would be,' said Mo, clearly directing her remark to Thomas, without actually turning to him, 'if it wasn't fer Jerry now knowin' where we are. All this', she nodded towards the bomb-blast damage all along the street, 'was becos of a tip-off.'

Beth froze, but Thomas remained grim and silent.

'Luckily,' continued Mo stiffly, 'the powers-that-be've got a good idea who's be'ind it. It won't be long before they catch up wiv 'im.' She turned and gave a long hard stare towards Thomas. 'But when they do, I 'ope they take 'im ter the Tower an' chop off 'is bleedin' 'ead!'

Knowing full well that Mo was getting at him, Thomas left them and walked away.

'Thomas!' called Beth, about to hurry after him.

But Mo grabbed her arm, and tried to hold her back. 'Let 'im go, Beff!' she growled angrily. 'Ain't you 'eard? Thomas is the one they suspect. '*E's* the one they reckon who's bin passin' on info ter Jerry.'

Beth, in a rage, pulled her arm away. 'You stupid cow, Mo!' she roared.

'You *know* it's true, Beff!' retorted Mo, hitting back. '*Everyone* knows it's true! The Paddies 'ave got a real bee in their bonnet about us English. Why don't they just pack up an' go back where they belong!'

'Mo, you're disgustin'!' snapped Beth. ' 'Ow can yer talk like that about people? It's prejudice like that that causes wars. Thomas ain't no traitor, he ain't no Jerry spy. 'E's a good, 'onest, 'ard-workin' feller, just like anyone else who works in that factory. An' you might like ter know that "Paddies", as you call 'em, are gettin' caught up in the bombs in London every night too. Only the uvver night Thomas's best friend got killed. D'you realise that if Thomas 'imself 'ad bin anywhere in these streets when those bombs come down, '*e* could've bin killed any time, just like the rest of us!'

'Yeah, but 'e wasn't, was 'e?' snapped Mo. 'It's funny 'e was the only male worker who wasn't on night duty in the factory when it got blasted!

'I'm sick of 'earin' people say that!' replied Beth angrily. 'It's nasty and vicious – and typical of people like you, an' yer ought ter be ashamed of yerself!' She turned her back on her and moved off. But she came to a sudden abrupt halt, and looked back. 'An' I'm tellin' yer this, Mo Mitchell,' she bawled. 'One er these days I'm goin' ter make you eat your words. An' when I do, I won't forgive yer fer wot yer've just said!'

Mo, her usually blood-red complexion now red to bursting point, was totally flabbergasted. But as she watched Beth rush off to join Thomas, not for one moment did it occur to her that what her best mate had just said might conceivably be true. 'There's no smoke wivout fire!' she yelled back, without any guilt at all.

Beth caught up with Thomas just as he was about to cross the road. 'Thomas!' As she reached him, Thomas continued to walk on, so she walked with him, her arm tucked around his waist. 'Don't take no notice of that silly cow,' she pleaded. 'If 'er brain was as big as 'er mouf, she'd make a fortune!'

'It's no good, Beth,' said Thomas, hands deep in his duffle-coat pocket, eyes glued, unseeing, to the pavement. 'When people get an idea in their head, nothin's ever goin' ter move it. Believe me, there are plenty more where *they* come from. And not only in the factory.'

'Just take my advice, Thomas,' replied Beth. 'Ignore it. You're bigger than all of 'em.'

Thomas brought them both to a halt. 'You think so?' he said, turning to her. 'D'you really think that's the way I should feel when I see the look in their eyes, see them whispering to each other every time I go into the canteen ter get a cup of tea? No, Beth. My dad may be a hell of a difficult feller, but he warned me that there'd be times like this. He warned me that people in this country can be just as biased as anywhere else. The way things are goin', I'm comin' around ter thinkin' the same way as him.'

Beth's expression changed. 'I 'ope yer won't do that, Thomas,' she replied. 'I 'ope yer'll know that not all people are the same, that there's one person who'll always believe in yer.' She leaned forward and kissed him, unaware that from the other side of the road, they were being watched by a woman sitting in a parked car. It was Jane Grigsby, the factory security officer.

Uncle Horace usually only went to his local pub in Tottenham, the Horse and Whistle, on Tuesday nights. That was when he teamed up with his mate Terry Barlow for the regular weekly darts match, which was always a very boisterous but amicable affair. But today was special. Today, he and Terry were there to celebrate a very special event at Walthamstow Town Hall the day before, Horace's first prize win for the best pumpkin at the Winter Vegetable Competition. As always on a Sunday lunchtime, the saloon bar was full, and would only empty when the customers, most of them middle-aged and elderly males, were thrown out by the landlord at three o'clock closing time, but with Ernie Peacock thumping out tune after tune on the pub's old Joanna, that was clearly going to be quite an effort. Today, Horace was reluctant to go home, because he'd enjoyed himself so much, with nearly everyone in the bar giving him a 'well done' pat on the back for his great achievement the day before. Terry, a large, ebullient man with rogue grey hairs growing on his cheeks in compensation for having very little on his head, was in great form. 'I tell yer, 'Orace ol' mate,' he said, his arm around Horace's shoulder as they downed yet another bitter, 'we're on to a good fing 'ere.' Tapping the side of his nose and pulling Horace closer, he slurred his words. 'You get yerself organised on that allotment of yours, an' we'll 'ave 'em queuin' up fer your veg. I can see it all now: GO TO HELL ADOLF. GET YOUR HOME-PRODUCED PRIZE-WINNING VEG HERE!'

Horace beamed with pride and puffed out endless palls of smoke from his pipe.

'We're a team, 'Orace,' said Terry, his checked flat-cap skew-whiff on his large head.

'An' I don't mean just darts. We're partners, mate – business partners – fifty-fifty on everyfin' we make. Done?'

'Done!' returned Horace, as he shook hands vigorously with Terry.

'An' I tell yer wot,' continued Terry, looking over his shoulder to make sure no one could hear him. 'Ter mark the new arrangement, I'm going ter get the stall spruced up, bit er paint 'ere, bit er paint there, a new tarpaulin cover fer the ol' roof.' He grinned mischievously, and tapped his nose again with one finger. 'Course I'm not goin' ter tell yer where I'm goin ter get the stuff ter do it!' He let out the most awful bronchial laugh, which for one brief moment prevented him from returning to his glass of bitter. 'I'm tellin' yer, mate, your missus'd be proud of yer. It just goes ter show, yer never know wot's waitin' round the corner for yer, yer never too old ter find somefin' new in life.'

Horace thought about Terry's words as he made his way back home. Although during the past hour or so he had had more than just 'one for the road', he was quite steady on his feet. And yes, he did feel pleased with himself. Even though it was only one part of an old vegetable competition he had won, it was the first time that anything like that had happened to him. Even when he was at school, he never won a race on sports day, never won a game of cards in the pub and, on the rare occasion that his darts team ever won a game, it had very little to do with his own contribution.

By the time he got to the corner of Beardsley Street, the first flurries of winter were beginning to fall. He stopped for a moment to look up at the sky; he had a great smile on his face as light particles of snow landed silently on his cheeks, only to be melted immediately by the warmth of his body. He found the crisp, fresh air invigorating, so he stood there for several minutes basking in the wonder of it all.

The moment he got home and opened his front street door, he could smell his Sunday lunch cooking in the oven. Having spent so much of his early life in rural Essex, he loved rabbit stew, and he always put it on to cook very slowly, together with some carrots, onions and turnips, all grown by himself in his back garden, and a stock made up from either Bisto or Oxo. But the first place he went to was, predictably, the front parlour, and the first thing he looked for was the competition winner's cup, taking pride of place in the middle of the mantelpiece, a thin ray of sun shining straight on to it through a gap in the lace curtains. With a broad beam on his face, he went straight to it, picked it up, and gave it a kiss. 'That's fer you, Maudie, my love,' he said, before replacing it. As he did so, Moaning Minnie wailed out across the rooftops outside, so he quickly disappeared into the scullery to get his rabbit stew, just in case Jerry decided to invite himself to Sunday dinner.

The journey back from Hertfordshire had turned out to be a nightmare for Connie and Ted. The worst part had been when they had been caught in the air raid whilst changing buses at Barnet to get on to the 609 trolleybus, for the sky suddenly erupted with ack-ack gunfire, and a ferocious aerial dogfight resulted in two 'pirate' raiders being shot down whilst crowds of people watched from the streets below. Connie was grateful she had Ted with her, for he had nursed baby Simon in his arms during the entire ordeal, shielding him beneath his overcoat, and getting him back to sleep every time he became restless. Nonetheless, until Moaning Minnie had wailed out the All Clear, Connie's nerves were on edge, and she couldn't relax until she and Ted got off the bus at the Nag's Head. As soon as they did so, however, they were hit by the inevitable smell of burning timbers which seemed to be coming from fires beyond Finsbury Park somewhere. 'Thank God we'll be out of all this by next weekend,' she said, as she and Ted hurried home along Seven Sisters and Hornsey Road, carefully avoiding lumps of white-hot jagged shrapnel as they went. 'I just hope Beth and Phil have done what you told them to do. My only fear is they'll try to take half the house with them when we leave.' When they got home, however, it was obvious that both Beth and Phil had done no such thing, for neither of them were at home.

'There's a note 'ere from Beff,' said Ted, at the kitchen table. 'She says she might be going ter the pictures round Savoy.'

'I thought as much,' replied Connie, carefully laying Simon down into his kitchen cot. 'She's always going to that place since it opened a few months ago. What about Phil?'

'She don't mention 'im,' called Ted, going to the kitchen dresser to pour himself a glass of brown ale. ' 'E's probably gone round ter see 'is gelfriend.'

Connie swung a startled look at him. 'He's what?'

Ted turned and met her look. ' 'Is gelfriend,' he replied, with a grin. ' 'Is superintendent up the fire station said somefin' about it. She's the daughter of one er the blokes up there. Sounds like a nice kid.'

'Ted!' protested Connie, horrified. 'Phil's only sixteen years old. He's far too young to be having girlfriends.'

Ted roared with laughter. 'Come off it, Con,' he spluttered. 'I was knockin' round wiv gels up the dance 'all while I was still at school. In any case, when yer fink wot Phil's bin fru over the last year, 'e ain't a boy no more. 'E's all grown up.'

'No,' said Connie, shaking her head. 'I don't want that. I don't want him to grow up before his time.'

'Come over 'ere a minute, Con,' said Ted. 'I wanna talk to yer.'

The moment she went to him, he put his arms around her waist, and kissed her. 'Kids seem ter grow up faster durin' the war. I don't know why. Maybe it's cos they never know from one day ter the next wot's goin' ter 'appen to 'em. Gord knows wot effect it'll 'ave on 'em in years ter come, but in the meantime we can't 'old 'em down too much, espeshally if one of us – or boaf of us – ain't around any more.'

Connie's face crumpled. 'Ted, what are you talking about?' she asked.

'I'm talkin' about when I go back to the unit on Tuesday,' he replied. 'It's more than likely I'm goin' ter be posted overseas. I can't tell yer where, but it could be I won't see you all for a time.'

Connie's expression showed that she knew what he was talking about, but didn't know how to respond.

'Just before I come 'ome last week,' Ted continued, 'we was all given a form ter fill in. It's s'pposed ter be our will.'

Connie gasped, and tried to turn away, but he stopped her.

'Don't be upset, Con,' he said, 'When yer fink about it, it's the right fing ter do. I mean, let's face it, anyfin' can 'appen when you're on active duty, can't it? It's best ter be prepared.'

'And how are *we* supposed to be prepared, Ted?' asked Connie. 'Me, Beth, Phil, the baby?'

'You'll be looked after, Con,' he replied. 'The army say they'll guarantee our wills are made absolutely legal, and that if anyfin' *should* 'appen to us, our relatives'll get all that's due to 'em. I just wanted yer ter know that I've left everyfin' I 'ave in the world ter you, Con, ter you *an'* the kids.'

'I don't want to know what you've left us, Ted,' said Connie tersely. 'I want *you*. I want the man I married, the man I love.' She went back to the cot and looked vacantly down at the baby. 'I'm very grateful to the army for being so considerate,' she continued, 'but have you or they ever thought about what would happen if something happened to *us* first?'

Ted went to her, and turned her round to face him. 'Nuffin's *goin'* ter 'appen to yer, Con,' he said. 'So don't ever let me 'ear yer talk like that!'

'Do you know what those dreams of mine were about, Ted?' she asked. 'Each night I lay awake, I could see Beth, Phil, the baby and I trapped in the wreckage of a building. I could hear us shouting out for help, but there was no one there. Since you came home, I've stopped having the dreams, but I still try to work out what I would do if a situation like that was real.'

'Yer don't have to work out anyfin' er the sort, Con,' said Ted, wrapping his arms comfortingly around her. 'An' yer know why? Becos we all fear the worst, an' the worst 'ardly ever 'appens.'

Connie snuggled her face into his shoulder. 'I hope you're right, Ted,' she replied, half to herself. 'I just hope you're right.'

The double-bill at the newly opened Savoy cinema had certainly attracted a crowd, for the queue for the first of the two Sunday performances had stretched right the way down Loraine Road, and the sweet shop on the corner opposite had done a roaring trade in black liquorice sticks, which seemed to be about the only confectionery that was not rationed.

Inside the cinema, Beth and Thomas had managed to find two one and sixpenny seats in the back row of the dress circle, which was a favourite haunt for courting couples. The building itself, which had surprised everyone by being opened during the first months of the war, was actually quite a plain design, with pastel-coloured walls, and a very conventional stage and screen proscenium, but the seats were comfortable enough, perfect for a slap and tickle in the dark, provided you got in the queue outside early enough before the doors opened. For the first time that day, Beth felt relaxed, mainly because Thomas had calmed down, and put behind him the malicious attack on him by her mate, Mo Mitchell. Despite the great attraction of the two 'B' movies, however, both films turned out to be rather boring, especially the one with Sydney Greenstreet and Peter Lorre, who were menacing everyone around them in the silliest story Beth had ever seen, but at least it gave her the chance to settle down in Thomas's arms, until an irritating usherette with a torch arrived to seat more patrons.

Halfway through the second of the two films, a warning flash suddenly appeared on the bottom of the screen. Beth and Thomas were too preoccupied at the time, and despite the fact that the flash remained for the best part of two minutes, they hadn't looked up in time to see what it had said. But ten minutes later, the same flash was repeated, and this time they were shocked to see who it was directed at: WILL BETH SHANKS GO IMMEDIATELY TO THE MANAGER'S OFFICE. AN IMPORTANT MESSAGE AWAITS YOU THERE.

It took Beth and Thomas no more than a few minutes to leap up out of their seat and rush down the stairs to the entrance door. When they got to the front desk, they were met by Beth's dad, who was waiting there with a large, red-faced man with rogue whiskers growing out of his cheeks. Both men were grim-faced, and the news they brought was devastating.

Chapter 14

Thick black smoke spiralled up into the night sky to be met by a heavy squall of freezing snow, which quickly settled on the rubble of four houses that had, until Sunday afternoon, formed part of a quiet, fairly insignificant little residential street tucked not too far away behind Seven Sisters Corner in Tottenham. But by the time Beth, her father, Phil, Thomas and Uncle Horace's old mate, Terry Barlow, had got there, the scene of utter chaos and devastation was too painful even for the most hardened members of the emergency services, who, with the help of Alsatian tracker dogs, and in the overpowering white glare of huge arc lamps, were struggling to retrieve any victim who might still have been trapped in the debris.

'It was a bloody magnetic mine bomb', said one of the weary firemen who was finishing a long three-hour shift at the top of a ladder, trying to rescue an elderly man who had been trapped on the top floor of the house where he lived. 'Came down in the back garden er number twenty-two. No one could er survived that.'

'Not even if they were inside a Morrison shelter?' asked Beth.

Obeying orders from his superintendent, the man decided to be more cautious in what he was telling them. 'Who yer lookin' for?' he asked.

'Uncle Horace,' replied Beth, whose pained expression told the man exactly what she was feeling.

' 'Orace Ruggles,' said Ted.

'Which number?' asked the man.

'Number eighteen,' said Beth, desperate for even a glimmer of hope.

The man prepared to get on with his work. 'If I was you,' he said, 'I'd go over an' check with the Speshuls. They've got the lists so far. Yer'll find 'em up the end, on the corner.'

'Lists?' asked Beth. '*Wot* lists?'

The man left hurriedly, leaving Phil to answer the question he had heard asked so many times before. 'Casualties, Beth,' he said.

The sombre group made their way along the street in the driving snow, helping each other over the rubble as they went, only stopping to cast a brief horrified look up at the houses that were still standing. Every one of them had received the full blast of the explosion, windows blown completely out of their frames, bricks and debris from chimney stacks scattered all over the pavement only to be quickly covered in a thin layer of white. Incredibly, one of the houses close to the huge crater in the ground, which had the whole of its front wall blown away, revealed a double bed perched precariously on the edge of a first-floor bedroom, the remains of tattered curtains dancing wildly in the ice-cold wind. Every so often Beth would turn to look back over her shoulder with disbelief and incomprehension at what had once been Uncle Horace's house, now reduced to nothing more than burning timbers and a heap of bricks and mortar; this was no more than what was yet to come. Beth's stomach was so wound up with shock that she wanted to cry, but something inside told her that if she was going to cope with what was now looking increasingly predictable, she would have to remain strong.

They eventually found their way to the corner of the street, where, but for the wind whistling eerily around the corner, the general mayhem of a major incident had been replaced by a strange, unnatural silence, where the attention of a crowd of silent onlookers was directed to the covered courtyard of a brewery close by. Ted approached a portly Special Constable, who was holding a clipboard in his hand, and whose tin helmet and cape was now covered in a thin layer of snow. 'Sorry, mate,' said the constable. 'Yer'll 'ave ter get back ter the other side er the road.'

'I'm lookin' fer a relative,' Ted stated, going straight to the point. 'Livin' in one of the 'ouses down Beardsley. Ruggles. 'Orace Ruggles.'

The constable's expression softened. 'Number?'

Once again, Beth answered the question.

The constable checked the list on his clipboard. He looked up. 'Over there, mate,' he said, indicating the courtyard just around the corner.

Ted nodded. 'Fanks,' he replied, about to move off.

'Sure yer want the little lady wiv yer?' asked the constable, looking at Beth.

Ted didn't even have to think about it. He just nodded.

At the tall iron gates of the courtyard, Beth, Phil, Thomas and Terry Barlow waited while Ted talked to another Special Constable. After checking his clipboard, and asking Ted for his identity card, the constable opened the gates. Ted calmly motioned to the others to join him. The scene inside the courtyard was morbid and tragic. Watched over by a silent group of St John Ambulance nurses, female Salvation Army and Women's Voluntary Service workers, two lines of victims had been laid out right the way across the yard, covered only by sheets, blankets, tablecloths, towels, and any item that could afford them their last moments of dignity. Ted went straight across to talk to a middle-aged male official who took him directly to one of the corpses that was covered by a large double blanket. From nearby, the other three watched whilst Ted and the official crouched down alongside the corpse. The official gave Ted a torch, and then held back the blanket just long enough for Ted to identify the face beneath. It took only a moment to do so. Grim-faced, he stood up, spoke a few words to the official, and thanked him. As he returned to Beth, Phil and Terry Barlow, the courtyard was throbbing with the quiet, anguished sobs of the relatives of other victims, who had just carried out the same distressing duty.

'Yes,' was all Ted could bring himself to say, as he reached the others. 'This bloody war!'

In a sudden outpouring of grief, Phil, tears streaming down his face, immediately threw his arms around Beth, and Thomas hugged both of them.

'I want ter be wiv 'im,' said Beth, to her father.

Ted shook his head. 'No, Beff,' he replied solemnly. 'Remember 'im as 'e was yesterday, not as 'e is now.'

'I don't want ter *see* 'im,' Beth insisted softly. 'I just want ter be wiv 'im alone – just fer a minute.'

Ted took a deep breath, and nodded agreement.

Beth gave Phil a final hug, then left the group to wander slowly off on her own to where Uncle Horace was laid out. When she reached him, she just stood over him silently. No words were spoken, but she was thinking a lot, thinking about only yesterday at the vegetable competition, thinking about all the times she had visited him in his beloved garden, and watched him whilst he pulled a cabbage or some Brussels sprouts for her mum to cook. And as she looked down at the lifeless shape beneath the rather ordinary blue woollen blanket, she remembered all those Sunday mornings, those seemingly endless Sunday mornings when she played on his old Joanna. She remembered that glowing look on his face as the two of them sang together, ' 'Til We Meet Again', and she remembered his look of excitement and intense pride as he stepped up on to the stage at the Town Hall to receive that precious little gold cup, the first prize he had ever had in his entire life. She stooped down, and blew him a kiss. 'Goodbye, Unc,' she whispered, her face crumpled up, and tears streaming down her cheeks. 'Take it from me, you're a winner, all right. Oh yes. Yer always 'ave bin, an' yer always will be.'

It was the early hours of the morning before Beth and Phil arrived home. Connie was waiting anxiously for them in the kitchen, and by the look on their faces, knew at once what had happened. 'Oh God!' she gasped. 'It's not true! Tell me it's not true, Beth.'

Beth shook her head, and took off her headscarf and coat which was soaking wet with melting snow. There was nothing she could say. Phil took off his uniform top coat and cap, and threw them over the back of a chair.

'But he had the Morrison shelter,' insisted Connie. 'I thought they were supposed to be so infallible?'

' 'E wasn't in the Morrison,' said Beth, flopping down on to a chair at the kitchen table. 'One er the ARP blokes who knew Uncle 'Orace said they found 'im in the scullery. 'E must've bin 'avin 'is Sunday dinner or somefin'.'

'Oh God – how terrible!' Connie cried. 'What a stupid thing to do!'

Beth looked up at her with a start. 'Uncle 'Orace wasn't stupid, Mum!' she snapped. 'Don't you ever say fings like that about 'im!'

'And don't you talk to me like that, young lady!' retorted Connie. 'I'm your mother – not a dog in the street!' She turned her back on Beth, and talked to Phil. 'Where's your dad, Phil?'

' 'E's stopped be'ind ter talk ter Uncle 'Orace's cousin,' replied Phil, who looked all in. 'They're goin' round gettin' all the papers they need for . . .' He broke down.

Connie went to him, herself fighting back tears. 'It's all right, son,' she said, putting her arms around his shoulders and trying to comfort him. 'It's all right. Come on, now. Why don't you go up to bed, and I'll bring you up a nice hot cup of cocoa.'

Phil recovered himself, sat up and wiped the tears from his cheeks with the back of his hand. He got up and lumbered out of the room.

Connie paused a moment, then looked back at Beth, who was still sitting with her elbows and hands supporting her chin at the table, 'You know, Beth' she said, 'you really shouldn't talk to me like that. I know you're upset, but so am I. I loved your Uncle Horace just as much as you. We *all* did.'

'You might've loved 'im,' replied Beth, 'but yer didn't know 'im. Not like me. We used ter talk an' laugh an' sing tergevver. 'E used ter listen ter me. Whenever I 'ad a problem, 'e always used ter listen ter me, ter tell me wot ter do.'

'I'm sorry to hear that, Beth,' replied Connie tersely. 'I'm sorry you've never been able to turn to *me* for that kind of advice.' Dabbing her eyes with the back of her hand, she went off to the stove to collect the kettle.

'No, Mum!' called Beth. 'That's *not* wot I mean.' Realising she'd hurt her mother, Beth got up from the table and went to her. 'Don't yer understand? There are some fings I just *can't* talk to yer about.'

'Oh really?' asked Connie, filling the kettle with water at the sink. 'What sort of things? Why you have an American mother who doesn't understand, doesn't *really* understand how things are done in North London?'

'Stop it, Mum!' snapped Beth. 'Don't talk like that!'

Connie swung round to her. 'Do you love me, Beth?' she asked point-blank.

'Er course I do! I've always loved yer. I love yer more than anyone in the whole wide world.'

'More than your dad?'

The stark reality of the question cut straight into Beth and, for one brief moment, she was completely at a rare loss for words. 'I love yer boaf the same,' she replied painfully.

'Then you've got a funny way of showing it,' replied Connie, lighting the gas beneath the kettle.

Beth was stung by this remark. She hesitated a moment, then went behind her mum, slid her hands around her waist, and rested her head gently against Connie's back. 'Why do people always 'ave ter quarrel whenever there's a deff in the family?' she asked softly.

Connie waited a moment before turning around to answer Beth's question. 'I guess,' she replied softly in her slow Texan drawl, 'it's because it's one of the only times when people have the courage to say what they really think of each other.'

Jessie Hawks was worried. In all the time she'd been coming down the warehouse shelter, not once had she been there without Connie and Beth Shanks being there too. But it was nearly nine o'clock in the evening, and still there was no sign of them. Fortunately, Moaning Minnie hadn't announced her presence so far, so Jessie presumed that the Shanks family were taking the opportunity to make the most of Ted Shanks's last couple of days home on leave. What she really missed, of course, was young Beth giving them all a sing-song on the old Joanna, something that she had come to look forward to as she made her way in the dark each evening down a freezing cold Hornsey Road. And it was now *very* cold outside, with the endless snow showers drifting in and out of the shop doorways, making it extremely difficult underfoot. The Lieberman brothers were feeling the cold too, playing a game of Snakes and Ladders with each other, wrapped up from head to foot in thick woollen blankets. 'Why we have to spend every night of our lives in a mortuary is beyond me,' grumbled Abe.

'Why not?' retorted his brother Bernie. 'If we're going to catch our death of cold, we might just as well hang around. It'll save a lot of time and money.'

'Please Mr Abe an' Mr Bernie!' scolded Eileen Perkins, who was watching her retarded child Rita crayon some pictures in a sketch-book. 'It's not very nice bein' so morbid when we 'ave no alternative but ter come down 'ere every night!'

The Lieberman brothers ignored her and carried on with their game.

Bill Winkler, on the other hand, was resigned to the situation. 'Wot diff'rence do it make?' he asked, puffing out clouds of smoke from his pipe. 'We all 'ave ter go sooner or later.'

'Well I'd sooner go later, if it's all the same ter you, Bill,' complained his wife Lil, who was still knitting the longest cardigan in history.

'Well,' persisted Bill, 'I still say that if me time's up, I don't mind when I go – as long as I can 'ave a good pint first! Wot say you, Jack?'

Jack Cutter, who had kept himself very much to himself after having shamed himself by getting blotto the night before, agreed. 'Right,' he mumbled.

'Cheerful bleedin' lot!' snapped Jessie, who was flicking through an out-of-date *Picturegoer* magazine, which was an unusual thing for someone like her to do considering she hadn't been to a picture house since talkies came in. 'Can't yer get nuffink on that wireless er yours, Lil? I wouldn't mind 'earin' a bit er Deanna Durbin.'

'Deanna Durbin!' called Abe Lieberman. 'She's nothing compared to Sophie Tucker!' He started to sing, 'My Yiddisher Moma'.

'Sorry, Jess,' called Lil Winkler above Abe's terrible singing. 'Can't get much reception on me wireless down 'ere. Too much interference. In any case, the battery's run out.'

'So wot's 'appened to our pianist, then?' grumbled Jessie, who threw down the magazine she had no interest in. 'The Shankses ain't ever bin as late as this.'

'There's a reason.' Jack Cutter's voice from his bunk in the corner was barely audible.

'Wot's that yer said, Mr Cutter?' asked Eileen.

'I said there's a reason they ain't 'ere,' repeated Jack. 'They've 'ad a deff in the family.'

Everyone stopped what they were doing and looked up.

'A deff in the family?' asked Lil. '*Who?*'

' 'Orace Ruggles,' said Jack. ' 'E wasn't really a member of the family, but 'e was very close. They'd known 'im fer years. Only yesterday they went up ter Walfamstow ter see 'im take first prize in a vegetable competition.' He shook his head slowly. 'Terrible tragedy. Ted told me it was practically a direct 'it on the poor bloke's 'ouse up at Tottenham. Apparently, 'e was a lovely man.' He sighed. 'Luckily, his missus passed away years ago.'

The atmosphere in the shelter changed immediately. Although in reality no one actually knew Uncle Horace, they all suddenly felt as though they did. A respectful silence was broken only by the methodical, slow dripping of water on to the floor from condensation running down the wall. Somehow, nobody wanted to speak, and for the next few minutes, they all withdrew into their own private worlds.

'Gord rest 'is soul,' said Jessie reverently, breaking the silence.

A murmur of agreement went up from everyone.

As Jessie spoke, Connie, Ted, carrying the baby in his arms, Beth and Phil came down from the door at the top of the steps. 'Good evening, everyone,' called Connie quietly.

Following a muted greeting from everyone, Jessie immediately got up to meet them, as did most of the others. Jessie waited a moment until the family had got themselves settled. 'Sorry ter 'ear your sad news, all,' she said.

Connie smiled appreciatively. 'Thank you, Mrs Hawks,' she replied.

'If there's anyfin' we can do, dear,' said Lil, coming across to them. 'Wot about a nice cup of tea?'

This time Ted smiled appreciatively. 'Fanks a lot, gel,' he replied, carefully putting the baby down into the cot alongside Connie's bunk. 'We've bin at the Rosie Lee all day!'

Jessie nodded to Lil to leave the family alone for a few minutes, which she did. The others followed suit.

Beth took off her coat and scarf, then helped her mother to do the same. Phil took off his coat and cap, then climbed up on to an upper bunk and stretched out there.

The family took their time to settle down and get themselves organised for the night, so it was some time before Jessie spoke again. 'Still snowin' out there, is it?' she asked.

Beth answered. 'Not so much,' she replied. 'Looks like it's freezing. Yer'd better be careful in the mornin'. It's not easy ter get around. Still, at least it's quiet up there.' She went across to the paraffin stove to warm her hands. Whilst she was doing so, both Lieberman brothers came to her, each carrying something in their hand.

'Have a wine gum,' said Abe, holding out a paper bag bulging with wine gums. 'Have more than one.'

'And take a Turkish delight,' added his brother Bernie, holding out a round tin.

'Just don't ask us where we got them,' said Abe.

'We might end up in *das Gefannis*,' added Bernie.

Beth looked puzzled.

'The gaol!' whispered Abe.

Despite the way she felt, Beth had to smile, so she took a wine gum from Abe, and a square of Turkish delight from Bernie.

The brothers then offered the same to Connie, Ted and Phil, before returning to their bunks.

As she munched on her goodies, Beth was amazed by the sympathy and sheer friendliness of 'the gang', as she now thought of them. It seemed so incredible how they adapted themselves to the Shanks's mood of grief and sadness, making sure that they were in no way intrusive.

A few minutes later, Moaning Minnie wailed out across the streets above.

'Ha!' grunted Jessie, glaring up towards the ceiling. 'I knew *that* was comin'! Don't believe in givin' us a night off, do yer, mate!'

The Lieberman brothers immediately grabbed their tin helmets and put them on, whilst Jack Cutter got off his bunk and lit a fag.

'Don't look like we're goin' ter get much sleep ternight,' said Lil Winkler, as they heard the oncoming drone of aircraft, followed by the incessant explosions of anti-aircraft shells.

'Mum . . .' groaned Eileen Perkins's girl, Rita, who was frightened, and quickly snuggling up to her mum.

'It's all right, darlin',' said Eileen, trying to reassure the child. 'It'll be all right.'

In her desperation to try and lighten the atmosphere, Lil Winkler turned on her wireless set. But it was utterly useless to expect anything to come out of it except a loud, garbled sound. 'No Deanna Durbin ternight, Jess,' said Lil. ' 'Fraid yer'll 'ave ter make do wiv Bill's grumblin'.'

'Beth,' said Connie, calling to her. 'Why don't you play something for everyone?'

Beth, who was still warming her hands at the paraffin stove, turned a look of total astonishment at her mum.

'Go ahead,' persisted Connie. 'It'll cheer everyone up.'

Beth shook her head violently.

'It's all right, Mrs S,' said Jessie. 'We quite understand. It's not the right moment, is it?'

'Why not?' asked Connie, addressing them all. 'It looks as though we've got another ghastly night ahead of us, so why shouldn't we make the best of it?' She turned to Ted, who was perched on the edge of her bunk. 'Don't you agree, Ted?'

Ted looked up at her, and gave her an admiring smile. 'Absolutely,' he replied, looking across to Beth.

Beth again shook her head, and went back to her bunk. But her mum intercepted her on the way. 'It's what Uncle Horace would have wanted, Beth,' she said softly. 'Remember how he always loved to hear you play. He once told me that when you sat at that keyboard, he felt as though he hadn't a trouble in the world. Play for *him*, Beth. Play for him *and* for everyone here. It's the right thing to do – believe me.'

Beth thought about what her mum had just said to her. But at that precise moment, she found it hard to equate what had happened to Uncle Horace less than twenty-four hours before with the need to raise the spirits of the people who were all huddled together down in that shelter. Was life really that like that, she asked herself? Was it right that she should get people to sing when Uncle Horace was lying in some awful hospital mortuary? But then she remembered how happy he was when she played to *him*, and how he had often told her that 'life's fer the livin, Beth, not the dead'. After a moment's contemplation, she slowly walked across to the piano.

Everyone watched her in awed silence as she sat down on the piano stool, opened the keyboard cover, and just sat there, staring aimlessly at the black and white notes that were waiting for her. But when she put her fingers on to the keyboard, all the life seemed to have seeped out of them. Then she felt someone's hands gently resting on her shoulders. 'Come on, darling,' whispered her mother. 'You can do it.'

Beth waited a moment, then in a sudden moment of impulse, started to play Uncle Horace's favourite song, ' 'Til We Meet Again'.

Everyone immediately joined in, and the sound they made was warm and nostalgic. Whilst Beth played, Connie's eyes welled up with tears before she left her, and returned to her bunk.

Ted put his arm around Connie's waist, then leaned close to whisper something into her ear. Connie looked up at him with a start, then nodded some kind of agreement.

Ted got up, went across to Beth, gave her a kiss on the top of her head, then made his way up the steps.

Beth watched him go. From the quiet way he had gone up the steps and left, she had a good idea what he was doing, and where he was going, but couldn't believe he was actually doing it. Once he'd disappeared through the door at the top of the stairs, she was so overwrought that she changed the mood sharply, and against the background of a barrage of ack-ack fire from the streets above, launched into a frenzied medley of every lively tune she could remember.

Chapter 15

It was a veritable winter wonderland, a rich blue sky, brilliant sunshine and a blanket of pure white snow that dazzled the eyes. As most of the traffic had come to a halt, Hornsey Rise was a perfect place to start a toboggan ride down the hill towards Seven Sisters Road, and even the back streets and alleys were gleaming in the rare early morning paradise. However, not everyone appreciated the beauty of it all.

'It's bleedin' murder fer me chilblains!' grumbled Jessie Hawks, as Jack Cutter helped her home along Hornsey Road, her galoshes covered in almost four inches of snow. 'Me feet're so cold, I shall 'ave ter put them in the oven ter warm up.'

'Just watch where yer walk, Jess,' said Jack. 'There was a lot er shrapnel come down last night. The kids won't be able ter find it under all this snow.'

'Shrapnel don't seem ter worry *some* people!' said Jessie, huffing and puffing as she picked her way precariously along the pavement, holding on for grim death to Jack's arm. 'Ted Shanks didn't get back 'til well after midnight. Gawd knows wot 'e was up to out 'ere.'

'Probably come out ter get some fresh air,' said Jack. ' 'E told me the uvver day 'e din't know 'ow we could all coop ourselves up down in that shelter every night. 'E said 'e'd sooner take '*is* chances in the trenches.'

Jessie sighed. 'That poor family,' she said. 'This is Ted's last day at 'ome. I can just imagine 'ow they feel. 'Speshully young Beff. She idolises 'er dad.'

★

On the way back home from the shelter, Beth hardly spoke to her dad, preferring to follow on behind him and her mum with her brother Phil. After a restless night tossing and turning in her bunk, she had come to the reluctant conclusion that unless he offered some kind of explanation about the woman he had been meeting, there was very little she could say to him. It wasn't easy for her, and she knew it; first thing in the morning her dad would be going back to his unit, and she had no idea when she would see him again. The thing that still troubled her, however, was how much, if anything, her mum knew about the woman her dad had been seeing. Should she tell her, Beth asked herself over and over again? It was not a decision she could take lightly, for this was a matter that concerned a marriage between two people who had been together for a very long time. She also felt that she just couldn't discuss what was going on with Phil, for he was too overwrought by not only having his fire station messenger's job taken away from him, but also the prospect of being made to leave London to live with their grandparents.

Some time later, Beth knew that her mum and dad were having some kind of intense conversation in their bedroom, because she could hear them through the wall of her own bedroom trying to restrain the sound of their voices. She looked around and saw all the things she had got out to take with her to Hertfordshire at the weekend, and it made her feel so miserable, all she wanted to do was to get out of the house. Although there was a perfectly good bathroom on the first-floor landing, she decided to make a rare visit to the public baths at the bottom end of Hornsey Road, where she could at least have a bit of time to herself. Quickly getting dressed again, she collected her towel and soap, and went downstairs, calling as she went, 'Just going down the road, Mum! Won't be long!'

Before either Connie or Ted could come out of their bedroom, Beth had gone.

It was quite a trudge down Hornsey Road, mainly because so many people were out trying to clear the pavements, which wasn't an easy task, for the overnight snowfall was starting a temporary thaw beneath the warmth of a friendly winter sun. Even as Beth approached the women's entrance of the public baths, she was beginning to doubt the wisdom of taking her clothes off in what would probably be an unheated, freezing-cold cubicle, but once she had stepped into the six inches of fairly warm bath water which had been drawn up for her by an attendant, the circulation in her body quickly acclimatised. She lay back in the bath, closed her eyes, and for a few glorious minutes allowed the warm water to help her soothe away the traumatic memories of the past twenty-four hours. Whilst she was lying there, however, she began to hear women's voices coming from the two adjoining cubicles, but when she tried to blot them out from her mind, she suddenly heard a voice that sounded familiar.

'You're right, Elsie,' said the familiar voice, which was soft and gentle. 'Yer only ever get one chance in this life. I tell yer, if I could live my time all over again, fings'd be diff'rent.'

Beth sat up with a jolt, desperate to listen in to the conversation.

'Me too,' replied the other, older woman's voice. 'Fer a start, I'd find meself an 'usband who 'ad enuff money ter keep me in the style to which I ain't accustomed. Anyfin' ter stop me 'avin ter do the ironin'!'

Both women laughed, and so did the other women bathers who could hear them from their own cubicles.

'Oh it ain't money I care about,' said the familiar voice. 'I wouldn't care 'ow skint 'e was, as long as 'e loved me. That's bin my trouble. I loved the wrong man, an' missed out on the one I really wanted.' There was a wistful sound in her voice. 'Mind you, I didn't really lose him. 'E just found someone better than me, that's all.'

'Come off it, gel!' croaked the older woman. 'They don't come much better than you, that's fer sure!'

By the rustling sound coming from next door, Beth was aware that the woman whose voice she recognised, had finished her bath, towelled, and was getting dressed.

'Well – yer know wot they say, Else,' said the familiar voice. 'Live fer terday. Yer never know wot's just round the corner.'

Both Elsie and all the other woman bathers agreed.

'See yer, then!' called the familiar voice.

'Right yer are, Vera!' returned the older woman. 'Mind 'ow yer go!'

At the mention of the familiar voice's name, Beth leapt out of the bath just in time to hear the door of the next cubicle open and close, but no matter how hard she tried, she couldn't get towelled and dressed in time to see the woman making her way out to the main entrance.

Leaving the smell of Lifebuoy soap and bath salts behind, Beth rushed out into Hornsey Road, hoping to catch a glimpse of Vera, the woman her dad had been meeting since he came home on leave. Unfortunately, there was no sign of her, for there were now too many people around, shovelling up snow from the pavements, trying to clear a path for the traffic to get on the move again, and generally making an effort to go about their business.

With sweat pouring down her neck after not taking enough time to cool down after her bath, Beth looked from left to right, up the hill along Hornsey Road, and down towards Seven Sisters Road, but the woman had clearly merged into the crowds and disappeared from sight. Distraught that her one chance to confront the woman had eluded her, she started to trudge off home in the mucky slush, her mind reeling from what she had heard coming from that next door cubicle: '*I loved the wrong man, an' missed out on the one I really wanted.*' What did she mean, Beth asked herself? What was Vera whatever-her-name trying to say? Was the one she really wanted Beth's own dad?

She walked on, oblivious to the fact that her mind was on fire and she was in danger any minute of bumping into a passer-by. '*Mind you, I didn't really lose 'im. 'E just found someone better than me, that's all.*' The words were beginning to haunt Beth. How was she going to live with them when she tried to sleep at night? She pondered all this, but as she walked on, her ankle-length galoshes splashed with dirty slush, she suddenly caught sight of a woman waiting at the bus stop near the corner of Andover Road. It was her – the woman! Without any regard to the hazard of rushing along in the snow, she slid her way along as fast as she could. There was now only one thought in her mind: who *was* this woman? If her dad had no intention of telling her, then she would find out for herself. But to her dismay, a number 14 bus finally managed to crawl its way towards the bus stop, where the woman joined others in the queue and got on.

'Wait!' yelled Beth at the top of her voice. But as she did so, she slipped on the thick muddy slush, and fell flat on her face. Several people immediately rushed to help her, but the more they tried, the more difficult it became for her to get to her feet.

The bus moved off, but despite crawling at a snail's pace on the slippery road surface, it was still travelling too fast and dangerous for Beth to get to her feet again and catch up with it.

'Wait!' she yelled as loud as she could.

The bus passed her. Inside, the mysterious Vera took her seat on the lower deck, unaware of the drama being played out on the pavement behind her.

Joe Sullivan slept late. He'd done six nightshifts on the trot at the hospital, and the strain of getting severely injured air-raid casualties on to stretcher trollys and wheeling them back and forth to the operating theatre was just beginning to take its toll. But although he needed his sleep, there was one appointment he knew he couldn't miss, and so he set his alarm clock to get him up and out of bed at midday. Once he had shaved, washed, and changed into some clean clothes, he was soon out of the house and on his way to the Flying Scot, his local pub just behind King's Cross Station. The overnight squalls of snow were rapidly turning to slush, and he was glad he had a pair of Wellington boots for the messy trek.

Owing to the weather, there were few of the lunchtime regulars in the saloon bar of the pub, which suited Joe well, for what he had to say to the man he had joined at a quiet table in the corner was not something to be overheard.

'What're yer talkin' about?' asked the man in the brown trilby hat and brown overcoat, whom Joe had last talked to in the dark outside the old Holloway Empire picture house. 'I've told yer before, Sullivan, quittin' fer you is not an option.'

'My son could've been killed the other night,' snapped Joe in his forceful Irish burr which differed so markedly from the other man's Northern Irish accent. 'But for the grace of God he could've been inside that factory when your apes from Berlin bombed the place.'

'Ah – the grace of God, is it?' replied the man, whose build was half that of Joe's, and who seemed to have a perpetual smirk on his parched yellow face. 'If I was you, I wouldn't give God the credit for your son's well-bein' the other night. We would hardly want ter cut off an important line of information like that, now would we? But I'm sorry yer boy lost his best friend.'

'What the hell are you sayin'?' asked Joe, eyes glaring.

The man with the trilby hat sipped a glass of Guinness, but kept a beady eye on Joe as he did so. 'Let's just say that the timing was planned,' he said. 'You could call it a little reminder, a reminder of what you owe the powers that be.'

'Now look here, *you*!' growled Joe softly, leaning across the table at the man. 'I gave 'em all I knew. I sent 'em that list of all the weapons I could find out about, about everything they were making in that factory that I could get out of Thomas without him knowing what I was up to. I could do no more. I don't *want* to do anything more.' He leaned even closer to the man. 'Look,' he said, voice lowered as much as he could. 'Your people got what they wanted. They've stopped production at the factory. The whole thing's bein' moved up north somewhere.'

'Ah!' replied the man, with another of those smirks. 'If only that were true.'

Joe's expression hardened. 'Wot're you talkin' about?' he asked.

Now it was the man's turn to lean forward. 'It's true they've moved some of the stuff out,' he replied. 'But that was a ruse, Joe, nothin' but a ruse. They goin' ter open up again, and when they do, they're goin' ter be makin' a new toy fer Churchill's brass hats.'

'I don't believe you!' retorted Joe angrily.

'Oh it's true,' insisted the man. 'Any minute now, the girls an' boys'll be gettin' the call ter get back ter work. If yer don't believe me, just ask Thomas.' He grinned. 'It's called *misinformation*, Joe – a little game of hide and seek thought up by those clever security people up there. A game to confuse us. But with your help, Joe, we're not goin' ter be confused – are we?'

Joe slowly sat back in his chair. His expression was quite numb.

The man in the trilby hat downed the rest of his drink, then got up. But before he went, he leaned down to Joe, and with lowered voice said: 'Our mutual friends will be in contact with you tonight, Joe. They have one or two things they want to discuss with you. If I was you, I'd make sure you listen ter what they have ter say.' He turned to go, but stopped. 'Oh, and by the way,' he repeated softly, chillingly. 'Quittin' isn't an option for you.' With one last smirk, he quietly left the bar.

Joe sat where he was for several minutes, trying hard to take in everything he had heard in the last few minutes. In front of him was a glass of bitter that he had not even touched.

Beth spent the afternoon tidying up the personal things in her room that she would be taking to Hertfordshire at the weekend; she did it with no enthusiasm at all, especially as her dad was the one who had arranged the whole thing. After what she had overheard in the public baths, she was desperate to know whether he would say anything to her about the woman before he rejoined his unit the following day. All afternoon she had heard the distant rumble of her mum and dad's voices talking in the front parlour downstairs, and she wondered how much, if anything, her dad would be revealing about the woman he had been meeting. Those anxieties came to a head when she heard her mum calling up the stairs.

'Beth! Phil! Come on down, you two. Dad wants to talk to you.'

Phil came out of his bedroom upstairs at the same time as Beth, and they met briefly on the first-floor landing. 'Wot's this all about?' he asked, his voice lowered.

Beth shrugged. As she had never discussed her dad's meetings with the woman with him, she hoped that what her dad had to say would prevent her from having to do so.

'D'you fink there's anyfing we can do about goin' ter Gran an' Grandad's?' he asked, as they went down the stairs. 'It's drivin' me mad just finkin' about it.'

'I doubt we can do anyfin', Phil,' she replied. 'Dad's set 'is 'eart on it.'

'Yeah,' replied Phil ominously. 'Well *I* 'aven't!'

Ted and Connie were waiting for them in the front parlour. Thanks to Ted's efforts at the coal yard, the room was beautifully warm, with the red glow of an already established coke fire in the grate taking the damp out of the moist, freezing cold air.

'Come on, mates,' said Ted, who was wearing a civvy shirt and trousers for the last time before he left the following day. 'Yer mum an' I want us all ter be tergevver. We can't talk much when we go down the shelter ternight.'

Connie, nursing the baby in her arms and standing alongside him in front of the fire, beamed affectionately.

'This week 'as gone so fast,' sighed Ted, 'I can't believe it was only last Tuesday I come 'ome.' He shot a look across at Beth, who was sitting straight-backed at the parlour table. 'We seem to 'ave spent most of our time in that ruddy shelter!'

Phil, who had flopped into an armchair, was not amused when his dad grinned at him.

'Anyway,' continued Ted, 'I just wanted yer ter know that when I go off termorrer, I'll be finkin' of yer. I'll be finkin' of yer an awful lot.' Beth's cold stare was making him feel uncomfortable. 'I don't know 'ow long I'll be gone,' he stuttered, 'but while I'm away, I want you two ter take care of yer mum and young Simon 'ere. In fact, I want yer all ter take care of each uvver. That's why I want yer out er this place. I can't bear the fawt of my family bein' in danger. Wot 'appened ter Uncle 'Orace', he said, falteringly, ' 'as only convinced me more than ever that gettin' you all safe an' sound is my top priority. War ain't fer people back 'ome, it's fer soldiers. At least *we* can see who we're fightin', we can give 'em just as good as *they* give – an' more!' He paused. 'The fact is, Beff, yer've no idea 'ow much I love yer. I don't want any 'arm comin' to yer. So just look after yerselves – OK?'

'Can I ask a question please, Dad?'

Phil's reply took both Ted and Connie by surprise. 'Er course, son,' said Ted.

'When we go out ter Gran an' Grandad's,' continued Phil, 'wot are we expected ter do wiv ourselves all day?'

Expecting something worse, Ted breathed a sigh of relief. 'I knew yer'd ask that, son,' he replied. 'So I'll tell yer. Yer grandad's spoken to an ol' mate of 'is in a bottle factory up at Welwyn Garden City. 'E says 'e can get yer a good job as an apprentice up there. It's a good way ter learn the trade.'

'Learn the trade?' gasped Phil incomprehensibly. 'In a *bottle* factory?'

'Don't look a gift 'orse in the mouf, son,' replied Ted. 'There are fousands er boys your age that'd jump at the chance. You'll make a stack er pals up there.'

'An wot 'appens when I get called up?' Phil reminded him.

'Don't be a Nellie, son!' scolded his dad. 'That's not for anuvver eighteen munffs at least. It'll all be over by then.'

Phil grunted and tried, without success, to catch his mum's eye, but she carefully continued to look down at the baby in her arms.

Ted turned his attention to Beth, but he was more hesitant with her. 'As fer you, Beff,' he said, less than confidently, '*you've* struck lucky, gel.'

Beth looked up, straight at him.

'Grandad reckons 'e can get yer a job in De 'Avillands' aircraft factory, right by the airfield.'

Beth remained silent and unresponsive.

'Isn't it marvellous, darling?' said Connie lyrically. 'It's only ten minutes from the house. You won't have to catch a bus in the freezing cold each day.'

'Loads er gels workin' over there, Beff,' enthused Ted. 'It's a dead cinch fer someone like you. After the type er work yer've bin doin' up Tally 'O, they'll grab yer wiv open arms.' For some extraordinary reason, he lowered his voice. 'Yer grandad says they're workin' on some secret new plane over there.'

'I know,' said Beth, stony-faced.

Ted pulled a puzzled expression. 'Yer know?' he asked.

'It flew over Thomas an' me when we went fer a walk in the fields near Gran and Grandad's. I wouldn't've fawt it was very secret by now.'

Ted felt as though the wind had been blown out of his sails. 'Oh – well,' he said with a shrug. 'So yer can see wot a good place it is ter work.'

'The factory up at Tally 'O was a good place ter work,' replied Beth. 'All me mates were up there.'

'The factory's closed now, Beth,' said Connie, 'so this is a good opportunity to make a fresh start.'

'Once somefin's over, Beff,' said Ted, 'yer can't bring it back.'

'I s'ppose not, Dad,' replied Beth pointedly. She caught his eye briefly before he turned away. In that brief flash of a moment, she remembered him as he was, as he used to be, the dad who used to take Phil and herself to the pictures when they were young, who used to go out into the streets to fight their battles if other kids' parents had a go at them, the dad who had a mania for doing jobs around the house that never got finished, like the time when he was decorating the room they were in now, and he accidentally stepped into a tin of white paint, which sent all the family into fits of laughter. So what was so different about him now, Beth asked herself? She looked up at the mantelpiece and saw all the framed family snapshots there, recalling so many of those happy times on day trips to the sea down at Southend, and feeding the pigeons in Trafalgar Square, and playing football with Phil in Finsbury Park. As she watched him fumbling for one of his bits of twisted newspaper that he used to light his fag, she remembered him as the dad who had always meant the world to her, so why should it all be so different now? If only he would tell her, if only he would tell her that the woman she'd seen him with didn't mean anything to him any more, that he was still the dad she knew, and a loving, faithful husband.

'So there it is, mates,' Ted said, lighting his dog-end from the grate with one of the bits of twisted newspaper. 'Yer've got nuffin' ter worry about. When yer mum an' I saw yer gran and grandad yesterday mornin', they said they'll 'ave everyfin' ready fer you all ter move in at the weekend. Yer've no idea 'ow they're lookin' forward to it.' He looked at Phil, who was slumped in the armchair, thoroughly miserable. 'Cheer up, mate!' he said brightly. 'Yer ain't walkin' the plank!'

Phil didn't agree with him. Going to live with his gran and grandad *was* like walking a plank, and the way he felt now, that was the option he preferred. But his dad was going away first thing in the morning, and there was no knowing if or when he would ever see him again. For that reason alone, he had a duty to show that he still loved the dad that had always been so good to him. Even so, all he could muster in reply was a forced smile.

'Of course,' continued Ted, 'yer've all got a rough day ahead of yer on Wednesday. 'I know 'ow much Uncle 'Orace meant to yer. I know 'ow much 'e meant ter me. It don't seem possible that this time on Saturday afternoon we was all up there in Walfamstow watchin 'im take that prize.' He took a deep puff of his fag, and looked up at one of the framed snapshots of Uncle Horace and his wife Maudie paddling in the sea at their favourite resort, Frinton. 'But', he continued, we've got ter be realistic. Uncle 'Orace wouldn't've wanted us ter sit around mopin' about 'im, so once they've laid 'im ter rest, yer've all got ter get on wiv yer lives. That don't mean we 'ave ter ferget 'im . . .'

'Yer don't ever ferget someone like Uncle 'Orace,' said Beth, who was finding it painful to keep her grief under control. ' 'E was such a part of us all.'

When she heard what Beth said, Connie's face crumpled up with emotion.

'Anyway,' said Ted, 'I just wanted yer ter know that when I leave termorrer, I'll be finkin' about yer all. Not only on Wednesday at the funeral, but *every* day. I'll do me best ter write to yer, of course, but, well, wiv the way fings are, nuffin's goin' ter be a dead cert, is it?' He looked across at Beth, whose eyes were lowered. 'So take care of yerselves, mates,' he said, trying hard to swallow a large lump in his throat. He quickly turned to look at the baby in Connie's arms. 'You too, mate! If yer only looked a bit like me, I'd take yer along ter scare off Jerry!' He looked around at the others, who had all been listening sombrely. 'Come on, you lot! Let's 'ave yer!' He opened his arms wide, inviting them all to join him.

Connie and the baby were first, then Phil, and finally Beth. He hugged them all together at once, his eyes welling up with tears. Beth could feel his breath on her forehead, and for one brief moment it recalled happier days. Unfortunately, however, it didn't give her any hope that, before he left tomorrow morning, he would speak those few golden words that she wanted so much to hear.

Joe Sullivan had a lot of thinking to do. By the time he got back home from the pub that afternoon, he was so full of rage he just wanted to smash the place up and get the hell out as soon as possible.

But before he could do anything like that, he had a lot of things to consider, decisions to make, important decisions that could affect not only his life, but that of his boy, Thomas. The first thing he did when he got through the front door was to go straight into the back parlour and pour himself a brandy, several bottles of which he had received as a bonus for services rendered from 'the people at the top'. The only problem was that he had never actually seen these so-called '*people*', and he had always made it a rule never to take gifts from strangers. So why had he done it, he asked himself? Why had he allowed his own personal feelings of hatred for one particular type of imperialist to be used to help the equally obnoxious political aspirations of another kind of tyrant? It was a thought that did not cross his mind when he was first approached by 'trilby hat' and his pals, acting on behalf of 'the people at the top'. And for what, he asked himself? What had he been offered that would help to change the map of Ireland and avenge the intervention of the British Government's hated Black and Tan police force during the 1920 rebellion? Did he really believe that once the Germans had invaded the British Isles, they would keep their promise to hand back Ireland to the Irish? Could he *really* trust 'trilby hat' and his masters, the 'people at the top', or were they ruthless enough to eliminate anyone who prevented them from spreading their cause from one part of the world to another? Yes, they were ruthless, he decided. By bombing that munitions factory, they had shown that they were ruthless enough to nearly kill his own son, his own kith and kin, despite their hollow assurances that they had timed the bombing for a night when Thomas would not be there. And then he got to thinking: since the start of the Blitz, how many good, innocent Irish people had lost their lives during the bombing of London and all the other towns and cities throughout Britain? Didn't he hear only the other day that twenty people in one Irish family had been wiped out by a bomb during the German aerial onslaught on Coventry? He sat at the parlour table, downed two glasses of good French brandy, then slumped forward, and with his head and arms resting on the table, he fell asleep.

When he opened his eyes, it was pitch dark. His back creaking like a ninety-year-old's, he slowly eased himself up from the chair, stumbled his way out into the scullery, and drew the blackout curtains. Back in the parlour he switched on the light and looked at his pocketwatch. Ten minutes to six. He shook his fuzzy head. Something was supposed to happen at six o'clock, but for the moment, he just couldn't remember what. And then it came to him. 'Jesus!' he cried, rushing for the door. He made straight for his topcoat, which was hanging on a hook in the passage, dug deep into the coat pocket, took out a torch, and turned it on. He quickly opened the cellar door alongside the coat hooks, and went down.

Turning on the light switch, which was situated at the top of the stairs, he hurried down, where a low-voltage electric lightbulb attached to a wire hanging out of a bare brick wall threw sinister shadows around the basement area which, until the arrival of the wartime shortages, had once had a hundredweight of coal delivered each week through a covered hole in the pavement on the street above. Seven minutes to six. He had to move fast, so he went straight to an old oven stove that was almost totally concealed against the wall in a dark recess, behind some wooden fruit crates and a step ladder. Quickly moving everything out of the way, he opened the stove door, and took out a small, battered leather suitcase, which he placed on a wooden workbench nearby. From out of the suitcase he lifted a complicated-looking contraption which was some kind of a transmitter. Cursing and blinding to himself, unable to assemble the thing as easily as he had done on so many other nights, he wrestled to attach the aerial, which seemed not to want to co-operate. However, with just one minute to spare, he had the power turned on, and was ready to receive a signal. Sitting down at the bench, he put on the earphones, and waited. Those sixty seconds turned out to be the most important of his life, for just as the first garbled sounds of a foreign man's voice echoed at low volume through the transmitter speaker, he had made a decision, a decision that was going to put both his own life and Thomas's at risk. No more passing on tit-bits of information from unwitting military patients at the hospital, no more pinning down the sites of military installations throughout the London area. His mind was made up. The garbled voice with a foreign accent was growing impatient.

'Dada! Are yer there, Dada?'

Joe nearly had a heart attack. That was Thomas calling to him from upstairs, and he wasn't due home until late that night. Furthermore, he hadn't locked the cellar door when he came down. What the hell! 'Coming, son!' he yelled, as he made a mad scramble to disassemble the transmitter. 'Be right with yer!' He only just managed to replace everything in time, for Thomas suddenly appeared at the top of the stairs.

'Dada!' called Thomas. 'What are you doin' down here?'

'Just tryin' ter find my old tool box,' returned Joe, as he climbed the stairs. 'Why? What's all the hassle?'

'Great news, Dada!' replied Thomas, as Joe reached him. 'I've just heard. We're goin' back.'

'Goin' back?' asked Joe. 'Where to?'

'To work, Dada!' gasped Thomas excitedly. 'They're reopening the factory and want us all ter go back ter work as soon as possible. Isn't it wonderful news, Dada? Isn't it wonderful?'

Joe was too shocked to respond. All his mind could think about was the man in the trilby hat, and his 'people at the top'.

Chapter 16

Ted Shanks had his own reasons for not wanting any of his family to go all the way to Waterloo Station to see him off. As far as he was concerned, he had already taken his leave of them the afternoon before, but to get on a train with hundreds of other tommies returning to their unit, all watching their loved ones slowly disappear into the distance, was more than he could take. However, it was a still a painful experience for him as he parted from them on the doorstep of their home in Moray Road. Saying goodbye to each one of them was an ordeal; he feared for their safety during the air raids, and told Connie to write to him the moment they had moved out to Hertfordshire. It troubled him to see Phil looking so upset; he and his son had always had such a good relationship, and it distressed Ted that he would not be around to see the boy in some of the formative years of his life. Taking his leave of Beth, however, was the most difficult. They had always been such mates, but ever since the night when she saw him with Vera, it was as if a wall had been built between them. He knew what she wanted from him, and it grieved him that he couldn't give it to her before he left. But one day, he hoped she would understand, and not think any the worse of him.

After Ted had gone, the house seemed bleak and empty. Later that morning, Connie gave her final piano lesson to young Freddie Cooper, who brought the news that he was being evacuated to Canada. Beth knew that this was a sad time for her mum, for there was no piano at Gran and Grandad's place out in Hertfordshire, and once they had gone there, music, which had always been so important in Connie's life, would have to be sacrificed. 'Is this *really* a good idea?' Beth asked, as she helped her mum to pack away her collection of sheet music into a cupboard beside the fireplace in the sitting room. 'I mean, is it worth leavin' all this be'ind, givin' up everyfin' becos we can't cope wiv the air raids?'

'We're not giving up, Beth,' replied Connie. 'We're just putting things on hold.'

Beth went to the piano to collect the last sheet music on the stand there. It was 'Onward Christian Soldiers', which young Freddie's mother had asked Connie to teach the boy. Beth took a cursory glance at the sheet, then put it back on to the stand. Then she looked down at the keyboard, and with one finger slowly tapped out a piece of music. The nostalgic mood led her to sit on the piano stool and play something she hadn't played since she was a child. It was a soft, emotional piece called 'La Golondrina', which was the first thing her mother had taught her when she had hopes in those early years that the child would learn how to play the piano by reading the notes, and not as she had subsequently done, by ear.

Connie looked round, surprised to hear what Beth was playing. Then she went across and watched over her shoulder. 'It's been a long time since I heard that,' she said wistfully. 'I could never remember how to play that without a music sheet.'

'I don't believe yer,' said Beth, without taking her hands off the keyboard. She consciously moved to the far edge of the piano stool, to allow her mum to sit beside her.

After a moment's hesitation, Connie waited for the right opening in the music, put her hands on the keyboard, and joined in a duet with her daughter. The sound they made together on the old upright piano was utterly beautiful, rising up from the carefully tuned iron strings, casting a magic spell around the room and all the memories that room recalled. From time to time both of them flashed a loving smile at each other, and as the music gradually reached the heights of sheer ecstasy, it was as though only one pair of hands was producing the lovely sound they were making. Finally, the piece came to an end. For one brief moment, Beth and Connie sat there in silence, their hands still resting on the keyboard. Then Beth slowly slid her arm around her mum's waist, and gently rested her head against Connie's shoulder. Connie immediately responded by leaning her own head against Beth. For several minutes they sat there without saying a word, allowing just enough time to forget the worries of the troubled world around them. But their overdue coming together was suddenly broken by the sound of someone banging on the front door outside.

Beth got up, kissed her mum on the top of her head, and went out into the passage. As she opened the front street door, she found Thomas there. 'Beth!' he gasped, rushing in excitedly. 'I've got some wonderful news!'

The security cordons were down, the small back streets cleared of all debris that had blocked the passage of traffic, and hundreds of workers were crowding back through the backyard entrance of the munitions factory, with the deep crater that had been made by the unexploded bomb now diffused and taken away. Amongst the throng were Beth and Thomas, who, to Connie's consternation, had rushed straight out of the house and got a trolleybus up to Tally Ho Corner. Once inside the factory, however, they were all herded into the canteen, where several members of the management staff were sitting at a long bench table set up on the stage, including the Chief Security Officer, Jane Grigsby, who seemed to make a special point of smiling at every single worker who entered the place. Beth soon caught up with several of her pals, including Midge Morton and Elsie Tuckwell, and between them and the stage she could just pick out Charlie Hatchet, the foreman, who was looking very pensive. Beth also caught a passing glimpse of Mo Mitchell, whose head was just visible between a plethora of excited, chattering girls, and who seemed to be doing everything she could to catch Beth's attention. Beth ignored her, preferring to look up at Thomas at her side, who gave her the sort of reassuring smile that had always made her go weak at the knees.

'Ladies and gentlemen!'

Beth immediately recognised the man who had stood up at the table to address them. It was the general manager, retired Major-General Richard Everton.

Once the workers' chatter had died down, the Major-General commenced his address: 'Let me say at once that it's very good to see you all back here again – and in one piece!'

A ripple of laughter and agreement came from everyone.

'I'm sure you all know the reasons why these premises have been closed for the past week or so, during which time quite a lot of clearing up has been undertaken with great care by members of the military, for whom we would all like to extend our most heartfelt gratitude. Without their help we would not be in the position we are in today.'

There was a nodding of heads in agreement from those seated each side of him.

'However,' continued the Major-General, 'this enforced period of closure has given us on the Executive a chance to discuss with the Ministry of Defence a range of options open to us after what, at first sight, seems to have been a serious breach of security.'

A buzz spread around the canteen hall.

'As you'll all be aware,' continued the Major-General, 'this situation has been of concern to us for some time now. The site of a factory such as ours, with the type of sensitive work we undertake for the war effort, makes us a high-risk target for the enemy, as does every single establishment of this kind around the country. Up until a week or so ago, you will have heard rumours that it was our intention to move the factory, and all the work we do here, to a different, safer location. However, in the light of the new circumstances at our disposal, and the vital new experimental work we have undertaken to carry out as quickly as possible, we now feel that such a move at this time would be detrimental to the timescale we have been given by our superiors. Therefore, we have decided to reopen the factory with immediate effect . . .'

He was interrupted by great gales of thunderous applause and joyous shouts of 'Cheers!'

'However,' continued the Major-General, holding the palm of his hand up to quell the response, 'if we are to continue to guarantee the safety and well-being of all of us who work here, there are certain measures that will have to be undertaken to ensure that security is kept at the utmost momentum. To talk about that, I want to hand you over to Chief Security Officer Grigsby.'

Remembering the series of security interviews that each worker had been subjected to over recent weeks, the moment Jane Grigsby stood up, she was greeted with a wall of silence. 'Hallo, everyone,' she began, in a rather too-chatty style. 'I can't tell you how lovely it is to see you all back here again, and ready to resume where you left off. I have so much respect for the way you've faced up to the challenges of a very difficult job.'

Both Beth and Thomas greeted this remark with a cynical, stony-faced silence.

'However, the fact that the enemy has managed to pinpoint this location is, I'm sure you realise, a matter of grave concern to us, and at the present time, we are undergoing a series of careful investigations to determine if and where the information came from. Now I don't want any of you to take what I'm saying as a personal attack on your integrity, but someone, somewhere, either within these walls or outside them, is responsible for what I sincerely hope is nothing more than 'careless talk', and until we can locate the source of that breach of confidence, certain measures will be put in place to ensure that such a thing never happens again.'

A buzz of speculation spread throughout the hall.

'Oh don't worry,' continued Jane, 'it's nothing too draconian. But from now on, each and every one of you will have to face a weekly security clearance.'

There was a wave of disagreeable murmurs from everyone.

'I know, I know,' continued Jane. 'But if that's the price we have to pay for our safety, then we have no alternative. How you can help, is to make quite sure that you never ever discuss with *anyone* what goes on within these walls. It doesn't matter how much of a relative or friend it may be, the security and safety of this factory, and all of you who work here, is absolutely paramount. The Ministry of Defence has already made special arrangements to step up our protection, both in the air and in the streets around us, but we rely primarily – on *you*. Remember those posters around you on the walls: CARELESS TALK COSTS LIVES. Good luck to you all, and keep up the good work.' She sat down to the same response as she had when she stood up – total silence.

'Thank you, everyone,' said the Major-General, hurriedly getting up from his chair again. 'The canteen will be open for business as usual the moment you clear, but in the meantime, please return to your duties, and if you need any further advice about what we've talked about today, please refer to your individual unit foremen. Thank you all very much.'

Everyone started to clear the hall and make their way to their respective workshops, where their foremen were waiting to allocate them new rosters. On the way, there was a lot of speculation from the girls about who had leaked the information Jane Grigsby had been talking about.

'Personally,' said Elsie Tuckwell, whose red curly hair was already tucked under her white work turban, 'I've got my suspicions about that Charlie 'Atchet.'

'Wot!' gawped pint-sized Midge Morton. 'Charlie 'Atchet ain't no spy. 'E can't even speak English proper, let alone German!'

'Wot makes yer fink it's Charlie?' Beth asked Elsie.

'Well, 'e never smiles, do 'e?' returned Elsie. 'Shows 'e's got somefin' ter 'ide.'

Beth had no answer to that. She just exchanged a bemused smile with Thomas.

'Well, I don't like it,' complained Midge. 'I don't like it at all. All this cloak an' dagger stuff, watchin' us wherever we go, wot we do, who we go out wiv. Gives me the creeps.'

Elsie shrugged. 'Well, fink yerself lucky yer don't go out wiv a Paddy,' she said. The moment she'd said it, she wished she'd bitten her tongue.

Fortunately, Thomas smirked, letting Elsie's tactless remark go in one ear and out the other, but Beth stiffened, and led Thomas off in a different direction. 'See yer later!' she called, as they went.

As it happened, Charlie Hatchet was hanging around the hall outside the canteen as Beth and Thomas came out. 'So 'ow d'yer feel about all that then, Beth?' he asked.

Beth shrugged. 'Nuffin' much,' she replied. 'They ain't told us any more than we already know, 'ave they?'

'Depends on wot yer *do* know,' replied Charlie. 'From all accounts, they've got enuff proof ter go after somebody in the factory.'

For some extraordinary reason, Beth automatically threw a quick look at Thomas, then back to Charlie. 'Proof?' she asked tentatively. 'Wot *proof*?'

'Couldn't say exactly,' said Charlie. 'But *I* 'eard the Yard's got their eyes on someone. They reckon there'll be an arrest any minute.'

Again Beth swung a troubled look at Thomas, whose expression had stiffened.

'Rum ol' business, if yer ask me,' said Charlie. 'I just can't believe any of *our* lot would wanna give the game away. I dread ter fink wot could 'ave 'appened if that bomb 'ad gone off inside the backyard the uvver night.' He turned to go. 'I must go an' get the rosters sorted out,' he said as he went. But he stopped briefly, and turned to call back. 'Oh, by the way, Beth. I was sorry ter 'ear about your bereavement. Terrible fing!'

Beth was taken aback. 'How did you know?' she called. But Charlie had already disappeared into the departing hordes of girls returning to their workshops.

'He's got a point, yer know,' said Thomas. 'What *would've* happened if that bomb had gone off?'

For one brief moment Beth didn't answer. She was still turning over in her mind how Charlie Hatchet knew that someone close to her had died. 'I dunno, Thomas,' she replied. 'But I'm glad you weren't on duty at the time.'

The sound of girls chatting excitedly filled the air, and as they filed out of the canteen, queues were already forming to clock on and to get into the lockrooms to change into work overalls and turbans. The few men that were there were now so depleted that they had no trouble at all in getting into their own lockrooms. But they all had a lot to talk about; they all had their own individual theories about who might have leaked the information that could have resulted in the factory being bombed to smithereens. Most of all, however, they were grateful that they weren't going to have to be relocated away from their own homes to some far corner of the British Isles.

'Beff!'

Just as Beth and Thomas were about to go out into the backyard, they were stopped dead by someone calling to them. When they turned, they saw big Mo Mitchell struggling her way through the tide of girls who were swarming against her.

' 'Allo, Beff,' said Mo, whose hefty body was capable of crushing anyone who crossed her path.

Beth shot her a look of steel. 'Wot d'yer want, Mo?' she snapped.

Mo looked from one to the other of them. 'I – I just come ter say sorry,' she replied awkwardly. ' 'Speshully ter you, Thomas. I shouldn't've said those fings I said about yer the uvver night.' She turned back to Beth. 'You was right, Beff – I *am* a stupid cow. My trouble is, once I get an idea in my 'ead, I can't let it go. I don't know wot's the matter wiv me. I s'ppose I've just got a big chip on me shoulder, that all I can do is ter try an' make mischief fer uvver people.' Beth didn't believe her, and turned to go. 'No, I mean it, Beff – 'onest I do. My mum says, "Always judge yerself before yer judge uvvers".' She turned back to Thomas again. 'I've got nuffin' against yer, Thomas, I swear it. I've got nuffin' against Paddies or anyone else – except Jerry, er course. In fact – d'yer know Pat O'Brien? 'E's that bloke in all those gangster pittures wiv James Cagney and Humphrey Bogart. I've always fancied *him*, every pitture 'e's ever bin in. An' d'yer know wot? 'E's a Paddy, so wot the 'ell am I goin' on about? No, my trouble is I'm so bleedin' jealous of Beff. I've bin jealous ever since she took up wiv yer. Yer'll just ave ter put it down to a stupid fat gel who don't know 'ow ter work fings out properly.'

For one long moment, Thomas stared in awe at her. With girls pushing them from all sides as they rushed past, he leaned forward and kissed her on the cheek. 'I'll tell yer somethin'', Mo,' he said. 'I've always had a thing about fat girls. Only don't tell Beth!'

Mo's face crumpled up, and, close to tears, she rushed off into the crowd.

Beth put her arm around Thomas's waist and they moved off into the backyard.

Outside, the air was slightly milder than of late, and the slush underfoot was gradually thawing. Thomas immediately took out his packet of fags and lit one. Both he and Beth were so relieved to be away from the hordes of workers milling around inside. At the back gates, there was a visible increase in the number of Special Constables and army reserves on duty there, and in the sky above, a barrage balloon was bouncing up and down through the thick grey cloud, a clear sign that the Ministry of Defence meant what they said about keeping raiders away from the factory. On the other side of the street, local residents were still slaving away trying to board up windows blown out through bomb-blast, while at the same time clearing the slush from the pavements before the evening freeze-up turned it all to solid ice.

To the relief of the factory workers, 'Stan's' their local newsagent shop was open again, albeit with boarded-up windows carrying the sign, BUSINESS AS USUAL. There were even kids in Wellington boots sliding up and down in the slush on the pavements, grateful that they had escaped the great exodus of evacuees which headed out of London at the outbreak of war. For a few moments, Beth and Thomas stood there in the cold, huddled up together, he smoking his fag, she standing facing him with her hands deep in his duffle-coat pockets, ignoring the odd wolf-whistles that came from one or two of the more envious male passers-by outside the gates. Beth felt so safe in Thomas's arms. After all the grief she'd experienced lately, the look in her eyes showed she found such comfort in his company.

'It's such a shame,' said Beth. 'All this excitement, and yet I can't be a part of it.'

'What d'you mean?' asked Thomas.

'We're leaving for the country on Sunday,' she replied. 'After all the arrangements Dad made with Gran and Grandad, there's no way Mum's goin' ter let me stay on in London an' come back to work 'ere.'

'Oh God!' replied Thomas. 'I'd forgotten about all that. Won't she let you stay on for just a few weeks, just until we see if the air raids die down a bit?'

'Not an 'ope,' replied Beth. 'I'm sure she's got it in 'er mind that if the family stay on in London, we'll all end up on the scrap 'eap.' She was about to sigh, but as she did so, he moved in and kissed her fully on the lips.

'Why don't we say hell ter the lot of 'em,' he said passionately, 'and just run away – away from my dada, your mum . . .'

'No, Thomas,' she insisted firmly. 'I could never do that. I love Mum, I love Dad, I love Phil an' Simon. I couldn't let 'em down.'

Thomas looked into her eyes, and it rekindled all the love he had felt for her when they first met. He leaned forward and gently kissed the tiny mole on the side of her chin. 'I won't let you go, Beth,' he said softly. 'I won't ever let you go.'

They kissed.

'Aren't you going to clock on, you two?'

Both of them swung back with a start to find Jane Grigsby approaching them.

'We want to get everyone back to work as soon as possible,' said Jane. 'We have quite a lot of catching up to do.'

'As a matter er fact, Miss Grigsby,' said Beth, 'I'll only be comin' back fer a coupla days. I'm goin' ter live wiv me gran an' grandad in the country. My dad arranged it all just before he went back from leave this mornin'.'

'Yes, I do know that,' returned Jane. 'But I shouldn't worry too much about that, if I was you. Your mother is quite happy to let you hang on for another week or so.'

Beth was shocked. As she looked at the woman who had cast so many doubts about Thomas in so many minds, she was aware that her complexion was not as clear and smooth as she had remembered. In fact the repetitious smile had a veneer of uncertainty, which made her look really quite vulnerable. 'My muvver?' she spluttered. 'Yer've talked ter – my muvver?'

'Yes, of course,' replied Jane quite casually. 'Didn't she tell you? We had a lovely long chat when I went to see her a few days ago.'

Beth swung a startled look up at Thomas.

'Mrs Shanks is actually a very practical and sensible woman,' continued Jane. 'She agreed that provided you are not put on any night duties, she's prepared to wait a week or so, just long enough to see how things are going.'

'You went ter see my muvver,' snapped Beth with mounting rage, 'without asking me first?'

'You're under age, Beth,' said Jane. 'I do know the law.' She turned to leave, but stopped briefly, and turned. 'Oh, by the way, I want you to know how sorry I am about your Uncle Horace. What a terrible shock it must have been for you and your family. He sounds like he was a lovely man.' She turned to Thomas. 'And you too, young man,' she said sombrely. 'Losing your best friend like that must have been a tragic loss. I do sympathise with you.' With that, she turned and walked off.

In total shock and disbelief, Beth and Thomas watched her go.

Abe and Bernie Lieberman had argued all day about how it was that the Germans were able to carry out air raids in bad weather. 'I still don't see how they can drop bombs through snow clouds,' insisted Bernie, as he and his elder brother trudged their way in the dark towards another night in the warehouse shelter. 'How can they possibly see their target? It's like being blindfolded, and in any case it's a wonder the bombs don't freeze as they come down.'

'When are you going to realise that the *Luftwaffe* don't care about targets, Bernie?' snapped his brother Abe irritably, whilst adjusting his tin helmet and juggling with his blanket at the same time. 'The *Luftwaffe* pilots are Nazis. They drop their bombs on anything and anybody. As long as they can get away before the Spitfires get to them, that's all that matters.'

Bernie grunted and walked on. In his mind, his brother was a know-all, he had always been a know-all, and would die being a know-all. Even so, what he said was probably true. Nazis didn't care about killing innocent people. That's why he and his brother had got out of Germany when the pressure was beginning to mount on the Jews.

As they approached the entrance to the warehouse, Moaning Minnie wailed out across the rooftops, so their shuffle became a rush to see who could get through the entrance door first. When they got inside, they were surprised to see Beth and her mother deep in animated conversation, which is something they rarely saw.

'Good evening, Mrs Shanks,' said Abe. 'Good evening, Beth.'

'Sorry to disturb,' added Bernie.

'Good evening to you both,' returned Connie, whose voice was uptight and tense.

'Evenin', gents,' said Beth, with very little warmth.

Once the two brothers had disappeared down the stone steps into the cellar, Beth and her mother carried on where they had just left off. 'Yer should er told me!' growled Beth, eyes blazing with rage. 'You let that woman come around ter see yer, an' yer say nuffin' at all ter me about it!'

'Why *should* I, Beth?' returned her mum forcefully. 'What they came to discuss with me was confidential. They wanted my permission, and I needed time to think about it.'

'Did yer now?' retorted Beth. 'An' so when she come back, yer gave 'er yer permission fer me to stay on at the factory?'

'That's what you wanted, isn't it?' snapped Connie. 'How many times have you moaned and groaned to me over the last few weeks how much you love your mates, and don't want to leave them?'

'An' 'ow many times 'ave *you* carried on about yer premonitions, yer dreams an' nightmares, or wotever yer like ter call them. Ohhhhh . . .' She did a caricatured impersonation of what her mum sounded like to her when she was expressing her fears about what she had 'seen' in her dreams. 'I'm scared, Beff. I'm so scared for the family . . .'

Connie rushed across to her, eyes blazing with quiet fury. 'Don't mock me, Beth!' she said. 'I'm not a stupid Yankee eccentric. What I've had are genuine fears for the safety of you, Phil, Simon and me. Everything I've ever done has been for the good of the family, and I won't have you make fun of it!'

'Fer Christ sake, Mum,' snapped Beth, with raised voice, 'I'm not making fun of yer! But you should er told me. Yer should 'ave told me wot was goin' on be'ind me back!'

'I couldn't,' insisted Connie.

'Why not?' demanded Beth.

'Because,' said Connie, raising her own voice for the first time, 'because . . .' She stopped briefly, and turned away. All around her, discarded junk such as a ramshackle old mangle, a chest of drawers riddled with woodworm, and several wooden crates, were making the place look like a dumping ground, and the whole first floor of the building was not only freezing cold, but smelt of damp and decay.

'Because', continued Connie, 'they wanted to talk to me – about Thomas.'

If Beth was angry when she started this barney with her mum, now she was enraged. 'Wot the 'ell're yer talkin' about?' she asked, quietly fuming.

Connie hesitated before answering. 'From what I gathered,' she continued, 'the security people have some concerns about – about Thomas's presence in the factory.'

Beth was finding it difficult to control her temper. 'Then why do they allow 'im ter stay there?' she asked.

Again, Connie took a moment to answer. Turning her back on Beth for a moment, she suddenly turned and looked back at her. 'Beth,' she said slowly, 'they want you to keep an eye on Thomas.'

Beth couldn't believe what her mum had just said. 'They – *wot*?' she retorted in disbelief.

'I want you to get something clear, darling,' said Connie. 'It's not Thomas they suspect. It's – his father. Apparently he's a strong Republican sympathiser, and it's just a possibility that Thomas – quite unwittingly – has been passing on information to him about what goes on in the factory. If that *is* the case, then it's more than likely that Thomas's father has been involved with – well, third parties, I suppose.'

Beth found all this impossible to take in. 'They want me to spy on Thomas so that they can get at 'is dad,' she asked. 'Is that it?'

'It wasn't put to me in exactly those terms,' replied Connie. 'What they said was that they wanted you around for the next two weeks or so, just in case you notice anything – out of the ordinary.'

Beth went to the top of the steps, and started to go down. 'Why couldn't they 'ave told me all this themselves?' she asked.

Again, Connie paused before answering. 'Because you would have told Thomas, because you love him,' she replied, adding pointedly, 'because they don't want you to be alone in all this.'

Beth came up the steps again. 'Let me ask yer somefin', Mum,' she said. 'Do *you* fink Thomas is a spy?'

'No, darling,' replied Connie firmly. 'But this war is cruel and nasty. If we don't take precautions, no matter how much we love someone, then an awful lot of people could be lost.' She went to her. 'I don't want to stay in London, Beth. I don't want you, or Phil, or our baby to stay. I hate the thought of living like a trapped rat each night, wondering whether we'll ever see the next light of day. But if we can save lives, then we have no alternative. Do what they say, Beth, do what they say. The sooner we get out of all this, the better.'

Chapter 17

Beth dreaded the thought of having to go to Uncle Horace's funeral, especially as he had requested to be cremated, the same as his beloved wife, Maudie, more than ten years before. Because there was no one to look after the baby, Connie decided that it was simply not practical for her to attend, but Beth, dressed in the only dark-coloured dress and coat she had, together with Phil, looking very smart in a black tie and navy-blue suit, did go, first to the funeral service in Uncle Horace's local church up at Tottenham, and then to the cremation service itself in Finchley cemetery. Beth was grateful that it turned out to be just a small family affair, organised by Uncle Horace's only really close relative, his cousin Lou, who was himself a widower. Most of the rest of the small group were a niece and nephew from Maudie's side, a couple of his neighbours from the same street who had survived the bomb blast, and several of Uncle Horace's dart-playing mates from the Horse and Whistle pub, including Stan Pakeman, his rival in the vegetable competition, and his closest mate of all, Terry Barlow, who was so distraught, he had to be comforted by his missus during the entire proceedings.

Fortunately, it was a beautiful November morning, with the sun bursting out of a crystal-clear blue sky, and when Beth and Phil got out of one of the funeral cars at the entrance to the crematorium, she was amazed how beautiful the abundance of huge chestnut trees looked as they shed the last of their autumn leaves and nuts, a sight that Uncle Horace himself would probably have appreciated more than anyone else.

Beth and Phil took their places in a pew near the front of the small crematorium chapel, sitting just behind cousin Lou and the other members of the family. It was the first time Beth had been inside such a place, and it seemed so alien and solemn to her after the quiet dignity of someone being buried in a grave. It also seemed a strange request for someone like Uncle Horace to make, for his whole lifetime was spent working with the soil of his gardens. The service also surprised Beth, for it was over in such a short time, and when Uncle Horace's simple elm-wood coffin was gradually concealed by a slow-closing curtain, Phil sobbed quietly to himself, together with Terry Barlow who had lost not only a good mate, but someone with whom he had been looking forward to working with.

As the mourners filed out of the chapel, everyone was reminded only too forcefully that there was a war on, for Moaning Minnie, which had wailed out just as the funeral cortege had entered the cemetery, had signalled the approach of another air raid, which resulted in a fierce dogfight in the sky above. More traumatic, however, was the queue of a new set of mourners waiting to enter the chapel, for according to the vicar who was officiating at the services, there were fifteen more such cremations due to take place that day, nearly all of which were for air raid victims.

Beth and Phil decided not to go with Uncle Horace's family for a drink and sandwiches in the Horse and Whistle back at Tottenham, but before they left, cousin Lou rushed after them to say something. 'I'd like yer ter 'ave this, Beth,' he said, digging into his overcoat pocket to hand something over to her. It was the small, brass-plated cup that Uncle Horace had won in the vegetable competition, and which had been recovered from the debris of his house. I know 'e'd've wanted yer ter 'ave it. 'E fawt the world er you an' your family. You were far closer ter 'im than any of my lot.'

Beth hesitated for a moment before she took the cup, but when she did the numbness that had prevented her from shedding any tears, gradually gave way. Tears welling in her eyes, she was unable to say anything to Lou as he kissed her on the cheek, and got into the funeral car that was waiting for him. Phil put his arm around her waist, and they strolled off to catch their bus back home. As they went, and with the thin, frantic vapour trails of dogfights raging overhead, another procession of funeral cars slowly wound its way through the main gates. There were so many burials that day, as there were every day during the Blitz. The quiet sobs of mourners at so many wartime gravesides settled on the melting snow, leaving stains of sorrow that would last for ever.

When Beth got into work that afternoon, she was surprised to find one of the workshops had been sealed off, with a huge NO ADMITTANCE: AUTHORISED PERSONNEL ONLY sign posted outside. Even more curious was that there was a Special Constable on constant guard at the door.

'Don't ask me,' begged Thomas, as he and Beth had a cup of tea together in the canteen during the short afternoon break. 'Don't ask me *one single thing* about what's going on in there, 'cos if Jerry finds out about it, yer can bet yer bottom dollar it'll be Paddy's fault.'

'Somefin' secret goin' on, that's fer sure,' suggested Beth. 'That's why they didn't want ter move us out. You 'eard wot ol' Everton said about doin' experimental work, and gettin' it done as quick as possible. I reckon they was in the middle of it when Jerry dropped those bombs. If they closed the place now, it'd hold everyfin' up. In fact . . .' a wave of uncertainty suddenly made her stop what she was saying. 'Anyway,' she said, trying to pass off what she had just said, 'who cares *wot* they're up to. We've got our own jobs ter cope wiv.' She was aware that Thomas was watching her closely, so she gave him a quick, reassuring smile. 'Anyway,' she bluffed, 'it's nuffin' ter do wiv us, mate.'

'Well, at least you're stayin' on for another couple of weeks,' said Thomas brightly. 'That's one good thing.'

Beth smiled back nervously, but just when she thought she had avoided an awkward moment, Thomas asked the question she hoped she would never have to answer.

'So did yer find out from yer mum why Mata Hari went ter see her?'

Beth thought quickly. 'Oh – it was – nuffin' really,' she spluttered. 'Apparently they're goin' round ter all the mums and dads of gels who work 'ere, gels under age, that is.'

'Why?'

Thomas's curiosity and the way he was watching her so closely was forcing Beth to scramble for credible answers. 'The fing is, a lot of us didn't get our mum's or dad's permission when we signed up. Mum 'ad ter sign a paper, that's all.'

'Bit late fer that, isn't it?' suggested Thomas. 'You've been workin' here for over a year now.'

'That's just it,' replied Beth. 'They're catchin' up wiv us.'

'Are you tellin' me you never got your parents' permission to work here?' persisted Thomas.

'*I* did,' she insisted, not very convincingly, 'but some of the uvver gels didn't. They're just checkin' up, that's all. Apparently it's against the law ter employ someone under age, 'speshully in a place like this. I reckon the real reason why Grigsby went to see Mum is because they can't afford to lose anyone workin' 'ere, 'speshully wiv all that's goin' on.'

Thomas sat back in his chair and smiled. He didn't believe a word she was saying.

'Well,' he replied, 'at least it means I've got you here for another coupla weeks. I just hope it's longer.'

'So do I,' sighed Beth. 'I don't wanna be away from you for one single minute.'

Thomas leaned across the table, and covered her hand with his own. 'Yer don't have ter worry about that,' he said with an affectionate smile. 'Cos it's not goin' ter happen.' He got up from the table. 'I'd better be gettin' back. Paddies are not s'pposed ter take too long over their tea breaks!'

Beth also got up from the table. They embraced briefly, and he started to go. 'Take care of yourself ternight, Thomas,' she called.

'Don't worry, I will,' he returned. 'We're as safe as houses here now – if yer know what I mean! In any case, I'm sure Jerry's got plenty of other irons in the fire. If he's hard up for a good target, he can always go up to that new steel plant up at Derby.'

'Too true!' called Beth, as she watched him disappear out through the canteen doors. After he went, she picked up their two empty cups and saucers, and returned them to the food counter. Then she made her own way back to the workshop.

Elsie Tuckwell was working at her bench when Beth returned, and the whole place was now a hive of activity, with the afternoon *Music*

While You Work radio programme blaring out from the loudspeakers.

'Got news fer you,' said Elsie, all smug and grinning. 'We've put you down fer the Chris'mas concert. After all we've 'ad ter put up wiv, we're goin' ter need a bit of a knees-up.'

'Sorry ter disappoint you, Else,' replied Beth, 'but it's on the cards I won't be 'ere.'

Elsie stopped filing down the bullet head she was working on. 'Wot!' she yelped. 'We can't 'ave the Chris'mas do wivout you. You're s'pposed ter be our firecracker, remember.'

Beth shrugged. 'Can't be helped,' she replied. 'That's life.'

'So where ya goin'?' persisted Elsie, tucking one of her red curls back beneath her work turban. 'Fink of all the people who want ter 'ear yer play the Joanna.'

'No, no darling!' Beth said in a mock Greta Garbo accent. 'I vant to be alone!'

'Cut it out, Beff!' snapped Elsie irritably. '*Why* can't yer be there? You goin' off wiv that Thomas or somefin'?'

'I wish I was!' sighed Beth. 'I don't even know if I'll see him at Chris'mas, an' even if I do . . .' She stopped dead and looked up. All the blood had suddenly drained from her face.

Elsie saw this, and became alarmed. 'Wot is it, Beff?' she asked nervously. 'Wot's up?'

Without saying a word, Beth rushed straight out to the ladies' lavatory. As soon as she got there, she went to look at herself in the mirror above the wash basin. Her eyes were large and intense, her mind racing. She turned on the cold water tap, cupped her hands, and splashed some over her face. She dried herself on the rather soiled roller towel, and looked again at her reflection in the mirror. Thomas. What was that he said as he left her in the canteen? She hoped her reflection would offer her some kind of an answer, but it didn't. But he said something at the time that she had dismissed because it was so trivial. But it wasn't trivial. It was important, so very, very important. In fact his parting remark had suddenly sprung to life in her mind, as though she had suddenly been struck by lightning.

★

Phil Shanks had been deeply disturbed and upset by Uncle Horace's funeral. Although during his cycle messenger's job he had seen many dead bodies being pulled out of the debris, the sight of Uncle Horace's coffin being carried into the crematorium had distressed him more than anything he could remember, mainly because it was someone very close to him. As soon as he and Beth got back from Finchley, the first thing he wanted to do was to get out of the house, and so after changing his clothes he went out, and made his way down to the Nag's Head, where he was just in time to get on a tram heading up towards Highbury Corner and the Angel, Islington. As the tram chugged its way along, he felt utterly desolate, and even if he could have looked out through the taped windows, he wouldn't have made the effort. He closed his eyes and leaned his head against the window, but the only images that were still burning in his mind were those that were formed at the cemetery during the morning. By the time the clippie had climbed the stairs and taken his penny ha'penny fare, it was almost time to get off, so he pulled up the collar of his uniform coat, adjusted the navy-blue knitted cap that his mum had knitted for him before the war, and followed the clippie back down the stairs. After pressing the Stop button, the tram came to a halt, and he got off.

Phil found himself in Goswell Road, passing on foot the old Sadlers Wells Theatre, but his actual destination was Clerkenwell Road, which was less than ten minutes' walk away. His gloom increased with every step he took, for during his time as a Fire Brigade cycle messenger, his duties had often taken him along this route, which had always proved extremely hazardous when bombs and shrapnel were raining down on all sides. In fact, once he had reached the junction of the two roads, his former headquarters base at Moorgate was only a stone's throw away, and his stomach churned over as he glanced up at all the familiar bomb sites he had carried urgent messages to on those frantic journeys from one part of the City of London to another. Everything now looked so calm and orderly, and as it was now approaching four o'clock in the afternoon, the sun was already beginning to disappear behind what was left of the tall office buildings, gradually leaving behind it pavements of crimson slush.

Turning right into Clerkenwell Road, it was not long before he came to the place he was looking for, which was a small closed turning tucked behind badly bomb-damaged, red-bricked commercial buildings. He was on time, for on the dot of four, he heard the school bell ringing, and within just a few minutes, the air was filled with the sound of laughing, chattering girls hurrying out through the front entrance of the school, heading for buses and trams and the tube station nearby. Phil carefully tucked himself in a concealed position behind a fire services water tank, waiting for the person he was looking for to appear. He didn't have to wait long, for the moment he saw Shirley coming out amongst the throng, in animated conversation with two of her friends, he felt the first surge of warmth and hope of the day. ' 'Allo, Shirl,' he called, as discreetly as he could with all the girls around.

The girl turned to look; her eyes lit up the moment she saw Phil. 'Phil!' She broke away from her two friends, who giggled when they saw the two of them get together. 'I've been thinking of you all day,' said Shirley. 'How did it all go?'

Phil shrugged. 'Can we go somewhere?' he asked.

A short while later, they were strolling hand in hand together by the River Thames along the Victoria Embankment. Phil was carrying Shirley's school satchel over his shoulder, and as they ambled along, all the buildings on the south side of the river were bathed in the deep-red glow of a crisp, cold sunset. Shirley was a lovely girl. At sixteen years old, she was already developing the mature looks of a young woman, with long flaxen-coloured hair, blue-green eyes, a porcelain complexion, and a speaking voice that Phil loved to think of as 'posh'. For most of the way from school, they said very little, just happy to be in each other's company, but when they stopped at the stone wall overlooking the river, Shirley slipped her hand around Phil's waist, and leaned her head on his shoulder. 'You just have to say to yourself, things can only get better,' she said.

Phil reciprocated by putting his arm around her waist too. 'I don't see 'ow,' he replied. 'The only good fing that's happened is we're not goin' ter Gran an' Grandad's fer anuvver coupla weeks. I just 'ope the war's over by then.'

Shirley sighed, and slowly shook her head. 'Not the way things are going,' she replied gloomily. 'All my family ever do is talk about an invasion. I don't know what we'd all do if *that* happens.'

They remained in silence for a few more minutes, taking in the traffic ploughing through the incoming tide of the cold waters below. A flock of seagulls suddenly appeared low in the sky from the Tower Bridge direction of the river, clearly making a daring trip away from their regular hunting ground in the Thames Estuary. The two youngsters watched the beautiful grace and movement of the smooth white creatures as they swooped low over the calm surface of the water, turned a deep crimson in the fading moments of the sun, only to rise up again and return in the direction in which they had come.

'Yer know wot I'd like ter do?' said Phil, quite suddenly.

They turned to look at each other.

'I'd like us ter get out of it all,' continued Phil. 'Find somewhere where we could go an' get married, an' settle down.'

Shirley laughed. 'Don't you think we're a bit young to get married?' she asked.

'I don't see why not,' replied Phil, feeling he'd been put down. 'If I'm old enuff ter be a messenger in the fire brigade, I'm old enuff ter get married.'

'Unfortunately,' said Shirley, 'I don't think our families *or* the law would see it that way.'

'To 'ell wiv families an' the law!' he snapped. 'If two people love each uvver, they should be allowed ter do wot they want.' He paused a moment. 'That is, er course – if yer *do* love me?'

Shirley looked straight into his eyes, smiled tenderly, then leaned forward and kissed him gently on the lips.

He responded, and held her pressed against him. 'You're about the only fing I've got now, Shirl,' he said, reluctantly pulling his lips away from hers. 'D'yer know that?'

'What about your mum and dad?' she asked. 'From all you've told me, I can't believe *they* don't love you.'

'They do – in a way,' he replied. 'But they're diff'rent ter wot they used ter be. Dad always used ter be such a mate; I never fawt of 'im as someone who was much older than me. But since 'e's bin in the army, 'e seems ter be set in 'is ways, treats me an' Beff as though 'e's just waitin' for us ter grow up an' get us off 'is 'ands.'

'How can you say such a thing, Phil,' replied Shirley, 'when he's been so concerned about you and your family staying on in London during the Blitz?'

'*You're* stayin' on,' retorted Phil. '*Your* dad ain't worried about the Blitz.'

'Oh my parents would take us away like a shot if they could,' Shirley assured him. 'The fact is, most of our relations live in London, so where else could we go?'

Phil looked away from her in frustration.

'What about your mum?' she asked. 'You said at one time you were very close to *her*?'

'I wouldn't exactly call it *close*,' Phil replied sourly. 'Anyway, she's more interested in the baby.'

Shirley was surprised to hear him say that. She turned him round to face her. 'You're not jealous of your little brother, are you?' she asked. Phil tried to walk on, but she held him back. 'Don't be hurt, Phil,' she said, pulling him to her. 'I'm only trying to think what I can do to help you.'

As they stood there, they were joined by a seagull, who was squatting on the wall beside them.

'Wos up wiv you then, mate?' asked Phil. 'Got lost, 'ave yer?'

Clearly insulted that he hadn't been offered at the least a slice of bread, the bird squawked crossly and flew off.

'D'you know what your trouble is?' asked Shirley, as they both watched the seagull rise up effortlessly into the sky, and race off to join up with the rest of its flock. 'You're bored.' She turned him round to face her again. 'You say you've got another couple of weeks to hang around. Is that right?'

Phil shrugged, and nodded.

'Then, as it so happens,' said Shirley, putting her arms recklessly around his neck, 'I know exactly the thing you should be doing to stop all this. Just follow me!'

★

The village of Lossheim was covered in a thick layer of white. The heavy winter snows had come early this year even for the north of Germany, and many of the small country roads had become impassable. The chimney pots in every house in the village were billowing out thick black smoke, which curled up into the night sky without a trace. At this time before the war, the villagers would have been doing advance preparations for their *Heiliged Abend* Christmas Eve celebrations, with fir trees taken from the surrounding forests to decorate with coloured lights both the inside and outside of every house. But the war had changed all that; the blackout had restricted the use of any light that might be of use to the RAF, who, these days and nights, were making far too many forays into the heavily fortified skies above the German fatherland.

With Christmas still over a month away, apart from a few seasonal pictures the children had painted during art class at school, the Buchner household was not yet showing too many signs of preparations. But the house was so beautifully warm with a roaring log fire, that the sight of St Nicholas flitting across the rooftops outside with his reindeer and sleigh would not really have surprised anyone.

Now discharged from the hospital after the forced landing in France in what was left of his aircraft, Heinz Buchner was enjoying his few days at home with his family, or at least he was relatively enjoying it. His two young boys, Richard and Dieter, were ecstatic to have their father home again, and he loved every minute he spent with them. Despite what his wife Helga had said about their narcissistic copying of the local national youth movement, he still found them to be two normal little boys who loved life and playing games after school. Unfortunately, Helga did not have the same opinion as her husband. 'I think we should take them away from school,' she said, after the kids had gone to bed and they had sat down to an evening meal together in front of the fire in the dining/sitting room.

Determined not to overreact, Heinz looked up casually from his meal. 'Why?' he asked.

'Because I think they'd get a better education from a private tutor,' Helga replied. 'I hear Herr Weiss is available. His fees are not at all too high.'

Heinz smiled sweetly at her. 'Why should we pay for a private tutor when they get a perfectly good education at the village school?'

'I've told you, Heinz,' replied Helga, who was looking decidedly drawn these days. 'The village school is not the same as it used to be. The curriculum for young children is far too grown up.'

'In what way?'

'They have to learn about politics – national politics.'

'What's wrong with that?' asked Heinz, finishing the last of his beef and dumpling stew. 'Isn't it good that they know what's going on in the world?'

'Heinz!' protested Helga, putting down her knife and fork, and staring at him across the table. 'They're only little children. At their age they should just be learning about reading and writing and how to talk properly.'

'You mean, they don't do that?'

Helga dabbed her mouth with her table napkin, got up, and went over to the fireplace. 'One of the mothers told me that they are shown photographs in the newspapers, photographs of what's happening in England.'

Heinz sipped his wine and sat back in his chair. His wife's concerns were beginning to get him down.

'Photographs of war and destruction, Heinz,' continued Helga, taking out a cigarette from a packet on the mantelpiece. 'Surely that can't be right?'

'I've told you before, Helga,' said Heinz. 'The British are our enemy. It's right that our children know about it.'

'Look, Heinz,' said Helga, quickly lighting her cigarette. 'I have no time for the British. As a matter of fact, as a race, I've always thought them arrogant and inferior. But when the children see pictures of innocent people lying dead on top of the debris of their homes, homes that *we've* destroyed, then I know that a line has to be drawn somewhere.'

'You're worrying too much, darling,' replied Heinz sweetly.

'Heinz,' protested Helga, 'it's not right that we . . .'

'I said,' snapped Heinz quietly but firmly, 'there's nothing wrong with our children. Just leave them alone to grow up strong and healthy.'

Helga suddenly felt hemmed in. As she drew fiercely on her cigarette, she took a passing glance around the ornate room, with all its many mementoes Heinz had won since the time he had been called up for military service with the *Luftwaffe*. And for those few moments, she hated the endless photographs of him in full uniform and the medals that adorned so many walls and corners, and especially the photographs of the children posing proudly with him. Her dilemma however, was that she still loved him. She loved him very much, and whilst she was staring into the fire, she was glad that he crept up quietly behind her, put his arms around her waist, and tenderly kissed the back of her neck. For a moment or so, they both stared contemplatively in silence into the flames in the log fire. They both felt confident in each other's company.

'War is doing this to us, Helga,' he said softly into her ear. 'It's doing it to so many German families. It's making us question our own beliefs.'

'Beliefs?' asked Helga.

'Our reasons for supporting the fatherland.'

Helga turned round to face him. 'What *are* our reasons, Heinz?' she asked tentatively.

'The survival of our way of life, Helga,' he replied earnestly. She was about to say something, but he put his fingers against her lips to prevent her from doing so. 'German families are being killed by the British too,' he reminded her. 'Believe me, when I fly over their city again, I'll be doing no worse than they.'

Helga was suddenly consumed with alarm. 'You're going back?'

He smiled affectionately at her. 'Soon.'

'But you still haven't recovered,' she spluttered nervously. 'And the weather . . . they say there's bad weather over the whole of Britain. They say it could last for at least another week. How will you – how will you be able to drop bombs if you can't see the target?'

Heinz gave her another warm, loving smile. 'I'll manage, my darling,' he replied. 'I'll manage.'

Chapter 18

'*I'm sure Jerry's got plenty of other irons in the fire. If he's hard up for a good target, he can always go up to that new steel plant up at Derby.*' Thomas's parting words as he took his leave of Beth in the canteen just a few days before, had come to haunt her. *She* had never heard of a new steel plant up at Derby, so how had *he*? After making discreet inquiries around the factory, none of her workmates had heard of such a place either, and it was only Charlie Hatchet who happened to mention it by chance when he was discussing a list of plants that were providing metal and other materials to the factory. The quandary now was what to do about it? Did she really believe that what Thomas had said was a slip of the tongue, and if it was, did she honestly now believe that he was not as trustworthy as she had thought? After a great deal of soul searching, she finally came to the conclusion that it would be unwise to say anything to anybody about her suspicions, not even to her mum, and not before she had had a chance to have it out with Thomas himself. That opportunity came on Thursday morning, when, as usual, she and Thomas travelled to work together on the same bus. 'Beth,' he said, quite out of the blue, 'I want you to come to a dance with me on Saturday evenin'.'

'A dance?' asked Beth, taken completely by surprise.

'A very special dance,' said Thomas. 'Actually, it's a weddin'. One of my mates is gettin' married up at King's Cross. The reception's just across the road in a Catholic Hall – followed by a dance – not *any* old dance, but one for the "Paddies".'

Under the present circumstances, Beth seemed unsure of how to respond. 'This mate of yours. Who is he?'

'Actually it's a girl,' replied Thomas. 'Her name's Sheila, Sheila O'Halloran. She's the sister of me mate Johnny, who got killed. She's a really honey. We went to school together, so did Michael, the bloke she's marrying. You and she'll get on like a house on fire. So – what d'you say?'

'I don't know, Thomas,' she replied. 'We 'ave ter work on Saturday, remember.'

'Come on now!' he pressed. 'We're both on early shift that day. We finish at four in the afternoon, and in any case we don't have to go to the wedding itself, just the reception.'

Beth was still hesitant.

'Shall I tell you something,' he said. 'The real reason I want you to come is because I think it's about time you met some of my mates – you might get a different idea of what Paddies are all about. Mind you, I can't guarantee what state they'll be in after a few pints of the hard stuff!'

Beth was torn apart by indecision. On the one hand there was nothing she'd like better than to go with him to the wedding of one of his mates, but on the other hand, she was still plagued by this nagging feeling she had about that devastating remark. 'I always 'ave ter go down the shelter wiv Mum,' she said, as an excuse. 'If there's an air raid . . .'

'There won't *be* an air raid!' insisted Thomas. 'Saturday evenin's goin' to be so quiet, you won't hear a penny drop – except when the gang start dancin'!'

'Wot makes yer so sure, Thomas?' she asked pointedly.

Thomas gently tapped the side of his nose with his fingers, and gave her a mischievous wink. 'Luck of the Irish,' he replied.

Connie was still reeling from Phil's news that the fire brigade were willing to take him back into his old job for two weeks, provided they received his mother's approval. Phil first broke the news to her whilst they were in the back garden, labouring with shovels in the cold to chip away at the drift of snow that had fallen two nights before, and piled up against the kitchen door, which had now turned to ice overnight.

'No, Phil!' barked Connie. 'I absolutely forbid it! If your dad knew what you'd done, you'd be in real trouble. You know very well he went to see your superintendent at the fire station and told him he wouldn't have you doing that dangerous job any more. It's so sly of you to go straight back to the station the moment your dad is out of the way.'

'I did *not* go straight back to the station, Mum!' insisted Phil. 'It was just that I was talkin' ter Shirley, and she took me to see her dad who works up there. '*E* was the one who spoke up fer me.'

'Oh did he?' snapped Connie. 'And why didn't this Shirley come and see me first? Why didn't her father come and talk to me? What do you take me for – an absolute idiot, someone who can be ignored and kicked around as though I don't even exist?'

'It's not like that, Mum,' pleaded Phil, who was already wearing his messenger's uniform. 'I fawt that – well, as we're not goin' ter Gran and Grandad's fer another couple of weeks or so, there seemed nuffin' wrong in goin' back ter 'elp out 'til then. After all, yer've let Beff go back ter the factory.'

'What Beth is doing,' retorted Connie, whose voice was surprisingly shrill, 'has *nothing* to do with you!'

From the scullery of the next door house, Jack Cutter was taking a sneaky look at his neighbours from behind the blackout curtains.

'Beth said you told 'er it was all right for 'er ter go back ter work 'til we go an' live with Gran an' Grandad,' Phil spluttered angrily. 'Why is it all right fer 'er an' not fer me?'

'Because *I* said so!' replied Connie firmly. 'And *I'm* your mother!'

Phil, angry and frustrated, threw his shovel to the ground, and strode back into the kitchen.

Connie sighed despairingly, put down her own shovel, and followed him in. 'Phil!' she called, just as he was about to rush out of the room. 'Listen to me, son! Please listen to me.'

Phil stopped where he was, but didn't turn to look at her as she came round to face him.

'Look,' she said in her quiet Texan drawl, trying to lower the heated exchange. 'I don't want to be the heavy-handed mother who wants to keep her children under her thumb. I don't want to stop you from doing anything you want to do. But you've got to bear with me, son. Every time you go out on that bicycle during an air raid, my stomach churns every minute 'til you get back. You know very well that I've never made any attempt to disguise how much I disapprove of using boys or girls of your age to go out into the streets, risking their lives day after day, night after night. But I let you do it because your dad wasn't around to support me, because maybe, because I'm not a native of this country, I didn't appreciate how important it was for our *own* boy to want to do his bit for the country. When your dad came home, however, it was different. He agreed with me that fighting a war is for grown men, and not for—'

'Fer kids, Mum?' said Phil. 'Is that wot you're sayin'?'

Connie, realising that she was making no impression on the boy, turned away, and went to look at the baby in his cot.

Phil followed her across. 'Mum,' he said calmly. 'I stopped bein' a kid the first time a bomb ever fell.' He took hold of her arm, and gently eased her round to face him. 'There's a piece of paper on the table fer you ter sign,' he said. 'All it's askin' yer ter do is ter give yer permission fer me to 'elp out up the station fer the next two weeks. Two weeks, Mum, that's all I ask.'

Connie turned away defiantly, and tried to leave the room.

'Yer've got ter let me do this,' persisted Phil. ' 'Cos if yer don't, I won't come back 'til yer do.'

Connie stopped dead in her tracks, and slowly turned. Then in one swift, decisive move, she went to the table, signed the piece of paper there, and left the room.

It was going to take Abe and Bernie Lieberman longer than forty-eight hours to be convinced that there was a lull in the *Luftwaffe* air raids. To their way of thinking, the fact that Moaning Minnie hadn't been heard since Wednesday morning meant nothing at all. They knew the mentality of the Germans, they knew that it was just another of their little plots, designed to make the people of London think that the Blitz was over. 'Don't you believe it,' said Abe, as he and his brother shuffled their way back to the shop up Hornsey Road, after spending another chilly night in the warehouse shelter. 'What they want is to put us off our guard, then, when we least expect it, they'll come back with a vengeance.'

Bernie grunted agreement. 'Thank God for giving us a home away from Nazis. I dread to think what it's like over there now.'

'In Germany, you mean?' asked Abe, his tin hat half covering his eyes, so that as he walked he could hardly see where he was going. 'Well, I don't think I want to know. At least this is a democratic country. We have nothing to fear here.'

They had got a few more yards along the road, when they noticed in the distance a small group of people were gathered outside their shop.

'What's going on?' asked Bernie, as they both increased their shuffle.

Within a few moments, they caught a glimpse of someone waving and hurrying towards them. It was Jack Cutter. ' 'Ang on just a jiff, mates,' he said, looking very troubled.

'Why?' asked Abe, who was becoming agitated. 'What's going on up there?'

Even as he spoke, they saw some of the group picking up various articles of clothing from the pavement and road outside the brothers' shop. Without another word, both of them rushed up the road as fast as their legs would carry them. On seeing Abe and Bernie approaching, the group of people stood to one side, to reveal a dreadful sight, for not only were there customers' clothes scattered all over the pavement outside, but the shop window was smashed. The brothers looked on in horror. 'My God!' gasped Bernie. 'What's happened here?' But worse was to come when one of the group reluctantly stood back to reveal what had been scrawled in white chalk on the shop door: JEW BOYS GO HOME.

One of those in the group was Eileen Perkins with her daughter Rita. 'Don't take no notice,' she said, putting a comforting arm around Bernie's shoulder. 'They're just a bunch er bleedin' lunatics!'

'*Who* are?' asked Abe, who was silent and smouldering with anger.

'Who did this?' asked Bernie. 'What does it mean?'

'It means,' said Jack Cutter, 'that whoever they are, they ain't got a brain in their 'eads.'

The two brothers gradually found their way into the shop, where heaps of clothes waiting for repair or alteration had just been ripped up and thrown everywhere. Bernie was too overwrought to say anything. He just took off his tin helmet and stared in disbelief.

Abe also stared around, but the look in his eyes told a very different story.

'We've called the flatfoots,' said Jack who, with Eileen and Rita, had followed them in. 'They should be 'ere any minute.'

'No police,' said Abe firmly.

'But they've got ter catch the devils who did this,' insisted Eileen. 'If I 'ad my way, I'd 'ang, draw and quarter the sods!'

'I said *no* police!' replied Abe forcefully. 'It made no difference before, and it won't now.'

'*Before?*' asked Jack, puzzled.

'We called the police lots of times back in the old country,' said Bernie. 'They came, but it made no difference.'

'But that was Germany, mates,' said Jack. 'We don't let that sort er fing go on 'ere. Once the law catch up wiv these buggers, they'll frow the book at 'em. If yer ask me, it's a bunch er kids. They're always comin' round collectin' shrapnel in the early 'ours er the mornin'.'

'In any case,' added Eileen, 'this is one er the fings we're fightin' against.'

Bernie exchanged a wry look with his brother. Both of them then tried to retrieve items of clothes from the floor, to check which of them they might be able to restore. Their biggest shock came, however, when they found their old sewing machine lying vandalised on its side beneath a pile of dresses, the machine itself broken away from its base, and the treadle hanging in two pieces.

Eileen looked away in despair.

Jack came across, and watched Bernie bend down to pick up the different parts of the machine and try to fit them together. 'We'll soon get that up an' runnin' again, mate,' he assured him. 'I've got a mate up the Singer repair shop. 'E'll get that goin' for yer again in no time.'

From under the carnage Bernie then retrieved a framed sepia photograph of an elderly man and woman, but the glass was broken and in pieces. He gave the photograph to his brother.

Abe looked thoughtfully at the photo. 'I wonder what *they'd* think of all this,' he said ruefully. 'This is our mother and father. They loved this country, even though they never ever came here. Mama said Britain was the only country in the world where you could be who you are, and not be ashamed of it.' He carefully laid the photograph down on the counter. 'I still believe she's right,' he continued, 'but wherever you go there are always people who think otherwise.'

On Saturday morning, Connie wheeled the baby in his pram down to do some shopping in Seven Sisters Road. Although the sky was grey and overcast, most of the slush from the earlier falls of snow had now been cleared, and any that remained were left in small, invisible clusters of ice that proved difficult for the naked eye to see. At Hicks the greengrocer's, she stopped to buy some potatoes and Brussels sprouts, but when she caught a passing glimpse of some good-sized pumpkins stacked precariously in a heap on a fake-grass display bench, it immediately reminded her of Uncle Horace, and his prize-winning brass-plate cup that now occupied a special place at home on the living-room mantelpiece. Further down the queue in front of her was old Jessie Hawks, who was well wrapped up in her well-worn navy-blue overcoat, a muffler around her neck, and a dark woollen scarf which completely covered her head. When she had bought her cabbage and onions, she waited for Connie to finish in the shop, before the two of them then strolled along together for a chinwag.

'Terrible, that fing about the two bruvvers,' said Jessie. 'I'd like ter get me 'ands on the bleedin' tykes who did that!'

Connie didn't know what she was talking about. 'The two brothers?' she asked. 'Mr Abe and Mr Bernie?'

'Wot they did ter their shop,' continued Jessie, picking her way carefully along the treacherous pavement. 'An' those words they found on their door.'

'I'm sorry, Mrs Hawks,' said Connie. 'I don't know about this.'

'Some louts broke inter their shop the uvver night, and messed up the place, said Jessie. 'Then they skipped off leavin' a dirty, filfy message on the front door: JEW BOYS GO HOME.'

'Oh my God!' gasped Connie. 'B-but why? Who would have done such an awful thing?'

'That's the question everyone's askin',' replied Jessie. 'No rhyme nor reason. Two good ol' boys like those two bruvvers – if yer ask me it's downright wicked! I mean, wot does it mean? Jews ain't no diff'rent ter anyone else. In fact, some of 'em are far nicer. When I was young, I used ter do cleanin' work fer a Jewish couple up at Stamford 'Ill – never a wry word between us in all the four years I was wiv 'em. I don't understand why people get a bee in their bonnet about uvvers who ain't the same as 'emselves, der you? I mean, 'ow can these buggers do a fing like that right in the middle of a war when that's what the war's all about?'

'Oh they can, Mrs Hawks,' replied Connie despondently. 'They can.'

Once they'd gone their separate ways, Connie made her way back to the Gas, Light and Coke Company to pay her gas bill. On the way she thought a great deal about what Jessie had told her about the Lieberman brothers, and it made her sick in her stomach. It also made her question in her mind the sort of person or people who could have done such a thing to them. The two brothers were not only two of the nicest men she knew, with a lovely dry sense of humour, but they were also wonderfully skilled craftsmen, who wouldn't know how to hurt anyone if they tried. But what had happened to them systematically led her to think about what was happening to Beth's boyfriend, Thomas, and the way fingers of suspicion were being pointed at him for the only reason that he was part of a population living in London who had a fringe element that were sympathetic to the enemy.

As ever, there was a small queue at the counter in the Gas, Light and Coke Company showroom in Seven Sisters Road. Connie got out her gas bill and purse, and joined it, keeping Simon's pram alongside her as she slowly moved forward. She was not aware that someone had entered the showroom when she came in, a middle-aged woman, who sat on a chair near the door, keeping a discreet distance from Connie until she had paid her bill. After putting her gas bill receipt and purse away in her handbag, she placed it with some of her shopping in the pram with the baby, then turned and made for the showroom entrance door. As she did so, the woman who had been waiting for her suddenly stood up in front of her.

' 'Allo, Connie,' said the woman.

Connie stopped with a start, and stared in surprise at the woman.

The woman smiled a sweet smile at her. 'You don't know me,' she said, 'but I feel I know you. My name's Vera. Vera Jeggs. Would you come and have a cup of tea wiv me?'

St Patrick's Hall was just a stone's throw from King's Cross, in a small cul-de-sac off Pentonville Road on the way up towards the Angel, Islington. By the time Beth arrived there with Thomas, the wedding of his former school friend Sheila O'Halloran to her fiancé, Michael Murphy, had already taken place nearby at the Roman Catholic church of Our Lady of Lourdes, but as there was still some food left over from the wedding breakfast, they were able to feast on the best food that was available on the ration.

Thomas proved to be right about Sheila and Beth getting on well together; Beth took an immediate liking to the girl, finding her sweet, lovely and totally unaffected. However, the real business of the day took off just as it was getting dark around five o'clock, when the drinking really started and Michael's best man, Donal, announced the first dance of the evening, which was a waltz, played by an all-Irish band consisting of four young men on piano, guitar, trumpet and drums. Needless to say, Thomas immediately took Beth on to the floor, and they caused quite a lot of attention as they seemed to glide together as if they had been dancing with each other all their lives.

When the dance was over, Sheila took Beth and Thomas over to meet her parents, a lively middle-aged Irish couple, who made her feel welcome the moment they saw her. Then she took her to meet Michael's parents, a seemingly well-off couple who, although very pleasant to her, were much more formal. After that, Beth met so many relatives and friends that for the rest of the evening she just couldn't keep up with who they all were. What did surprise her, however, was the fact that practically everybody in the hall seemed to be Irish, and practically every young man amongst them had a joke of some sort to tell. Beth did her best to put aside all her uncertainties about the guests, and from time to time she felt waves of guilt about what the security people at the factory had asked her to do.

'Thomas tells me they call you a "firecracker" at the place where you work.'

This comment from Michael, the bridegroom, embarrassed Beth, but she passed it off as best she could. 'That's not the only fing they call me!' she joked.

Some of the young Irish blokes and their girlfriends laughed. They liked her quick repartee.

'But what does "*firecracker*" mean?' asked one of them.

Thomas answered for her. 'It means she's a live wire,' he said. 'You should hear her play the piano.' He turned to Beth with a mischievous grin. 'Charlie Kunz has got nothin' on you, has he, honey?'

' 'Cept 'e gets paid more than me!' retorted Beth, quick as a flash.

There was more laughter from the others.

'Well he would, wouldn't he?' suggested another of the blokes. 'He's a Nazi.'

Everyone went silent. Beth was stony-faced.

'Who said Charlie Kunz was a Nazi?' asked one of the girls.

'Well, with a name like that,' said the young bloke who started the conversation, and whose nickname was Skip, 'he'd have to be. Let's face it, the Germans are good at most things – especially droppin' bombs!' Although he laughed at his own joke, it was not shared by the others, who all looked away embarrassed.

'I would have fawt anyone who's caught bein' a Nazi in *this* country would be put in a camp or somefin',' said Beth cynically. 'No matter 'ow well 'e plays the pianer.'

'In any case,' added another young bloke, 'just because you're a German doesn't necessarily mean you're a Nazi.'

Beth was about to answer, but the band suddenly swung into life with a crazy outburst of wild sounds.

'Jitterbug!' yelled the group.

Most of them rushed off to get on the dance floor, leaving Beth and Thomas behind. But one young Irish boy, who couldn't have been more than fifteen or sixteen years old, and who had large, protruding ears, rushed up to Beth, and tried to grab her hand. 'Jitterbug!' he yelled excitedly.

'Not on your Nellie!' protested Beth, trying to pull away from him.

'Go on, Beth!' yelled Thomas, urging her on above the heavily amplified sound of the band. 'Let 'em see what a firecracker you *really* are!'

'Jitterbug!' yelled the boy with the big ears, dragging her on to the floor straight into the middle of a whole lot of youngsters doing the latest American high-energy dance.

With Thomas, Michael and Sheila looking on, for the next few minutes Beth found herself being thrown over the boy's shoulder, dragged along the floor through his legs, and being twisted and turned in the most frenetic so-called dance she had ever done. But she certainly took to it all quite naturally, so much so that everyone turned to watch her and the boy, forming a circle around them, applauding and laughing as the crazy dance progressed. When it all came to an end, the hall erupted to the sound of everyone cheering and applauding. Without realising it, Beth had made a hit with the Irish community, so much so that the bride's mother came across to help her up off the floor, and to congratulate her. 'Wot a sport you are!' said the portly little woman, whose face was chubby and friendly. 'If I was twenty years younger, I'd give this lot a run for their money!'

Immediately deserted by her Jitterbug dancing partner, Beth was taken back to Thomas by Sheila. 'Wot a lovely mum yer've got,' said Beth. 'She's got so much go in 'er.'

'Yes, she's grand, isn't she?' replied Sheila, with her bright Irish accent, handing Beth over to Thomas, who was waiting for her at a table at the edge of the dance floor. 'Considering she lost her brother only a short while ago. He was on HMS *Hood* when it was torpedoed.'

Beth swung her a look of horror. ' 'E was in the navy?' she asked, completely taken aback. 'The *Royal* Navy?'

'Why not?' asked Sheila. 'There are plenty of good Irish boys up front as well, yer know. Just because they weren't called up doesn't mean they couldn't volunteer.'

That was something Beth *didn't* know, and when she remembered how she was supposed to be keeping an eye on Thomas, it only confused her even more.

For the rest of the evening, some of the heavy drinkers seemed to be enjoying themselves more and more. And when it came to a line-up for the Irish clog dancing, but with highly polished shoes replacing the clogs, the air was echoing to calls of 'Come on, Paddies! Let's have yer, boys!' All the blokes danced with great aplomb and precision in the line-up, helped considerably by the endless quantities of Guinness, brown ale and bitter they had been consuming ever since the start of the festivities. Beth was exhilarated by the sheer excitement and natural rhythm of it all.

Before the bride and bridegroom stepped into their wedding car to depart for their four days' honeymoon in a hotel 'somewhere in Surrey', Sheila made a special point of casting her wedding bouquet towards Beth, who caught and held on to it. Beth couldn't believe how much she had enjoyed an evening which, when Thomas had first mentioned it, she had been dreading. It was the first time she had been in contact with so many 'Paddies', and, with one or two exceptions, what she saw of them she absolutely adored. Nonetheless, she still had that one vital question that was hanging over her, the question of that parting remark in the canteen a few days before, and, if she was ever to have peace of mind, she could not delay that question for a moment longer.

She waited until they were on their way home. It was after midnight when they left the wedding reception, which was still in full swing, despite the fact that the bride and groom were no longer there. As there was very little chance of finding a bus at that hour, they decided to walk home. Although it would be quite a long walk, taking the best part of an hour, it was a fairly simple one along Upper Street and Holloway Road. It was a cold, crisp night, with a freezing frost settling hard and fast on the pavements and on the rooftops, where the moon's bright white light was so dazzling, it could almost have been daytime. But so far at least they had actually got through an evening without the sound of Moaning Minnie, and the fact that there had now been no air raid since the previous Wednesday, gave them hope that this was the start of a lull in the *Luftwaffe*'s bombing campaign.

As they strolled along at a brisk pace, an arm around each other's waist, Beth still clutching Sheila's wedding bouquet, it was not until they had almost reached Moray Road that Beth finally plucked enough courage to ask him the all-important question. 'By the way, Thomas,' she murmured tentatively. 'Can I ask yer somefin'? 'Ow did yer knew there's a new steel plant up at Derby?'

At first, Thomas hadn't quite taken in what she had said. He just kept walking, but gradually slowed his pace. 'What d'you mean?' he asked.

'The uvver day,' continued Beth, gripping his arm more than she realised, 'when we was in the canteen, you said somefin' like: "If Jerry wants a good target, 'e can always go after that new steel plant up at Derby." I mean, nobody else in the factory knew about it, and a coupla nights later, Jerry tried ter bomb it. So – 'ow did *you* know, Thomas?'

Thomas brought them to an abrupt halt. 'What d'you *think* I meant, Beth?' he asked calmly, without giving any reason to believe that he had taken offence.

'It was j-just w-wot yer said,' she replied falteringly. '*I* didn't know nuffin' about no steel plant up there. I've never even 'eard of it.'

'So why are you asking me?'

Beth hesitated. 'I fawt we weren't s'pposed ter know about – about secret places. An' if we did, we ought ter keep quiet about 'em.'

'Careless talk costs lives,' said Thomas. 'Is that it, Beth?'

Beth was suddenly upset by the sudden cold tone of his voice. She jumped as a cat shrieked at her side, leapt off the coping stone of a front garden, and rushed off down the road.

'D'you think it's something I should be aware of, Beth?' asked Thomas menacingly, removing his arm from around her waist and turning to look at her. 'D' you think it's not good for someone like me to talk "carelessly", just in case someone happens to be listening nearby?'

As he talked in that cold tone, Beth saw the reflection of the moon in his eyes, the pupils glistening like balls of light. It made her feel uneasy.

'Gee whiz,' he mocked. 'I hope I didn't use too much careless talk while we were at the dance tonight. Suppose one of my mates – my *Irish* mates – had heard what I was saying: A new steel plant up at Derby? Where's the nearest phone to Berlin, boys?'

'Don't be silly, Thomas!' pleaded Beth. 'That's not what I'm saying!'

'Isn't it?' said Thomas quietly, gently holding both her arms. 'Did you tell that to Mata Hari, to those people who're convinced that every Irishman in London is working against the national interest?' Beth tried to pull away, but he strengthened his grip on her arms and held on to her. 'Is this *their* idea, Beth?' he asked, leaning close to her. 'Is that why you came to the dance tonight, because they wanted you to keep an eye on me and all my mates . . .'

'No!' protested Beth.

'Because they wanted to know who I am, and the sort of people I mix with?'

'No, no, no, Thomas!' begged Beth, finally pulling away. 'It's not you, Thomas,' she insisted desperately. 'It's not you they're after. It's – it's yer dad.'

Thomas froze.

'They've bin watchin' 'im,' she continued. 'They've bin watchin' yer 'ouse. I don't know wot they think they've got, but it's *not* you, Thomas. It's *not* you!'

Thomas hesitated before replying. 'Thanks for being so reassuring, Beth,' he said. 'Thanks for trustin' me, and for tellin' me how your mates in security feel about *my* dad!' He turned, and started to walk off back down the road.

Beth immediately went after him. 'Please, Thomas!' she pleaded, holding on to his arm. 'Please listen ter me . . .'

He stopped, and turned to face her again.

'Would it interest you to know,' he said, quite calmly, 'that your friend in security told me about that plant when she interviewed me a couple of weeks ago?'

Beth was so taken aback, she withdrew her hand from his arm.

'Yes,' continued Thomas. 'As a matter of fact, she talked quite a lot about it, because it was one of the places some of the workers could be transferred to if and when the factory had to close. She made a special point of telling me that the plant *wasn't* on the secret list, so I didn't have to worry if I talked about it when I was with "close" friends like you.'

Beth tried to talk to him, but he wouldn't let her.

'D'you know what I told those people up at the dance tonight, Beth?' he said. 'I told them that I was the luckiest bloke in the world ter find someone like you. I said, for me, you were the nearest thing ter heaven, that you were really somethin' quite special. But I was wrong, Beth. I couldn't possibly spend the rest of my life with someone who could never trust me *or* my dad.' He turned and walked off.

Beth watched him go, and tried one last time to appeal to him. 'Thomas!' she called.

He turned one last time. 'You're not a firecracker, Beth,' he called. 'You're just a damp squib!'

He hurried off, watched by Beth whose eyes were filled with tears. She turned and made her way to the front door of her house. With one last, forlorn look along what was now an empty road, she gently smelled the flowers of Sheila's wedding bouquet, took the front street-door key out of her coat pocket and let herself in.

Chapter 19

Jane Grigsby didn't always like the work she was doing. It was a job that was more or less created when war was very clearly on the horizon at the beginning of 1939, and once she'd gone through formal training with the special security division at Scotland Yard, her main preoccupation had been to ensure that the workforce were kept safe and secure from infiltration by any alien espionage. The trouble was, the very nature of her job meant that nothing and no one on the premises was free from the most intense scrutiny, and that meant at times not only the infringement of people's privacy, but also tampering with human emotions. With that in mind, she was not in the least surprised when she found Beth Shanks waiting to see her when she arrived for work on Monday morning. After all that had been going on over the past week or so, Jane was expecting trouble from Beth, but she was prepared for it.

'Why are you playin' games wiv my life, Miss Grigsby?' asked Beth as she followed Jane into her office.

'First of all,' said Jane, taking the girl's aggressive tone in her stride, 'why don't we just sit down and talk about things?'

'I don't wanna talk about *anyfin'* wiv you!' snapped Beth, refusing to sit down in the chair in front of Jane's desk. 'All I want from you are explanations. I want ter know why you told Thomas about that steel plant up in Derby, knowin' that 'ardly anyone else in the factory knew about the place?'

Jane shrugged, but because of Beth's angry outburst, was not, for the moment, given a chance to answer anything.

'I don't s'ppose it's of any interest ter you,' continued Beth unabated, 'but becos of wot you've done, Thomas 'as ditched me!'

'I'm sorry to hear that, Beth,' said Jane, going to the door and quietly closing it.

'I bet you are!' growled Beth.

'Sit down, please,' said Jane, as she went to her own chair behind the desk.

Beth crossed her arms defiantly, refusing to sit down.

'I said sit down – *please*,' repeated Jane quietly, calmly, but firmly.

The way Jane looked up at her finally convinced Beth that she meant business. Reluctantly, she sat down.

'The first thing I think you should know,' Jane began, 'is that keeping Thomas under scrutiny is not *my* idea. It's the orders I've received from – well, shall we say – a higher authority than myself. Now as it so happens, neither I nor anyone else believe that Thomas is responsible for the leak of information from this factory . . .' Beth was about to protest but Jane stopped her. 'But,' she continued, 'he *is* responsible for passing on information – albeit unwittingly – to his father. I won't go into that now, because I know you're already aware of that situation. However, for that reason, and that reason alone, it *is* necessary for us to use Thomas as a kind of – I suppose you call it – a pawn, a pawn in a very precarious game of espionage.' She got up from her desk, and moved aimlessly around the room. 'You asked me the reason why I fed that information about the steel plant *to* Thomas. Well, it was an experiment, one that proved to be justified, because a few nights after I told him, the Germans specifically targeted that plant.'

Beth swung round on her chair and threw a look of horror at her.

'Yes, Beth,' said Jane, staring down at her. 'It was the first time they had had enemy activity in that area, and thank God no real damage was done, and none were killed or injured. But it happened, and as much as we hate to admit it, the information I fed to Thomas found it's way to the *Luftwaffe*.'

'But Thomas would never've . . .'

'I *know* that, Beth,' insisted Jane. '*I* know that Thomas is not a spy, and so do you. But somehow – don't ask me how – that information was relayed by someone, and in our opinion that someone was Thomas's father.'

Beth sat back in her chair. 'But you told Thomas the place wasn't secret, wasn't important.'

'It wasn't, it isn't,' replied Jane, who frequently ran one hand through her short bobbed hair. 'Which meant that it was more than likely Thomas would feel free to mention it, no matter how casually, to you – or his own father. And for all we know,' she moved back to her chair behind the desk, 'Thomas may even have mentioned it in the same way to any one of those people at the wedding the other night.'

Beth looked up with a start.

'Don't look so surprised, my dear,' said Jane with a wry smile. 'I'm told you had a very good time there, and quite right too. There's a time and place for all this cloak and dagger stuff.'

By Monday morning, Abe and Bernie Lieberman were getting over the shock of finding their tailor's shop ransacked by anti-Jewish sympathisers. With the help of some of their loyal and concerned neighbours, they soon got the place cleaned up, and even managed to salvage those of the customers' clothes that had been treated so badly. Furthermore, Jack Cutter had kept his word and made immediate contact with his mate up at the Singer centre, who came personally to repair the old sewing machine so that it was up and in running order again within twenty-four hours. However, there was still the most enormous anger amongst the neighbours as to who the thugs were who had carried out such a vicious attack on the livelihood of two well-loved residents.

'I still say it's that Mosley,' said Bill Winkler's wife, Lil, who had just been down on her hands and knees scrubbing the shop floor with carbolic. 'It's just the sort er nasty fing 'is lot'd get up to.'

'But Mrs Winkler,' said Connie, who was neatly folding up some of the customers' repairs that were waiting for collection, 'Sir Oswald Mosley has been in prison since May, and thankfully, it looks as though he'll be there for some time.'

' '*E* may be in prison,' added Jack Cutter, who was busily sawing wood to board up the shop door, 'but 'e's got plenty er sympathisers around, don't you worry!'

'Bleedin' yobs, yer mean!' called Eileen Perkins, who was at the back of the shop making the brothers a cup of tea. 'They really fancy themselves in them black uniforms. They fink it makes 'em look tough!'

'Tough, my arse!' growled Jessie Hawks, who seemed to be there only as some kind of an unofficial foreman. 'Put 'em up against some *real* men, an' they'd run fer their bleedin' lives!'

'Well,' said Lil Winkler, 'all I can say is the longer they keep 'em all locked up the better. We'll all feel much safer for it.'

'You won't be able to lock them *all* up, Mrs Winkler,' said Abe, who was cutting out material for repair work, whilst his brother Bernie was hard at work on the sewing machine. 'Fascists are everywhere. They call themselves sympathisers, but when the German army march in down Oxford Street, they'll be out there with their *Sieg Heils* and their Nazi salutes.'

'*When* they march in?' spluttered Eileen, who nearly burst a blood vessel with outrage as she brought across two cups of tea. 'Over my dead body!'

'You think it's going to happen, Mr Abe?' asked Connie, tucking the baby up in his pram. 'D'you really think the Germans are capable of invading?'

'Just take a look at Czechoslovakia, Poland, the Benelux, France,' said Bernie.

'Yeah,' said Jack, 'but none er them 'ad the English Channel. Yer can do a lot wiv twenty miles er water.'

'You think the English Channel will stop the Nazis?' asked Abe, peering over the top of his metal-rimmed spectacles. 'It's a machine we're up against, my friend, a great big war machine, bigger than anyone has ever known. Its ultimate aim is to conquer the entire world.'

'I don't fink the Yanks'd put up wiv it!' said Eileen. 'Wot say you, Mrs Shanks?'

'I just hope it never comes to that,' sighed Connie. 'For all our sakes, I hope it won't be too long before the US come to our rescue.'

Behind Connie's back, Eileen exchanged a wry look with Lil Winkler.

'Well, I tell yer this much,' said Jessie, getting *her* ha'pennyworth in.

'The next time them two grinnin' hyenas come spoutin' at *my* front door, I'll frow all I've got in me bleedin' po pot over 'em!'

'Grinnin' hyenas?' asked Jack, sawing through his last plank of wood. 'Who's that, then?'

'Kids – no more than sixteen!' continued Jessie. 'Shiny-faced little sods they were. Goin' on about 'Itler, an 'ow 'e ain't nearly so bad as people try ter make out.'

Everyone immediately looked up at her.

'Oh don't worry,' said Jessie, meeting their looks. 'I told 'em wot I fawt of 'em in no uncertain terms! I told 'em my 'usband fought in a war ter get rid er people like them. I told 'em Kaiser Bill weren't much better than 'Itler.'

Jack flicked a quick, anxious glance across at the two brothers, who were both staring in astonishment at Jessie. 'When *was* this, Jess?' he asked.

'Coupla weeks ago,' replied Jessie. 'I remember it well, 'cos it was the mornin' after we 'eard about that big raid up West 'Am. So yer can imagine the mood I was in fer those little tykes!' She suddenly realised that everyone was staring at her. 'So – wot's wrong?' she asked them all, quite innocently.

'Why didn't yer tell us at the time, Jess?' asked Jack.

'Well yer didn't ask, did yer!' snapped Jessie haughtily.

Jack looked around at the others, who were still gaping in astonishment at the old lady.

'So wos all the fuss?' asked Jessie. 'I ain't done nuffin' wrong, 'ave I?'

'Only that these two geezers sound like a coupla Mosley's lot,' said Jack, trying not to sound too critical of the old girl. 'Wot's more, they might be the same two that done up this shop.'

For one brief moment, Jessie went absolutely silent and grim. Then she gave her reply: 'So wot are we waitin' 'round 'ere fer, then? Let's go down 'Ornsey Road an' tell the cop shop!'

Beth spent most of Monday afternoon looking up at the clock in her small arms workbench at the factory. The time was dragging as it had never dragged before, for, after all she had heard from Jane Grigsby during the morning, she couldn't wait to catch up with Thomas at the bus stop on the way home, to tell him that she had been set up by the security people, that she *did* trust him, that she *did* love him, and that she hoped he would forgive her and let them go back to the way things always used to be. However, the signs were not good; Thomas hadn't turned up for either lunch or tea break that day, and when she *did* catch a brief glimpse of him in the corridor outside his own workshop earlier in the afternoon, he pretended not to have seen her, and quickly disappeared before Beth had even had a chance to go and talk with him. On top of that, the small talk from the other girls in the workshop, together with the incessant piped music from the tannoy system around the place, was getting her down, for even though the girls were her mates, there was no way she could confide in any of them as far as her relationship with Thomas was concerned.

'Personally,' said Elsie Tuckwell, who was trying to clear her bench of metal shavings, 'I wouldn't've minded bein' moved up ter somewhere like Skegness.'

'Skegness?' asked Midge, pausing briefly to wipe a dewdrop from her nose with the back of her hand. 'Wot's so special about Skegness?'

'The navy, my dear!' replied Elsie lustfully. 'There nuffin' I like better than a good sailor in a pair of bell-bottoms. In fact I just love the bottoms – full stop!'

All the girls around them laughed, even Beth. But not Midge. 'That's very vulgar, Elsie,' she said prudishly. 'Yer shouldn't talk about men's posteriors like that.'

'Why not?' called one of the girls from an adjacent workbench. 'They talk about ours!'

More laughter from the others.

They were interrupted by an internal management announcement on the tannoy speakers around the walls, which gave triumphant news of a huge raid on Hamburg and Lubeck the night before, in which rail yards and munitions depots were devastated. Although this brought a huge cheer from the girls, there was a muted response from Beth.

'Wot's up, mate?'

Beth turned to find big Mo Mitchell standing beside her. 'Sounds like good news, don't it?'

'I s'ppose so,' replied Beth, carrying on with her work. 'It just means that more an' more people're gettin' killed.'

'Well if they're Germans,' said Mo, 'good riddance! Yer don't fink their blokes who come over 'ere care much about us when they drop those bombs, do yer?'

'I just 'ate the idea of *anyone* gettin' killed,' replied Beth, ' 'cept fer 'Itler, and Goering, and Goebbels, an' all that lot.'

Mo smiled at her. 'That don't sound much like our firecracker,' she said, meaning no harm. But to her surprise, Beth turned on her.

'I wish yer'd stop callin' me that, Mo!' she snapped. Then she raised her voice so that the other girls could hear. 'I wish yer'd *all* stop callin' me that! I'm *not* a firecracker. I'm not anyfin', so fer Gawd's sake, leave me alone, will yer!'

She suddenly realised that all the girls around her were staring in astonishment at her, so her only response was to slam down the tools she was working with, and rush off to the lavatory. Once she was inside, she locked herself inside one of the cubicles, and sat there fully clothed, on the toilet seat. She was so churned up inside, she felt like crying; in fact she just wished she could burst into tears. But just when the tears were about to well up in her eyes, she heard someone come into the lavatory and enter the cubicle beside her. For a moment, there was silence. But then, someone spoke.

'Is that you, Beff? It's me, Midge. I'm the 'alf-pint, remember? Blimey, don't it pong in 'ere!'

Despite her tears, Beth smiled to herself. It also made her aware that the place did hum a bit, and there was a lot of graffiti on the cubicle door, which was not somehow suited to nice young girls!

'Yer shouldn't take no notice of us lot,' said Midge. 'I agree wiv yer, "firecracker" is a stupid name. I'm goin' ter tell 'em out there ter stop callin' you it, 'cos you're nuffin' like a firecracker.' She paused. 'Mind you, I've bin called a few names meself in me time – Tich, 'Alf-pint, Grumpy, even Munchkin from *The Wizard of Oz*. I can't say I like it, well, not *all* the time, but when yer come ter fink of it, it's a kind er way people 'ave of showin' they like yer. An' I can tell yer, Beff, there're plenty er people out in those workshops who like *you*. I s'ppose we call yer "firecracker" 'cos yer make us laugh, an' anyone that can do that, 'speshully these days, 'as ter be someone special. The trouble is, when you're a joker, people seem ter ferget that yer 'ave feelin's; they laugh even when you're not happy. I *know* you're not happy, Beff, but if there's anyfin' I can do ter 'elp, anywhere, any time, yer know where I am, don't yer?' She pulled the lavatory chain, and called out. 'See yer later!'

By the time Midge had opened the door and come out of the cubicle, Beth was waiting for her.

Tears streaming down her face, Beth leaned down and hugged 'Half-pint' as hard as she could.

At five o'clock on the dot, Beth left her workbench with all the other girls, changed out of her work apron and turban into her day clothes, clocked out, and rushed out through the backyard exit. There were several hundred girls streaming out of the place at the same time, so it took a lot of effort to try and get ahead of them, but when she did finally manage to make some progress, she was rewarded with the sight of Thomas in the fading evening light, waiting at their usual bus stop with some of the elder men from the factory, and just about to get on to one of the two trolleybuses that were lined up there.

'Thomas!' she called, over the heads of the girls swarming towards the open air bus station. 'I'm here, Thomas!'

Thomas turned, and saw her hurrying towards him, but he hesitated, looked unsure what to do, and then got on to the bus.

Just as the bus was about to pull away, Beth managed to jump on and immediately rushed up the stairs, hoping to meet Thomas in one of their usual seats on the top deck. But when she got there, there was no sign of him. She frantically searched every single seat, but all she saw was nearly everyone lighting up fags at the same time, so she rushed to the back of the bus, and finally managed to get a glimpse out through the protective tape on the back window. Her heart sank, when, down below, she saw Thomas looking up forlornly at the bus that was just pulling away from the stop, and then getting on to the bus behind.

Beth took only a moment to understand what, by his action, Thomas was saying to her, before sitting down in the nearest seat, for what was clearly going to be a very lonely journey home.

★

Unbeknown to Beth, it was also a pretty lonely journey home for Thomas. On the way, time and time again he turned over in his mind the question she had asked him that night after the wedding reception: ' *'Ow did yer know there was a steel plant up at Derby?*' How could she do such a thing, he kept asking himself? How could she believe what other people were saying about him? 'No smoke without fire'? He could almost hear Beth's workmates egging her on. How could he talk to her, how could she expect him to pick up their relationship, especially after what she had said about his dad? He refused to even think about such a thing.

By the time he reached King's Cross on a number 14 petrol bus, it was almost dark. The whole area was already blacked out, and only dim concourse lights could just be made out within the precincts of the mainline station, where the evening rush hour was mixed with home-going commuters and servicemen returning to their units from leave. The news-vendors were doing a roaring trade, especially *The Star*, which carried banner headlines about the raids over Hamburg and Lubeck, but Thomas was in no mood to buy an evening newspaper.

When he got to the corner of his street, he found it deserted and completely blacked out, but the nearer he got to his own house, he thought he saw someone disappear fairly quickly back into the main road at the far end. Then he felt something brush against his leg, and although he couldn't really see what it was in the dark, he could tell that it was 'Whisky', his next-door neighbour's moggie. 'Nothin' for yer ternight, mate,' he said briefly, bending down to stroke the animal, who was displaying his usual cupboard love.

Once inside the house, he drew the blackout curtain at the passage door, then switched on the light and went straight into the back parlour. It was obvious his dad hadn't been home since he left at midday for the start of his shift at the hospital, for the place was freezing cold. So the first thing he did was to stoke up the oven grate, and add some black market coal. In the scullery, his dad had left the usual badly scrawled note: *Dinner in oven.*

Since dinner turned out to be not in the oven, but to be a tin of spam, three unpeeled potatoes and a tin of peas on the table, he opted instead for a slice of bread and beef dripping from the larder. Then he found himself what remained of a bottle of brown ale in the dresser cupboard, and sat down to his feast at the back parlour table.

After a moment or so, his eyes glanced up at the framed snapshots of his mam and dad on the mantelpiece over the oven range, and he sat there pondering why, if his dad was now so distant from his wife, why he kept those snapshots on view. And then he got to thinking about his dad, and what Beth had passed on about him being under suspicion by the security authorities. It made him mad to hear the man accused of being some kind of spy, when Thomas knew only too well that, despite his hot-headed views on Northern Ireland, he didn't deserve to have his character attacked in such a scurrilous way. Even so, it did make Thomas look back over recent events with his dad, trying to remember if he had ever said anything that could in any way be misconstrued as passing on information to the enemy. But the more he made himself think about it, the more he was convinced that the whole thing was crazy and ridiculous. After all, what possible secret information would a hospital ward porter have that could be of any interest to the Germans? He even smiled at the thought: '*The British are losing the war because they're running out of bandages!*'

The whole idea was getting more absurd by the minute. His dad may have a lot of failings, he may be opinionated and set in his ways, but the one thing he certainly wasn't, was a traitor. But then he got to thinking about Beth again, and all that rubbish she had talked about the steel plant up at Derby, and how Jerry had tried to bomb the place after he'd heard about it from Jane Grigsby. God! How stupid can you get! He got up in a rage, ran his fingers through his hair and stomped out of the room. But in the passage, he suddenly came to a dead halt. It was as though something had just hit him, and hit him hard, something that was so trivial that it probably didn't mean anything at all. Even so, he *did* remember passing comment about that steel plant one evening when he was eating a meal with his . . . an automatic reaction suddenly made him swing round and stare at the cellar door. After considering it for a moment, slowly, methodically, he went to the door and opened it.

As he stood at the top of the cellar stairs, he stared blankly into the dark, which was only broken when he turned on the light switch. He went down carefully, and soon realised why he had never ventured down into the place, because the smell of damp and decay was stifling. The low-voltage bulb cast eerie shadows all around the old brick cellar walls, but as he wandered around, there seemed to be nothing there that was very unusual. He went to the small stack of newly arrived coal, which, because it had been obtained on the black market, had been shoved under cover of dark by his dad, through the round iron grating in the pavement above. He looked up at the grating, from where thawed snow had recently been seeping down on to the cellar floor.

'*No smoke without fire.*' For some unconscious reason, those bloody awful words kept going through his mind, and so, in one swift movement, he turned back to the stairs again, and started to go up them. But he had only reached halfway when he came to a stop. Turning round, he focused on something that had only registered marginally for a split second when he saw it just a moment before. It was an oven, an old oven stove, only just visible behind some wooden fruit crates and a step ladder. For one moment, he seemed hypnotised by the thing, until he finally came to, and gradually went down the stairs again. He took his time approaching the corner where the oven was placed, and even when he got there, he took a moment before he moved anything. Then, piece by piece, he removed the crates and the ladder, and stood looking at the oven stove. He leaned down and opened the oven door. It was almost no surprise at all when he came across a small, battered leather case there inside, so he lifted it out and took it across to a workbench nearby. Once he'd summoned up enough courage, he unfastened the case and opened the lid. The shock was immediate; all the blood seemed to drain from his body. What he found there made him gasp aloud: 'Holy Mother of God – no!'

Chapter 20

On Monday evening, it was nearly half past six by the time Beth got back home from the factory. After the distressing experience of seeing Thomas deliberately get on to another bus to avoid travelling with her, she just wanted time to be alone, to think of any way that she could make things right between them again. But, she asked herself, how was she going to be able to do it if Thomas wouldn't even talk to her, and even if he did, what if he didn't understand a word she was saying? After she got off the bus at the Nag's Head, she decided to take a bit of a detour on her way home, and so, using her torch to light her way along the pavements in the blackout, she turned off into Enkel Street past the back entrances of Marks and Spencers and Woolworths department stores, where rubbish collectors outside were loading their horse-drawn carts with the stores' leftovers. For one brief moment, her torch beam picked out the eyes of one of the black dray horses that could hardly be seen in the dark, so she stopped to have a word with him. 'I tell yer wot, mate,' she said, as she gently stroked his nose and ear. 'I'd sooner 'ave your job any day. At least yer don't 'ave no one ter answer back to.' She strolled down Roden Street and stood for a few moments listening to the early evening boozers in the nearby Enkel pub. It was a comforting feeling to know that, after the continuing lull in the air raids, they might be able to see an evening through without having to rush off into the nearest public shelters.

She timed her arrival home for after six-thirty, for despite the lull in the air raids, her mum was still insisting on taking the baby down into the warehouse shelter each evening. However, Beth knew that her mum would be in good company, for some of the other regulars were of the same opinion as herself: 'Better ter be safe than sorry.' Beth knew she would have to go along and join them eventually, but for the time being she was content not to have to rush.

Once she'd got to the end of Moray Road, she thought she felt the first drops of either rain or sleet, so she quickened her pace. Once inside the house, she found the light in the hall passage on, which meant she had to close the front door quickly. She took off her coat and hat and hung them up, but the moment she went into the kitchen she knew that her mum had been cooking something, for there was a wonderful smell of onions, potatoes and tomatoes, together with a note on the table which said in Connie's handwriting: 'It just needs warming up for ten minutes. See you down there later.'

Sure enough, when she opened the oven door, she found her supper, a dish of corned beef hash, which her mum, being an American, had pre-cooked to perfection. Collecting the box of matches from their usual place on the ledge above the cooker, she got down on her hands and knees, lit the oven, and closed the oven door. After making herself a cup of tea, she sat down at the kitchen table and waited for the hash to finish warming up. Once again she was tormented by thoughts of the awful day she had just had. In particular she was wondering what the reaction of Thomas's father would be if Thomas told him that he was under suspicion for passing on information to the enemy, and that both he and their house was under constant observation by the security people. She was so absorbed by all these nagging thoughts, that she almost forgot her corned beef hash, but just as she had got the teacloth ready to take the dish out of the oven, she looked up with a start towards the ceiling, distracted by what sounded like a thump on the floor upstairs. She put the dish back into the oven and rushed out into the hall.

She looked up at the first-floor landing, but there was no sign of anyone there. Knowing that her mum was down in the warehouse shelter, and Phil was on duty at the fire station, her first inclination was that it was a fall of snow frozen on the roof which had suddenly fallen into the back garden. After waiting a moment or so, just in case she had interrupted someone who had broken into the house, she made her way back slowly to the kitchen. Before she had got there, however, there came another thumping sound. This time, she decided to investigate.

Quietly climbing the stairs, she checked her parents' room first, and then her own, relieved to find that there was no one there. Then she looked up the small flight of stairs that led to the upper landing, where Phil's room was situated, together with a small boxroom next to it. To her surprise, she saw a light beneath the door of Phil's bedroom, and so, with some relief, she went straight in. 'Yer stupid git!' she said as she entered. 'Why didn't yer tell me yer was . . .' She stopped dead, and couldn't believe what she saw. Two faces appeared over the top of the bedclothes. It was Phil and his girlfriend Shirley.

'Blimey!' gasped Beth, immediately getting out and slamming the door behind her.

Some time later, there was something of a similar situation at the Sullivan home in King's Cross. Joe Sullivan arrived back earlier than usual from his shift work at the hospital because he had something to do, something that should have been done days ago. Fortunately, the moment he found the house in darkness, he knew that Thomas had probably gone out for the evening with Beth, and so after taking off his coat and woollen cap, he went straight to the cellar door and opened it. To his shock and horror, he found the light on, and as soon as he stepped on to the landing and looked down, he saw Thomas sitting at the workbench below, the contents of the small leather case spread out in front of him. 'Come on down, Dada,' he called. 'Yer don't want to be late for your appointment, now do yer?'

Joe Sullivan came down the stairs. 'What the hell are you doin' down here?' he snapped, with smouldering anger. 'You know damn well this place has got nothin' ter do with you!'

'How long has it been goin' on, Dada?' Thomas asked the moment Sullivan had reached him.

Sullivan looked at the transmitting equipment Thomas had laid out neatly on the workbench. 'This is none of your business,' he said, as quietly and reasonably as he could manage. 'I don't have ter explain a damned thing ter you.'

'Is that a fact?' returned Thomas. 'Even when your own son could have been killed by those bombs around the factory the other night?'

Sullivan turned away. 'I didn't know about that,' he replied. 'I didn't know they were goin' ter . . .'

'*They?*' asked Thomas. 'Who are *they*, Dada?'

Sullivan turned back to him. 'You're playin' with fire, son,' he said forcefully. 'Keep out of it.'

'What about that steel factory up at Derby?' persisted Thomas. 'When I happened ter mention it to you in passing, never did I think a couple of days later yer pals would be over ter bomb it. Have yer no conscience, Dada? Have yer no reason?'

'Oh I have plenty of reason, Thomas,' retorted Sullivan. 'The domination of *my* country by people far worse than the Nazis!'

'Mother Mary!' cried Thomas in sheer disbelief.

'You don't think what I'm sayin' is true?' asked Sullivan tersely. 'Then let me tell yer somethin'. D'yer remember that woman yer met when I took yer back ter the old country when yer were little? Her name was Sadie, Sadie Malone. She and her husband were born and brought up in a small village just south of Comber in County Down. Old Mick was a grand feller, a great one for the Guinness, very popular with all the lads. He used ter fish every weekend in the estuary up there, had his own boat. But his real job was in the Town Hall, somethin' ter do with the electoral register, makin' lists of everyone livin' in the area. He also happened ter strongly believe in Ireland for the Irish, and that proved his downfall – shot down in cold blood by the Royal Irish Constabulary because he refused to let them stop him delivering anti-Brit pamphlets in the village. In *this* country, Thomas, they call that justice. Old Mick was just one in hundreds. Freedom of speech? Forget it!'

'And you think that that man's death is justification for killing hundreds of innocent people?' asked Thomas.

'It happened, son,' retorted Sullivan. 'I didn't dream it!'

'Dada,' persisted Thomas, going to him. 'Nazis are evil.'

'So are the Brits!' returned Sullivan.

'The Nazis kill because they're murderers, because they want power, because they want to be a superior race. They kill women and children, they kill Jews because they're jealous of their intellect and culture, they kill because they want to "cleanse" the world, so that they can start it all over again – in their own perverted way.'

Sullivan stared Thomas out for a moment. 'When you're *my* age, boy,' he said, 'yer don't forget what happened all those years ago.'

'You don't have to forget, Dada,' replied Thomas, 'but it does no good ter dwell. The moment after somethin' happens, it becomes history. What happened to your friend, Dada, *is* history. Yer can't bring him back, yer can't make things right again. What's happenin' in the world today is somethin' very different; it's frightenin' and dangerous. Can't you understand that if you help people like the Nazis, you're damning yourself to a conscience that can never be free as long as you live.'

Sullivan turned away again. 'It's so easy for a young generation,' he snapped. 'What the eye doesn't see, the heart doesn't grieve after.'

'You think I don't grieve, Dada?' asked Thomas, pursuing him. 'You think I haven't stopped grieving ever since I lost my best friend in a bomb that was probably dropped by one of *your* pals? Grief isn't the prerogative of one particular generation, Dada – and neither is revenge.'

Sullivan refused to listen to any more that his son had to say. He turned and started to make his way up the stairs.

'So what are you goin' ter do, Dada?' called Thomas. 'What are you going to do about the people who are watching your every movement?'

Sullivan stopped dead on the stairs.

'They *are* watchin' you, Dada,' continued Thomas relentlessly. 'Don't ask me how I know, but I *do*!' He walked across to the foot of the stairs and looked up at his father. 'And d'you know what they'll do to you, Dada, once they have enough proof? They'll string you up from the highest scaffold they can find!'

For the first time, Sullivan felt totally on the defensive. Crushed and confused, he sat down on one of the stairs, and held on to the wooden banister. In the course of just a few minutes, his entire world had fallen apart. He didn't know what to think, he didn't know what to say, all he knew was that what his son had said was true.

And yet, as he sat there, he found it impossible to look his son in the eyes. He found it impossible to say that over the past few months he had done everything in his power to turn away from his own bitterness and hatred. 'You don't understand, do you, son?' he asked remorsefully. 'You don't understand how I felt when these people first approached me. What they said made sense. The Brits have treated us like dirt. All they've ever wanted is power, power to hold on to land that doesn't belong to them. That's why I wanted to join the struggle.' He looked up at Thomas with a pained look in his eyes. 'But I never wanted to kill innocent people – yer've got ter believe me, son. It all just – got out of hand.'

'But why didn't you tell me, Dada?' asked Thomas, moving as close as he could to him. 'Why did you have ter keep things bottled up inside? Why couldn't you just have shared them with me?'

Joe paused a moment, then looked Thomas straight in the eyes. 'Because it was too late, son,' he replied, his expression cracked with desperation. 'They said they'd kill you if I didn't do what they wanted.'

'What?' asked Thomas, taken aback. '*Me?*'

'Oh not in so many words,' replied Sullivan bitterly. 'But I knew what they were sayin', and I knew that I love you too much to gamble with your life.'

Thomas came to the foot of the stairs. 'Who are they, Dada?' he pressed. 'You *have* to tell me.'

Sullivan hesitated. His expression was no longer that of the swaggering bigot. It was of desperation and fear. 'People who'll never give up,' was all he was prepared to say.

In one swift movement, Thomas went across to the workbench, collected all the bits and pieces of the transmitter together, and threw them back into the suitcase.

'What're yer doin'?' asked his father, standing up.

'I'm gettin' rid of all this stuff,' he replied busily. 'I'll pack it up in the bagwash. If I go out with it, no one's going to take any notice. I'll take it down to the embankment, and dump it in the river. The most important thing is to get you out of here as fast as we can!'

'W-what're you talkin' about?' spluttered Sullivan, who was suddenly like a child as his son started to organise things. 'This is crazy! You said yerself, everyone's watchin' the house.'

'Just collect as many things together as you need,' said Thomas breathlessly. 'But don't take them with you, just go to the hospital as though you were going off on night shift. I'll find some way of getting the things to you later.'

'But – where am I goin'?' asked Sullivan. 'If they're all keepin' an eye on me –'

'Leave the hospital during a tea break, a meal break – anything,' said Thomas. 'Then make your way up North. You've got plenty of mates up there who'll be willing to help you. Just lie low for as long as you can, until everyone realises you've gone.'

'And then what?'

Thomas stopped what he was doing. 'And then you disappear, Dada,' he said, going to him. 'You go back home, to the *real* home that you've never really left.'

Beth was reeling from the shock of finding her young brother in bed with his girlfriend. It wasn't just the fact that they were under-age to do such a thing, but the sly way in which Phil had gone about it, and after the two of them had put on their clothes and come down to the parlour, she gave him a real right rollicking. 'If it was Mum that came in an' found yer,' she ranted, 'she'd've 'ad your guts fer garters!'

'Well it wasn't Mum, was it?' snapped Phil, who curled up with his arm around Shirley on the sofa. 'An' you can talk. You ain't no saint!'

'We ain't talkin' about *me*,' growled Beth. 'You're boaf under age. If the law found out what yer've bin up to, they'd lock yer up and frow away the key!'

'Please, Beth,' pleaded Shirley, who looked decidedly uncomfortable sitting so close to Phil after what had just gone on in his room upstairs. 'If anyone's to blame, it's me. Phil asked me to come back here, and I said yes.'

Beth looked at the girl, whom she had only just met for the first time, and found that she really rather liked her, not just because she was a pretty little thing, but because she showed a kind of humility. 'I'm not *blamin'* anyone, Shirley,' she replied. 'I mean I'm only Phil's sister, not our mum or dad. But – well, you're still at school . . .'

'She's sixteen – same as me!' insisted Phil defiantly, as though that was some kind of permission to do what they wanted.

'Sixteen ain't legal, Phil,' Beth reminded him.

'Neivver's eighteen,' he retorted.

'Wot yer talkin' about?' asked Beth.

'*You* was only eighteen,' said Phil with a smug grin, 'when you an' Thomas slept tergevver upstairs. An' *that* was when there was no one in the 'ouse at the time. Don't fink I don't know, 'cos I do!'

Beth was furious, not because what Phil had said was untrue, but because, since that day, Thomas and she had never had the chance to be alone together to do such a thing again. She threw a quick look at Shirley, who was so embarrassed, she didn't quite know where to look.

'Yer cheeky bugger!' barked Beth, turning on Phil. 'Yer know very well if Dad knew about wot yer've bin up to, 'e'd kill yer stone dead!'

' 'E *does* know.'

Both Beth and Shirley looked at him in utter astonishment.

'I told 'im when 'e was 'ome on leave.'

Shirley was shocked. 'Phil!' she said, aghast.

'You told Dad that you and Shirley were – sleepin' tergevver?' asked Beth.

'I told 'im that I wanted to – if she'd let me.'

Beth was finding it a bit hard to take all this in. 'And wot did 'e say?'

' 'E said it was up ter me,' replied Phil, without a shred of guilt, 'provided we didn't do anyfin' too silly and took precautions. "Live fer today", that's 'is motto.

Beth slumped back into her chair. As she looked at her young brother, she couldn't believe that this was the same boy she used to bully when they were small kids together, the same boy that used to harass her so much that she often walloped him behind their parents' backs. The only difference now was that he wasn't a boy any longer. His features were that of a young man who had decided views about how he wanted to live his life, without interference from anyone around him. Phil now reminded her of their dad in more ways than one. 'Wot about *your* dad, Shirley?' she asked. 'Don't tell me yer've told 'im too?'

'You're joking!' replied Shirley. 'If *my* dad knew what I was . . . well, I think he'd never want to see me again. He's got so many old-fashioned ideas. Even though he's a fireman, I think he forgets there's a war on. You never know what tomorrow's going to bring.'

'In any case,' said Phil, suddenly leaping up from the sofa, 'I don't see wot all the fuss is about. As soon as I've made a bit of cash, me an' Shirl are goin' ter get married.'

Beth looked up like a shot. 'You're wot?'

'We're goin' ter get married,' repeated Phil. 'Wos wrong wiv that?'

'Well, don't yer fink Mum an' Dad may 'ave somefin' ter say about that?'

'They can say wot they like,' replied Phil cockily, taking out a packet of fags and matches from his trousers' pocket. 'But it won't make no diff'rence. I love Shirl, an' she loves me. As far as I'm concerned, that's all that counts, an' if anyone don't like it, that's their problem – not ours.'

Beth watched him light up a fag, something she had never seen him do before. For her, it was a revelation. In fact everything about him now was a revelation. Despite the fact that they had grown up together, she didn't really know him any more.

Despite the promise of rain earlier in the evening, by the time Beth reached the warehouse air raid shelter, the skies were clear again, the moon full, and every star in the galaxy was putting on a show of dazzling magnificence. On the way, Beth could hear that all the customers in the pubs were enjoying themselves, only too pleased that the way things were going, air raids were a thing of the past.

Down in the shelter, things were also in a buoyant mood. The regulars had no real excuse for being there, and their nightly sojourns had really turned into a social gathering. In many ways, their close relationship was quite endearing, for each of them had taken to bringing their own contribution to help pass the night away. Eileen Perkins, for instance, had brought two packets of digestive biscuits, which had practically disappeared from the shops since the start of the war, but which she had apparently managed to get by using her feminine charms on Mr Braithwaite, the local grocer, who clearly fancied her like mad; her young daughter Rita brought a bag of liquorice allsorts, which came from 'under the counter' from 'Pop's' sweet shop further down Hornsey Road; the Lieberman brothers brought their usual Turkish delight; Lil Winkler had some potato cakes, made with, amongst other things, marmalade, saccharine tablets and beef dripping; and Jack Cutter had brought three quart bottles of brown ale which, to Jessie Hawks's disapproval, he and Bill Winkler were getting through rather more quickly than she would have liked. However, Jessie herself didn't come empty-handed, for even she had made a pile of fish-paste sandwiches which went down like a bomb. Connie's contribution was a very special one – two huge vacuum flasks of homemade pumpkin soup, made from one of her mother's recipes back home in Texas. When Jessie was offered *her* cup of soup she ungraciously sniffed at it very suspiciously before taking a tentative sip, wary of tasting something that she was unfamiliar with for the first time. But at least she was able to wash it down with a nice cup of tea, a job which Beth had allocated to herself. However, it was not long before she was back to 'tinkling the ivories' again, which was something the regulars looked forward to most of all. But whilst she was playing, she just couldn't clear her mind of all the awful things that had happened during that day, especially the sight of Thomas getting on that bus after work up at the Tally Ho, and the prospect that the two of them might never talk to each other again . . .

It wasn't the best of nights to make an escape, no matter how discreet. With a full moon beaming out of a clear dark night sky, the entire street outside the house in King's Cross was so illuminated it could have been done by arc lights. As he peered through a chink in the blackout curtains, Thomas wasn't as yet sure how he was going to play this game of hide and seek, to get his father out of the house without too much notice being taken. Eventually, however, he decided that the only way *was* to draw attention, and so when his father came out of the house a few minutes later, he would make it perfectly clear that Dada was merely on his way to night shift at the hospital.

Whilst he was waiting for his father to get ready for his last departure from the house, Thomas sat in the dark in the front parlour trying to work out how he was going to deal with the security people once it was known that Joe Sullivan had slipped away from work during a late-night meal break. It was *he*, Thomas, who would have to answer the questions, *he*, Thomas, who would have to look into the eyes of people like Jane Grigsby and tell them that he hadn't the faintest idea where his father had gone to. Worse still, was how he was going to come to terms with the way he had reacted to Beth when she had warned him that his father was the one who was under suspicion, and not him. *She* was right, and *he* was wrong. It was a thought that had been haunting him ever since he found that transmitting equipment down in the cellar. But the thing that was worrying Thomas most of all, was how he was going to apologise to Beth. He was only too aware that never in his life had he been one to apologise; he was far too proud for that. Nonetheless, there had to be a way, he had to *find* a way, because if he didn't he would lose the one person who meant more to him than anyone else in the whole wide world.

A few moments later, Thomas and his father stood in the passage hall by the front door. Not a word was spoken between them as they stood there, staring into each other's eyes, allowing a lifetime's relationship to skip past them without comment. Thomas turned off the passage light, and with a sudden flourish, opened the front door to let his dad out. Sullivan, dressed in his usual everyday clothes, went straight out into the street. Thomas followed him out on to the doorstep, and called out clearly to be heard by whoever was watching from the shadows, 'See yer later, Dada! I'll leave somethin' in the oven for yer.'

Sullivan didn't turn to look back, merely waved his hand casually.

For one brief moment, Thomas watched him go. He felt his stomach churn, his heart burning with emotion. That was his father, his dada out there, now nothing more than a dark shape bathed in the full light of a November moon, like a mirage that never existed. But it *did* exist. The man he could see becoming a smaller and smaller figure as he strolled down the street was a man who had allowed his life to be ruined by disillusionment and hate; there was no turning back now. As Joe Sullivan turned the corner and disappeared into the main road,

Thomas had no idea if or who might be waiting for him during the coming days, or whether or not he would ever get the chance to see his dada again.

After an hour and a half of knocking out one sing-song after another on the old Joanna, to tumultuous applause and calls of '*Good ol' Beff!*', Beth flopped down exhausted on the lower bunk where her mum was sitting.

'Well done, darling,' said Connie, her voice low. 'You really are an inspiration. I don't think anyone can imagine this place without you now.'

'They will,' replied Beth, 'when we go out ter live in 'Ertfordshire!'

Connie sighed. 'I'm sorry you and your brother feel like that,' she said. 'Your grandma and grandad are two very kind people. They really do care about us all.'

'Oh, it's not them,' Beth said, trying to reassure her. 'It's just the way fings are.'

'You mean, you hate the thought of leaving London?'

'No, that's not wot I mean.'

Connie swung a surprised look at her.

'I've bin finkin' about it,' said Beth, kicking off her shoes and crouching on the mattress. 'It'll probably be fer the best. It'll probably be much safer out there.'

Connie was surprised by this change of attitude. 'Does Phil feel the same way?' she asked.

Beth shrugged. 'Phil 'as 'is own ideas,' she replied.

Connie tried to work out what Beth meant. 'Was he home when you left this evening?' she asked, after a pause.

Beth had to think quickly before replying. 'No,' she answered quite casually. 'I fink 'e said somefin' about stayin' on ter do some work on 'is bike up at the station.'

Again, Connie was deep in thought. 'I do worry about that boy,' she said. 'Did you know he has a girlfriend?'

Beth tried her best not to sound too positive. 'Oh – yeah?' she replied vaguely.

'Her name's Shirley,' continued Connie. 'She's the daughter of someone who works up at the fire station. I have a terrible feeling they're getting just a bit too close.'

'Wot makes yer fink that?' asked Beth.

'Oh, I don't know,' said Connie, taking a passing look into the baby's cot. 'It's the way he talks at times, about all the things he wants to do when the war's over, about getting married and settling down. He's far too young to be thinking about that at his age, especially when he's out risking his life night after night.'

'The way fing's're goin,' said Beth, ' 'e won't 'ave ter do that much longer.'

'Oh I wouldn't be so sure,' said Connie prophetically. 'Mr Adolf Shickelgruber isn't finished with us yet. No, but I *do* worry about Phil. I must write to his father about him. In fact, I have quite a lot of important things I have to tell your father.'

Beth let that remark pass without too much thought.

'Mrs Shanks.'

They both looked across to Lil Winkler, who was standing by the piano.

'Wot say we persuade *you* ter play somefin' for us?'

Everyone looked over to Connie, and agreed.

'Oh no, Mrs Winkler,' replied Connie. 'You know what my kind of music sounds like. It just depresses the lot of you.'

'That's not true!' insisted Lil, coming across to her. 'I listen ter lots er fings on the wireless, and they're not all boom boom te boom. Some of the fings they play on *Force's Favourites* on Sunday mornin's are really lovely. 'Andel's "Largo", I always 'ave a good cry when I listen ter that.'

'Well, yer know wot they say, Lil,' called Jack flippantly. 'The more yer cry, the less yer p . . .'

'Don't be so vulgar, Jack!' scolded Lil.

To Connie's surprise, Abe Lieberman got up from sitting on his own bunk, and came over to her. 'You know what would be absolutely wonderful, Mrs Shanks?' he asked. 'Brahms's Lullaby.' Do you know it?'

'Of course she knows it, you idiot!' called Bernie from his bunk.

Abe raised his eyes to heaven and ignored his brother. 'Yes?' he asked, smiling invitingly to Connie.

Connie, embarrassed, shook her head.

'Come on, Mum!' said Beth, urging her on. 'Yer don't need no music. Yer know *that* one by 'eart!'

'Please?' pleaded Abe.

With calls of 'Come on, Mrs S!' to urge her on, Connie stood up.

Like the perfect gentleman he was, Abe offered Connie his arm, which she took, letting him lead her across to the piano. 'Oh well,' she said, as she sat down on the piano stool, 'you asked for it!'

As her fingers touched the keyboard, everyone settled down to listen. The reaction from them all was immediate, for the soothing sound of 'Brahms's Lullaby' cast a potent spell on an unreal atmosphere, so much so that even Jack Cutter stopped playing 'Patience' to look up and listen, whilst the others began to hum the melody. It was a moment of pure magic for them all, especially Beth, who watched her mum playing with not only rapt attention, but with intense pride. However, just as the piece was drawing to an end, the sound of Moaning Minnie cut across that magic. Connie finished playing and then turned to look around at the others.

Everyone's eyes were gazing up forlornly towards the ceiling. The so-called lull was clearly over. Their few days of relief and joy were about to come to an end.

Chapter 21

In the aftermath of the *Luftwaffe*'s latest bombing campaign, fires had broken out all over London. Amongst many of the worst-affected areas was, as ever, the East End, where a series of direct hits by high-explosive bombs on the docks and warehouses caused death and destruction on an unprecedented scale. In Islington, Jessie Hawks was none too pleased when she arrived home from the warehouse shelter the next morning to discover that the windows of her house had been blown in for the fourth time, and when Bill Winkler got home, he was furious to find that his chimney-pot had not only been dislodged from its stack, but had careered through the roof, passing right through two floors, and ending up in his front parlour below. The expletives flying around the streets that day were, to say the least, somewhat derogative of Hitler and his bomber pilots, especially as it meant that the regulars of the warehouse shelter would once again be condemned to an endless life underground.

After helping her mum to clear up the broken roof tiles that had come tumbling down into their front garden, Beth went off to work at the munitions factory. On the way, there were appalling scenes of devastation where terraced shops and houses had vast smouldering gaps, and tracker dogs and their army handlers were scrambling over the debris trying to locate any sign of life beneath. After a while, it all proved too much for Beth, and so for the rest of the journey she simply turned away from the taped-up bus window.

Fortunately, the factory itself was unscathed, but as she clocked in and went into the women's locker room to change, she hoped she wouldn't bump into Thomas because, quite frankly, she wouldn't know what to say to him. But the moment she reached her own workbench, the girls were breathlessly waiting with some news for her.

' 'E's in trouble!' croaked Elsie Tuckwell excitedly. 'If yer ask me, they're goin' ter charge 'im any minute.'

'Who's in trouble, Elsie?' asked Beth anxiously. 'Wot are yer talkin' about?'

'It's Thomas, Beff,' said big Mo, attempting to temper Elsie's exaggerations. 'But I'm sure there's nuffin' ter worry about.'

'They stopped 'im at the gates when he got 'ere about 'alf an 'our ago,' said Elsie, rambling on at full steam. 'It's all ter do wiv 'is dad. Looks like'e's in real trouble.'

'Where d'yer 'ear all this?' asked Beth.

'All the gels're talkin' about it,' said Elsie. 'Some of 'em saw it 'appen. 'E's waitin ter go inter the security office now!'

'Oh fer goodness sake shut up, Elsie!' snapped Midge Morton who came up to join them. 'It's got nuffin' ter do wiv Beff, so why don't yer just leave 'er alone!'

'I agree wiv that!' added Mo, wholeheartedly.

Midge's and Mo's sturdy defence of Beth met with some resentment from Elsie. 'Well, I'm not tellin' yer somefin' that everybody don't know!' she moaned.

Once Elsie was out of the way, Mo took Beth to one side. 'Keep a look out for Charlie,' Mo said to Midge. 'We're just goin' out ter 'ave a quick fag.'

Midge gave the thumbs-up sign, and went on watch for Charlie Hatchet, the foreman, leaving Mo to lead Beth out through the workshop door that was an emergency exit into the backyard.

Beth was glad that she had her warm jumper and slacks on under her work aprons, because it was bitterly cold outside.

' 'Ave a fag,' said Mo, getting out her packet of Woodbines.

Beth shook her head. 'Yer know I don't.'

'Yer should,' said Mo, lighting up. 'It 'elps yer ter cope.' She looked around, and lowered her voice. 'It's also marvellous after sex!' She laughed at her own joke, and almost swallowed a mouthful of smoke as she did so. 'Seriously though,' she continued, 'yer mustn't worry about Thomas. 'E knows 'ow ter take care of 'imself.'

' 'Is dad's a spy, Mo,' replied Beth. 'I tried ter tell 'im, but 'e refused ter believe me. That's why 'e's bin 'auled inter security now. They won't rest 'til they get their last drop er blood out of 'im. But there's nuffin' *I* can do about it. 'E won't even talk ter me.'

'D'yer love Thomas, Beff?' asked Mo, right out of the blue.

'Wot d'yer mean?' she asked.

'It's a simple question,' replied Mo. 'D'yer love 'im or don't yer? Yes or no?'

Beth knew what the answer was, but because of the way things were between them she just couldn't bring herself to say it. 'Oh Gawd,' she sighed, moving a few steps away. 'Who knows?'

Mo followed her. 'D'yer know somefin'?' she asked. 'Thomas come up an' talked ter me yesterday. It's the first time 'e's done that since we started workin' 'ere. I don't know why 'e did it, when yer consider those rotten fings I said about 'im the uvver week. But 'e 'ad somefin' ter say, so I listened.' She paused a moment to take a light puff of her fag.

There was a great deal of activity in the yard, with girls rushing from one workshop to another, a few middle-aged men carrying machine parts through one of the side doors, and in the background, a burly armed guard was on duty at the outside entrance to the top secret workshop.

'It was all about you,' said Mo. 'About 'ow disappointed 'e was that yer'd let 'im down.'

Beth swung a look at her.

'But 'e didn't mean a word of it,' continued Mo. 'An' d'yer know 'ow I could tell?' She moved closer. 'It was by the way 'e never stopped talkin' about yer, never stopped talkin' about all the good times yer'd had tergevver, the places yer've bin to, the laughs, the trust yer've always 'ad in each uvver. Somebody who talks like that ain't goin' ter give up lovin' you *that* easily, no matter 'ow bitter an' twisted they feel inside. Take my word – wotever's goin' on in that security office right now, ain't goin' ter change the way fings are between 'im an' you.'

'We'll see, Mo,' said Beth, downcast. 'We'll see.'

★

In the security office, Thomas was being interrogated by Jane Grigsby, watched over by two Special Branch police officers, one in uniform, the other in civilian clothes.

'Where is he, Thomas?' asked Jane, leaning across her desk at him. 'Your father left the house for work in the hospital about ten o'clock last night, but he'd already done his shift for the day. Within a short while of arriving at the hospital, he disappeared, probably through an exit in Manor Gardens that was unlikely to have been watched by – those who were keeping a constant lookout for him. Where is he making for, Thomas?'

Thomas sat in his chair facing her across the desk, his expression completely bland and un-giving. 'I don't know what you're talkin' about,' he replied.

The plain-clothes officer took over. Although he was clearly middle-aged, he had well-greased black hair and moustache which somehow made him look younger. 'We've searched your house, Thomas,' he said formally. 'We *know* what was in that cellar, and so, I suspect, do you.'

'I thought you were supposed to produce a search warrant for that sort of thing,' replied Thomas tersely.

'Your father's a murderer.'

Thomas swung a look at the second, older man, a uniformed police superintendent, whose features were not easy to see because he was standing behind Jane with his back to the window.

'The information he passed on', said the superintendent, who was of the old school of bobbies, unafraid of going straight to the point, 'was probably responsible for the deaths of hundreds of people. Does that give you any cause for concern, Thomas?'

Thomas turned away brusquely.

'When we catch him,' persisted the man in uniform, 'once a judge and jury find him guilty, he'll go to the gallows.'

'And you expect me to help you find him?' replied Thomas sharply.

'It depends who you feel the most allegiance to – *this* or the *old* country?

Contrary to what the man may have thought, his question didn't ruffle Thomas at all. In fact, he had been expecting it. 'I've lived here for the best part of my life,' he replied. 'I'm as much a part of *this* country as anyone who was born here.'

'But would you go to war for it?' pressed the man, who thought his question was quite a clever one.

Thomas turned to look at him. 'Yes, I would,' he replied without a moment's hesitation. 'Like a lot of my Irish friends in the British army.'

'Then why haven't you done so already?' asked the man. 'Is it because your father would object?'

Thomas snapped right back. 'My father has nothing to do with it!' he said, knowing only too well that what he was saying wasn't true.

The man's expression stiffened.

The plain-clothes officer took over again. 'Thomas,' he said with a softer approach than his colleague, 'last night, your father left the house and went to do his night shift at the hospital. But he'd already done his shift for the day. Where did he go to?'

'I've already told you, I've no idea.'

'But he must have talked it over with you?'

Thomas shook his head. 'My father never talked about *anything* with me. If he had, he wouldn't be in the trouble he's in now.' He sighed.

'Is he getting a safe passage across the Channel,' asked the uniformed man brusquely, 'or is he trying to get back to Ireland?'

'Out of the two,' said Thomas, 'I hope he goes back to the old country. At least there's not much chance of any harm coming to him there.'

'I wouldn't be so sure,' replied the uniformed man. 'We're not the only ones who'll be looking for him – or you. If I was you, I'd be on your guard. Your father's friends won't be too pleased when they know he's gone.'

Thomas swung a glare at him. 'I'm not scared of them – *or* you!' he snapped back angrily.

'Look, Thomas,' said Jane, trying to cool the atmosphere. 'I've always said that I don't believe for one moment that you personally have been in any way involved in your father's activities. But the fact that he *is* your father makes you just as much of a security risk.'

'So what's that supposed ter mean?' asked Thomas.

'It means,' replied Jane, with a genuine look of regret, 'that with immediate effect, you won't be able to work in this factory any more. It also means that, until we know what has happened to your father, we can't allow you to make any contact at all with Beth Shanks.'

With the resumption of the air raids, Beth had no wish to hang around the factory once she had finished work in the evening. Sure enough, however, just as the girls were about to leave the workshop, Moaning Minnie wailed out, sending them all scurrying down into the factory air raid shelter, which was a cut above what Beth was used to in the old warehouse in Hornsey Road, for it was a massive area, equipped with everything from electric light, a wind-up gramophone, an upright piano, and plenty of stores and provisions just in case a bomb should fall on the place and they were all trapped down there. It was said that the shelter was as safe as houses for the walls and ceilings were reinforced with wire set in concrete, which cut no ice with Beth and the other girls who thought it was a daft place anyway to put a shelter beneath a munitions factory.

Once they had all got settled on their long wooden bench seats, Beth kept an anxious lookout for Thomas, for not only had she had no word as to what had happened to him during the morning, but he hadn't turned up for either the tea or meal breaks. It was therefore left to Midge to find out what she could, and when she joined Beth, Mo, Elsie and the other girls in the shelter, it turned out that she hadn't really found out very much.

'All I know,' said Midge breathlessly, 'is that he left the factory with two fellers about 'alf past ten. One of 'em was a copper.'

'Was 'e in 'andcuffs?' asked Elsie eagerly.

'Don't be so daft, Elsie,' replied Midge dismissively. 'They just left the buildin', and that's all anyone seems ter know.'

'So 'e never went into work at all?' asked Mo.

'Not by the sound of it,' returned Midge.

'So where *did* they take 'im?' asked Elsie, who was applying lipstick without the use of a hand mirror.

'I know yer won't believe this, Elsie,' snorted Midge, 'but the coppers don't always share their little secrets wiv *me*!'

In the background some of the girls were quietly taking the mickey out of two of the senior management team, who were just coming down into the shelter.

'I 'ope we're goin' ter get overtime fer this!' joked one of the girls out loud.

During the laughter that followed from the other girls, the two managers smiled back bravely, trying to join in a joke that was just a little too near the knuckle.

'So wot're yer goin' ter do?' Mo asked Beth. 'S'ppose Thomas don't come back. S'ppose they've kicked 'im out or somefin'?'

Beth shrugged. 'Wot can *I* do if they 'ave,' replied Beth who, like many of the girls, was sitting on her hands to keep warm. 'If 'e won't talk ter me, there ain't much I can do about it.'

'But it's like I said,' replied Mo. 'I'm positive 'e *will* talk to yer, if yer can only get ter see 'im. Why don't yer go up to 'is place in King's Cross, 'ave it out wiv 'im? At least yer'd then know where yer stand.'

'No, Mo!' replied Beth firmly. 'I'd never do that.'

'But why not?' asked Mo.

' 'Cos the last time we talked,' said Beth, 'e made it quite clear that 'e couldn't trust me any more. I don't intend ter beg, Mo. If anyfin's changed, if Thomas really does now understand wot I was tryin' ter do fer 'im, then it's up ter 'im ter get in touch wiv *me*.'

As she spoke, one of the girls from the same workshop came up to her. 'Beff,' said the girl, whose name was Linda. 'Will yer come an' give us a tune?'

Beth immediately shook her head. 'Not now, Lind,' she replied adamantly. 'I 'onestly don't feel up to it.'

'Oh *please*!' begged the girl. 'It gets so borin' down 'ere. It'll make the time go so much faster.'

'Put somefin' on the gramophone,' suggested Beth, desperate to avoid yet another sing-song. 'There's a whole pile er records over there.'

'Yeah,' sighed the girl, 'an' we've 'eard the whole bloomin' lot of 'em over an' over again! If I 'ear "Don't Fence Me In" once more, I'd sooner take me chances outside!'

After a great deal of nudging and encouraging, Beth finally succumbed. After all, she told herself, she did her best to raise the spirits of her neighbours in the shelter back home, so why shouldn't she do the same thing for her own workmates? Quite unconsciously, her face suddenly lit up, and she looked like the Beth they all knew.

'All right!' she announced, leaping up from her seat. 'If yer all gluttons fer punishment, then yer've asked fer it!' Urged on, applauded, and cheered with calls of 'Good ol' firecracker!', Beth practically ran over to the piano and opened the lid. 'Come on then, you lot!' she yelled. 'Let's 'ear yer!'

As Beth launched into 'She'll Be Comin' Round the Mountain', the whole shelter erupted to the sound of raucous singing, some of the words clean, some of the replaced words hardly becoming to young ladies. During all this, ack-ack gunfire echoed around the streets above, but it was neatly outwitted by the girls of the munitions factory, whose defiant voices rose above it all, not only across the London rooftops, but across the English countryside and beyond, to places where music was also being used to soothe the night away . . .

If the cute sounds of Shirley Temple singing 'Animal Crackers in My Soup' didn't quite drift up gracefully from the cellar of the Buchner household, it was no fault of the two children who were reluctantly listening to it. Despite the fact that the Americans were not at war with Germany, their culture was being discouraged by the Third Reich government as 'decadent'. However, whatever the views of the politicians, American and even some British pop stars were popular in Germany, and no matter how much Heinz Buchner disapproved of Shirley Temple or Deanna Durbin or Fred Astaire and Ginger Rogers, his wife Helga drew comfort by listening to them. Alas, the same could not be said of Richard and Dieter, the Buchners' two children, who seemed to prefer the sound of ack-ack gunfire in the fields above to the alien sounds of a foreign child singing a song in a language that, at their school, had been judged offensive to the State. Buchner himself also found it offensive that he and his family were forced to sit incarcerated in their own cellar, simply because the first enemy bomb of the war had actually fallen on their village of Lossheim during the recent massive RAF attacks on Hamburg and Lubeck. He had now come to realise that retaliation for the *Luftwaffe* raids on London and Coventry were an option for the British, but the fact that they were actually doing it close to his own home and family was an outrage. He was relieved that this was his final night at home before rejoining his base in northern France; now that he was reasonably well-recovered from his recent forced-landing, there was nothing he wanted more than to take revenge.

Once the gramophone record had finished, Helga sorted out another one, and wound up the gramophone player.

'Can we have a song in German, please, Mother?' asked Richard, who at seven years of age was two years older and thinner than his small brother, Dieter, who was quite a dumpy little thing. 'I don't understand what that silly girl was singing.'

'Shirley Temple is not a silly little girl, Richard,' replied his mother. 'You said you liked her when I took you to see her at the cinema when you were little.'

'Well I don't now!' the boy snapped. 'I like to hear bands, so that I can march.'

'Me too!' agreed Dieter.

'Yes,' agreed Helga reluctantly, 'but songs are nice too, especially when you can join in and sing with the words.'

'But I don't understand the words,' grumbled Richard, 'so how can I join in?'

Heinz grinned, and put down the newspaper he had been reading. 'That's good thinking, son,' he said to the boy. 'But your mother's right. There are all kinds of music in Germany. One day you'll grow up to appreciate composers like Richard Wagner and Richard Strauss. It will be a whole new world for you.'

Both boys exchanged a puzzled look, pulled a face, and went to their bunk beds to play with their toy soldiers.

For the next few moments, there was silence between all of them. Because of her sons' objections, Helga decided not to put on any more gramophone records, so she returned to the socks she was just finishing off knitting in time for her husband's departure the following morning. A little later, the barrage of gunfire from above seemed to subside, and when Helga turned to look at the two boys, they were fast asleep. She quietly moved her wicker chair closer to her husband's. 'I wish you didn't have to go tomorrow, darling,' she said in hushed tones. 'I'm going to miss you so much. The children are never the same without you.'

'Nonsense,' he said affectionately. 'They adore you, you know they do.' He moved closer to her. 'But I want you to remember something, Helga. You must let them grow up like all the other children at school. You mustn't isolate them.'

'All I want them to do,' replied Helga, 'is to survive this war. I want *all* of us to survive it.'

'What makes you think we won't?' asked Heinz.

Helga flicked her eyes up towards the ceiling; there was an eerie silence from the sky above. 'Sometimes I get scared,' she replied. 'Especially when we have to come down here at night.'

'Darling,' said Heinz, now whispering. 'I want you to promise me that from now on, whatever happens up top, you'll come down here with the boys every night. The RAF – they have ways of sneaking in without being noticed. I don't want you taking any chances.'

Helga was about to reply, but he continued talking.

'That's why I've asked my mother to come and stay with you.'

Helga froze. The one thorn in her life since she married Heinz had been his mother, a widow for twenty years, who had political opinions far beyond her station in life; a woman who was firm and dogmatic, who would make quite sure that everything she, Helga, ever did, would be reported back to her son. At a time like this, it was a terrifying prospect for her.

'I know it's one more mouth to feed,' continued Heinz, 'but Mother will be a big help to you, especially with the children.'

'Heinz,' Helga replied irritably, 'I'm perfectly capable of looking after my own children.'

'There are going to be more and more air raids, Helga,' said Heinz. 'You need someone with you for support.'

'I'd prefer that person to be you,' she replied.

As she spoke the barrage of ack-ack gunfire resumed from above. Both of them looked up in unison to the ceiling.

'When we've invaded Britain,' said Heinz bitterly, 'all this will be a thing of the past. But we have to stop them doing this. You have to understand that, Helga.'

She leaned closer. 'All I want,' she said softly, 'is for you to come back home safely to us.'

He kissed her. 'D'you see this?' he asked. From around his neck, he showed her his lucky charm, a small gold Bavarian beer glass and chain. 'You remember how you gave this to me when we went to the Beerfest in Munich before the war?'

Helga nodded, her eyes welling up with tears.

'Well,' he said, holding out the charm for her to see, '*this* is going to bring me back to you. And d'you know why? Because you and our boys are with me wherever I go.'

Helga gently kissed the charm for good luck. But she did it without any conviction at all . . .

Fortunately, the air raid that had confined the munitions factory staff to the shelter after work hours, lasted little more than half an hour or so, during which time Beth had raised everyone's spirits tremendously by thumping out tune after tune on the piano for a mass sing-song. As soon as the single wail of the All Clear siren came, there was a mad scramble to get out of the place, out into the street and on to the buses. Again, Beth was lucky, for she managed to get on her usual 609 trolleybus almost immediately.

When she got off the bus at the Nag's Head, it was pitch dark, for there were quite a lot of heavy snow clouds around. She got out her torch, and hurried along Seven Sisters Road, only grateful that there was no ack-ack fire to contend with. However, just as she had reached the 'John Essex' men's outfitters store at the junction of Seven Sisters and Hornsey Road, she caught a flash of someone's face illuminated in the dim glare of the half-masked dipped lights of a taxi that was just picking up a passenger. Her heart missed a beat, because, although it really was only a quick glimpse, she was positive that the face she saw was that of the woman called Vera, whom she had seen with her dad outside the warehouse factory a couple of weeks before. Without giving herself time to think it over, she rushed off up Hornsey Road to follow the woman. Remembering what had happened when she fell over in the slush the last time she did such a thing, now she moved carefully, resisting the urge to call the woman's name, just in case it was the wrong person.

Whilst she was trailing the woman at a respectable distance in the pitch dark, Beth's thoughts were dominated by the thought of her dad with this woman, and how long their relationship had been going on. Once again her stomach was churned up inside, and once again she asked herself all sorts of questions as to why her dad had kept it all such a dark secret, kept it from his wife, kept it from his family. But she was now determined about one thing – this whole business had gone far enough, and since her dad had solidly refused to come clean about it when he was home on leave, then she would confront this woman and find out the truth for herself. Whilst she was pondering all this, however, the dark figure that she was following moved on a little faster, and turned off to the left down Tollington Way.

'Beff! Is that you, dear?'

Beth came to an abrupt halt, as the beam of someone's torch was shining directly into her eyes.

'We're just on our way ter the shelter. Are we goin' ter see you an' yer mum down there later?'

Beth recognised the voice immediately. ' 'Allo, Eileen,' she replied. 'Yes, if Mum 'asn't already gone, I'll follow 'er down later.' She tried to move on. 'Yer'll 'ave ter excuse me now. I've gotta . . .'

Once again Eileen delayed her. 'Remind me ter tell yer all about the puppy Rita found near our 'ouse. We're goin' ter keep it, ain't we dear?' She shone the torch on Rita's face, but the child covered her eyes with her hands.

'I'm sorry, Eileen,' called Beth, rushing off. 'Gotter dash!'

'See yer later, then!' returned Eileen hurriedly. 'Oh – an' don't ferget it's ol' Jessie's birfday terday!'

As much as Beth liked Eileen Perkins, she could have murdered her for delaying her just at a time like this. She was even more furious when she realised that no matter where she flicked her torch beam, the woman was nowhere to be seen. Quickening her pace, she turned off into Tollington Way, but the figure she had been following had disappeared. She came to a standstill, utterly frustrated; once again the woman had given her the slip. Gathering herself together, she moved on until she came to Moray Road. By the time she had reached her own front garden gate, there was another light sprinkle of snow, so she quickly went to the front door and let herself in.

As she did so, her mum was waiting for her in the hall. 'Hallo, darling,' said Connie, with a curiously bright expression. 'Oh – don't tell me it's snowing again?'

'You're a bit late, ain't yer?' replied Beth, taking off her coat and headscarf. 'I fawt you'd be down the shelter long ago.'

'I've got everything ready,' replied Connie. 'It won't take us long to get down there. Mustn't be *too* late, though. It's Mrs Hawks's birthday today.'

'Yes, I know,' Beth sighed. 'Eileen Perkins told me.' She turned to go up the stairs. 'Could yer put the kettle on fer a cuppa, please, Mum?' she called out as she started to go upstairs. 'I'm just gonna 'ave a quick wash down . . .'

'Could you wait for that, darling?' called Connie. 'Just for a few minutes.'

Beth came to an abrupt halt and turned.

Her mum was at the foot of the stairs, looking up at her. 'There's someone in the living room I'd like you to meet.'

Beth came slowly down the stairs and followed her mum into the living room.

'Beth,' she said hesitatingly. 'I want you to meet an old friend of your dad's. This is Mrs Jeggs, Mrs Vera Jeggs.' She turned to the woman who had just got up from the armchair. 'Vera. This is our daughter, Beth.'

The woman smiled sweetly, came across and offered out her hand to Beth. ' 'Allo, Beff,' she said. 'It's so nice ter meet yer prop'ly – at last.'

Chapter 22

Beth was so shocked, all she could do was stare. When she came to, she shook the woman's hand limply.

Vera Jeggs was a slightly built woman in her forties, whose hair was jet black, straight, and hung neatly just over her shoulders. But it was her complexion that was her most notable feature, for it was a pure white, in such marked contrast to her hair, and her eyes were so dark and large, they seemed to protrude out of their sockets. 'I was really sorry that night,' she said with a voice that was at first straight out of the East End, but on close scrutiny tinged with just the faint suggestion of a Mediterranean accent. 'Yer dad *should've* introduced us. I told 'im so after yer'd gone.'

Beth looked across at her mum for some kind of explanation.

'Vera and I met kinda accidentally a week or so ago,' said Connie, whose own accent contrasted so much with Vera's. 'We had tea together. There was an awful lot to talk about.' She threw a quick glance at Vera. 'An awful lot that I was so grateful to hear.'

Beth turned to Vera, who nodded.

'Now I want Vera to tell you what she told me,' said Connie, moving to the door, 'so I'm going to leave you two together for a while.'

'I won't be too long, Connie,' said Vera. 'I've got me own lot ter get back to.'

As she watched her mum leave the room, Beth was quite dazed by what she had come home to.

Vera returned to the armchair she had been sitting in, but just as she did so, she broke into a nasty fit of coughing, so she quickly took out her handkerchief from her handbag, and covered her mouth with it. When she had recovered, she looked up and found that Beth was still standing in the same place, looking in bewilderment at her. 'Yer know,' Vera said, 'I reckon wot I wanna tell yer is best 'eard sittin' down – all comfortable like.'

Beth hesitated a moment, then went to sit on the sofa. It was only then that she really noticed that Vera was neatly dressed in a heavy woollen grey cardigan, pale long-sleeved blue blouse, and navy-blue skirt.

Before she said anything, Vera delicately wiped her lips and tucked her handkerchief back into her handbag. 'Me an' your dad were mates,' she began. 'Oh it was years ago, before you was even born. I'd only just got over 'ere from Malta – that's where I was born. I'd only bin married a year.' Her eyes lowered sorrowfully. 'My 'usband was in the Royal Navy – the British 'ad a lot er ships docked down there. 'E was me mum an' dad's choice – not mine. I s'ppose yer could call it a kind of 'arranged marriage', only it was one that *I* didn't arrange meself. Trouble is, Mum 'n' Dad fawt I'd stand a better chance in life if I went ter England, and this bloke – 'is name was 'Arry Jeggs – seemed ter them the best way ter do it. But I really 'ated the bloke, I truly 'ated 'im!'

'Why?' asked Beth.

It was the first time Beth had said anything, and it took Vera by surprise. 'Why?' she asked. 'Well, when someone keeps givin' yer black eyes fer absolutely no reason at all, I s'ppose it don't exactly endear 'im to yer, do it?' She felt she was going to cough again, but before she had retrieved her handkerchief, the feeling subsided. 'Anyway,' she continued, 'we went ter live in Shoreditch. Wasn't a bad place – two bedrooms an' a livin' room at the top of this 'ouse. There was even a barffroom on the first-floor landin'. That was a *real* luxury, I can tell yer – especially after wot *I'd* come from. Anyway, after that it was down'ill all the way. Petty Officer Jeggs soon got fed up wiv wot 'e'd really married me for, and started lookin' around fer somefin' better. Yer know wot sailors are!' She chuckled at her sad little joke, very nearly bringing on another fit of coughing. 'The trouble started when I told 'im one night that I knew wot 'e was up to. 'E suddenly swung 'is fist at me, an' said a bleedin' little whore like me's got nuffin' ter write 'ome about.' She shook her head in despair. 'That went on fer quite a time. If it 'adn't bin fer your dad . . .'

'Should you really be tellin' me all this, Mrs Jeggs?' Beth asked, who was beginning to feel deeply embarrassed. 'I mean, wotever went on between you an' Dad is none er my business.'

'Oh but it is, my dear,' Vera assured her gently, moving to the edge of her chair. 'Yer know – somehow – I fink yer've got the wrong end er the stick, 'cos *nuffin'* – absolutely *nuffin'* – went on between me an' your dad. Wot 'e did fer me was somefin' I'll never ferget. 'E saved my life.'

Beth was puzzled.

'Yes Beff,' continued Vera, 'I'd've bin dead an' buried by now if it 'adn't bin fer 'im.' She gently leaned her head back. 'We first met when 'e come round ter do a bit er decoratin' for the old couple who lived on the ground floor where me an' 'Arry lived. In those days, yer dad was a jack-of-all-trades – willin' ter do anyfin' as long as 'e got paid fer it. Anyway, soon after 'Arry left the navy and got this scaffoldin' job, I used ter see yer dad from time ter time, 'ave a bit of a chinwag about the wevver or wot 'ave yer. Then when 'Arry got me pregnant the first time, yer dad used ter carry the shoppin' up the stairs for me, somefin' 'Arry would never've dreamed er doin'! Then one day, yer dad stopped an' ad a cuppa tea wiv me, an' 'e told me 'is entire life story, an' I told 'im mine. We got on like a 'ouse on fire, but I never told 'im about 'Arry goin' off wiv all these uvver women. After I 'ad my second baby, though, fings got nasty. I fink it was just that 'Arry was fed up livin' wiv me, an' wanted ter get out. Trouble was, there was nowhere fer 'im ter go, so 'e just got more and more frustrated so that every time I even said anyfin' to 'im, 'e just walloped me – time and time again. That's where yer dad stepped in. When 'e saw me wiv these black eyes an' fings, 'e got really angry, an' asked me why 'Arry was doin' this ter me. Well, one day yer dad come over an' saw 'Arry after 'e come 'ome from work. I told 'im not to, but 'e wouldn't listen. It ended up in a fight, a really awful fight. 'Arry got the worst of it, er course – yer dad was quite a bruiser in his time. Anyway, before yer dad left, 'e warned 'Arry that if 'e so much as laid one more finger on me, 'e'd 'ave 'is guts fer garters.' She smiled to herself. 'I remember cryin' a lot, not fer me, but becos your dad was the only person who 'ad ever stuck up fer me.'

Beth watched her carefully as she gently removed hair away that had fallen across her face. 'And was that the end of it?' Beth asked.

'Unfortunately not,' replied Vera solemnly. 'A coupla weeks after that, 'Arry beat me up again, but this time 'e went just a bit too far. 'E went fer me wiv a carvin' knife, an' shoved it in my side.'

Beth gasped in horror.

'Like I told yer mum,' continued Vera, 'the ol' couple downstairs must've 'eard me and the kids screamin', 'cos they went an' got yer dad, who'd just gone round the corner ter get a packet er fags. When 'e rushed up the stairs – it was . . . just terrible. 'E beat the livin' daylights out of 'Arry – cuts and bruises – 'is face was all bashed up. Yer dad wanted ter go an' bring up a copper, but I begged 'im not to, so 'e threw 'Arry out of the 'ouse, practically frog-marched 'im in ter the street. A coupla days later, 'Arry came an' collected 'is fings an' buggered off. I ain't seen 'im from that day ter this. That was almost twenty years ago. It's also the last time I ever saw yer dad – until that night we met outside the warehouse in Hornsey Road.'

Beth got up from the sofa, absolutely shattered by what she had just heard. She tried to compose herself by warming her hands over the paraffin stove. 'Mrs Jeggs,' she asked. 'Why're yer tellin' me all this?'

Vera sat up straight in the armchair. ' 'Cos I nearly died that night. They rushed me ter the 'ospital an' they say I lost two pints er blood. After that, yer dad looked after my little boy an' little girl. They worshipped 'im. If it 'adn't bin fer 'im, I wouldn't be 'ere ter tell the tale.'

'But why *now*?' persisted Beth. 'Why didn't my dad tell me all this while 'e was 'ome on leave? After all that time, you came an' met 'im twice. Why?'

Vera got up slowly from the chair and stood with her. 'Because when I said goodbye to yer dad all those years ago, I never 'ad the chance to fank 'im. I never 'ad the chance ter fank 'im fer me – *an'* the kids. I never knew wot 'appened to 'im. I never knew wevver 'e'd married, wevver 'e'd had kids of 'is own, or where 'e was livin'. It was only when we moved over this way ourselves a few years before the war started that I first started 'earin' 'is name mentioned, 'ow 'e'd married an American woman, an' 'ow 'e did 'ave grown-up kids. An' then some time after that, I 'eard about 'im bein' called up. It wasn't 'til I was standin' in this fish an' chip shop queue down at Anderson's that I over'eard this ol' lady talkin' about someone wiv yer dad's name, who was comin' 'ome on leave. From that moment on, I was determined ter see 'im.'

'But yer never come ter see Mum first?' asked Beth, who was still unsure about this woman's story.

'No,' replied Vera.

'Why not?' asked Beth.

'Because until I'd 'ad a chance ter talk to yer dad,' replied Vera cautiously, 'I didn't know wevver 'e'd want 'er – or 'is family – ter know about 'is past life.' She paused a moment. 'There were uvver reasons too.'

Beth lowered her eyes uneasily. 'Yer mean,' she suggested awkwardly, ' 'cos you an' dad . . .'

Vera turned to look at her. 'No, Beff,' she replied earnestly. 'Whatever our relationship was, yer dad never loved me.'

'An' *you* didn't love 'im?'

Vera looked down into the flickering flame of the paraffin stove. 'I didn't say that,' she replied. 'I've always loved 'im – from the first moment I ever laid eyes on 'im.'

'But,' said Beth, ' 'e *should've* told us. I'm not a kid any more. Neivver's Phil. We've got a right ter know these fings.'

Vera bravely put her arm around Beth's waist. 'Let me tell yer somefin', dear,' she said softly. 'Some men find it difficult to put inter words what they want ter say. I know, 'cos after I lost sight of 'Arry Jeggs, I've met enuff men ter know 'ow they bottle fings up inside – some women too. You're dad's a bit like that. What I remember of 'im from those days is that 'e's a very – private man, 'e wants ter keep fings from 'is family that might embarrass 'im. But 'e's also a very special man. Yer mum's special too – I knew that the moment I talked to 'er. She understands. She understands a lot of fings.' She turned to look again at Beth. With a warm, affectionate smile, she hugged her, and Beth responded. 'Don't worry, dear Beff,' she said softly. 'I shall go on lovin' yer dad fer the rest of me days, but I would never allow 'im ter love me too – not even if 'e wanted to.'

Beth, dazed by all she had heard, looked up at her and returned her warm smile. It was only then that she saw a smudge of blood on the woman's chin.

Once Vera had left, Beth and Connie started the trek round to the warehouse for another night in the shelter. This time Connie resisted the urge to carry baby Simon in her arms, and took him instead in his pram. On the way, Beth was still reeling from the extraordinary encounter with the woman who, until just a few hours before, had been in Beth's mind a shadowy, dangerous figure from her dad's past. All she could think of now, however, was how she had misjudged her dad, and how the first thing she would do when she got home in the morning, would be to write a letter to him, and tell him how proud she was of him.

'She's quite a person, isn't she?' said Connie, as they turned into Hornsey Road for the last few minutes of their journey. 'I mean, in her own way she must have loved Dad very much, when you think how she's kept that picture of him all those years.'

Beth turned with a start. 'Pitture?' she asked, puzzled. '*Wot* pitture?'

Connie was surprised. 'Didn't she show you that locket around her neck,' she asked, 'with the tiny picture of Dad when he was young?'

'No, she didn't,' replied Beth. 'D'you mind that?'

'Why should I?' asked Connie. 'Even if there *had* been anything between her and your dad, what difference would it make?' She sighed. 'Especially now.'

Beth didn't really take in what her mum was trying to say. 'Wot d'yer mean?' she asked.

Connie hesitated before answering. 'She's going to die, Beth,' she said.

Beth brought them both to an abrupt halt. 'Wot're yer talkin' about?' she asked.

'Did you hear that cough?' asked Connie. 'Did you see the blood on her handkerchief? She was diagnosed with consumption a few years ago. Now she has no more than six months or so to live.'

Beth gasped. She was devastated.

'Don't you understand, darling? That's why she's been waiting to see your dad. She came not only to say thank you, but also to say goodbye.'

They had stopped, and Beth was so taken aback, that for a moment or so she couldn't move. Eventually, however, Connie moved on with the pram, and Beth, in a daze, followed her.

A few minutes later, they reached the entrance to the old warehouse. Beth helped her mum to get the pram through the door, but lingered just long enough to take a deep breath of crisp, fresh air before disappearing inside. Overhead, the heavy snow clouds had dispersed as quickly as they had come, leaving stars clinging to a clear night sky, and the streets below lit by the dazzling power of an incandescent moon.

After a mainly cloudy day with intermittent rain and showers, it was now also a beautiful, clear night in northern France. Although the fields were muddy after the recent heavy falls of snow, the first signs of an early yield of corn during the coming spring were already struggling to keep warm as their shoots gradually began to show their heads. However, the *Luftwaffe* base near St Omer in the Pas de Calais was quite oblivious to the surroundings. A squadron of Messerschmitt fighter-bomber aircraft had been lined up on the tarmac for several hours now, waiting for the weather to clear, their crews fully briefed about their forthcoming night's mission over London and the British Home Counties, leaving the maintenance crews the difficult job of keeping the wings of the aircraft clear of ice.

With the hour of 'Action Stations' rapidly approaching, Oberleutnant Heinz Buchner sipped his final pre-departure *schwarzen Kaffee* with his fellow pilots in the Officers' Mess, the air of bravado that had pervaded during the day now replaced by cool practicality. They mostly talked about their targets for the night, railway bridges and power and water installations in all parts of London, and an ordnance factory near the racing-course at Epsom in Surrey. This, of course, was all official talk. Unofficially, the bombs were to be dropped wherever they would do the most harm, not only to life and limb, but also to morale, for morale is what this war was all about. Smash the British morale, said the Führer, and we have won the war. Unlike some of the young pilots who had been joking earlier about 'making the British suffer until they begged for mercy', Heinz Buchner wanted that war to end as soon as possible.

A few minutes later, Heinz returned to his cramped room in the officers' quarters to collect, amongst other things, his flying helmet, goggles and aerial maps of London. Foreboding had never been part of Heinz Buchner's nature, and when he took one final look at the framed photograph of his wife and two young sons on his bedside cabinet, he picked it up briefly, looked at it, smiled, and kissed it confidently. 'See you soon, my darlings!' he said. But the moment he had replaced it on the bedside cabinet, in his mind he could hear Helga's parting words to him: '*I'm going to miss you so much. The children are never the same without you.*' It was almost as though she were in the room with him. But when the tannoy on his wall burst into life, giving him orders for immediate take-off, he was more than ready. With one, last, quick look around his room, he rushed straight out of the building.

' 'Ands, Knees, an' Boomps-a-Daisy!' Jessie Hawks's birthday party was in full swing. To say that the old warehouse shelter in Hornsey Road was a bizarre place to hold such an event was an understatement, but the prevailing atmosphere gave no hint that everyone was having any less than a slap-up good time. Jessie herself was not revealing her age to *anyone*, though she winked at Abe, who knew, and when Jack Cutter asked why not, he got short shrift from not only Jessie herself, but Lil Winkler and Eileen Perkins, who reminded him that gentlemen didn't ask ladies personal questions like that.

The evening so far had been a huge success, not only because of Beth's vigorous accompaniment on the old Joanna for the repeated knees-ups, but because none of the regulars had got it into their heads that Moaning Minnie wouldn't dare to wail out tonight – especially during Jessie's special 'do'. The grub was pretty good too, with the neighbours turning up trumps with all their homemade cooking, only made possible by everyone pooling their food-ration coupons. Needless to say, there was also plenty of booze on show, provided this time mainly by Bill Winkler, who had practically begged, borrowed and stolen from his black market contacts, who, apart from the usual brown stuff, had managed to get him a couple of bottles of gin, which even Jessie herself partook in. To Jack Cutter's delight, it made her quite tiddly, so much so that he ended up on his knees in front of her, singing in the most dreadful wobbly tenor voice: 'If You Were the Only Girl in The World'. In fact, Jack's participation was only part of the regulars' cabaret, which included Eileen Perkins's little girl Rita doing an appalling Shirley Temple impersonation, Bill Winkler trying to make sense of a tune on his mouth-organ, and even the Lieberman brothers doing the most moving rendition of 'My Yiddisher Moma' in Yiddish. But the highlight of the evening was undoubtedly when Lil Winkler brought forward a large jam sponge with one single candle on top. After being overwhelmed by all the birthday cards and presents she'd been given, especially the pair of pink-coloured bloomers chosen and contributed by Eileen Perkins, Jessie found herself at the mercy of her neighbours, who yelled and shouted, 'Speech! Speech! Come on, Jess! Let's 'ave yer, gel!'

After being helped up from her canvas chair by Jack Cutter, and crushed with embarrassment into doing something that she had not been called upon to do in her entire life, Jessie looked around the beaming faces all around her. 'Well, you lot,' she began, in a rasping, uneven voice tinged with gin, 'I don't know wot I'm s'pposed ter say ter yer. People like me don't make speeches. After all, I'm only an ordin'ry workin'-class woman . . .'

Groans from Jack of, 'Oh blimey! 'Ere we go again!'

'Leave 'er alone, Jack!' scolded Eileen.

'Take no notice, Jess,' urged Lil Winkler, gently encouraging the old lady. 'You just go on, dear.'

Jessie waited a moment, burped, then went on. 'Well I *am* an ordin'ry workin'-class woman, wevver yer like it or not!' she said, glaring at Jack. 'So makin' speeches ain't my line.' She took another look round everyone in the shelter. 'Yer see, no one ain't ever taken such notice er me like this before. Er course, my Sid used ter buy me a present on me birfday every year – *when* 'e remembered!'

Laughter from everyone.

'The fing is,' continued Jessie, 'I've bin on me own fer so many years now, I've almost fergotten wot it's like ter 'ave people round me. When yer get ter my age, yer spend an awul lot er time sittin' in a chair just finkin', finkin' about the past, an' all the fings yer used ter do, all the fings yer wished yer could've done but never got round to doing. Sometimes yer eivver end up laughin' yer 'ead off about some daft fing that 'appened to yer years ago, or yer find yerself cryin' yer bleedin' 'eart out 'cos someone yer used ter love ain't round no more. That's why . . .' she swung from side to side, looking around at them all, 'that's why I feel pretty rich ternight. It's funny, ain't it, 'ow it takes a war ter bring people tergevver. I mean, I 'ardly ever passed the time er day wiv any of you lot til we started comin' down this shelter. I don't know why. Maybe it's 'cos we're like the Yanks call us – "reserved"?' She exchanged a passing smile with Connie. 'Keep ourselves ter ourselves. I s'ppose that's wot it's all about. But then, somefin' inside gets us all ter open up our 'earts tergevver, and I come down 'ere – ter this nasty smellin 'ole – an' I meet some of the nicest bunch er peop . . .' she stopped, dabbing her eyes with the back of her hand. 'I don't know why I'm goin' on like this,' she said, 'but yer did ask fer it, remember. The fact is, this place *ain't* really nasty an' smelly. In fact, it's become more like a 'ome than I've 'ad in a long time – an' that's fanks ter you lot.'

Jack helped her sit down again. For a moment there was silence, except for the sound of one or two of the regulars sniffing back their tears. But suddenly, the shelter erupted into applause, cheers and shouts of 'Good ol' Jess! Gord bless yer, gel!'

At this point, Beth, who had listened to all this from her seat at the piano, launched into a rousing chorus of 'Happy Birthday To You!', to which everyone joined in with vigour, almost raising the thick concrete ceiling, and probably sending tremors all along Hornsey Road.

Heinz Buchner always preferred flying over the English Channel when he knew he was on the return journey back to his base. Tonight, however, as he scoured the clear night sky for any sign of the dreaded RAF Spitfire fighter aircraft, the water down below didn't look quite so welcoming. In fact, during the past week or so, the English Channel had become the focus of several fierce major battles, when squadron after squadron of *Luftwaffe* Stuka dive-bombers with strong fighter aircraft cover, had attacked British convoys in the Dover straits, causing immense damage to the merchant ships who were trying to enter port at the time, but which had also been at the expense of a high number of German aircraft shot down by ground artillery units, with the loss of many pilots, some of whom had been known personally to Buchner himself. At this moment, however, the watery giant below was sleeping and calm, and as he turned to look from side to side of his own Messerschmitt aircraft, he gave the thumbs-up signal to his colleagues, who could be seen quite clearly in the dazzling white moonlight, heading towards their different targets, towards their different destinies.

As they approached the British coastline, Moaning Minnies wailed out all along the way, and within moments, the dark, menacing intruders were surrounded by the terrifying glare of ground-based searchlights which criss-crossed the sky frantically searching for their prey, accompanied by hundreds of small puffs of relentless anti-aircraft flack, which burst into life all around them, leaving Heinz Buchner no choice but to reach for the lucky beer glass charm around his neck . . .

Beth was worn out. She had been playing the piano for Jessie Hawks's birthday party for the best part of two hours, so much so that she felt as though her fingers were about to fall off her hands. Apart from that, she had mixed emotions about her day. As she lay resting on her bunk in the warehouse shelter, listening to her neighbours in animated conversation about all the local gossip, her mind couldn't help churning over what was happening to Thomas, and whether they would send him to prison because of what his father had done. She also dwelt unremittingly on the extraordinary story of Vera Jeggs, the woman she had made herself despise, the woman she had totally misjudged. And then she thought about her dad, and how she had totally misjudged him, too. It was a soul-destroying thought for her to know that it would probably be a long time before she would see him again, to tell him that she would never forgive herself for not trusting him. Whilst all these things were racing through her mind, she felt her mum perch on the bunk beside her.

'It'll be a long time before I forget this evening,' said Connie. 'Vera Jeggs is just about the bravest person I have ever met. I don't mean just because she's dying – God knows that's ghastly enough for someone her age – but because she's never stopped loving someone whom she knew she could never have.' She leaned down closer so that Beth could hear what she was saying. 'D'you know what she asked me just before you came home this evening? She asked if, before she dies, she could bring her own son and daughter to meet me and the family. I said, I'd be proud and honoured, and I know you and Phil would be, too.'

Beth, upset to hear all this, turned her face away.

'D'you know something,' said Connie, gently turning her back to face her, 'I'm terribly proud of you – and Phil, too. I've learned so much from you both over the years, not just about being British, but from the way people show such love for you. Especially you, Beth. The warmth you've brought into this shabby place down here has never ceased to amaze me. Despite all the things that trouble you, despite all the things that anger you, you never cease to amaze me. Sometimes, when I see you playing that piano, I wonder what the hell I was doing all those years at music college. One thing you've taught me is how wonderful it is that music is something that can be shared, that a good popular song can be just as uplifting as a piano sonata.'

Beth was taken aback by what her mum had said, especially as she had never heard her talk in such a way before.

As she spoke, Jessie approached. 'I'm goin' ter turn in now, folks,' she said wearily. 'I reckon I must be gettin' a bit old fer all this gallivantin''. Anyway, I just wanted ter say fanks from the bottom of me 'eart fer all yer've done, fer all *everyone's* done. If somebody 'ad told me I was goin' ter spend me birfday doin' a knees-up in a warehouse dug-out, I'd've told 'em they're stark ravin' bonkers.' She turned to Beth. 'An' as fer you, young lady,' she said, leaning down with difficulty to stroke Beth's hair, 'I reckon you're the tops!'

Beth took the old lady's hand, and gently kissed it. ' 'Night, Mrs 'Awks.'

Just as Jessie started to move back to her bunk, Moaning Minnie wailed out along the streets up top, but it had to compete with the groans and moans of the regulars, who didn't want to hear it – especially on the birthday of their much-loved neighbour and friend.

Heinz Buchner had managed to steer his way through the coastal flak, but by the time he got to the outskirts of London, all hell broke loose, for although the change in the weather was providing excellent visibility of the ground below, it was also helping the enemy ground units to pick out and target dozens of the overflying *Luftwaffe* attack aircraft, many of which had already spiralled down out of control in flames, or just exploded in mid-air. The next few minutes, however, would be vital for Buchner. He was steering a course north-east into London, where his target was the huge gas tanks just behind the goods yards at St Pancras Station. Unfortunately, however, owing to the many evasive moves he had had to make en route, his own fuel was beginning to run low, and soon he would have to decide whether he had enough left with which to get home or not. That decision was made very soon, when a piece of shrapnel from anti-aircraft fire just clipped the edge of one of his wings, leaving him no choice but to drop his bombs, and get out of the area as quickly as he could. Once he had reached the Seven Sisters and Holloway Road junction on his map, he unclipped the lever on his bomb bay . . .

In the warehouse shelter in Hornsey Road, the noise from the skies above was now building into such a crescendo that everyone was perched on the edge of their bunks, constantly staring nervously up at the ceiling, some of them with fingers crossed, others, like Connie, saying a silent prayer to herself. These were tense moments for them all, for it seemed as though the barrage of ack-ack fire was heralding a new and more terrifying campaign, where waves of 'pirate' aircraft were ploughing the skies, and dropping their bombs wherever they wished.

'I've never known it like this before,' said Eileen Perkins shaking from head to foot, as she hugged her Rita as tight as she could.

'Is this it, d'yer fink?' asked Lil Winkler, eyes transfixed anxiously on the ceiling. 'Are they softenin' us up fer the invasion?'

'Well,' added Jack Cutter, 'somefin's up, that's fer sure.'

As he spoke two huge explosions from nearby rocked the place, bringing chips of plaster and brick down from the ceiling. Everyone automatically covered their heads with their hands, but as soon as the first shock subsided, they pulled themselves together again.

'I'd like ter get me 'ands on those buggers!' said Bill Winkler, who was not averse to using bad language in front of the ladies, but when he did it usually meant that he was scared. 'If I 'ad the strength, I'd like ter frow their bleedin' bombs straight back at 'em!'

'Well, 'opefully,' said Eileen, 'that's exactly wot our boys're doin' ter them over there!'

The droning of planes above was gradually subsiding, so everyone started to relax a little, except for Abe and Bernie Lieberman, who continued to crouch on the stone floor with hands over their ears, their tin helmets firmly in place.

In the brief silence that followed, Jack Cutter's voice seemed almost intrusive. 'They're goin',' he said, voice only just audible. 'We're all right now. Nuffin' ter worry about.'

Nobody had noticed old Jessie, who was still in her canvas chair, slowly shaking her head, eyes staring up ominously at the ceiling.

At the far end of the shelter, Connie, who had thrown herself across the baby's cot, gradually emerged, to be met by Beth, just climbing out of the lower bunk. 'Well, I reckon that's it,' said Beth. 'If yer ask me, we're all gettin' our knickers in a twist over nuffin'! This is Mrs 'Awks's birfday, remember.' She glared up at the ceiling and shook her fist. 'There ain't *nuffin'* you can do up there, mate – not on a day like this! Come on, everyone!' She started to move back towards the piano. 'Let's tell Jerry wot we fink of 'im!'

She had no time to reach the piano, for they heard the distant whistle of a bomb hurtling down from what sounded like one solitary plane passing by overhead. Everyone stopped moving, almost stopped breathing. As the whistling sound grew louder and louder, more shrill, and more precise, all eyes were transfixed on the ceiling, now covered in a mass of human shadows from the flickering flames of the paraffin stove. They were hoping, and praying . . .

And then it happened – a massive, blue flash, a deafening explosion. The screams and shouts of everyone in the shelter was almost dwarfed by the crashing and rumbling sounds of falling masonry.

'Oh my Gawd!' yelled Eileen hysterically. Her child Rita was screaming uncontrollably.

Someone called, ' 'Elp!', but it wasn't clear who.

In that flash moment of horror, it was the sounds that were the most frightening, the most horrifying. And when a kind of silence returned, all that could be heard were rambling groans, and cries of 'I can't move! I can't move!'

Connie called out, 'Beth! Where are you? Can you hear me!'

There was no reply.

'Oh my God!' called Connie, weeping. 'Beth! Where – are – you?'

In the chaos of sounds that followed, the cries, the sobs, the groans, it was obvious that the whole place was immersed in dust and rubble, which caused an immediate outbreak of coughing and spluttering.

Through the pitch dark, Jack Cutter's voice could be heard calling out: 'Don't move, anyone! Whatever yer do, don't move!' He turned on his torch.

The sight he saw was like the worst possible nightmare.

Chapter 23

In the pandemonium that followed the terrifying explosion, the screams were replaced by coughing and spluttering from the clouds of what must have been plaster and brick dust that had engulfed the old warehouse air raid shelter. And in the middle of it all came the frenzied sound of Connie's baby yelling his head off, and Connie herself calling out desperately, unsuccessfully, for Beth. In the pitch dark, no one could see anything except for the distorted ray of light from Jack's torch beam, which struggled to pick out what was happening through the dark gloom and fluttering grey dust. 'Wait where yer are, everyone!' Jack called. 'Wait 'til this stuff settles!'

As he slowly looked around, the first person Jack saw was Beth, crumpled up on her side in the middle of the floor, dazed, covered in plaster and tiny bits of rubble. 'Beff!' he called, rushing to her.

Hearing that Jack had found her, Connie also called her name. 'Beth! Beth, darling! Is she alive, Jack? Is she alive?'

'She's all right, Mrs S!' returned Jack. 'Just 'ang on!' He stooped down, directed his torch beam on to Beth's face – she was covered in dust, and she had a small gash on her forehead, but she was alive. 'You all right, mate?' asked Jack, as he attempted to lift her head.

'Am I alive or dead?' she groaned, trying to pull herself up.

'Don't be silly,' he joked. 'You're much too young fer the knacker's yard!' He gradually helped her to her feet, and led her over to her mum, who was desperately covering the baby with a blanket to shield it from the dust.

Jack continued to shine his torch around. As far as he could see the ceiling remained intact, but several of the old timber beams that had been used to take the weight, had either simply buckled or had collapsed from their fixtures on the ceiling itself.

'Over 'ere, Jack – quick!' The desperation in Eileen's voice sent him hurrying over the rubble to her. When he eventually picked her out in his torch beam, he found her with the Lieberman brothers, who seemed to be crouched on the floor. When he took a closer look, however, he found Bernie, the younger brother, groaning in agony, with one of the large timber beams lying across the upper bunk, which had in turn crashed down across his leg, pinning him to the floor.

'Christ Almighty!' gasped Jack, crouching down to help Abe, who was straining without success to lift off the heavy beam. ' 'Ere, mate!' he said to Eileen, handing her the torch. ' 'Ang on ter this fer a minute!'

On the other side of the shelter, Beth helped her mum to cope with the baby, shielding them both with another blanket which she had pulled off her own bunk.

'Mrs Hawks!' cried Connie anxiously, struggling like everyone to breathe in the stifling air.

Beth quickly found her own torch, and went across to where Jessie had been left when the explosion came. To her surprise she found the old lady still sitting in her canvas chair, bent forward, covering her head with her hands and arms. 'Mrs 'Awks!' Beth called out loud as she reached her. 'Are you all right?'

'Course I'm all right!' came the reply. The old lady sat up and squinted at Beth in the beam from her torch. 'I ain't made er matchsticks, yer know!'

Jack and Abe were struggling hard to ease the heavy timber beam off Bernie Lieberman's leg, but the weight of the thing was more than just the two of them could cope with on their own. Bernie was writhing in pain, and it was clear that they needed immediate help to shift the beam. 'Bill!' called Jack, turning round to look in the direction of Bill Winkler's bunk.

There was no reply.

'Bill?' Jack called again.

Still no reply. Then he heard what sounded like someone sobbing, so he quickly got up, grabbed the torch back from Eileen, and hurried across to Bill and Lil's bunks as fast as he could. When he got there, he found Lil, covered in dust, kneeling on the floor, her face buried in her hands, weeping quietly to herself. Alongside her was the recumbent figure of her husband, Bill. 'Lil!' Jack cried. 'Wos 'appened, gel?'

Lil kept her face covered with her hands without replying.

Jack crouched down and shone the torch beam on to Bill's face. It was like stone, his eyes fixed wide open. Jack sighed deeply, and tucked his arm firmly around Lil's shoulder. 'Poor ol' bugger,' he said, puzzled and horrified to see what had happened to his old mate. 'But I don't understand?'

Lil slowly looked up. Her tears were trickling down her face through a cover of dust. ' 'E's always 'ad a dicky 'eart,' she said. ' 'E just didn't want anyone ter know.'

Jack hugged her to him, and held her like that for a moment or so. Then he pulled a blanket off the bed, covered Bill with it, and helped Lil to get up and sit on the edge of her bunk. Beth was there; the moment Jack moved away she took over, sitting down with Lil, who was now sobbing freely. 'It'll be all right, Mrs Winkler,' Beth said, hugging Lil to her. 'I reckon 'e's in a better place than we are right now.'

Nearby, Jack, helped by Abe Lieberman and Eileen, was struggling to use one of the fallen beams to wedge it under the bunk which was pinning Bernie's leg to the floor. The pain was so much that Bernie's cries became more and more frantic, which was distressing the others terribly, especially his older brother. In the end, Beth, and even poor Lil Winkler came across to help. The task seemed impossible, for every move they made, the beam settled more and more on to Bernie's leg. However, after one last immense physical and mental effort from everyone, Bernie screamed out in agony as the huge beam was very slowly prised up just enough for them to be able to pull him out from beneath the bunk. 'Don't move, Mr Bernie,' said Beth, helping the others to make him more comfortable on the floor. 'We'll get yer ter the 'ospital in no time!'

As the dust gradually settled, they became aware how bitterly cold the place had become, for the paraffin stove had been knocked over on it side, its flame extinguished, fortunately without causing a fire. Jack urged everyone to find their own torches as quickly as possible, as this was clearly going to be the only form of light they would have. 'Wot 'appened?' asked Eileen, who was still shaking, and doing her best to calm down her girl, Rita. 'It sounded as though we 'ad a direct 'it?'

'Well if it wasn't,' said Beth, 'I don't know wot the 'ell it *was*! Just look at the place!'

All of them, including old Jessie, flicked the beams from their torches around the shelter. But for minor cracks, all the walls seemed to be quite intact, and the floor was strewn with debris from overturned sleeping bunks and personal possessions, all of it mixed up in fallen plaster and lumps of reinforced concrete from the massively thick ceiling above them. 'Let's see if we can get out of this place,' said Jack, as he struggled to get to the foot of the old stone steps which led to the main floor and exit. It wasn't easy for him, for the steps were littered with bits of masonry and lumps of bricks which had taken the full blast of the explosion up top, and had been virtually blown through the door, which itself was lying over the steps. When he finally managed to reach the landing, he was shocked by what he found. Turning around to look down at the others who were watching him anxiously, he called out energetically, 'Everyone – shine yer torches up 'ere!'

They all obeyed at once, flooding the entrance with their torch beams.

'Jesus wept!' Jack said to himself, as he looked at the cellar entrance, which was completely blocked by a mountain of debris and rubble, huge lumps of concrete which were lodged solid, with not an inch of space to get through.

'Wot is it, Jack?' called Connie anxiously, from the other side of the shelter.

'Can yer see anyone?' called Eileen, living in hope.

Jack looked in despair at the blocked entrance, and shook his head. 'No,' he replied. 'I can't see anyone.' He turned to look down at the eager faces hanging on his every word down below. 'It's blocked.

There's no way we're goin' ter get fru this lot. It's up ter them up top now. 'Til *they* do somefin' – we're trapped.'

Despite the ferocity of the night's air raid on the capital, which was still going on, it took the emergency services no more than a few minutes to reach the scene of the serious 'incident' in Hornsey Road. Although the direct hit by a high-explosive *Luftwaffe* bomb seemed to have come down on to some houses just behind the old warehouse, the warehouse itself had been reduced to a huge pile of rubble and burning timber. Within a short while arc lights had been moved into place and tracker dogs were brought in to scramble over the mass of twisted iron, timber beams, bricks, concrete and debris. The first item of any interest to be uncovered was an old iron mangle.

'Do we know if there was anyone inside this place?' asked a senior Police Officer from Hornsey Road Police Station just a short way down the road. 'I know some of the locals use the cellar as an air raid shelter.'

'No way of telling, sir,' replied one of his bobbies, as fire engines and ambulances arrived on the scene. 'I know they carried on using it right through the lull.'

'Bloody hell!' blurted the police officer. 'Better find out for sure, and get lists as soon as you can! That includes the relatives!'

'Yes, sir!' The bobby raced off as fast as he could to work on a near impossible task.

'Wot we got 'ere, then?' called one of the firemen as he rushed across from his engine.

'Disused warehouse,' replied the police officer. 'Piano factory up until about a year or so ago.'

'Any pianos in there now?'

'Not to our knowledge – only junk. Only thing is we're not sure if there's anyone down there. The owners let the local residents use the place for an air raid shelter.'

'Christ!' exclaimed the fireman. Against the background of heavy ack-ack fire thundering in the sky above them, he and the police officer scrambled their way together up to the top of the mountainous pile of debris, which was still hot and difficult to stand on. 'If there's anyone in that cellar,' said the fireman, shaking his head gloomily, 'they're goin' ter 'ave a long wait 'til we can get ter them. It's goin' ter take some heavy liftin' equipment ter get rid of this lot.'

'Well, if that's what it needs,' replied the police officer stiffly, 'then that's what we've got to do. That is, providing there really *is* anyone down there.'

Soon after midnight, Thomas was woken up in his bedroom to find two burly Special Police Constables standing over him in the dark, shining a torch beam straight into his bewildered face. 'Jesus Christ!' he spluttered. 'I know you've got my front-door key, but do yer usually break into a gent's private bedroom in the middle of the night?'

The constable who spoke was not amused. In fact he was downright rough with him, pulling back the bedclothes and growling at him. 'Up! Get dressed as quick as you can!'

Thomas did as he was told. Freezing cold, he leapt out of bed, and searched in the dark for his clothes which, as usual, he had just thrown on to a chair before he went to bed.

The other constable drew the blackout curtains, while his fellow constable switched on the light.

'Where are we going?' asked Thomas. 'I thought I was supposed to be under house arrest or somethin'?'

'Stop blabberin'!' snapped the aggressive constable, 'and get yerself downstairs *tout suite*!'

Thomas was practically pushed out of the house, and straight into a waiting police car. When he got into the back seat he was astonished to find he had a fellow passenger. It was Jane Grigsby, from the munitions factory.

As they drove off at speed, the barrage of ack-ack fire was tearing the night apart, and the sky was as dramatically red as a 'shepherd's warning'.

In his heart of hearts, Heinz Buchner knew that his time had come. The hole in the portside wing of his aircraft, which had been punctured earlier by a piece of flying shrapnel from an ack-ack shell, had now ripped wide open, and flames were gradually fluttering towards the cockpit. The fuel tank had also been ruptured, causing the aircraft to rapidly lose height and, with the machine shaking violently all around him, Heinz was only too aware that it could explode in midair at any moment. Desperately struggling with the controls, he knew that his only hope now was to try and reach the Kent coast and attempt to ditch the aircraft into the English Channel, where he would at least have a slim chance of survival. Every moment that passed was a bonus as, by his own calculations, the English Channel was still more than ten minutes' flying time away. All he could do now was sit back in his cockpit, close his eyes and contemplate his memories of a life that seemed to be gradually ebbing away from him. Inevitably, in his mind's eye he saw Helga and their two boys, enjoying one of their happy family outings together at a riverside café in Lubeck – Richard and Dieter tucking into too many cream cakes, which always resulted in them ending up sick in the car on the way back home. He was aware of so many sublimely cherished moments flashing through his mind, like autumn leaves floating in the wind. He could *see* Helga, he could *see* his two boys, he could almost touch them, smell them – they were here with him now, urging him on, begging him to live. But once those memories cleared, he was left with the image of three men in uniform and swastika armbands standing before him, arms raised in a Nazi salute to acknowledge his own: his Führer Adolf Hitler, alongside Hermann Goering and Joseph Goebbels. They were also urging him on, imploring him to make the supreme sacrifice for the Fatherland. But when his eyes suddenly sprang open, stark reality returned with suffocating horror, for a fire had broken out in the aircraft engine, and the flames were cascading straight back towards the cockpit window. Then suddenly he saw it – the sea! There it was, the glorious sea – shimmering below in the bright moonlight. With one last supreme effort, he fought hard to slide back the cockpit window in order to leap out, for the aircraft was now in a nose dive and only moments from crashing into the sea. Desperate to cling on to life, he managed to climb out of the cockpit and leap out. Almost simultaneously, the aircraft crashed into the sea, exploding into a ball of fire. 'Helga . . . !

Richard . . . ! Dieter . . . !' Heinz's strangulated yells struggled to overcome the sound of his burning aircraft, and as his fingers desperately searched for Helga's beer glass charm around his neck, his final poignant cries of '*Ich liebe dich! Ich liebe dich* . . . !' echoed across the dark, murky waters of the English Channel, and fluttered into the oblivion of a merciless, cold November night.

'What time is it, darling?' Connie asked Beth.

As Jack had suggested that everyone conserve the batteries in their torches wherever possible, Beth switched on hers for just a brief second to look at her watch. 'It's almost one o'clock,' she replied wearily.

Connie sighed. 'God knows how long we're going to have to stay down here,' she said tensely, whilst trying her best to breastfeed her baby in the dark. 'It's going to take them hours to dig us out.'

With the dust now settled, the atmosphere in the warehouse cellar had changed from terror to incomprehension. Whilst Jack Cutter did everything in his power to search around every wall for another way out of the place, Eileen Perkins proved to be a wonderful comfort for Lil Winkler, who refused to leave her husband Bill's side, despite the fact that he was stretched out on the floor like cold stone, covered by an old tartan blanket. But the most poignant sound of all was coming from Abe Lieberman, who knelt rigidly alongside his seriously wounded younger brother, holding his hand, rocking to and fro gently, humming a religious Yiddisher song in an effort to help relieve Bernie's acute pain.

A few minutes later, old Jessie, who had fallen asleep in her canvas chair, suddenly sat up with a start. 'Wot's that?' she cried brightly.

'Wos up, Mrs 'Awks?' asked Beth, rushing across to her. 'Anyfin' wrong?'

'Can't yer feel it?' said Jessie, her head swivelling around in the dark. 'Where's it comin' from?'

Beth, fearing for the old lady's state of mind, turned on her torch and looked at her. 'It's nuffin', Mrs 'Awks,' she said. 'Everyfin's goin' ter be all right, just you wait an' see. Try an' get some shut-eye, dear. By the time yer wake up it'll all be—'

Jessie didn't allow her to finish her sentence. 'No!' she mumbled. 'Yer don't understand. There's nuffin wrong wiv me. I can feel a draught – not a big one, but I can feel fresh air . . . It's comin' from somewhere . . . over there . . . be'ind the bunks.'

Beth immediately swung her torch round to Jack Cutter. 'Jack!' she called.

'Yes, I know,' replied Jack, who was already investigating what he himself had also felt.

Everyone's torch beams were suddenly turned on and directed eagerly towards Jack.

'Wot is it, Jack?' Beth said, hurrying across to join him.

'I dunno,' replied Jack curiously, using the fingers of one hand to feel along an outside concrete wall behind the sleeping bunks. 'But it's definitely colder back here.'

Connie, who had just finished feeding the baby, stood up with him in her arms. 'I felt it too, Mr Cutter. There must be an opening or something along there.'

Beth was investigating too. 'It's 'ere!' she suddenly yelled. Directing her torch beam along the wall, she picked out with her fingers a tiny narrow slit in the wall from where a cold draught of outside air could be felt seeping through. She then tried peering through the slit.

'Can yer see anyfin', Beff?' asked Jack.

'No – nuffin',' returned Beth. 'It's pitch dark out there, except . . . I did fink I saw just a flash er light . . .' She suddenly yelled out at the top of her voice through the slit: ' 'Allo! Is anyone there? 'Allo!' She pulled back with a sigh. 'No, nuffin',' she said despondently.

'P'raps if we all shouted out at the same time?' suggested Eileen.

'Don't fink it'd do much good, gel,' replied Jack. 'It's still night out there, an' we don't know wot's on the uvver side er this wall.'

Eileen persisted. 'But by now there must be millions er people up there tryin' ter get to us?' she said hopefully.

Jack shook his head. 'The fact that we can't 'ear nuffin' ain't a good sign,' he warned gloomily.

'Wot about the ceilin'?' asked Jessie. 'If we all shouted, wouldn't they 'ear us up *there*?'

Everyone's torch beams flicked up automatically to the ceiling.

'Don't ferget this buildin' was three storeys 'igh, Ma,' said Jack, looking up. 'Unless I'm mistaken, that concrete's probably about two feet thick. I just 'ope it's goin' ter be strong enuff ter 'old the weight 'til they've cleared all that stuff away.'

One by one the torch beams were turned off.

Outside the warehouse, all the emergency services were now hard at work. Fortunately, the 'regulars' from the London Fire Brigade, together with members of the Auxiliary Fire Service, had managed to get most of the fires under control, but were still having to dampen down the fallen hot masonry. The biggest danger now threatening them, however, was the front of the building itself, which had been left as a skeleton frame right up to the top floor, but with the entire building gutted behind right down to what had previously been the ground floor. Although Hornsey Road had been cordoned off, scores of local residents were gathered around to watch the rescue operations, some of them still wearing their night clothes, dressing-gowns and blankets draped over their shoulders. Despite the bitter cold, the deafening sound of ack-ack gunfire, and the constant menacing drone of enemy aircraft overhead, the eyes of every single person there showed horror and frustration, the hope that if anyone *was* trapped inside the old warehouse, they would be rescued without too much delay.

In the middle of all the mayhem, the LFB in charge of operations frequently called out to the crowds to go home, for there were still enemy aircraft overhead, making it dangerous for them to hang around with so much ack-ack shrapnel coming down.

But nobody took much notice, and even when an incendiary bomb crashed down on to the pavement and burst into a powerful white glare just a short distance beyond them, his shouts of 'Get the hell out of there!' still seemed to have no effect. But he was soon distracted by another commotion, when an AFS messenger boy suddenly appeared, pushing his way through the crowd yelling, 'Let me through! Let me through!'

'What's going on?' snapped the overworked LFB officer. 'You got a message for me, boy?'

'No, sir!' spluttered Phil Shanks breathlessly, his tunic uniform, cap and face covered in dust, a white scarf around his neck for covering his mouth. 'Me family's down there!'

The officer's eyes widened. '*Your* family?'

'Yes, sir!' replied Phil impatiently. 'Me mum, sister an' baby bruvver.'

'So there *are* people down there,' the officer said half to himself. 'You're absolutely sure about that?' he asked, returning to Phil, now with great urgency.

'Yes, sir!' insisted Phil, emphatically. 'Absolutely! My mum always goes down there wevver there's a raid or not. An' I know she was goin' down ternight, becos one of our neighbours was 'avin 'er birfday there wiv all the uvvers.'

'The – others?' The officer was suddenly lampooned into action. 'How many of them, d'you know?'

'I've no idea, sir!' called Phil, shouting above the noise from overhead, whilst going with the officer to consult with his men. 'Eight or nine, I reckon.'

'Pierson!' yelled the officer to one of his firemen.

'Sir?' came the immediate answer.

'How long before we get the heavy lifting equipment?'

'Not until the morning, sir,' replied the man.

In frustration, the LFB officer briefly took off his fire helmet and ran his fingers through a shock of white sweaty hair. 'That's too bloody late!' he bellowed. Then, turning to look across the road at the crowd of onlookers, he yelled: 'Go and get that lot to help! But tell them to put helmets on – *and* some bloody coats. I don't want 'em all dying of pneumonia on me!'

As he rushed off, Phil turned with the intention of joining in with the rescue. The moment he'd climbed up on to the first lot of rubble, however, a frantic voice called to him from behind.

'Phil!'

Phil turned with a start to find Thomas staring up at him.

'Is she down there?' asked Thomas desperately.

Phil, his face beginning to crumple up with fear and tears, nodded back. Thomas held up his hand. Phil took it, and pulled him up.

As volunteers were recruited for the rescue operation from the other side of the road, someone anxiously watched Thomas and Phil scrambling up to the top of the huge pile of debris. It was Jane Grigsby.

The night seemed to be the longest Beth had ever known. Even though it was barely four o'clock, she already felt as though she had been down in that hell-hole for an entire lifetime. It must have seemed the same way to the others as well, for the fear of being incarcerated alive was denying them the chance of any sleep. For nearly an hour, Beth sat with Abe Lieberman whose younger brother Bernie had lost so much blood that he had obviously sunk into unconsciousness. Thanks to her mum providing a bottle of cologne from her handbag, Beth reckoned she had at least managed to clean the gaping wound in Bernie's leg, if only temporarily, but her dread was that he might not be able to last out until the morning. The morning! It seemed like a lifetime away. In her few moments of daydreaming, Beth wondered what the morning would look like, and whether she would ever live to see it. She felt all the emotion welling up inside her again as she thought about Thomas, whether he would have been told about what had happened to her in the shelter that night, and even if he had been, whether he would care a damn. All she knew was that whatever he thought of her, she still loved him, she loved him – to death. But she did manage a brief smile to herself as, in her own mind, she was telling him that if he dared to get himself someone else after she'd gone, she'd come back and haunt him. She thought about her dad, too, and how devastated he would be if . . . if . . . How she loved him, how she loved her mum, too, despite the dismissive way she had talked to her over the recent years. The past! So much to look back on, but so little time to do it. Her eyes welled up with tears, but there was nothing she could do about it. Everything seemed to be so stacked against them.

'You know,' said Abe Lieberman, his voice so low that it couldn't be heard by the others. 'I've talked so much to God in the last few hours that he must be sick of my voice. I asked him why he had to do this to me, to me *and* Bernie. After all, hadn't two old stitchers like us suffered enough back in Germany all those years ago, hadn't we paid enough for all our sins? I hadn't realised what wicked people we are.'

Beth reached out gently for his hand. 'There's nuffin' wicked about *you*, Mr Abe,' she insisted softly. 'You *nor* Mr Bernie. In fact everyone round 'ere loves yer boaf. We all say you're the best "stitchers" in the business!'

Abe leaned down and gently kissed her hand.

A few minutes later, Beth left the brothers and wandered quietly around the shelter. When she got to the far end near the foot of the stone steps, she gazed down forlornly at the old upright piano, which had also been one of the casualties of the explosion. It was a poignant sight for her, to see it lying on its side, with a huge piece of concrete embedded in its keyboard. She bent down, and with a wistful smile, tenderly stroked the top of the 'old Joanna' with the tips of her fingers. Moving on, she stopped briefly with Eileen, who had finally managed to get her girl Rita to sleep in what was left of her lower bunk. 'Are you all right?' Beth asked quietly.

'Well I wouldn't mind a plate er fish an' chips,' joked Eileen. 'Apart from that . . .' she sighed. 'Oh well, wos the use er complainin'? It won't get us out of this bleedin' place.' She moved slightly to make herself more comfortable. 'I've just bin tryin' ter imagine wot my Ernie's goin' ter fink of all this. Gawd knows where 'e is now, but 'e's always writin' ter tell me that if fings get any worse, ter pack up an' take Rita up ter Nottin'am, ter live wiv my Aunt Ethel and Uncle Alf. D'yer know wot I've always written back to 'im? I said, I'd sooner die than do a fing like that.' She chuckled to herself. 'Just shows 'ow wrong yer can be!'

Beth moved on.

'D'yer know the one fing I regret about my life?' said Jack Cutter, when Beth crouched down to make contact with him. 'The fact that I never married. It was me own fault, er course. There was this gel – it was a long time ago er course – long before I become the stupid ol' git I am now. She was eighteen, an' I was nineteen. 'Er name was Jas – that's short fer Jasmine – stupid bleedin' name, I know, but I liked 'er – no, I *loved* 'er, an' I know she loved *me*, 'cos she told me so, an' when I asked 'er ter marry me, she said yes like a shot. Anyway, she was from a diff'rent class ter me, if yer know wot I mean. 'Er ol' man was somefin' big up the City, an' her ol' lady come from some big 'ouse up Kilburn way. Well, ter cut a long story short, when 'er ol' man died suddenly of a 'eart attack, Jas got all funny, an' said she owed it ter 'em not ter fink about marryin' *anyone* while 'er mum was still alive. I said that was a stupid idea, 'cos 'er mum might live fer years after that. But she wouldn't 'ave none of it, and made it sound like the real reason was becos I wasn't good enuff for 'er. So that was it. *I* walked off, an' so did she – it was as simple as that. I only saw 'er once after that. She got married to a bloke double 'er own age. But 'e turned out ter be somefin' in the City too, so she was all right. But me? Nah – never again. I've done all right on me own. 'Ard an' fast ol' bachelor, that's me.'

'I'd say yer've done more than all right,' replied Beth, her voice low. 'The way yer keep that 'ouse next door to us is a credit to yer.'

'Fanx, Beff,' replied Jack. 'But a 'ouse ain't no substitute fer a good little woman, is it?'

'Wot's that smell?'

Everyone sat up with a start as Eileen's girl, Rita, who rarely spoke, if ever, called out in alarm.

'Wot is it?' asked Beth, rushing across to her. '*Wot* can yer smell?'

'Gas!' yelled someone from the crowd of volunteers from the local residents outside, who, together with the exhausted members of the emergency services, were struggling to remove the rubble and debris piece by piece from the collapsed warehouse. 'I can smell gas!' repeated the man.

For a brief moment, everyone stopped what they were doing, and turned to look at the man, who was at the foot of the pile of rubble.

'Where's it coming from?' yelled one of the ARP men who was one of many helping out.

'I can smell it, too!' called a woman volunteer from the St John Ambulance team, who, like the others, was using her bare hands to remove bricks and concrete. 'It's down here on the pavement somewhere! I can't believe anyone's still alive down there!'

Despite the grave doubts of everyone who was toiling away with the debris, within seconds several members of the rescue services were investigating the gas leak. They eventually located the source, which seemed to be coming from somewhere beneath the pavement, and which probably led down into the basement of the building itself.

'Gas board!' called the LEB officer.

A man from the Gas Company was already making his way over. 'I'm here!' he called as he approached. He was carrying a bucket of sticky clay, which was always on standby during a serious 'incident'. He immediately crouched down on the pavement, and as soon as one of the group moved a paving stone, with a shovel and trowel, he set about digging down into the hard soil.

During all this, Phil and Thomas were frantically removing lumps of bricks, concrete and scorched timber from the top of the gradually receding pile of debris.

'It'll take fer ever ter move all this stuff!' said Phil, still fighting back his emotions, his fingers bleeding from hours of grappling with sharp rubble.

'I was just thinkin' the same thing meself!' said Thomas. 'If they're down in the cellar, it could be there's another way into the place. At least we could try ter make contact with them.'

Phil didn't have to say anything. He just got up quickly and joined Thomas, who was already making his way down to the pavement.

The smell of leaking gas was causing considerable alarm and discomfort amongst the group of 'regulars' trapped in the cellar below. Most of them quickly tied scarves around their mouths, whilst Beth and Jack made a frantic search of the place to see where the gas was coming from.

'I knew I should've brought me bleedin' gas mask!' bemoaned Jessie, behind the scarf covering her mouth. 'They said on the wireless yer should never go anywhere wivout it!'

'It's too late now, Jess,' called Eileen. 'Anyway, we might as well be gassed as ter be buried alive!'

At that moment, all heads looked up towards the ceiling as, for the first time, they heard sounds coming from above. At first it seemed like someone scrambling around, but gradually it became a series of heavy thumps.

'There's someone up there!' said Lil Winkler, who slowly got up and went over to join the others.

The thumping sounds continued.

'You're right, Lil!' said Jack Cutter, who was trying not to show too much excitement.

More thumping sounds, getting closer and closer.

'They're tryin' ter get fru to us!' called Eileen. More thumping sounds. 'Can yer 'ear 'em? They're tryin' ter get fru to us! Down 'ere!' she yelled out loud. 'Down 'ere!'

The others immediately joined in, and soon everyone was yelling and shrieking out loud, trying to attact notice.

The thumping sounds came to an abrupt halt.

'Wot's 'appened?' asked Beth. 'They've stopped.'

'Wos goin' on up there?' asked Jessie.

Everyone got more and more depressed as the silence continued.

'Let's keep on shouting,' insisted Eileen. 'They won't know we're down 'ere unless we do!'

'It won't do no good, Eileen,' Jack explained. 'There's no way they're goin' ter 'ear us fru all that concrete.'

'But if *we* can 'ear *them*,' said Eileen obstinately, 'why can't *they* 'ear *us*?'

'Because if the air raid's still on up there,' replied Jack, ' 'ow d'yer fink they're gonna 'ear fru all that ack-ack?'

Both Eileen and everyone else felt their spirits ebbing away.

'What d'you think's happened, Beth?' asked Connie, from behind her scarf mask. 'Are we trapped down here for good?'

' 'Course not!' Beth replied. 'They'll find a way fru to us eventually.'

'Eventually may be too late,' replied Connie.

Beth perched down next to her on the lower bunk. 'I fink we're just goin' ter 'ave ter wait 'til the mornin',' she sighed. As soon as it's daybreak, they'll be able ter move much faster.'

'But how will *we* know when it's daybreak?' asked Connie. 'We won't be able to see it.'

That was a question Beth couldn't answer. Her only hope was that the slit she had found in the brick wall behind the bunks would provide some kind of hope the moment there was any sign of daylight. But what then, she asked herself? Would anyone be able to hear them just because there was light in the sky?

'It's strange how it's all coming true,' said Connie, gently rocking the baby to and fro in her arms, and adjusting the handkerchief she had put over its mouth for protection. 'You remember my dreams?'

Beth had known that sooner or later that would come up, but whether she liked it or not, she had to admit that her mum's dreams had become somewhat prophetic. 'It don't do no good ter fink about that now, Mum,' she pleaded. 'Wotever 'appens, we're goin' ter get out er this.'

'But it *has* happened, darling,' persisted Connie. 'It's happening to us right here and now. We're trapped down here, and we're never going to get out of here alive. *That's* what I saw. *That's* what I feared.'

'Shall I tell yer somefin', Mum?' said Beth, gently sliding her arm around Connie's waist. 'I reckon wot 'appens in dreams is always the opposite. Yer mustn't give up. We owe it ter Dad not ter give up.'

'I know what you're saying is right, darling,' replied Connie, voice cracking, 'but I can't help hating the thought that I'll never be able to say goodbye to him.'

Beth squeezed her arm around her mum's waist. 'Don't ever let me 'ear yer say that, Mum,' she said firmly. 'There's no such fing as *never*.'

On the other side of the shelter, Jessie was beginning to cough and wheeze. The smell of gas was getting stronger . . .

Chapter 24

Outside the warehouse, the man from the gas company finally managed to dig down far enough to reach the puncture in the gas plate, which had clearly been damaged during the bomb explosion. With strict instructions for everyone not to use a bare flame anywhere near the gas leak, the man began the task of sealing the puncture with handfuls of sticky clay. Until the work was complete, the site remained in total silence.

Nearby, Thomas and Phil, together with one of the firemen, discovered a narrow gully at the foot of a flight of stone steps at the side of the former warehouse, which in the past had clearly been used as some kind of drainage maintenance area, built below ground floor level, and flanking a long, high, yellow brick wall faced with concrete and plaster. With just a couple of hours to go before sunrise, Thomas and Phil began a frantic search to find a way into the cellar.

Inside the cellar itself, the group entombed there were becoming drowsy from the effect of the gas fumes that had been leaking from somewhere beneath the stone floor. To try to combat these effects, each person took turns in placing their mouth against the open slit in the wall to inhale as much fresh air as they could. It was a desperate situation, especially as Abe Lieberman had solidly refused to leave his brother and participate in the lifesaving attempt. However, just as Beth was about to take her turn at the slit in the wall, Jack Cutter, who had been listening to the faint distant hissing sound coming from the leak, suddenly yelled out jubilantly: 'It's stopped!'

Everyone rushed across to him, all pointing their torch beams towards the narrow gap in the floor from where the small jet of gas seemed to have been coming.

'Yer can't *see* nuffin',' Jack said. 'But it's definitely stopped 'cos I can't 'ear nuffin' no more. They must've turned off the supply up top or somefin'.'

'I fink you're right, Jack,' agreed Beth. 'I just 'ope they 'aven't given up on us,' she added gloomily.

There were mixed feelings when the thumping sounds resumed again up top.

'Anyway, listen, everybody!' called Jack above the cheers. ' 'Til we get rid er the fumes, we've got ter carry on takin' in fresh air from the wall. Beth – you go across first. It was your turn.'

Beth hurried across to the wall, and placed her mouth against the slit. Just as she was doing so, however, she thought she heard a distant sound on the other side. Taken completely by surprise, she quickly peered through the slit, and immediately saw something. 'There's someone out there!' she yelled. 'I can see a light!'

With that, everyone rushed towards the wall, and started yelling their heads off. 'We're 'ere! Down 'ere! Get us out of 'ere!'

On the other side of the wall, Thomas thought he heard a distant noise of some sort, but couldn't determine what. Both he and Phil went back and forth along the wall with the two firemen, desperately searching for some way of getting in. But as quickly as the noise began, it wasn't heard again.

With their hopes dashed, the group inside the cellar moved back reluctantly from the wall. The stress and strain of what was happening to them was now beginning to wear them down, and the first to weep openly was Eileen, who held on to her girl Rita as tight as she could. 'Wot's the bleedin' matter wiv the fools!' she sobbed. 'Are they deff or somefin'?'

'Don't get upset, Eileen,' pleaded Beth, going over to her. 'I may 'ave bin wrong. I fawt I saw somefin' out there – but I could've bin wrong.'

The thumping sounds from the surface up top were now getting more and more frequent.

Even old Jessie's nerves were saturated to boiling point. ' 'Ow much longer they goin' ter be muckin' about up there?' she groaned, covering her ears from the deafening sounds. 'Why can't yer 'ear us?' she yelled up at the ceiling.

Jack Cutter suddenly shouted out: 'Stay where yer are, everyone! Just keep still!' He was pointing his torch beam up at the ceiling, where, to his horror, large cracks were beginning to appear. 'Oh no!' he said to himself. 'Get back ter the uvver side – by the wall!' he yelled, clearly alarmed.

'Wot is it, Jack?' asked Beth, hurrying across to him. 'Tell me!'

'It looks as though the whole bleedin' lot's goin' ter come down on us!' he replied.

Beth followed the direction of his torch beam with her own. She gasped. 'Wot're we goin' ter do?' she asked.

'Just get out of this bleedin' place!' Jack bellowed at the top of his voice.

Conscious that their predicament was also now getting Jack down, Beth hurried across to her mum, who was still rocking the baby gently in her arms. 'Stay where yer are, Mum,' she said softly. 'We're goin' ter get out of this soon, I promise you!' She turned the torch beam on to her watch. 'It's almost dawn,' she said. 'The sun'll be up soon – *if* there is any!'

Outside the front of the building, the gas company official had successfully sealed the gas leak beneath the pavement by slapping a poultice of sticky clay all around the plate. This meant that work had now continued on removing the slowly receding pile of rubble that had collapsed on to the ground floor of the old warehouse.

Meanwhile, Thomas and Phil had found their way round to the opposite side of the building, still frantically searching for a way into the cellar. The back of the warehouse was totally impassable, blocked by debris and rubble from two residential houses on the street behind that had taken a direct hit from the same bomb. It was now almost dawn, and in a few minutes' time the sun would be struggling to break through a thin layer of grey early morning cloud. With this in mind, Thomas and Phil made their way back to the wall where they had first begun their search. 'See if you can get one of the dogs round here!' Thomas called to an ARP man. 'It'll soon be light. We'll get a better chance to see if there's any way we can find a way in.'

In the cellar shelter, all the group stranded there were lined up together with their backs against the long brick wall, where the thin slit was providing the only fresh air that was available. Despite Jack's pleas to conserve their batteries, everyone had their torch beams directed on to the ceiling above, where cracks were continuing to appear down the centre, which was made worse by the deafening sound of debris being removed above them.

' 'Al . . . lo!' shrieked Eileen, for the umpteenth time. 'Why – can't yer – 'ear us? Are yer deff, yer stupid sods?'

The others joined in with yells, shouts and whistles, making any sound they could that might attract their rescuers, but they were now too breathless and weak from the gas fumes to create the kind of noise that was needed to seep up through the heavy concrete barrier to those who were battling to reach them from the surface.

'Let's leave it, everyone!' shouted Jack, who, with Abe Lieberman, was doing his best to support the unconscious Bernie propped up against the wall. 'Let 'em get a bit closer, then we might be able to make contact!'

'By the time they get any closer,' old Jessie reminded them, 'we could be buried by that bleedin' ceilin' up there!'

Everyone went absolutely silent, as they stared up at the flakes and chips of plaster and cement that were breaking off the heavy concrete ceiling. The only sound that could be heard now was made by Eileen's girl, Rita, who was sobbing quietly.

Beth remained with her mum, who was desperately clinging on to the baby in her arms, their backs against the wall, hoping in some way, like the others, that a miracle would save them before that ceiling caved in on them. Holding her mum so close, Beth could feel Connie's heart beating against her, so she gently leaned her head on her mum's shoulders. In that strange moment, there was an intimacy between them that hadn't been there for a long time.

'Did I ever tell you,' asked Connie softly, whilst competing with the heavy thumping sound of debris being removed up top, 'the *real* reason why your dad and I gave you your name?' She didn't wait for an answer. 'It wasn't just because we liked the name itself, it was because when I read *Little Women*, I thought that that little girl in the book was so special. She had qualities of such goodness, such an appreciation of life, exactly what I always dreamed a child of mine would have. Your dad felt the same way, too. Of course, he's never read a book in his whole life – he much prefers to read his silly old newspapers – but soon after we were married, I used to read the story aloud to him in bed every evening.' She chuckled to herself. 'He said, if our first child was a boy, we'd call it Bert, but if it was a girl, she'd be Beth, like that girl in the book. So here you are. And you *are* special, Beth, and *you* have always had an appreciation of life. And what's more,' she added with a loving smile, 'you've turned out to play the piano in your own wonderful way, just like your namesake in the book. That's why I'm not afraid down here. As long as I'm with you, I'm just not afraid.'

'Look!'

The sound of Lil Winkler's voice swung everyone's attention to her. To their astonishment, a hairline ray of light had penetrated the wall through the slit, and was settled across her face.

In the background, Eileen gasped, and wept.

'Oh God!' said Connie quietly to herself.

Nearby, Abe Lieberman, only just audible, was reciting a Yiddish prayer.

'The sun's comin' up,' said Lil, almost in a trance, hardly daring to move in case the ray of light streaked across her face should disappear. 'I never fawt I'd see it again.'

'Surely they know we're down 'ere by now?' sniffed Eileen, crying with her girl Rita. 'Why can't they stop that noise? Don't they know they're goin' ter kill us if they bring that ceilin' down on top of us?'

The thumping sounds above were relentless, but the more the work up above continued, the more precarious the ceiling looked.

'Why don't yer 'ave a go at that slit again,' Jack suggested quietly to Beth. 'It's worf one more try.'

Beth left her mum and the baby for a moment, went to the slit in the wall, and called out as best she could through it: ' 'Allo! Is anyone out there? Can yer 'ear me?'

On the outside of the wall, Thomas came to an abrupt halt. Although he and Phil had already moved past the slit in the wall without noticing anything, for one split second, he thought he had heard – *something.*

'Wot is it?' asked Phil.

'I – I don't know,' replied Thomas who had a peculiar look on his face. 'I thought I heard . . .' He turned around and scanned the wall. He could see nothing, nothing at all – so he moved on.

Inside the cellar, Beth gave up her efforts to be heard through the slit in the wall, and reluctantly pulled away. 'It's no good,' she said. 'Unless we've got somefin' ter make the 'ole bigger, they're never goin' ter 'ear us.'

There was a sudden cracking sound from the ceiling. Everyone's torch beams flicked up there.

'You're puttin' too much bleedin' weight on that floor!' yelled Jack, frustrated that despite all the strenuous efforts of everyone in the shelter to make themselves heard, their desperate calls were apparently still not filtering through to the emergency teams on the surface. 'Oy . . . you lot!' he bellowed. 'Stop it, d'yer 'ear! Fer Chrissake – stop it!'

'Wos the matter wiv 'em?' screeched Eileen, angry and sobbing at the same time. 'There must be some way we can make 'em 'ear!'

'It ain't no use gettin' upset, Eileen!' snapped old Jessie firmly. 'We've just got ter pull ourselves tergevver, and pray they'll get us out of 'ere.'

'Pray?' Eileen snapped back, sobbing her heart out. '*Who* are we goin' ter pray *to*? There can't be no God up there. If there was, 'E'd never let us suffer like this.'

'If only we 'ad the old Joanna,' said Lil Winkler with a sigh. 'I bet they'd soon 'ear Beff 'avin' a go on *that*!'

Beth heard what Lil had said, and for a moment thought about it. Yes, she said to herself, it was true that her much loved Joanna *would* have made a good old racket, and if that lot up on top couldn't hear it, then they must be a lot of idiots. But a Joanna was, after all, only a musical instrument, and human beings came before Joannas. 'We don't need no pianer to get us out of 'ere, Mrs Winkler,' she said, suddenly springing to life.

'We don't?' asked Lil, confused.

'No, we don't!' replied Beth firmly. 'We've still got our voices, ain't we? So why don't we sing?'

'Sing!' Jessie nearly swallowed her false teeth. 'Wot d'yer fink we are – Bing Crosby an' the Andrews Sisters!'

'We don't need Bing Crosby, Mrs 'Awks,' Beth assured her, 'an' we don't need the Andrews Sisters. All we need are ourselves – our *own* voices – the voices God gave us!'

'Well 'E didn't give Jack Cutter much ter write 'ome about, did 'E!' quipped Jessie.

'Come on now, everyone!' called Beth. 'It's at least worf a try. Just imagine that it's last night all over again – Mrs 'Awks's birfday party, me at the Joanna, an' all the lot of yer 'avin a right ol' knees-up, singin' yer 'eads off!' She immediately led off the proceedings by bellowing out, '*THERE'LL ALWAYS BE AN ENGLAND . . .*'

One by one, everyone gradually joined in. Thoroughly weary though they were, short of breath and wheezing from the gas leak, their eyes still fixed firmly on that precarious ceiling, they struggled as hard as they could to make some kind of sound.

'Come on then, you lot!' Beth shouted at the top of her voice. ' 'Ow d'yer expect anyone ter 'ear *that* rubbish. It's gettin' light out there! Let's sing – ter the dawn!'

Despite the chaotic situation they all knew they were in, Beth roused them all to produce a stirring sound that shook the old cellar to its very foundations, as they sang their heads off to the strains of 'There'll Always be an England'.

In the gully outside, this time it was Phil's turn to come to an abrupt stop. With eyes almost popping out of his head, he swung round to look along the wall.

'Wot is it, Phil?' asked an astonished Thomas. 'Can you hear somethin'?'

Phil didn't answer. He just rushed back along the wall, stopping at one place after another to listen, his ear pinned against as many minute holes in the brickwork as he could find.

'What *is* it, Phil?' demanded Thomas, rushing after him.

'Fer Chrissake, Thomas!' blurted Phil excitedly. 'Can't yer 'ear it?'

'Hear *what*?' Thomas snapped back impatiently. 'I can't hear a damned . . .' He stopped dead. 'Jesus Christ!' he gasped, putting his ear against the wall.

'It's them!' spluttered Phil, bursting with excitement as he punched at the wall as he moved along it.

'I *can* hear somethin'!' yelled Thomas. 'Beth! Are yer in there, Beth?'

' 'Ere!' Phil shouted out excitedly from further along the wall. 'There's a place, a crack in the wall . . . yer can 'ear it . . . listen!'

Thomas practically pushed him aside to place his ear against the thin crack that Phil had found halfway down the wall. The moment he did so, his face broke into a look of absolute ecstasy. Then he put his mouth over the crack, and shouted: 'Beth! Beth . . . it's me . . . Thomas! Can yer hear me?'

On the other side of the wall inside the cellar, Beth swung with a start towards the slit in the wall.

'Beth! Can you hear me, Beth?'

Although the voice she could hear was distant, there was no doubt in her mind whose it was. 'Thomas!' she yelled back, elated.

Jack immediately brought the singing to a halt, as everyone crowded around Beth at the wall.

'Can yer 'ear someone? Wot're they sayin'? Who is it? Tell 'em ter get us out of 'ere!' The desperate calls from the others were practically overwhelming Beth, and she turned round and raised her hands, begging them to keep quiet.

'Thomas?' Beth called as loud as she could through the wall. 'Can yer 'ear wot I'm sayin'?'

The distant, distorted voice called back. 'Yes, Beth – I hear you!'

'Then listen, Thomas!' continued Beth. 'Listen carefully. There's a whole bunch of us down 'ere, an' yer've got ter get us out as fast as yer can . . .'

As she spoke, there were the first sounds of cracking in the ceiling.

Eileen screamed. 'It's comin' down!' she shrieked.

'Thomas!' called Beth frantically. 'Tell those people up top ter stop movin' around. The ceilin's about ter come down at any minute. 'Urry, Thomas! Fer Gawd's sake – 'urry!'

Within just a few minutes, a team of rescue workers armed with vast sledge hammers were battering down the brick wall flanking the cellar. To calm everyone's nerves inside whilst this was going on, Beth got them all to sing again. Amidst tears of joy and relief, they sang Uncle Horace's favourite song, the lilting, poignant ' 'Til We Meet Again'.

As soon as the slit had been knocked open wide enough, Thomas pushed his hand through. 'Beth! Oh God, Beth!'

On the other side of the wall, Beth took Thomas's hand, kissed and gently caressed it.

A short while later, three huge holes were hammered out in the walls, allowing the hasty rescue of all those who had been trapped inside for so long. One by one they were helped out, squinting in the early morning light; a warm greeting from a bright and friendly sun. All of them were then taken straight to a team of doctors and nurses who were waiting in ambulances that were lined up along the road, and as each one of them appeared, they were cheered and applauded by the rescue workers, emergency teams and local resident volunteers who, throughout the night, had slaved away with bare hands to remove the debris and fallen masonry from the ground floor of the old warehouse, unaware that their strenuous efforts were very close to bringing the roof of the cellar down on all those trapped beneath it.

The moment Abe Lieberman watched his younger brother being brought out on a stretcher, he at last allowed himself to weep. At this time, Bernie was still unconscious, and Abe had no idea whether he would live or die. But as he climbed into the ambulance to travel with him and the nurses to the hospital, he took a brief look up at the sky, and said a quick, silent thank you to his God, who, after all, had not forsaken him *or* his brother.

Old Jessie Hawks was helped out of the cellar by two ARP men, but when they tried to lead *her* off to the ambulance, she gave them a piece of her mind. 'Yer don't put me in no ambulance!' she growled.

'I've got two good feet, an' I intend to use 'em ter go back ter me 'own 'ome!'

Last to leave the cellar was Lil Winkler, who had the agonising task of watching the covered body of her husband, Bill, being taken to an ambulance on a stretcher. As she walked in solitary procession behind him, she took a passing look up at the sky, which was bright and blue, but her face crumpled up when she realised that for the first time since she and Bill were married, they would not be sharing the start of a new day together. The moment the ambulance drew away, Moaning Minnie wailed out the All Clear siren across the rooftops.

When Beth and Thomas were in the ambulance, together with her mum and the baby and Phil, she took one last fleeting look back at what was once the old warehouse, the home for many months of a group of people who, until a short while before, had been virtual strangers. Now they were friends, firm friends, perhaps for the rest of their lives, for they had all travelled to the brink together – and survived.

Once all the ambulances had departed, a loud, thundering crash was heard in the cellar below the old warehouse, as that heavy concrete ceiling finally kept its promise, and collapsed.

Most of the survivors of the warehouse bomb were kept in hospital for little more than twenty-four hours, mainly all together in the same Accident and Emergency ward, the only exception being old Jessie Hawks, who solidly refused to go to hospital when, as she insisted, there was absolutely nothing wrong with her. Phil spent much of that time with his mum, sister and baby brother, until he had to get back to his duties with the AFS. Thomas was also there visiting Beth, for what turned out to be a reunion in which they determined that the question of trust between the two of them would cease to be an issue in their lives. Beth was astonished to hear how Jane Grigsby had persuaded Special Branch to allow him to leave his house arrest, when she had received news late at night about the bombing of the old warehouse, and the possibility that Beth and her family might be amongst the victims. However, his visit had to be a short one, for, until his father's whereabouts were known, he would have to be kept under close scrutiny.

During her only night in hospital, Beth slept soundly. But she did have one brief dream, in which she saw her dad peering through the window of the music college where he first met her mum. It was a strange dream, for the next minute she saw him sitting alone in the empty hall, listening to her playing the piano, and when it was all over, he stood and applauded, and she beamed with happiness, and ran down the steps off the platform, and straight into his arms. It was so romantic, and when Beth suddenly felt someone touching her lightly on her shoulder, she woke up with a huge smile on her face.

'Someone to see you,' whispered the ward nurse who was on night duty. 'It's most irregular for visitors at this time of night,' she said, as she led Beth out into the corridor, 'but for something like this, rules are there to be broken.'

Beth was shown into a small visitors' room, where she found her mum being hugged by her dad. Overjoyed, she leapt straight into his arms. 'Dad!' she gasped, her face immediately crumpling up with tears. 'I fawt I'd never see yer again.'

'From wot *I've* bin 'earin',' said Ted, fighting off tears himself, and hugging her as tight to him as he could, '*that* was pretty much on the cards!'

'But 'ow did yer get 'ome?' asked Beth excitedly. She couldn't stop looking him up and down, and thanking 'someone up there' for answering her prayers.

'The C.O. called me in first fing this mornin',' explained Ted. 'Once 'e'd told me wot'd 'appened down 'Ornsey Road, I was on that train back to London the minute he gave me permission fer compassionate leave. It's a lucky fing, though. We was just about ter be shipped out.'

'Shipped out?' asked Beth. 'Where to?'

Ted hesitated, and smiled. 'Yer don't ask a man in khaki fings like that,' he joked. 'You know "Careless talks costs lives"?'

Beth's face dropped. No one knew better than she about things like that.

They all sat down together to talk awhile, with Ted getting up every so often to take a look down at the baby in his cot alongside Connie. As Beth and her mum related all the horrors of the previous night, Ted's face remained ashen white, and it wasn't hard to imagine what fears were going through his mind. Beth wanted to ask him so many things about what he'd been doing, but time and time again she was reminded how it was virtually impossible for him to answer most of those things. Most of all, however, she wanted to talk about Vera Jeggs, to open her heart about the way she, Beth, had behaved towards him before he went away. But Ted was still restrained in how much he wanted to talk to his family about Vera, and when he did, it was only to say, with lowered, sorrowful eyes, that 'some people are born to bad luck'.

Before he left them, Ted brought up the subject of the family moving out to live with Grandma and Grandad in Hertfordshire, which brought the same immediate response from Beth. 'Please don't ask me ter go, Dad,' she said with difficulty. 'As much as I love Gran and Grandad, I could never be 'appy actually livin' wiv 'em.'

Ted's face stiffened. 'An' I could never be 'appy', he replied, 'knowin' that, after all my family've gone fru, if the same fing 'appened again, I might be miles away, an' there'd be nuffin' – absolutely nuffin' – that I could do about it.'

'But there's a difference now, Ted.'

Both Ted and Beth turned to look at Connie, taken by surprise at her remark.

'You see, darling,' continued Connie, 'we're not frightened any more. None of us – me, Beth, Phil – even junior here. This war is doing something to us – don't ask me exactly *what* – but it *is* bringing us closer and closer together.'

Ted looked at her in absolute astonishment. 'But yer can all be close if you're out er London,' he said. 'Every day you're at the mercy of somefin' like yesterday.'

'Yes, I know, Ted,' Connie replied. 'But the difference now is that none of us are prepared any longer to be intimidated. We're a kind of – team. We're willing to take our chances, like all the other people in this city.'

Ted was stunned. 'But wot about your dreams,' he asked, 'your nightmares?'

For one brief moment, Connie's expression changed, but then she stretched out her hand, and gently held his. 'What happened to us in that shelter is one dream that came true,' she said. 'I promise I won't let any more happen like that.'

Beth looked at her mum in disbelief.

Ted sat back in his chair, trying to take in what he was being told. 'That's all very well,' he said, 'but it's not very fair ter me, not knowin' from one day to anuvver wot's 'appenin' to yer all, not knowin' wevver I'm ever goin' ter see the people I love again.'

Connie paused a moment. 'I know, darling,' she replied. 'We feel exactly the same way about you.'

A week or so later, an official-looking car approached along the long winding lane which led to the Buchner house in Lossheim. Helga Buchner had watched it coming from the moment it turned off the main road, which for the past few weeks had been covered with several centimetres of snow. Because of the road conditions, it seemed to take for ever to reach the drive in front of the house, but the moment the two uniformed officers got out of the car, she had no doubt why they had come. After they had delivered their message, which was short and to the point, the two men left, and once again she watched the car struggle to make its way back to the main road.

Heinz's mother, who had been present during her meeting with the two men, made a discreet exit to her room the moment they had left. Helga didn't know whether she would be shedding any tears, for she was an undemonstrative person, and ever since she had arrived to stay with the family after Heinz had left for his previous mission, she had come to realise that emotion was something Heinz's mother would never show in public. However, soon after Frau Lotte Buchner had left the room, Helga could hear her sobbing quietly to herself as she climbed the stairs.

In the sitting room, Helga spent several minutes looking at the black leather suitcase the two men had brought with them, and which was now placed on the highly polished oval table. She went to it, and gently eased the tips of her fingers over the silver embossed initials there: 'H.B.' She unclipped the case, and opened it. Inside were the possessions that Heinz had packed when he first went off on duty to his base nearly a year before. His body had been picked up at sea, kept afloat by a tattered parachute, and the Red Cross had returned his things to the German authorities. She recognised most of the clothes – two v-necked pullovers, several long-sleeved shirts, underwear, a smart two-piece grey suit, black leather gloves, and so on. His uniform was offered to her, but she declined, however the one thing that did catch her eye was a small brown paper bag that had been laid neatly on top. She stretched out for it, and opened it. Inside was a thin gold neck chain, attached to the beer glass charm she remembered giving him. For several moments, she held it in the palm of her hand, just looking at it quite coldly. It seemed to look so lonely there, as though it was trying to say something to her. But then she heard a movement at the door. When she turned round, she saw her two young children Richard and Dieter standing there, hand in hand, side by side. Not a word was spoken. All they did was to stare inquisitively.

Only then did tears well up in her eyes. But as she looked across at her two boys through those tears, she resolved to bring them up to think of their father as a hero. She would not paint him as someone whom they should follow along a path of beliefs that were misguided; a path dominated by cruel and perverted men whose only goal in life was power. Oh no. Helga was determined that, whatever their future paths would be, Heinz's sons would grow up to think for themselves.

Although Beth was thrilled to hear Thomas's news, she knew that he himself would have mixed feelings about it. Special Branch had informed him that they had located the whereabouts of his father, but as he had managed to get to the Republic of Ireland, and because of the present complex state of Anglo-Irish relations, it was doubtful that any action could be taken against him without a lengthy extradition application, which would probably be turned down anyway. Under those circumstances, Thomas had been told by Jane Grigsby that, although he was free to leave his house and go about his daily life again, he would have to forfeit his job at the munitions factory, for which, in any event, Thomas was not at all unhappy. However, after the threats Joe Sullivan had received from his Irish Republican 'sympathisers', there was still the issue of how Thomas was going to deal with his own safety.

'Oh,' he said over a Sunday midday meal with Connie, Beth and Phil. 'I don't think that's somethin' I'm going ter have ter worry too much about – for now.'

'Oh?' asked Connie curiously. 'And why's that?'

Thomas exchanged a quick, knowing grin with Beth. 'Well yer see, Mrs Shanks,' he said mysteriously, 'I've joined up.'

Connie dropped her knife on to her plate of beef and roast potatoes. 'You've – what?' she gasped.

'Thomas 'as bin accepted inter the Royal Irish Fusiliers,' said Beth, who had been let into Thomas's secret just a few hours before.

'The Royal Irish Fusiliers?' asked Phil. 'Wot der *they* do in the war, then?'

Thomas looked a bit taken aback by Phil's question.

'Wot d'yer fink they do, stupid!' snapped Beth. 'They fight. They fight bleedin' 'Itler!'

'Really?' replied Phil, munching a potato that was far too hot for his mouth.

'There *are* quite a lot of Irishmen who are fighting for this country, you know, Phil,' Thomas reminded him. 'Not only from the north but the south too.'

Phil shrugged, and let it pass.

Connie was still too shocked to eat. The thought of another young man going to war appalled her, not only because he was obliged to, but also because he had volunteered. 'Why, Thomas?' she asked. 'If you don't have to go, why put your life at risk?'

'People are putting their lives at risk every day and night of their lives, Mrs Shanks,' he replied. 'There's very little I can do to make up for what my father did, but at least I can try.'

'Your father was – misguided, Thomas,' said Connie. 'I hope you'll forgive me for saying that, but there are some men and women in this world who don't stop to consider the harm they can do to people's lives, just because they believe in a "cause".

'I agree with yer, Mrs Shanks,' said Thomas, 'but there are always people like me who have ter pick up the pieces after the worst is done. I've lived in this country fer the best part of my life now. I feel I owe it at least *something*.'

Beth looked across the table at Thomas, and knew that everything that first attracted her to him was true. Thomas was a man of principle, someone who had a passion for life, a love for people, who could laugh and cry, who could bring a little joy to a humdrum world – that was something she discovered when they went to the wedding of his friend, Sheila and Michael. Getting to know Thomas had been a rich, if sometimes unsettling experience. What was it about the Irish that made them such good company, she asked herself? It wasn't just that they were cute, like the leprechauns that everyone teased them about. No, like Jewish people, they had a purpose in life, and they had charm. Yes, there were always the hotheads, but they were few and far between. What Thomas gave everyone was his sincerity.

A short while later, Beth walked with Thomas to his bus stop. As they walked down Hornsey Road, it all seemed so different to that terrifying night down in the old warehouse cellar, for everything was clear again, even if the old warehouse itself had been reduced to nothing more than a pile of rubble. At the bus stop, they spent quite a time huddled up close together, for it was getting dark, and the cold snap was clearly going to go on and on. They kissed so hard and for so long, that Thomas missed one bus, and had to wait for another, but they didn't mind, because they had all the time in the world together, until . . . until Thomas went away.

On her way home, Beth took a passing look up at the sky, grateful that, so far, there was no air raid. Even so, it wouldn't matter if there was, for, as her mum had told her dad, '*We're willing to take our chances like all the other people in this city*.' When she reached her front garden gate in Moray Road, she heard Jack Cutter calling to her quietly from next door.

' 'Allo, Beff!' he called. 'Did yer 'ear they've caught those two thugs who done up the bruvvers' shop? They've bin charged, an' they're goin' up before the magistrates termorrer mornin'.'

'Oh that's t'rrific, Jack!' replied Beth. 'Who are they?'

'Nobody!' replied Jack. 'Just a coupla bleedin nobodies!'

After Jack had gone back inside, Beth stood on the front doorstep for a few minutes, looking all around her: at the long terrace of houses with boarded-up windows still waiting to be repaired from previous bomb blasts, at the chimneypots all along the rooftops, belching out thick black smoke into a clear blue sky, and at the scattering of local kids with their buckets who were scouring the pavements, gutters and front gardens for remnants of shrapnel that would be taken to the nearest ARP posts for eventual recycling for the war effort. Without realizing it, she had a broad grin on her face, which was still grimy after her night of sheer horror. She closed her eyes and turned her face upwards to bask in the warmth of the gradually rising sun. And in the darkness of her mind, she saw many things. She saw Thomas bidding farewell to her at the bus stop in Hornsey Road, that parting kiss that convinced her that, although she was going to miss him, once the war was over, he *would* one day return safely to her. With her fingertips she gently touched her lips, feeling the love he had left behind. And then she thought about the night she had just survived, about the extraordinary companionship and determination of her neighbours who had endured so much with her and her mum and young Simon. The 'regulars' were a wonderful bunch and she would never forget them; their refusal to give up even in the depth of despair, their good old London humour, and the way they just sang, sang their hearts out in the face of adversity. These were people who deserved the best out of life, a future that would repay them for their courage and perseverance. Whatever happened in years to come, no one would be able to rob them of the credit they were due, for the people who had lived through the Blitz had shown that they could cope with anything that was thrown at them.

With the smile still lingering on that cheeky, obstinate face, Beth opened her eyes and found that she was looking straight up into the sun. She squinted, and for one passing moment reflected on the man who had dropped his bomb on the old piano factory. What kind of a person was he? she wondered. Did he have no family of his own that he could obey orders to kill innocent men, women and children? Wherever he was, whatever he was doing now, she hoped that he would regret what he had done.

She opened the front door and went in. But before she closed it, she couldn't resist one last glimpse at the world outside. For one fleeting moment it seemed crystallised in time. How long would this painful war last? she wondered. What kind of a world would it be in fifty or sixty years' time?

Only time would tell.

Epilogue

The teenage American girl had three-quarter-length trousers that laced up around her calves. Her sweater was pretty casual too, stretching down over her bottom to her thighs, which did nothing to accentuate what was actually quite a trim little figure. But her appearance was nothing compared to the young American man who was with her, whose shorts were so baggy and long they looked about twelve sizes too big for him. His long t-shirt did nothing for him either, despite a bold picture of a fist emblazoned across the chest which carried the legend: STUDENT POWER. However, they certainly didn't look out of place in the streets of present-day London, where teenage fashion was somewhat different to the 'Make Do and Mend' of the war years. Nonetheless, Lisa Duffield and her boyfriend, Luke Pitt, had taken a real liking to these old back streets, mainly because most of them still had the sign of what the area must have looked like in the 'old' days.

Walking amongst the bustling activity in Seven Sisters Road gave Lisa one of her biggest thrills, because she had seen letters that her great-aunt Connie used to write home to her sister, Melanie, Lisa's grandmother, during and after the Second World War, describing the shops, the people, the quaint customs, and to see it all come to life was, for Lisa, just 'amazing'. Of course the area wasn't quite the same as Great-Aunt Connie had described it, for although there were still plenty of shops, a lot of them had foreign names above the windows, and something that looked like a big supermarket in the photos that her great-aunt has sent, had taken the place of what must have been a department store. Also, there were many different nationalities around, some with white skin, some black, some brown, some with frizzy hair, some with spiky hair, some with slanting eyes, but it was all so – so modern, which, in Lisa's mind, was just how it *should* be. However, her boyfriend Luke wasn't quite so convinced. In fact, he reckoned the place looked no better than the downtown area of Boston where he came from.

For Lisa, the trek along Hornsey Road was the most galvanising, for it gave her the opportunity to try and identify individual shops, and the site of the public baths, and the police station next door which had been bombed with the loss of so many lives, and where in 1941 the King and Queen paid a personal visit to the survivors and relatives of the victims. Luke was getting a bit fed up with all this information that was being pumped into him, mainly because Lisa was reading it aloud from a notebook, as though she was some kind of guide. But no matter how hard Lisa tried, she just couldn't find the spot where the old warehouse had been before it was bombed. There were so many new buildings along Hornsey Road now, and most of the people who had lived there at the time had either passed away, or gone to live in the country. But Lisa insisted on standing still for just a few moments, just to close her eyes and try to imagine what it must have been like on that fateful night, when Great-Aunt Connie, and cousins Beth and Simon were trapped down in that awful cellar. She tried to picture her mother's cousin Beth, and how she had played that piano – that ol' Joanna – night after night, with everyone down there singing their hearts out to keep their spirits high. What an incredible person Beth must be, Lisa said to herself, and how wonderful it was going to be to meet her the following day. Despite the rush of traffic that was doing its best to ruin the atmosphere, for one brief moment, Lisa felt that she was there on that cold November night, listening to 'Moaning Minnie' wailing out from the roof of the police station, listening to the enemy planes droning overhead and the constant bang, bang, bang of the anti-aircraft gunfire. For one brief moment she was there, thanks to the vivid way Great-Aunt Connie had described everything in her letters.

As Lisa followed her street map, and turned her and Luke into Tollington Road, her heart was beginning to pound faster and faster, for within just a few minutes she would be standing outside the house where her mom's sister and family lived during all those turbulent times. Even though she had seen her cousin Phil's snapshots of the house, she tried to picture in her mind's eye what it would *actually* look like. But when they finally arrived at the end of Moray Road, she was really quite disappointed to find a very neat terrace of ordinary red-bricked houses, which were no different to so many of the little back streets she had already seen scattered around North London. She and Luke strolled slowly along, taking in the small front gardens, some that were simple concrete walk-ins with a little round flowerbed in the middle, and others that were so crammed with beautiful coloured flowers they looked as though they would be good enough to display in a flower show.

Arriving at the house itself was, for Lisa, a feeling of homecoming. She stared up at the front façade and was transported to another world. This was the house where her grandma's sister had lived with Great Uncle Ted and their family all those years ago. Was it possible, she asked herself, was it really possible that that terrible war in Europe *and* the Far East had ended sixty years ago this very year?

'Hey, man,' Luke said quite suddenly in his wild New England accent, as he watched Lisa gazing up at the house. 'I hope we're not gonna stand out here all day? What say we go get a burger and fries down the main street?'

'Patience, Luke!' said Lisa, whose voice was clear and pure New England. 'When are we gonna get the chance again to see a house that means so much to my family?'

Never, if Luke had anything to do with it, although he didn't say as much. He was suddenly aware that Lisa was halfway up the garden path to the front door. 'Hell, Lisa!' he whimpered. 'What're ya doin'?'

'Ssh!' replied Lisa, putting one finger up to her lips to silence him. She went up to the door, and to her surprise, immediately detected the smell of cooking. She knocked on the door, and when a young Asian man opened it, she was practically knocked out by the smell of garlic and curry.

'Yes?' asked the man, with a thick accent, eyeing Lisa suspiciously.

'I'm sorry to bother you,' replied Lisa, a little offput by the sight of several ladies in saris who had joined the man at the door. 'My name is Lisa, Lisa Duffield. My relations on my mother's side . . . to cut a long story short, my great-aunt Connie and her husband Ted used to live in this house – with their children, Beth, Phil and . . .'

'They don't live here now!' said the man, who had a beautiful shock of dark hair and a bushy moustache to match.

'I know that,' said Lisa with a polite little laugh. 'My aunt has been dead for years.'

'So what do you want?' asked the man impatiently.

Lisa hesitated a moment. She didn't really *know* what she did want, and even if she did, what difference would it make? This was no longer where Great-Aunt Connie and the family lived. They had gone long ago. That was the past, and this was the present. She smiled at the man and shook her head. 'Nothing, really,' she said. 'I'm sorry to have wasted your time. Goodbye.' The young man was about to close the door, but as she was leaving, Lisa called back to him: 'Are you going to watch the celebrations next week?'

'What celebrations?' asked the man.

'It's the sixtieth anniversary of the end of World War Two. There are going to be a lot of processions and entertainments up in London.'

The young man shrugged. 'What's that got to do with me?' he asked. 'I wasn't even alive in those days.'

Lisa smiled back at him. 'Cool!' she said, as she left.

'Don't be so ridiculous, love!' called the man before closing the door. 'It's a beautiful day!'

'Satisfied?' asked Luke, as he and Lisa walked back along the road.

'It's weird,' she replied. 'He doesn't even know about the anniversary.'

'Why should he?' asked Luke. 'What would a guy like that know about the Second World War?'

'Nothing I guess,' said Lisa, taking his hand and striding off with him. 'But I know someone who will.'

The sea was calm at Palm Bay in Kent. In fact it was so calm, the incoming tide was finding it almost impossible to create even the smallest ripple. That's just the way Beth Sullivan liked it. She hated living down by the sea when there were storms, because the sounds reminded her of the Blitz. But one of her greatest joys was to come down to their favourite seat on the promenade with Thomas, and idle away a couple of hours during the morning, before going back to cook lunch for them both, which, considering their advanced years, was usually something quite light. This is how they lived these days, happy and content, but at a much slower pace than in the past.

As usual, Thomas had read his newspaper from end to end, and had nodded off. Beth often looked at him and worried about why he had to nod off quite so often, until she pinched herself to make herself realise that both she and he were now two old pensioners in their eighties, and didn't have the energy they used to have. She stared across to the sea. She had stared at the sea an awful lot since she and Thomas had moved out of London all those years ago, but it didn't mean much to her, because at heart she was still a London girl, born and bred. In any case, she was always asking herself, what the advantage was of living down by the sea just because you were old? In fact the sea could be very boring at times, one big black wilderness at night, one big blue or grey wilderness by day. And when the wind blew, oh boy, how it blew! Many a time she had seen the promenades in Kent flooded by high tides, and it scared the living daylights out of her. Not as much as the bombs, though. No, they were something quite different. She turned to look at Thomas, who was just emerging from his forty winks. He, like her, was a bit on the plump side these days, and beneath his checked flat-cap his hair had thinned out quite considerably. But in her eyes, he was just as good-looking as ever. 'So where've yer bin terday?' she asked, her assumed cockney accent as strong as ever despite years away from Islington.

Thomas was having a good after-nod stretch. 'Nowhere particular,' he replied, his Irish voice a little gruff after smoking too many fags for too many years. 'I think I was in that procession in London next week, marchin' alongside me mates from the old regiment.'

'Must be bonkers!' said Beth, who was actually very proud that her man had done his time in the Royal Irish Fusiliers during the war. 'Yer wouldn't get me up the West End wiv all *those* crowds – speshully wiv all the nutcases around these days.'

'And wot about your distant cousin from America?' he asked.

'Wot about 'er?' asked Beth.

'*She'll* be goin' ter the big show. And don't forget she and her feller are coming to see you tomorrow.'

'That's diff'rent,' replied Beth. 'If I was 'er age, I'd probably do the same fing. D'yer remember us sleepin' out fer the Queen's Coronation?'

Thomas grunted. 'Will I ever ferget it!' he said. 'Stretched out on the pavement in the pourin' rain all night.'

'Yes,' insisted Beth, 'but it was worf it. In those days we 'ad pride in our Royal Family, pride in our country.'

'So what does that mean?'

Beth wasn't prepared for that question. 'I don't know, really,' she replied wistfully. 'Just that fings ain't the same any more, I s'ppose.'

'Isn't that inevitable?' asked Thomas.

'Why *should* it be?' Beth asked haughtily. 'There's nuffin' wrong wiv bein' proud of what and where yer come from.'

Thomas grinned to himself. How he loved this girl. How he had always loved her, even during those troubled times when both of them thought they had abandoned trust in each other. He loved the way she had never really left Islington, that her heart was still there, but that she had accepted that such a move was necessary years ago when the doctors had warned Thomas that sea air was more conducive to Beth's angina than the smell of London traffic. 'D'you have any regrets in your life, Beth?' he asked.

'That's a funny question,' she replied. 'Are yer expectin me ter pop off or somefin'?'

'Don't be so crass,' he replied tetchily.

'That's a good word fer so early in the mornin'!' she replied flippantly.

'No, I mean it,' said Thomas crossly. 'There are a lot of things *I* regret.'

'Such as?'

'Not knowin' what Dada was up to all that time,' he replied despondently, 'even though it was right under my very nose.' With the tip of his walking-stick, he started making shapeless figures on the paving stone. 'Not havin' the chance ter see him before his so-called mates gunned him down in cold blood.'

Beth didn't say a word. For years this had been a taboo subject between them, and because she loved and respected Thomas so much, she intended that it would always remain so.

'Of course,' continued Thomas, turning to her, 'they're not the only things I regret. Your piano, for a start.'

'My piano?' asked Beth, turning to look at him.

'You should never have got rid of it when we left London.'

'I didn't get rid of it,' she replied. 'You know I gave it to Susie. With my arthritic fingers it's far more use to her than me now. She'll learn 'ow ter play it all right. She takes after 'er Great Gran'ma.'

'*And* her Grandma,' Thomas reminded her, with a smile. 'God knows what you'd've done without your music over the years.'

Beth smiled to herself, and looked out at the sea. 'Fer me,' she said wistfully, 'playin' the pianer was like floatin' in the air. Oh these days, Joannas don't mean a fing ter the young – it's all electric guitars an' silly dances.'

'Like the jitterbug?' Thomas said, grinning, reminding her, as he had done many times before, of the dance she did with the crazy young Irish boy at Sheila and Michael's wedding all those years before.

She smiled. 'The piano was somefin' else, Thomas,' she continued. 'Sometimes, when I was down that shelter listenin' to 'em all singin' while I was playin', I felt as though me 'ands din't belong ter me. Some'ow – they just took over.' She paused a moment. 'Yer know, it's wonderful ter 'ear people singin'. It sort of – brings 'em all tergevver, 'elps 'em ter ferget all their troubles, even if it's only fer a few minutes. I remember my ol' mum sayin' ter me: 'A good popular song can be just as uplifting as a piano sonata.'

They had been talking so much together, that they hadn't noticed a flock of about eight seagulls who had waddled up towards them along the promenade. The moment they were close, Thomas felt into his overcoat pocket, and brought out a small bag of bacon rinds that Beth had cut off before breakfast that morning.

'Yer'll 'ave Ken Livingstone after you!' Beth said, as he started feeding the gulls. 'The Mayor of London don't like birds. 'Speshully in Trafalgar Square.'

'What about you, then?' he asked.

'Don't be silly,' she replied, 'I love birds.'

'I'm not talkin' about birds,' he said. 'I mean – what regrets do *you* have?'

Beth hadn't thought about that one before, well, not seriously. 'Got a pencil an' paper?' she asked. 'This could take all day!' She leaned back on the bench, crossed her arms and looked back into the past, as she had done so many times before. 'I regret 'avin' to've read that telegram ter Mum when Dad got killed in Norf Africa. I regret not seein' 'im just once more ter tell 'im 'ow much I loved 'im. I regret not bein' able ter fill the gap 'e left in Mum's life.'

'She lived to a ripe old age,' said Thomas, slipping his arm around his wife's shoulders. 'Eighty-six isn't bad, yer know.'

'They were lost years, Thomas,' replied Beth, staring out to sea. 'The moment she knew Dad wouldn't be comin' 'ome, in 'er mind, there wasn't much left for 'er except teachin' the piano.'

'And Simon,' he reminded her.

Beth smiled to herself. 'Oh yes – Simon,' she said. 'She was proud of 'im all right. 'E certainly turned out ter be the brains of the family.'

'Not many kids from our walk of life get the chance ter go ter medical college.'

'*An'* set up their own practice,' she replied. 'I still find it 'ard ter believe – *Doctor* Simon Shanks. And now '*e*'s got grandkids, just like us.' She chuckled wryly to herself. 'Mum would've loved that.'

'I bet yer dad would've too.'

'Oh yes,' sighed Beth. For one brief moment, she was alone with her thoughts, seeing all the family together years before, back in dear old Moray Road. 'I'll tell yer wot though,' she said. 'I still miss all the gang up 'Ornsey Road. Sometimes I lie awake at night finkin' about 'em, finkin' about those times we spent tergevver down the shelter. It's 'ard ter believe that most of 'em've gone – ol' Jessie 'Awks, Jack Cutter . . .'

'Those two Jewish tailors,' added Thomas. 'What were their names now?'

'The Lieberman brothers – Abe and Bernie,' said Beth. 'It's amazin' 'ow Bernie managed ter live fer the rest of 'is life with only one leg, the fact that 'e survived at all when that ton er weight come down on 'im in the shelter. Wot a pair those two were.' She sighed. 'Ah, they don't make 'em like that *these* days.' She looked up at the sky where thin wisps of white clouds were racing past in a gathering breeze. To her it symbolised the rapid passing of an entire lifetime. 'And that poor woman – Vera, Vera Jeggs. I'm glad we got ter know 'er and 'er family before she died. It some'ow seemed right that we should. Dad would've said so.'

'Yer know *your* trouble, don't yer, Mrs Sullivan,' said Thomas, gently taking her hand and rubbing it to keep it warm. 'You live in the past far too much. Yer can't bear ter leave it all behind.'

She swung a look at him. 'Thomas, m'dear,' she replied fervently. 'Yer couldn't be more wrong. Yer don't ever leave people be'ind that yer love.'

He took her meaning and smiled back at her. 'You're right, ol' girl,' he replied affectionately. 'Of course you're right.'

'Although, I tell yer this much,' she continued. 'The one thing I *do* regret is 'avin' four kids.'

'Yer what!' protested Thomas, giving her a shocked, scolding look.

'I'd've preferred to 'ave 'ad ten!'

'Ten!' Thomas nearly had a fit. 'What d'yer take me for – Superman?'

'Just fink,' she chuckled, putting her arm around him, 'we could've 'ad our own football team.'

'Well, they couldn't've been worse than what we've got now,' said Thomas.

They stared briefly into each other's eyes, their life flashing before them.

'The only fing I've never regretted,' said Beth, 'is gettin' 'ooked up wiv you.'

'Get away with yer,' said Thomas, grinning at her. 'Yer say that ter all the boys.'

'Even though you're gettin' ter be a miserable bugger in yer ol' age.'

'Thanks a million!' he replied, trying to turn away.

'But I wouldn't change anyfin' we've done tergevver all these years,' she said, pulling him back, and kissing him lightly on the tip of his nose. ' 'Cos if I did, I'd never be able ter tell yer 'ow much I love yer.'

Despite two elderly ladies glancing disapprovingly at them as they passed by, Beth and Thomas kissed. For a fleeting moment they were young lovers all over again, and the world belonged to them. Then they leaned back, he with his arm around her shoulders, and, as they had done on so many occasions in the past, they started to hum softly together the song that dear old Uncle Horace had loved so much, ' 'Til We Meet Again'.

The gulls quickly dispersed, leaving the sweet sounds from two old people to drift across the sands, to drift across the sea, and on to the old streets of London, the London of long ago, the London that Beth would never forget, if she lived to be a thousand years . . .